UNRAVELED

HERITAGE OF POWER BOOK 4

LINDSAY BUROKER

Unraveled

Heritage of Power, Book 4
by Lindsay Buroker
Copyright © 2018 Lindsay Buroker

ACKNOWLEDGMENTS

THANK YOU, DEAR READER, FOR continuing on with my Heritage of Power series. Before you jump into the story, please let me thank my beta readers, Cindy Wilkinson, Rue Silver, and Sarah Engelke for giving early feedback, and my editor, Shelley Holloway. Also, thank you to Deranged Doctor Design for the cover art. We hope you enjoy the story!

CHAPTER 1

LIEUTENANT RYSHA RAVENWOOD MURMURED AND made soft exclamations as she studied one of two journals she'd recovered during the last week's mission. The scribbles of her enthusiastic pencil filled the hostel room as she took notes. At least, they did at the moment. Often, the shouts, thumps, and screams from the other rooms and the alley outside drowned out her quieter noises.

"It's disconcerting to hear someone making such pleasure-filled sounds while reading a book," Major Kaika said, pausing her push-ups to lock her arms in the board position, or the "rest position," as Rysha's instructor in the elite troops training program called it. As if one could rest while one's arms were quivering from holding up one's weight.

"It's a journal, ma'am, not a book."

"That makes it much better. I hope that's not the one from the dragon-rider outpost. Didn't you say the title translated to *How to Be a Delusional Cultist in Six Easy Steps*?" Kaika lowered herself halfway and held the position.

"That wasn't the *precise* translation." Rysha felt guilty for sitting cross-legged next to the shuttered and barred window with her books instead of joining in with the exercises. By now, she had missed so much of her training that she feared she would have to wait a year for the next session to start. "The front half of the cult book does have the history, bylaws, and ceremonies for the Brotherhood of the Dragon, but it's the back half that's more interesting. It's written in Middle Dragon Script and was copied from a much older version of the book, I believe— maybe the original from over three thousand years ago when the cult was founded. I've only got a few pages translated."

"And that's what has you more excited than being handed a freshly dipped dragon horn cookie from Donotono's Bakery?"

"Actually, that journal is disturbing. I do need to go over it so we can return it to—"

"Return it? You want to walk past a hundred angry cultists to put it back in their sacrifice room?"

"I was thinking we could leave it outside for them to find. Or drop it in the entry hole."

Kaika grunted and rolled onto her back to torture her abdomen muscles with leg raises.

"The journal I'm reading now is the one we found in the dragon's lair. I believe the man who dropped it…" Rysha hesitated, reconsidering her word choice. The man hadn't *dropped* it. It had been in his pack when he'd been slain, and then the scavengers living in those tunnels had eaten the flesh from his skeleton and chewed on his bones. "I believe the previous owner was traveling in the same party as Trip's mother."

"His surrogate mother?"

"Apparently so."

Since they had all been there for the discovery of Trip's heritage, and the fact that he was one of nine half-human-half-dragon offspring that had been born thousands of years earlier, she didn't think she needed to bring it up. Trip hadn't stopped calling the woman who had found and raised him his mother, so Rysha would use the same word.

"The journal isn't particularly organized," she added, "and there aren't any dates, but it's quite fascinating. It details a lot of the research the party did that led them to find the dragon's lair in the first place. Unfortunately, it doesn't name the members or talk about if someone brought the team together or if the individuals formed it themselves. There *is* mention of someone financing the expedition, possibly someone local. I flagged that. I need to find a map to see if I can put together the clues. I'm also still looking for a confirmation that Trip's mother was indeed in the party."

"Is there any reason we need that information now?"

"Well, I think Trip would like to know it, and I find the events that resulted in his existence in our time to be quite fascinating."

"I see. *Trip* is the reason you're making those noises."

The look that Kaika slanted her was hard to read, but Rysha thought she saw disapproval in it. Kaika didn't object to dalliances with men—she seemed to dally more frequently than the next person—but she didn't believe dalliances should turn into an obsession—or affect a woman's career.

Rysha didn't think she was obsessed, but she *had* been willing to risk punishment and expulsion from the elite troops training program when she'd chosen to stay here in Lagresh to help Trip unravel the Dreyak mystery. If Kaika had been able to find passage back to Iskandia, she would have already left and reported that Trip and Rysha were... AWOL, essentially. The minute Trip had said he intended to stay here to investigate Dreyak's death, he'd been on a personal mission rather than one assigned by a commanding officer. That meant Rysha was too.

Was that a mistake? Rysha had made the decision in the moment, acting on instinct—and feelings—rather than well-thought-out arguments.

"The *events* that resulted in his existence are fascinating to me," Rysha repeated firmly. "He's not just some boy I'm making moon eyes over. In addition to his greater than average potential to help Iskandia in the coming years, he has all those half-dragon baby siblings over there who could also grow up to help the country." She waved at the compact stasis chambers, stacked against the wall like kegs in a brewery, hoping she could imply that her interest in Trip's past was part of some grander scenario, one from which Iskandia would benefit.

"So, the half-lizard baby brother in that one on the end is what's attracting you to Trip? Or is it that furry panda-looking thing?"

Rysha sighed. "Ma'am."

She didn't argue further. Kaika didn't seem to have maternal instincts. Rysha hadn't thought she did, either, but when she'd looked at the human babies nestled in the stasis gel, their features just discernible through the semi-transparent lids, she'd felt the urge to protect them. More than that, she wanted them to be hatched from those prisons where they'd been held in perpetual hibernation for thousands of years, and she wanted them to have wonderful childhoods and good lives.

A boy and a girl—twins, perhaps—were in side-by-side chambers on the top of the stack, each with dark curly hair and their thumbs in their mouths, and they reminded her of her little cousins, Frian and Themala, when they had been little. She could easily imagine the babies growing into toddlers and playing in her family's valley, chasing squirrels in the orchard and swimming in the lake.

"Why don't you take a break from the books and come exercise?" Kaika asked. "We can do unarmed combat drills too. I'd like to see you return to the capital, having equal or greater ability than the rookies that have been training the whole time we've been away on these missions. If you don't pass the test at the end of the spring, then you've got to wait another year to reapply to the program, and there's no guarantee that you'll be selected again. Do you want to go back to overseeing a crew of thugly gun huggers on the wall of the fort?"

Rysha hadn't minded her job as an artillery officer, especially since aiming guns effectively employed her mathematics background, but she'd mostly gone into that specialty because it was one of the few combat jobs open to women. She'd believed that background would make her more appealing to the elite troops recruiters. Everything had been a careful calculation, with the end goal to become only the second woman to pass the training and be accepted into the unit.

And Kaika was right. She was potentially giving all that up because of Trip.

She could tell herself that his path and potential were greater than hers and that he could use the support of someone who cared about him, someone who might eventually love him, but was she positive that was the truth? Maybe she just liked having sex and snuggling with him, and she was deluding herself about the rest. After all, since she'd been chosen to wield the *chapaharii* blade Dorfindral, she, too, had the potential to play a great role in protecting her country and her people from dragons and other enemies.

Rysha rubbed her face. Why couldn't she have it all? Trip *and* the elite troops?

"It's not too late," Kaika said quietly.

"For push-ups?"

Kaika snorted. "Never too late for them, but I meant to get back home in time to rejoin the training and graduate from the program. You haven't yet... Nothing has happened that I would need to report.

Admittedly, I don't know what Blazer will report to General Zirkander about soldiers turning into bed buddies in the field, but since we haven't been able to secure transportation yet, you haven't technically chosen to go AWOL with Trip. We're all stuck here until there's a boat heading our way that we can get on. But once I find one, if you choose not to get on it..." Kaika shrugged. "I *have* to go back and report in, and Blazer tasked us with getting all those canisters home."

Rysha grimaced, imagining that Trip would object to them being taken away without him. Would he even allow it?

"I'll train with you, ma'am."

Rysha closed the book. She would stay up nights to finish reading the journals if she had to—she could sleep during the voyage back to Iskandia. Besides, how valid was her argument that she needed to finish studying them when she hadn't even read the one that had come from the outpost, the one she'd essentially stolen and should return before they left?

"I haven't given up my dream, not for Trip or for anyone else," Rysha added. "I want to make it into the elite troops."

"Good."

Kaika rose to her feet and lifted a hand, as if to wave Rysha over to join her, but she paused in the middle of the gesture. Frowning, she grabbed her *chapaharii* blade, Eryndral, and strode to the window. She leaned her ear toward the shutters, some of the desert's harsh sunlight slipping through and creating the slashes of light Rysha had been reading by.

Rysha raised her eyebrows and mouthed, "What is it?"

"I hear voices," Kaika said quietly.

Rysha spread her hand, palm up. She'd been hearing voices all day and through most of the night too. Deals being cut and threats being delivered. Twice, gunfire had woken her with her heart slamming against her rib cage. She didn't think the people in this city ever slept. Especially not in this neighborhood.

Their hostel was close to the waterfront, so Kaika could go down every morning and check for passage on new ships that came in, but the location was the only good thing about it. The room itself was a sewer pit with the lumpy mattresses on the floor providing the only furnishings, if they could be considered that. They were made from dried cactus pads, with some but not *all* of the thorns removed before they'd been stuffed into the cases.

"It's quieter than it's been all day." Rysha had been doing her best to block out the interruptions.

"That's what concerns me. Two different groups of idiots tried to mug me this morning when I was on my way down to the harbor. To say this city is dangerous is an understatement."

Kaika had neglected to mention that earlier.

"Were they random mugging attempts, or did they target you for a specific reason?" Rysha looked Kaika up and down.

They were both clad in their gray uniform trousers but not the jackets or caps that would have left no doubt that they were in the Iskandian army. Kaika wore a creamy button-down shirt with the sleeves rolled up, a tattoo of the first grenade ever invented inked in black on one of her ropy forearms. Even if she hadn't been carrying the sword and her pistol, she wouldn't have looked like an easy mark, not with her six feet of height and athletic build.

Rysha was close to six feet tall, too, and strong and agile if not quite as lean, but her spectacles always seemed to make people think she was a librarian rather than a warrior. She could easily imagine muggers targeting *her*.

"I assumed they wanted the sword." Kaika tapped Eryndral's scabbard. The blade only glowed green when a magical item or someone with dragon blood was nearby, but the scabbard still looked old and valuable, with elaborate runes running down the sides. "But it's also possible someone thinks we have something worth money in our room. Numerous street toughs were watching from the shadows as we unloaded the wagon last night."

Rysha glanced again at the stasis chambers. They'd done their best to keep them covered, and she doubted anyone could have guessed what they were, but someone could have assumed they were valuable. Twice that morning after Trip had left, someone outside had attempted to open their locked door.

The doorknob rattled, and Rysha jumped.

"Sword," Kaika said, pointing to where Dorfindral leaned against the wall in its scabbard.

Rysha grabbed it and belted it on. She pulled the blade out a couple of inches to see if it was glowing. It was, but she remembered that it had been glowing a little ever since they had recovered the stasis chambers.

Every time Rysha picked it up after it had been set aside for a while, it sent an urge through her to heft the sword overhead and smash it into the magical containers.

As that urge came over her now, she started to whisper the new "stand down" command term that she'd chosen and that Trip had programmed into the sword. But she hesitated before finishing it. She might need the sword alert to guide her movements if someone with magical means attacked them.

"Stand back." Kaika stepped away from the window, facing it and the door, and drawing her own sword.

Eryndral also glowed green, and Kaika's jaw clenched as she glanced back at the stasis chambers. But she narrowed her eyes in determination and faced the door.

Something slammed against it. The lock snapped off, and the door flung inward.

Kaika tossed a compact cylindrical object Rysha hadn't noticed her pull out. An Iskandian military smoke grenade. Something else was tossed into their room at the same time, an oval object that almost knocked into the cylindrical one.

Rysha had no idea what the other object was, but she scurried back, worried it was something deadlier than a smoke grenade.

Kaika had the opposite reaction. She sprang forward and smacked the oval projectile with the flat of her blade before it struck the floor. It flew back out through the doorway, Kaika's accuracy impressive.

Several alarmed shouts sounded in the alley, coming from at least four different voices.

An explosion boomed scant feet from their doorway. Light flashed, and shrapnel—or were those pieces of the wall?—hurtled into the room as smoke flooded the air.

Rysha lifted an arm to shield her face as shards pelted her body and clanged off the stasis chambers.

Not showing a similar self-preservation instinct, Kaika leaped through the doorway, her sword cutting for a target before she landed fully in the alley. A thud sounded, followed by a yell of pain. Not hers.

The smoke wrapped around Kaika as she lunged toward someone else, and Rysha lost sight of her.

Realizing Kaika might need help, Rysha ran toward the doorway. Her instincts should have been to attack right away rather than to defend. But Rysha halted before crossing the threshold. The stasis chambers. If she left the room, someone might sneak in and get them—or damage them.

Hoping Kaika wouldn't believe her cowardly for staying inside, Rysha crouched next to the doorway, Dorfindral ready to strike at intruders. The smoke stung her eyes and her throat, and she had to fight the urge to cough. She didn't want their enemies to know she was there.

Clangs and shouts came from the alley. Something—or someone—flew into the bars of the window, and the shutters rattled.

Rysha bit her lip as the battle raged outside and seconds passed with her doing nothing. Should she peek out and see if she could help? The smoke hadn't yet dissipated, and she doubted she would see anything.

She was on the verge of leaning out when a scuffling sounded in front of the doorway. Rysha crouched lower, ready to spring.

But the intruder didn't come inside. A gun fired, and bullets slammed into the back wall.

Cursing, Rysha glanced toward the stasis chambers. She had to do something—if they were hit, they might be destroyed. But she couldn't fling herself into fire. Bullets kept streaking through the doorway.

From up high, she realized as most of the bullets slammed into the wall at head height. And they were coming straight in, not from an angle. The gunman had to be right in front of the doorway.

Hoping she wasn't being suicidal, she shifted and dove through the doorway, staying low and turning the wild fling into a roll. Right away, she slammed into someone's legs. She had enough mass and momentum to knock the person back, and something clattered to the ground nearby. The gun, she hoped.

She sprang to her feet, swinging toward her opponent as she did so. Dorfindral cut into flesh. A man's arm? She couldn't tell in the thick smoke.

A man cried out right in front of her. The smoke stirred, and Rysha sensed him leaping back. She leaped after him, swinging again, a fierce protectiveness welling within her and lending strength to her movements. Whether by accident or design, this thug had been trying to destroy the chambers, trying to kill *babies*.

Her foe had been scurrying back, but he must have bumped into the far wall. A thud sounded, then a shout of alarm. Rysha thrust Dorfindral point first, and the blade sank deep into flesh.

She might have stabbed again, to wound the man deeply enough that he would never want to return, but the clamor from Kaika's skirmishes had quieted, and Rysha heard the rustle of clothing behind her. Someone trying to get into the room?

She yelled and wheeled, running back for the door. The smoke had cleared enough for her to see the shadowy figure of a man in dark clothing. He'd reached the threshold, but he heard her yell and whirled, a dagger and pistol in hands.

Anticipating a shot, Rysha sprang forward but also to the side. He fired. A scream of pain came from behind Rysha—had he hit his own ally?

She didn't pause to consider it, instead leaping in and slicing Dorfindral toward that pistol. A normal blade would only have knocked a firearm aside, but the *chapaharii* sword sliced through the metal, cleaving the barrel in two.

The man's eyes bulged in surprise, but he reacted quickly. He dropped the pistol and tried to knock Dorfindral aside with his dagger as he sprang toward Rysha. She had to dance back, but she evaded the attack and whipped her sword in, keeping it between her and the man.

He yanked out a second dagger, the blade almost long enough to qualify as a short sword, and advanced on her. He used one weapon to block her attacks and stabbed and slashed with the other. Rysha tried not to give ground—she sensed that he wanted to push her away from the doorway so someone else could slip into the room.

For the first time, she looked into the eyes of one of their attackers, clear blue eyes like an Iskandian might have. She didn't let that make her pause, other than to note the grim determination in the man's face. Instead, she launched into one of the sword routines she'd worked on with Colonel Therrik, one for use against a foe with two weapons.

He tended to block with his right hand, and she suspected that was his dominant side. She struck hard and toward his left, forcing him to block with the other hand. He was less accurate and swatted as often as he connected. She had to watch out for the attacks from his right-hand dagger, but she had the advantage of reach. As long as she kept Dorfindral in front of her, he struggled to touch her when he slashed.

Her foe growled at his lack of progress, and his attacks grew faster, almost frantic. Rysha felt daunted as she struggled to keep up, having to parry and move her feet rapidly so as not to give ground. Fortunately, he lost his accuracy and missed a few important blocks. Rysha feinted toward his ribs on his left side, then, as he twisted his body away to avoid Dorfindral's tip, she whipped her blade down, sinking it into his thigh.

Hollering curses, he stumbled back. She pressed the advantage and feinted high, then attacked low again, catching him in the hip.

He pulled an arm back, and she almost didn't recognize his intent in time. He threw one of his daggers. Rysha ducked, desperately jerking Dorfindral up to protect her head. More by chance than because of skill, her blade deflected the weapon, and it clanked against a nearby wall.

Though shaken by the near miss, Rysha forced herself to lunge after him, knowing she had the advantage. He was down to one weapon.

But he halted, his eyes bulging in surprise—and pain—before Rysha could strike again. His remaining weapon fell from his fingers, and a second later, he followed, crumpling to his side.

Major Kaika stood behind him and in front of the doorway to their room. The smoke had cleared, revealing five fallen men in the street. Kaika bent and pulled a dagger out of the back of the one Rysha had been fighting.

"Sorry," Kaika said. "Normally, I would have let you finish—good training—but there are a lot of eyes watching this alley."

Rysha grimaced and glanced behind her, and then in the other direction as well. Girls, boys, men, and women crowded both ends of the alley, peering toward them with wide eyes. Most of them scattered when Kaika looked their way, but who knew how many spies had been in the group? From what Rysha had heard and seen, this city was run by a few crime lords and powerful business people. Possibly, those were the same thing here.

"I'll forgive you this one time, ma'am," Rysha said, though all she'd been thinking about was surviving the encounter and defending the babies, not getting *training*.

"You're a gracious lieutenant." Kaika kept her voice low so they wouldn't be overheard.

Right, it wasn't a good idea to announce to the world that they were Iskandian soldiers.

"Yes, ma'am," Rysha whispered. "That's how they taught us at the academy."

Kaika wiped her blade off on the dead man's shirt, but paused before rising from a crouch. There was nothing notable about their assailants' clothing, nor did all of them have the same hair or skin color. Rysha had noticed Lagresh was quite the melting pot with complexions from all over the world.

But something must have given Kaika a clue. She shoved the man over and cut his shirt part way open, revealing a brand in the center of his chest below his collarbones. It was a familiar mark. The symbol of the Brotherhood of the Dragon.

"I was hoping we wouldn't see these people again." Kaika rose to her feet and frowned at the fallen men.

It might have been useful to question one of them, but Rysha didn't think any had survived. The first one she'd stabbed had taken a bullet to the throat, courtesy of his comrade. And Kaika's foes all appeared quite dead.

"They wanted Trip dead from the moment they saw him," Rysha said, stepping through the doorway to check on the stasis chambers. "Maybe they can sense when someone with some of Agarrenon Shivar's blood is nearby. Or at least a couple of them can."

As she recalled, most of the cultists had been mundane—Dorfindral hadn't reacted to their presence, just as the blade hadn't been bothered by these attackers—but Trip had mentioned the leader having power. Had another leader stepped forward? One who could direct his people to the stasis chambers?

"You'd think they would want to *worship* someone with their god's blood," Kaika said. "Not get rid of the person."

"Maybe. The first zealot I encountered on the cliff called Trip a usurper. Maybe they think offspring of the dragon are inferior and should be gotten rid of? Or maybe they worry that such offspring might try to take control of the cult?"

Kaika grunted dubiously. Rysha wasn't enamored with the hypothesis herself. She had no evidence. Maybe she should have been reading the Brotherhood journal instead of the other one. But from the beginning, she'd been far more interested in the outpost and the dragon riders who had created it than in the cult that had moved in later. She would have been perfectly happy if she had never encountered the Brotherhood of the Dragon again.

Unfortunately, the Brotherhood seemed to have other ideas.

Rysha touched a dent in one of the stasis chambers, grimacing. Most of them appeared undamaged, and they continued to hum faintly with whatever magic powered them. The dent looked to have come from one of the bullets. She peered inside, her gut clenching because it was one of the human babies. The dragon-human hybrid babies, Rysha corrected, but it—he—looked perfectly human as he floated there in the transparent gel.

It was the boy she'd been thinking reminded her of Frian. She shifted to check on the one that she'd thought might be his twin, the curly-haired little girl. But the chamber wasn't next to the boy's, as it had been earlier. Had Kaika moved them around?

Rysha backed up and counted the rows. "Twenty-five... twenty-six..." Dread surged through her limbs. "Where's twenty-seven?"

"What?" Kaika leaned against the doorjamb—she had been watching the alley—but now she frowned over at Rysha.

Rysha checked again, peering into the tops of the chambers, hoping she had simply counted incorrectly. But she hadn't.

"One of the chambers is missing. It was here just a few minutes ago. I'm sure of it."

"Someone got in, took one, and got out without us noticing?" Kaika asked skeptically. "I was right outside the door. Fighting, yes, but I pay attention to my surroundings when I'm in a skirmish."

Rysha silently admitted that someone could have gotten by *her* without her noticing, especially with all that smoke, but said, "Could someone have used magic?"

"I—" Kaika frowned and tapped Eryndral's hilt, the sword back in its scabbard. "Damn, maybe so. It buzzed a little warning in my hand while I was fighting. I assumed it was implying my opponent had some dragon blood."

Rysha rubbed the back of her neck, that feeling of dread increasing to one of horror.

She had promised to keep an eye on the babies—to *protect* them—while Trip figured out who killed Dreyak. What would he think when he got back? Would he be disappointed in her? How not?

Rysha hoped he could use his magic to locate the stasis chamber. But what if it was too late? What if someone transported it out of the city? Or what if someone took it to the harbor, pried open the lid, and dumped the baby out?

Tears of fear and panic formed in her eyes.

"You have any way to get in touch with Trip?" Kaika touched her temple, sounding much calmer than Rysha felt.

"No, not unless he reaches out to me telepathically." Rysha didn't know what his range was for that, especially when she was toting Dorfindral around.

"I can go look for it while you guard the others, but we're not going to want to stay in this room indefinitely. It's clearly not safe now." Kaika waved toward their fallen assailants outside and also to the busted door. The initial kick that had thrust it open had also ripped it from its top hinge, and it hung askew. "People know we're here, and someone could bring a team back for the rest of the babies. We need to get Trip here to assemble his wagon so we can move."

Kaika waved at the disassembled metal wagon he had made from scrap ore carts in the dragon's lair. He'd taken its sides and wheels off so they could bring it into the room, fearing it would have been stolen in seconds if they left it outside unattended. Little had they known that would be the least of their worries.

"I better go while there's still a chance of catching up to—" Kaika frowned toward the rooftop on the opposite side of the alley and drew her sword again.

"More trouble?"

"Someone up there is spying on us. Someone who may have seen the kid being taken. Stay here." Kaika ran across the alley and leaped to a window, using its vertical bars to pull herself up. She kept climbing to the next story and then the next, disappearing onto the rooftop.

Rysha stared bleakly at the limestone wall of that building, feeling very alone and very much a failure.

CHAPTER 2

*W*E COULD SIMPLY GO IN *the front door,* Jaxi spoke into Trip's mind. *Majestic and powerful mages don't usually squat on smelly rooftops, their shirts stuck to suspicious tarry substances as they spy on people meandering into work.*

You believe I'm majestic and powerful? Trip asked, watching as a man in the gray and white uniform of one of the city's law enforcers strode toward the front door below his rooftop perch. Jaxi, one of two soulblades in scabbards attached to his belt, had been critiquing his information-gathering techniques all morning.

No, but I thought you might aspire to be those things.

As much as it pains me to agree with such a young and immature soul, Telryn, Azarwrath spoke up from his other hip, *I agree that this skulking is beneath you.*

I don't think I can walk in and start asking questions. Trip had considered that a couple of times, because he wasn't learning anything useful from brushing the minds of the enforcers coming to work or those already in the building. None of them were thinking about Dreyak, even though someone from the two-story enforcer structure had presumably been responsible for chaining his body to the prominent post at the city docks. Trip had hoped he would catch a few of them thinking of Dreyak today, if only to wonder why he'd disappeared from his ignoble perch during the night.

Before dawn, Trip had cut him down and searched his pockets, hoping for clues about who had murdered him. But if Dreyak had died with anything on him, thieves or his killers had removed it. After that, following Cofah tradition as much as he understood it, Trip had burned the body and scattered the ashes in the gentle waves lapping at the dock supports. Had there been anything he could have kept to send home to Dreyak's family, he would have done it, even though he already worried the Cofah would suspect his team of having something to do with his death.

Trip couldn't help but feel that he'd failed the Cofah warrior. It wasn't as if Dreyak had ever asked for his assistance or had a kind word for him, but he *had* helped his team retrieve those *chapaharii* blades from the pirate fortress and then bury the dragon portal in the Antarctic. He deserved more than to have met his death in this remote city of criminals.

You most certainly can question these people, Azarwrath said. *And if you do so, your words will elicit the thoughts you need in their minds.*

And what about after I'm done asking questions? At some point, they'll realize I have dragon blood. Remember what was carved into Dreyak's chest? Witch. I don't think these people like magic. If the enforcers start searching for me… I don't want to lead armed men back to the others. Or the babies.

I do not think you need to worry about these mundane beings, but I can show you how to remove the enforcers' memories of you questioning them.

That's… creepy. And disturbing. I don't want to tinker with people's memories. Trip shuddered at the idea that he might have the power to do so.

He spotted movement out in the harbor, one of two massive barges adjusting its position. One had something like a palace atop it with towers and spires, the roofs glinting golden under the sun's rays. The word *barge* hardly seemed adequate. The second looked like a floating warehouse that could store massive amounts of goods. Neither appeared seaworthy. He wondered if they were permanently anchored in the harbor.

We've had this discussion, Telryn. Some tactics that would not be acceptable when used on allies should be employed on enemies, thus to avoid greater pain and destruction later on.

It seems a fine line. And are these enemies? They're just people who work here.

The people who work here are employed by criminal organizations, Jaxi put in. *I've been browsing through the thoughts of a man doing the books in an office in the back, and it looks like four different business owners are responsible for the salaries of these supposed public protectors. You may want to start your questioning with the bookkeeper. Besides, some street urchin on a different rooftop has noticed you and is currently wondering if the enforcers would pay her for informing them that they have a spy on their building. You should probably threaten her with your power and majesty.*

Trip looked across the square in front of the enforcer building and immediately spotted a girl of nine or ten on a sloped red tile roof. She flinched when their eyes met. He glimpsed scrawny limbs and ragtag clothing before she scrambled over the apex of the roof and behind a chimney. Her curiosity may have outweighed her wisdom, for she poked her eyes around the chimney to look at him again.

I'd rather feed her than throw power at her, Trip thought. *She looks hungry.*

She looks hungry for the coin she'll get for reporting you, Jaxi said. *Don't be soft-hearted, especially in this town. Everybody is on someone's payroll here.*

I didn't know you were an expert after only a day here.

Trip fished in his pocket for one of the few coins he carried, choosing a silver one since it would have value even if nobody here dealt in Iskandian currency. He held it before his eyes, then gathered a channel of air under it. He let go, pleased when it hovered there, bobbing slightly. A few weeks ago, he wouldn't have believed he could do such a thing. He squinted at the coin, willing the air to sweep it over the square and toward the opposite rooftop.

I've been paying attention, Jaxi said as the coin reached the chimney.

At first, the girl ducked out of sight, but she must have realized what it was, because she scurried out over the tiles toward it.

What have you been doing? Jaxi added. *Dreaming of your lieutenant's voluptuous naked curves?*

Trip lost his concentration. The coin fell, clanking onto the tiles and rolling down toward the gutter.

He rushed to reestablish his concentration and stop it before it disappeared and the girl couldn't reach it. She was faster than he and ran down and snatched it before it landed in the gutter. She raced back, disappearing behind the chimney, but Trip could sense her there, staring with disbelief at the coin in her hand.

Refusing to respond to Jaxi's comment, he focused on the girl and projected a few words into her mind.

I would appreciate it if you didn't mention seeing me, he thought.

Surprise and fear lurched into the girl's mind. She raced off the rooftop and slid down a vertical drainpipe at the corner, but she was so scared that she slipped and fell to the uneven stone street, twisting her ankle. That didn't keep her from running away, but her ankle hurt with each step.

Trip slumped. He hadn't meant to scare her and certainly not to hurt her.

Was this what it meant to be a sorcerer? That no matter how well-intentioned his actions, there was the potential to do as much harm as good?

Sorry, Jaxi said. *I just wanted to warn you she was watching. I didn't think you'd fling coins at her.*

I don't think the coin was the problem.

No. Now you've learned why we rarely make telepathic contact with those who aren't expecting it. The average person finds it alarming to hear a voice in their head, no matter how wise and sublime the owner of that voice is.

Are you describing you or me? Trip asked.

Me of course. Nobody would describe you *as wise.*

Trip wished he could feel indignant about that comment, but he feared "nobody" was correct.

All right. He scooted across the rooftop, grimacing when his shirt stuck to the tarry substance Jaxi had noticed, and found a drainpipe of his own to skim down. *We'll opt for the direct route. Are you both prepared to save my butt if I get into trouble?*

Naturally, Azarwrath said as Trip headed for the front door of the whitewashed stone building.

Indeed, Jaxi agreed. *We're prepared to save your butt day and night. It's why Sardelle sent me along, you know.*

I thought she sent you because you incinerated a diaper, Trip thought. *While it was still attached to her baby.*

No. She agrees that I'm not the ideal babysitter, but she sent me to make sure you don't turn into a megalomaniac dragonling that we have to worry about.

Trip stubbed his toe on the single step leading up to the door. Jaxi hadn't admitted that before, and his stomach knotted at the idea that Sardelle—and through her, possibly General Zirkander as well—didn't trust him.

Does she deem that likely? Trip asked softly.

Not at this time, but we're concerned that an old Cofah soulblade flung himself into your hands. We don't know what Azarwrath's motivations are or if he'll try to manipulate you into being something you're not. Or at least, something you weren't. *Like loyal to Cofahre instead of Iskandia.*

Trip paused with his hand on the door latch, expecting Azarwrath to chime in with a disgruntled comment. But he realized Jaxi had been directing the words solely at him.

I don't think he's angling for that. Trip rubbed the metal latch with his thumb, the back part of his mind noting a few pits and rusty spots that he could have smoothed out with the proper tools. *Does General Zirkander share Sardelle's concern?*

Nah, he said you're a good kid and would tell Azzy to toss himself in a volcano if he tried to turn you into a Cofah sympathizer.

Ah. Trip closed his eyes, surprised at how much emotion welled within him at the simple statement. That Zirkander barely knew him but believed that with such certainty. *Good. It's true.*

He didn't know how anyone could think he would betray the country where he'd grown up, where his grandparents still lived. And his army colleagues and friends. He wanted to be a *hero* to Iskandia, not a traitor.

It's just a mild concern, a hedging of possibilities, Jaxi assured him.

I understand. And he did, but he couldn't help but feel deflated that Jaxi had been sent to keep an eye on him rather than to assist and guide him.

With an alarmed lurch, he realized Jaxi might be suspicious of his motives for staying here, for wanting to finish Dreyak's mission for him, or at least find out what had happened to him. Did Jaxi believe Azarwrath might have been the one to suggest it?

He remembered being surprised when he'd learned he was subconsciously protecting his thoughts now and that the soulblades could no longer read him all the time, unless he made an effort to let them see into his mind. Or if he was distracted thinking about things like voluptuous naked curves and, as Jaxi had said, left his bank vault door flapping open. Being opaque to the soulblades now might make them—make *Jaxi*—less certain of him.

The door opened, almost knocking Trip off the top step.

A stern-faced man with bare muscled arms the size of tree trunks—or, in this place, two-hundred-year-old barrel cactuses—stepped out. No less than six daggers and two pistols hung from his belt. He frowned, pausing to eye Trip and the two swords sheathed at his waist.

That's not the bookkeeper, is it? Trip asked the soulblades as he said, "Sorry, sir," out loud.

Does he look *like a bookkeeper?* Jaxi asked as Azarwrath offered a simple, *No.*

"Is this the enforcer headquarters?" Trip asked. It was a stupid question, but nothing else popped into his mind. He hadn't concocted a cover story to explain why he might want to enter.

Because powerful mages don't need cover stories, Telryn.

Simply tell him to step aside while you ooze some power at him, Jaxi added. *You did it on the way into town with Kaika and Rysha.*

When I did that, I wanted people to sense that it would be unwise for them to wonder about us and our wagon. I wanted to protect the babies.

Well, now you can want to protect your butt cheeks. Do it.

"Yes. But we don't work with your kind." The enforcer squinted at Trip. "You better get off our steps and ply your trade elsewhere."

Trip had been in the process of taking a deep breath and attempting to project his aura outward, but the reaction startled him.

"My kind?" he asked, not able to hide his puzzled tone.

"Bounty hunters." The enforcer waved at his swords. "Seen enough of you to know one. Damn independent rogues. *We*—" he thumped himself on the chest, "—handle collecting criminals here. And getting paid for it."

Distaste trickled from the enforcer along with a vibrant memory. He had recently been stalking a wanted man and had been about to apprehend him when a bounty hunter leaped from the shadows, driving a dagger into his target's chest. The enforcer had battled the bounty hunter for the right to decapitate the wanted man, but had lost the fight, nearly being knocked unconscious. He'd watched his rival slice off the target's head and stalk off with his prize.

"Ah." Trip noticed the memory hadn't included anything about the beheaded man actually being a criminal, just that someone powerful had wanted him dead. "I have a quick question for someone inside. Step aside, please."

Trip tried to let some of his aura slip through, as he'd done the day before, but he'd had a better reason for it the day before. Now, he felt like a bully trying to use his powers for his own gain.

The enforcer squinted suspiciously at Trip even though his legs moved, as if of their own volition, and he stepped to the side of the door. Trip met the man's stare, silently urging him to continue away from the building. The enforcer headed down the stairs.

Realizing the man would be as likely to know about Dreyak as any of the enforcers, Trip turned and asked, "You don't know anything about a shaven-headed Cofah warrior that was killed and strung up by the docks, do you?"

"Just that he was worth two hundred vreks," the enforcer said, shrugging. "I didn't get him. Fraxog did, I think."

"Is he here today?" Trip pointed his thumb toward the door.

"Nah, he's always out on patrol. Does extras so he can get all the wanted thugs roaming around after dark. He'll probably be able to buy a palace soon with all the bounties he collects." The man curled his lip, eyeing Trip's swords again, and Trip could sense his sway over him slipping away.

"I'm a traveler, not a bounty hunter." Trip willed the man to believe him. "Who paid Fraxog the bounty?"

"Paymaster Jamrok." The enforcer waved. "Last office in the back."

The enforcer turned his back to Trip and stomped off, wallowing in bitterness and thinking again of the wanted man he'd lost out on.

So long as he wasn't after Trip, Rysha, or Kaika.

I feel disgruntled that I've been mistaken for some thugly bounty hunter, Jaxi thought.

Perhaps you should have glowed at him. Trip stepped inside to a large marble-floored room with light coming through the slitted windows in the walls. *Wisely and sublimely.*

Undoubtedly so.

A couple of enforcers at desks frowned in Trip's direction when he entered. Once again, thoughts of cover stories came to Trip's mind, but he envisioned a human version of Azarwrath frowning at him, eyes dark under bushy gray eyebrows.

Instead of opening his mouth, Trip willed the people not to notice him. He tried not to think how contradictory it was for him to use his powers—and make his aura *more* noticeable—while doing this.

The enforcers turned back to the books and papers on their desks. Trip let out a relieved breath. He'd done it with the cultists, when he'd ordered them to give up the search and return to the bowels of their mountain sanctuary, but that had been for the good of his team. Why did manipulating people for his own gain seem harder? And... wrong?

The soulblades, apparently not privy to his thoughts, did not comment.

Trip strode down a wide corridor, ignoring mostly empty side offices and angling toward the one he'd seen in the bounty-hunter-hating enforcer's thoughts.

He walked in without knocking, startling a man sitting at a desk. The paymaster, presumably.

A vault door was open behind him, and he whirled to slam it shut before reaching for a pistol secured in a hidden holster under his desk.

"Relax, my friend." Trip held the man's gaze, willing him to be at ease, to see him as a welcome visitor rather than a mistrusted stranger.

For a few seconds, the paymaster didn't move. His hand hovered under his desk, an inch from the pistol's holster.

"I am in need of your services." Trip was tempted to offer money, since that seemed to be how things were done around here, but he had very little and none in the local currency. General Zirkander hadn't had an extended stay in Lagresh in mind when he'd sent Trip off on this mission.

The paymaster settled back into his chair, leaving the pistol in its hidden holster. He eyed Trip's sword scabbards, taking a long look at each one before speaking.

"Unless you work for Terror Tay, Bhodian, the Silver Shark, or the Overseer, I can't help you."

Aren't those charming names? Jaxi observed. *What happened to Bhodian? He didn't keep up with his membership dues for the Brutish Nickname of the Month Club?*

"I've actually been in contact with the Silver Shark," Trip said.

The paymaster had thought of a beautiful bronze-skinned woman with black hair shot with silver as he said the name. *Her* name. Lustful fancies had accompanied the image with a focus on full breasts and a dress that accented them. Though Trip wasn't sure he wanted to encourage the paymaster to spend more time thinking of her, the images accompanying the other names had been fuzzier. Besides, the woman had looked Cofah. It was a stretch, but maybe Dreyak had known of her and contacted her.

"Oh? The Shark doesn't usually take on new people and has no reason to acquire a mage of his own."

The paymaster waved casually and still appeared relaxed, but his eyes were intent. Because Trip had seen his thoughts, he recognized the trap.

"*She* finds useful people... useful." Trip was so focused on letting the paymaster know that he knew the Shark's sex that he forgot to organize the rest of the sentence to have more punch.

Do yourself a favor, and don't go into speechwriting when you retire from piloting, Jaxi said.

No plans for that.

Wise.

The paymaster snorted and didn't acknowledge that Trip had seen through his little trap. "I can imagine what *use* she finds for you, Green Eyes."

It took Trip a moment to realize what the man was suggesting. When he *did* realize it, he blushed like a twelve-year-old boy getting a speculative wink from the girl next door. So much for striding in like a majestic and powerful mage.

Stop blushing and pay attention, Jaxi advised. *He knows you're manipulating him and that you have power.*

"A Cofah warrior was killed here recently," Trip said, acknowledging Jaxi's words with a mental nod. "Were the enforcers responsible? My new acquaintance wants to know."

He doubted his words would convince the paymaster to spill information, especially if he was being careful because he believed Trip was a sorcerer, but if answers to the questions rose in the man's thoughts, that might be enough.

"I believe your *acquaintance* already knows all about that. One of her messengers dropped off the payment in advance for the Cofah's death and came by to ensure that Gull and Voxin, our two resident mages, helped with defeating him."

"That's not what she told me," Trip said, feeling far more on the defensive than he should have, considering he was leading this questioning session. But he could see from the paymaster's thoughts that he was telling the truth. A squirrelly man with two missing front teeth had brought the payment by several days earlier, and the man was known to work for the Shark, among others.

"Maybe you're just her latest bedroom toy, Green Eyes."

A flash of sullenness entered the paymaster's thoughts, and Trip sensed that *he* wished to be a bedroom toy for the woman. That was surprising since his vision of her seemed to be of someone around fifty. She was still striking, no doubt, but Trip would have expected the enforcer to lust after younger women.

"Not a confidant," the man added.

"Why would the Shark want to kill a man from her own homeland?" Trip asked, hoping to confirm whether or not she was Cofah. Just because she had bronze skin and straight dark hair didn't assure she came from the empire's home continent.

The paymaster shrugged. "She's a businesswoman. I'm sure she puts threats to her financial interests ahead of personal feelings toward her countrymen."

It was all Trip could do to keep his mouth from dropping open. Business? What could Dreyak have been saying or doing that would cause someone to find him a threat to his—or her—business? He felt lost in this entire conversation.

"Assuming she has any feelings left for her countrymen." The paymaster shrugged again. "She's been in Lagresh longer than I have." The man eyed Trip's swords again. "You'll have to talk to her if you want to know why she pays to have the people killed that she does. We don't interrogate our benefactors around here."

Trip almost asked where he could find the woman, but remembered he was supposed to be an associate of hers already. "I'll do that. Tonight, when we're enjoying each other's company at her place." He winked and smirked, trying to emulate the expression Leftie adopted when he was certain he would be sleeping with a woman that night.

Stop that, Jaxi said. *You look like you got something in your eye.*

Fortunately, the paymaster wasn't as much of a critic. A surge of envy flooded him, and he imagined himself traveling out to the woman's floating warehouse to romance her in her upstairs loft.

Trip grimaced. He was glad to learn the woman's location, but chagrined that she lived somewhere it would be difficult to reach unobserved. He would either have to steal someone's boat to get out there or levitate across the harbor with the soulblades' assistance—he wasn't that accustomed to using channeled air on *himself* yet. Either option would have to wait until dark.

"Thank you for your assistance." Trip started to lift his fingers in an Iskandian military salute, but stopped mid-gesture and instead brought his hand to his stomach and bowed.

Did they bow in this country? He had no idea.

You better stick to piloting and shooting things, Jaxi said. *You would make a horrible spy.*

Are you this critical with Sardelle? Trip asked, backing away from the desk.

She values my criticism. It helps her grow as a person.

Trip was beginning to appreciate that Azarwrath was proving to be a less verbose soulblade. Maybe because he was older, he needed more naps.

Really, came Azarwrath's dry response.

Trip grinned because he'd intentionally let that thought slip out. It pleased him that he was starting to have some control over when other telepaths could read his mind and when they couldn't.

When have you caught me sleeping? Azarwrath added. *I simply don't feel the need to fill your head with inane chatter, unlike a certain* other *soulblade.*

My chat is pithy and wise, Jaxi said. *And also relevant. Trip, use your spymaster skills on that paper before you leave.*

Already in the doorway, Trip paused and looked back as the paymaster slid a sheet of paper out of a folder on his desk. Trip expected a wanted poster, but the page held two images on it, not of people. Were those swords? He squinted, but couldn't see the ink drawings well from there.

Use your senses or enhance your vision, Azarwrath advised.

Trip was about to ask how, since he'd previously only used his senses to detect life and nearby terrain, not distant artwork, but Azarwrath did something to his eyes first. He felt a little itch, and his vision sharpened so that he clearly saw swords—no, a sword and a scabbard—drawn in the picture. Something about the runes or hieroglyphics on the scabbard was familiar.

That looks exactly like Kasandral, Jaxi thought.

The chapaharii *sword that Captain Ahn and Colonel Therrik share?* Trip had seen it in the hangar when he'd briefly met Captain Ahn. As he scrutinized the drawing, he realized one of the runes matched a rune on the side of Dorfindral's scabbard. Maybe it was on Eryndral's too.

Yes, Jaxi replied. *Note the reward on the top.*

I see it. Five thousand vreks. What is that in nucros?

I'll have you know that nothing embossed in the runes on my *scabbard claims that soulblades are experts on global exchange rates.*

In other words, she does not know, Azarwrath said.

Do you? Trip asked.

About seven thousand nucros.

Do you actually know that or are you making it up? Jaxi asked suspiciously.

Do not forget that I worked with pirates for many years, Azarwrath said without any hint of pride. If anything, he sounded chagrined. *Pirates are well aware of what the goods they acquire are worth around the world. They sometimes sail to different countries to get better rates.*

The paymaster looked up and frowned at Trip. "Don't you have a sexy businesswoman waiting for you?"

"So it seems," Trip murmured and hurried out.

As he walked down the hallway toward the exit, he realized why the paymaster had scrutinized the soulblades. He must have been wondering if they were *chapaharii* swords and if he could get any money for them if he managed to acquire them. The common person probably didn't know that mages couldn't touch *chapaharii* weapons. Further, they might think any fancy-looking sword was one.

Trip frowned. What if *all* of the enforcers were looking for *chapaharii* blades now? Kaika and Rysha could be in trouble.

CHAPTER 3

RYSHA PACED BACK AND FORTH in front of the stasis chambers while watching the door she'd manhandled back into place. She gnawed on something the locals called Tacky. Dried fish jerky seasoned with something that seemed a mix of sugar and fire chilis. It was awful, stale, and not truly identifiable as fish, but it was available everywhere. She couldn't say that it filled her stomach, since it took ten minutes to chew down a piece, but it gave her mouth something to do while she worried about the missing stasis chamber.

The journal and the cult book lay open on one of the lumpy mattresses, but she had a hard time studying, knowing she had failed Trip and one of those helpless babies. Worse, Trip and Kaika had both been gone longer than expected. Rysha had expected—*hoped*—Kaika would return within minutes with the stasis chamber in her arms.

Thumps, voices, and clangs kept coming from the alley. Rysha had thought the bodies out there would deter foot traffic for a while, but earlier, after someone had exclaimed in wordless delight, she'd opened the shutters to peer out. She'd spotted a woman and man— wife and husband?—levering a body into a wheelbarrow while a couple of kids rifled through the pockets of the other fallen men.

"…good money for these bodies, and those knives are gems," the woman had said, indifferent to the blood spattering the cobblestones and the bullet holes riddling the surrounding walls.

Rysha had backed away and closed the shutters, not wanting to know what kind of economy paid "good money" for bodies. Nor did she want to know what could be done with dead human beings to turn a profit.

A thump sounded on the door, and Rysha grabbed Dorfindral.

She had set the sword aside earlier, hoping to make herself more accessible in case Trip attempted to communicate with her from a distance. It buzzed as she gripped it again, as if to admonish her for not keeping it close.

Rysha took a deep breath. The idea of defending the room—the stasis babies—again without Kaika's help unnerved her, but she vowed to do it. She wouldn't fail again.

It's me, a gentle voice spoke into her mind. Trip.

A surge of excitement flowed into her arms as Dorfindral hoped in vain that it would finally get a chance to rid the world of a vile half-dragon human.

She glared at the blade and set it aside. All the quality time Dorfindral had spent with Trip, and the silly sword didn't yet know he was an ally. Or didn't care. She wished Trip had reprogrammed its personality and not just the command words.

The door seems to be malfunctioning. His tone turned dry, and she suspected he had already examined it and determined the problem. She also suspected he didn't yet know about the missing baby.

You're skinny, Rysha thought back while she mustered the courage to bring it up. *I can open the shutters, and we can see if you can fit between the bars over the window.*

Skinny? That denotes scrawniness. I assure you that I'm lean, wiry, and strong.

Don't worry, Trip. It wasn't your massive brawn that attracted me to you. I won't think less of you if you can slip between these bars.

My lean, wiry, strongness—I didn't claim massive brawn—couldn't possibly fit between those bars. I believe they're there to keep people such as myself out of the hostel rooms.

People such as yourself? Trip, you realize that you are officially in your own category these days, right? It's a very special category that few can enter.

Rysha headed for the door, intending to tug it open, if the warped hinge would allow it. She glanced at it as she approached, then halted in surprise. It was... reshaping itself. The bent screws re-formed, and the hinge smoothed itself to the jamb and door again.

The door opened easily and soundlessly on hinges that were more obliging than they had ever been.

That makes it a rather lonely category. Trip stepped inside. His lopsided smile, a mixture of self-deprecation and wry but resigned amusement, tugged at her heart.

Rysha stepped forward and hugged him. "Categories are for simpletons. We're all individuals. Unique souls with unique places in the world."

"Hm." Trip returned her hug, resting the side of his head against hers. "Did you know your room has bullet holes in the door?"

"This is hardly my room. Major Kaika is the one who rented it." Rysha took a deep breath and groped for an opening. She had to tell him.

"Where is she?" Trip looked around, though it wasn't as if there were any places to hide in the room.

There was her opening.

"She chased someone who was spying on us from a rooftop. After killing several people who attacked us. And whose bodies were later carted away to be sold for parts." Rysha tried to keep her tone calm and flippant—that seemed to be the way for Iskandian elite troops, and for pilots, as well—but her voice cracked as she continued on to the important part. "We lost one of the stasis chambers. We didn't even see someone get in. Kaika said her sword sensed a little magic. I was too busy fighting to notice anything, and it was smoky, and—" She took a deep breath and forced herself to slow down. "I'm sorry, Trip. It was one of the human babies, a little girl. Kaika was hoping the spy saw whoever got the stasis chamber and that she can get it back."

Rysha closed her eyes, her spectacles mashed into Trip's shoulder. She didn't want to see his expression, his disappointment.

"It sounds like you had an eventful day." He stroked the back of her head and didn't say anything condemning, even though he had to feel distress. He'd only been gone a few hours, and they had let someone steal one of his defenseless little siblings.

Easy, Trip thought gently into her mind. *It could have happened if I'd been here too. It looks like the odds were against you. I didn't expect so much interest in them. I shouldn't have left you two alone. I'm glad you're all right.*

Even though Rysha wouldn't forgive herself, the fact that he wasn't blaming her filled her with relief. She wanted to be strong and independent like Kaika, who had probably never leaned against a man for support in her life, but it felt good to remove her spectacles, rest her head against Trip's shoulder, and let him stroke her hair.

"If Kaika can't find it—find her—will you be able to sense the stasis chamber's location in the city?" she asked.

Trip hesitated. "Maybe. There's more magic in this city than I would have expected, dragon-blooded people and also artifacts. A lot of noise like that makes it hard to pinpoint specific items."

"I hope Kaika brings it back."

"I'll find the baby, even if she doesn't." His determination came through in the words, and Rysha sensed how much it meant to him. Trip might not blame her, but that didn't mean he wasn't upset by the loss.

"Major Kaika wants to move, no matter what," Rysha said. "These people—one of them had a Brotherhood of the Dragon brand on his chest—singled out our room and were determined to get in. I don't know if they knew exactly what we had and believed them valuable or if it was just a guess after seeing us unload the wagon. I doubt that's all it was. Someone was willing to throw away men's lives to get in here."

"It's possible they knew about the stasis chambers, but it's also possible they wanted the *chapaharii* weapons and, when they realized they wouldn't get one, grabbed the only other thing in the room besides our packs."

Rysha leaned back. "What makes you think they came for the swords? Until the fight this afternoon, we'd never had them out of their scabbards."

"I saw a poster in an enforcer's office. It was nothing about us specifically, but it had a picture of a *chapaharii* sword on it, the blade next to the scabbard. Jaxi identified it right away. It looked a lot like the one I saw Captain Ahn carrying back at the flier base."

"Kasandral?"

Trip nodded. "There could be a number of them that look like that, but there was a reward of five thousand vreks listed above the drawings. Someone is paying for *chapaharii* weapons, and we happened to stroll into the city yesterday with two."

"It was in the local currency? Not nucros? It would be upsetting if King Angulus issued a reward for them while we happened to be over here."

"Yes, the local currency, though I suppose it's possible that whoever is offering the reward plans to act as a middleman and then ship them off to a government in need of protecting its people from dragons. At a large markup." Trip frowned and gazed at the stasis chambers. Worrying someone meant to sell the one that had been stolen? "This seems like the kind of place for that."

"I was just having similarly disparaging thoughts about Lagresh. At least paying for a valuable sword that can be used for fighting dragons seems more morally acceptable than paying for human bodies. Or magical babies."

Trip's brow furrowed. "Is it morally acceptable if two women are attacked in their hostel room in order to acquire those swords?"

"No, but maybe whoever offered the reward was thinking more of archaeological treasure hunts to old ruins than murders."

Rysha thought again of the dead man with the Brotherhood brand on his chest. As large as the organization was, it seemed their coffers would be deep already and they wouldn't need to chase rewards. The man's brand could have been a coincidence and nothing more. Or maybe the attack hadn't had anything to do with the *chapaharii* swords. Maybe the thief had gotten exactly what he wanted.

"In this town?" Trip asked. "I doubt it. Besides, who would think the enforcers would be experts on ancient sword-filled ruins?"

"Maybe someone in the office has an academic background and a hobby." She arched her eyebrows at him. "You don't know, just because someone wears a uniform, where their expertise lies."

"I don't think we should use you as an example for what's typical in a law or military force. You also belong to a category that doesn't house many other people."

"Did you just call me odd, Trip?"

"Yes, but I was trying to be subtle about it."

"Try harder. My cogs aren't rusty, you know."

"I've noticed. Your cogs are very nice." He glanced at her chest with speculation in his eyes.

Rysha wouldn't have minded more than a glance. A nice long leer, perhaps. Though her Aunt Tadelay would be scandalized if she learned her niece admitted that to a man.

"Really, Trip. The things engineers say to seduce a woman."

Trip looked at the stasis chambers again, let go of her, and stepped back instead of leering or launching a seduction campaign. He walked to the stack of stasis chambers, shifted some away from the wall, and leaned over to pull out a business card that had fallen behind them. It hadn't been visible—he must have detected it with his senses. Or maybe the soulblades had.

"Harbor Warehouse One," he read, then flipped it over. "Ten thousand vreks."

Rysha joined him to peer at the card. The amount—a reward?—was scribbled on the back in pencil. The calligraphic words on the front had been printed at a print shop.

"Is that an address?" She rose on her toes, hope and excitement returning for the first time since the theft. "Maybe that's where the stasis chamber was taken." She dropped down on her heels again. "But it would be awfully convenient if the thief left his destination behind. I suppose it could have fallen out of a pocket, but I'm inclined to think it's a plant. Maybe someone wants us to think that's where it was taken, that whoever owns the place was responsible. It's probably on its way to somewhere on the opposite side of the city." Still… if Kaika didn't find the stasis chamber, they had to check. What other leads did they have? Unless Trip could magically locate it.

Rysha looked at his face, noting his silence.

He had flipped the card back to the front and was staring down at the three typeset words. "If this is the floating warehouse I think it is… I already needed to visit it. Now, it seems, I have two reasons to go."

"You mean *we*, don't you?" She had been at least partially responsible for losing the baby. She would help him get her back.

"You're welcome to come. I talked to an enforcer and got some clues out of his thoughts. I believe the Silver Shark lives and works out there. She's a powerful businesswoman who is one of the four major players that run just about everything in the city. I have no idea why she would want one of the babies, but she may be the one who ordered Dreyak's death. I doubt she'll want to talk to an Iskandian pilot about either event, so the evening could get interesting."

"I should definitely come then. And bring some of Kaika's explosives."

Rysha hoped Kaika returned in time so she *could* go with him. He wouldn't want to delay, but they couldn't leave the rest of the stasis chambers unguarded.

Rysha also hoped that Kaika hadn't run into anyone looking to cash in on the *chapaharii* bounty. Even if she had, it was hard to imagine her not being able to handle the problem. Still, anyone could have some bad luck. She thought sadly of Dreyak.

"When do you get your own explosives?" Trip asked.

"Probably after I graduate from the elite troops training and whatever demolitions school Major Kaika went to. I imagine that if I walked up to the armory now and asked for explosives, the supply sergeant would lock me inside."

"Sergeants don't usually lock up officers."

"Not even young lieutenants who are shiftily asking for bombs?"

"Young?" Trip arched his eyebrows. "Didn't we decide you were rather geriatric for a lieutenant?"

"I'm twenty-seven. That's a normal age. You're just overly young for a captain."

"Are you sure? I thought we determined I should be making you a cane."

"It's possible there's a reason Dorfindral keeps suggesting I beat you mercilessly."

"Jealousy?"

"That's not it."

"Huh."

He lifted his arms to offer a hug, and while Rysha was debating if she wanted to accept it after he'd called her old, he lowered his arms and turned toward the door. He pulled it open, revealing Kaika standing there, her hand raised to knock. She wasn't carrying anything. Rysha sighed.

"You make a prompt butler, Trip," Kaika said, walking in.

Her shoulders had a weary slump, and soot smeared the side of her face, but she did not appear injured.

"I'll keep that in mind as a backup profession in case I ever get kicked out of the army." He smiled, as if it were a joke, but Rysha detected worry in his eyes. Maybe he feared that was a possibility because of his decision to stay here and settle Dreyak's affairs. And what if it took days or weeks to find the stasis chamber? He wouldn't be willing to go back to Iskandia while one of his siblings was missing.

"Being a sorcerer isn't your backup profession?" Kaika asked as Trip shut the door.

Full darkness had fallen outside.

"I don't think that's a valid profession these days."

"You sure? You should ask Sardelle. Maybe she'll start something up now that there's more than two of you in the country. There could be a guild with benefits. Better pay than the army offers. Which, admittedly, wouldn't take much. I ran into a panhandler with a monkey in downtown Pinoth once, and he told me how much he made for playing a flute and dancing with his furry sidekick on a busy street corner. It was depressing."

Kaika unbuckled her sword belt and flopped down on one of the thin, poky mattresses. She looked toward Rysha, her eyebrows lifting. To ask if Rysha had told him about the missing baby? She nodded once.

"It's a good thing you were recently promoted to major, ma'am," Rysha said. "Better pay, right?"

"I think the panhandler is still making more than I am. People do love monkeys." From flat on her back on the mattress, Kaika held up Eryndral. "Did you two know there's a reward out for these swords, right now? Not ours specifically, I don't think, but any sword with runes on the scabbard is being targeted and brought to the enforcers. They're offering three thousand vreks to anyone who brings one in."

"Interesting considering whoever pays the enforcers for them offers five thousand," Trip said.

"You *did* know." Kaika slanted him a disgusted look. "Why didn't you warn us?"

"I only learned about it this afternoon, ma'am," Trip said. "I warned Rysha."

"Because she's the one who you have warm, snuggly thoughts about at night?"

"Because she was here."

"You and your pet soulblades couldn't have located me in the city and tucked a telepathic warning into my brain? I would have listened."

Trip tilted his head thoughtfully. "Actually, I believe we *could* have found you, since you're familiar to us and carry that sword. I'll warn you next time something like this comes up. Though Jaxi says she wouldn't warn you if a piano was about to fall on your head, not after you called her a pet."

"Ah, that's fair. What does the other one think?"

"That a piano would be a flattering accessory on you."

"Those swords are impudent."

"Yes, ma'am."

Kaika sighed as she sat up and looked at Trip. "I guess Ravenwood told you, but someone sneaked in and stole one of the baby boxes while we were fighting with miscreants in the alley. I'm afraid I didn't see sign of the thief when I was out there."

"I understand, ma'am. We do have a possible lead. An address." Trip walked over and handed her the card.

"This was left in the room?"

"Behind the stasis chambers."

Kaika's lips twisted into an expression of skepticism.

Having voiced similar skepticism, Rysha understood perfectly. "It could be a trap. Or, at the least, misdirection. But it's our only lead."

"It's also somewhere I wanted to visit, regardless," Trip said. "I believe this may be the address of the woman responsible for Dreyak's death. I want to go find her tonight and question her. Also, if someone brought her the stasis chamber, it will be easy for me to sense it when I'm in the same building—or barge—as it is. Is it all right for me to go, ma'am?"

Kaika quirked a single eyebrow. "You're asking me for permission?"

"You're the highest-ranking officer here, and Blazer left you in charge."

"*I'm* aware of that. I just thought *you'd* forgotten it."

Trip's cheeks grew a touch red. "No, ma'am. I didn't—don't—want to disobey orders. I just want to do the right thing. For Dreyak and Cofahre *and* for Iskandia. I don't want the fact that we gave Dreyak a ride over here and were the last ones to see him alive to turn into an international incident when Prince Varlok learns he's dead."

"Yes, yes, I've heard your reasons for assigning yourself this mission, Sidetrip."

"And it's more than that now. I *have* to get the stasis chamber back before I can leave."

Kaika grimaced. "You've got a bunch of other ones that need to be taken back to Iskandia as soon as possible."

"I can't *abandon* one."

Rysha's gut twisted as she thought of the innocent baby girl. "The one the thief got was one of the human babies, ma'am." Maybe that would make a difference to her.

"*Half* human," Kaika grumbled.

Trip spread a hand, his face growing bleak. *He* was half human, after all.

"Yes," Kaika told him, "you may go off tonight and look for your little sibling and find Dreyak's murderer if you can. But you need to accomplish your goals quickly. We can't allow ourselves to get bogged down here for weeks. Our people need us back home. There's a dragon threat, in case you've forgotten. Besides, Blazer ordered us to get those stasis chambers off this dusty brown continent as soon as possible. It's better to take the ones we have than to risk losing more. Once I can arrange passage, we all need to be on the boat heading home. If that baby box is still missing, or if our superiors deem Dreyak's death as important as you seem to think it is, maybe they'll give you permission to come back with a team of pilots, but that's not my decision to make. And it's not *yours*. If you're not with us on the boat, you'll be looking into that butler's gig whenever you finally *do* get back to Iskandia." Kaika spoke firmly, meeting Trip's eyes, and he shifted under her gaze.

Since Kaika was so often flippant, it was easy to think she would be less likely to drop the disciplinary hammer, but that look made Rysha certain that she wouldn't forget it if they stepped on her authority. Kaika's gaze turned toward Rysha, including her as well as Trip, and she also found herself shifting uneasily.

"I don't think I'd make a very good butler, ma'am," Rysha said.

"Did your castle not have one who taught you the ways of the profession?" Trip smiled and touched her elbow.

"The manor *did* have a butler. And a maid. But I used to tell them all about the things I learned in the books I was reading, and they started avoiding me."

"How odd," Kaika said.

"I thought so."

Trip grew more serious and said, "I'll get to the bottom of all this tonight."

"*We* will," Rysha said. "If Major Kaika doesn't mind standing guard, I still want to go with you."

"Major Kaika would rather get a massage and a rub-down at a spa." Kaika closed her eyes.

Rysha hesitated. Maybe she shouldn't presume that Kaika would let her go off with Trip. "What happened out there, ma'am? Did you ever catch up with that spy?"

"No, I did not. I chased her over a dozen rooftops, through a stinking cannery, up the smokestack of a refinery, and into a park filled with hoodlums engaged in a full-contact sporting event. She cried, 'She's got one of the swords!' and more than fifty men, most with more fingers than teeth, gave chase. They didn't just want to catch me; they were perfectly happy to kill me to get the sword. They kept throwing rocks and knives whenever they got the opportunity. I spent three hours trying to lose them. I think one had dragon blood because he *had* to be tracking me with more than mundane means. He stuck to me like gum to the bottom of your finest parade boots. I finally got him alone, turned on him, and knocked the rest of the teeth out of his mouth. Then I used Eryndral to cut his belt off. By then, I was cranky, and I was tempted to cut off other things. Eryndral was glowing a little and agreed with the sentiment. Instead, I told him not to pester the handlers of *chapaharii* blades because they were powerful warriors. And then I took his pants."

"Er, what, ma'am?" Rysha asked.

"I'd cut the waistband when I slashed his belt, so they were falling off anyway. I figured that being pantsless would keep him from following me, and it seemed a less extreme punishment than cutting off his flesh pole or killing him outright. I hope he has a family that will mock him soundly when he arrives home."

"Our butler definitely would have mocked me if I'd come home without pants," Rysha said.

Kaika looked at her.

"He was the one to open the door, so he would have been the first to know."

"Yes, good. I hope this fellow's butler mocks him." Kaika closed her eyes again.

Trip opened his mouth, but Kaika must have anticipated his next question.

"Go, go." She waved her hand again. "I'll stay here on guard while you have grand adventures. Be back by dawn. I want to go to the docks early in case any new ships come in during the night."

"Yes, ma'am," Trip said, "but grand adventures weren't what I had in mind."

"Even if we got the opportunity to cut off someone's pants?" Rysha asked.

Trip smiled faintly, but he looked more worried than amused. He glanced toward the stasis chambers, perhaps feeling daunted by Kaika's timeline.

CHAPTER 4

W AVES ROLLED UP THE SANDY beach and lapped at the supports for the docks. Rysha stood in the shadows with Trip, and he briefly imagined that they were back home and taking that romantic sunset beach walk he'd dreamed about.

But here in Lagresh, the sun had set hours ago, and gunshots and screams of pain rang out from the city behind them. Giant cannons loomed on manmade rock formations around the harbor, their silhouettes dark and brooding against the moonlit sky. He remembered how they'd fired on the fliers without warning when Wolf Squadron had approached. There was nothing romantic about this place.

It was just as well. He needed to focus on his mission. He didn't have much time, and he needed to get the baby back.

Not just "the baby." His little sister. Even though he hadn't known she existed until a few days ago, his gut clenched at the idea of losing her forever, of never getting a chance to know her.

He'd been an only child his whole life, moving every year or two as a kid. How often had he longed for siblings? Brothers and sisters to play with in the yard. Brothers and sisters who didn't care how odd he was because they all shared the same blood. Because they were *all* odd.

Even if he didn't play anymore, not in the childhood sense, he loved the idea of watching little brothers and sisters play. Of seeing them grow up. Of knowing he had kin, that he wasn't all there was of his blood—of *him*—in the world.

Trip blinked away moisture forming in his eyes, surprised by how emotional the thoughts made him.

Focus, he reminded himself again, and locked his gaze on the harbor and the two vessels floating on the far side of it, well away from the docks. They were the same two barges he had noticed earlier in the day, one looking like a palace and the other a warehouse.

From here, he couldn't read their names to see if Harbor Warehouse One was printed somewhere on the hull of the darker, boxier one, but he and Rysha had looked at the street signs along the waterfront and hadn't found a match. It seemed likely the card he had found was for that barge.

Judging by how close it was to the other one, Trip suspected they were owned by the same person. The Silver Shark. He wondered what her Cofah name was and if she had been anyone in their society before emigrating here.

A woman's scream punctuated the night, and Trip winced. It was hard to imagine anyone but the depraved *wanting* to emigrate here.

"This isn't quite how I imagined our romantic walk on the beach going," Rysha said from his side.

He bumped his shoulder gently against hers, pleased she had also been thinking about their future romantic beach outing.

"Though the lights on that floating palace are pretty," she added. "Do you think that blue one is magical? Or is that just a special lens?"

"I'm not sure."

Trip had been focusing on the warehouse, but he eyed the spherical light she'd indicated. He didn't sense that it was magic. In fact, he couldn't sense much about the palace at all, such as how many people were in it. Over in the warehouse, he was aware of two people playing a card game near the front door. He also sensed dozens of animals in cages in the back. He'd hoped to sense the missing stasis chamber, but if it was out there, it wasn't in the warehouse.

In the palace... he not only couldn't sense anything inside, but trying to do so made his brain itch. It almost repelled him. The experience reminded him of the quarry with the banded iron formations, the formations that had offered up ore appropriate for crafting the magic-loathing *chapaharii* weapons.

But that was silly. They were at least fifty miles from there and no longer in the magic dead zone that surrounded the quarry. It was more likely that another sorcerer had placed a magical camouflage over the place.

Does either of you sense more about that floating palace than I do? Trip silently asked the soulblades.

I sense that those spires are pretentious and ridiculous, Jaxi said.

Your vast magical powers tell you that?

Indeed, they do. If yours aren't telling you the same thing, there's a problem.

I sense... Azarwrath was slower in sharing his verdict. *Little. I believe the same as you, Telryn, that it's likely we are dealing with a mage.*

Trip sighed. He should have known it wouldn't be easy.

He could tell there wasn't a woman on the warehouse barge, but he had no idea about the palace. Would it be worth going out to investigate the loft the paymaster had imagined even if the Silver Shark was nowhere around? And even if he didn't sense the stasis chamber out there? A bedroom might hold condemning documents or other clues.

It makes sense that an advantage such as magic would be useful in gaining power here, Azarwrath said.

I sense something, Jaxi thought.

Aside from crimes against architecture? Trip asked.

Yes. In the back of the warehouse barge, there are animals. A surprisingly large number of them.

Trip nodded. *I sensed them too.*

Animals with dragon blood.

He reached out a second time. He had missed that.

It's an eclectic—or should I say eccentric?—collection, Jaxi said. *Several giant lizards, winged lions, a couple of furry relatives of baboons, probably from Dakrovia or one of the equatorial islands around its northern end. Oh, I think those scaled panthers might be slightly magical versions of the one that attacked Rysha by the spring last week.*

She'll be glad to hear there's a more deadly variation of that three-hundred-pound fanged beast.

Doubtful. I haven't told her about the panthers yet. But all of the animals are caged and definitely have dragon blood. Does this woman run a circus of the odd and unusual?

I hope not. She might want to add me. Or a half-dragon little girl, Trip added to himself.

He winced, imagining his little sibling being turned into a circus performer or freak show entrant. Back at the hostel, he hadn't thought twice about leaving the stasis chambers with Kaika and Rysha, both because they were capable soldiers and because he hadn't believed anyone had known about the babies. A foolish belief. He should have known better. *He* could sense the chambers' magic when he was close enough. And as the paymaster mentioned, there were other sorcerers in the city.

You wouldn't look good in a cage, Jaxi said.

I agree. Pilots have to be free to fly. Trip decided to avoid the animals if they could. They shouldn't have anything to do with Dreyak's death or kidnapped babies, but they might alert the two guards to their presence if he and Rysha sneaked out there.

Maybe those animals would like to be free.

I imagine if we let them out here in the city, they would be hunted and killed. And only the native creatures would be able to survive in the nearby desert. I'll hope the owner is treating them humanely, whatever her reason for having them is. Admittedly, he didn't know if this Silver Shark was the owner. The paymaster's memories hadn't included thoughts of animals.

The owner that may have killed Dreyak for no good reason?

Rysha turned toward him, probably wondering about his long silence.

"Jaxi, Azarwrath, and I have started our spying early," he said.

"So I assumed. Does that mean we don't have to go out there?"

"No. I don't sense the woman or the stasis chamber in the warehouse, but since so many clues point to her and to this place, I think we should go out and snoop."

Rysha made a face. "Is it wise to pick trouble with one of the most powerful people in the city?"

"Financially and politically powerful, not magically powerful." Trip touched the hilts of the two soulblades. "We'll have the advantage if we're somehow discovered and there's a confrontation."

"You're not getting cocky on me, are you?"

"I hope not. Azarwrath once said he would let me know if I became arrogant and full of myself."

"Azarwrath did? That sounds like something Jaxi would say."

"I'm sure she would chime in."

Most definitely, Jaxi said. *I like your lieutenant. She's getting to know and respect me.*

She just said you would be quick to point out my failings.

She oozed respectful thoughts while she said it.

"Listen," Trip said, "I know it's not exactly legal, but we can't come here every night and wait to spot her. I'm not positive this is her full-time residence."

"She's not in the palace, either? I would think a rich businesswoman would be far more likely to live in a palace than a warehouse."

"It's possible." Hadn't he just been thinking that the way those two barges were anchored so closely together suggested the same owner? "But I can't sense anything on it, so I want to start with the warehouse."

"Ah, interesting." Rysha shifted her hand to Dorfindral's hilt.

"Do you sense magic out there? Or does the sword?"

"Not that I've noticed thus far, but we're also not that close."

"Let's get closer then. Warehouse first. For snooping."

"How are we getting out there?"

Trip almost said the soulblades could levitate them over, but remembered Dorfindral's presence would make it impossible to use magic on Rysha. And he couldn't imagine her leaving the sword behind. Nor did he want her to, not with dragon-blooded animals and who knew what else on the palace barge.

"We could swim, but a boat would be more convenient. Either way, we'll have to be quiet. There are two guards playing cards inside the warehouse." Trip had no idea if there were guards on the palace barge. He hadn't heard voices come from that direction, nor had he seen anyone with a light walking around on the deck.

"My vote would be for dry snooping, but there's only one ship tied up here tonight." Rysha pointed toward a schooner moored at the far end of the dock. "It probably has lifeboats, but I saw lanterns on the deck as we were walking over here, so I think there are people awake. I suppose we could borrow the whole schooner with your magical influence..." She didn't sound enthused by that idea.

"Let me see if I can come up with an alternative."

Trip directed his senses into the water, toward the bottom of the harbor. Unsurprisingly, he saw all manner of junk down there, including bottles, crates, barrels, and wrecks. Trip suspected a few battles had taken place in the harbor over the centuries.

He detected a lifeboat that hadn't made it to shore, likely due to the cannonball hole in the bottom of it. Though it was covered with barnacles and the metal brackets were rusted over, the hole appeared to be the only thing that would render it incapable of floating. If he could turn it upright and dump the water out.

Can you two help me? Trip asked.

With what? Jaxi asked. *Your bank vault door isn't open. Were you afraid to show me the latest issue of that metalworking magazine that you stuck inside?*

No, I understand that my mental decorating tastes aren't for everyone. Trip pointed out the boat to the soulblades and envisioned his plan.

You should be able to handle this on your own, Azarwrath said.

Are you encouraging me to grow as a sorcerer or are you simply uninterested in helping?

I don't like touching disgusting things. An image of the barnacles filled Trip's mind.

That's an excuse, Jaxi said. *He's old and doesn't want you to know he needs his nighttime naps.*

Something akin to a growl filled Trip's mind.

The boat stirred, breaking away from all manner of growth attaching it to a larger wreck on the harbor floor, then floated upward. Azarwrath moved it under the dock supports before it broke the surface, so it wouldn't be visible to those in the schooner. Trip meant to help, but Azarwrath worked quickly, and the barnacle-covered lifeboat soon rested upside-down on the sand next to them.

You're welcome, Jaxi said smugly, as if she was proud she'd convinced Azarwrath to do the work for him.

I was *encouraging Telryn to grow as a sorcerer,* Azarwrath said stiffly. *And also practice using his power.*

I'll use it now, Trip thought, hoping to head off an argument about age and naps.

He knelt beside the old boat, resting his hand on it and examining it with his mind more than his eyes. In the shadows, his eyes could barely distinguish it from the sand.

"Please tell me that isn't our ride out there," Rysha whispered.

"Not yet." Trip closed his eyes and concentrated.

Her groan wasn't heartening.

Not daunted, he examined the lifeboat's wood and iron parts. The craft was more wood than metal, which was more difficult for him to manipulate. He couldn't melt wood and shift it into other shapes.

Trip searched the bottom of the harbor again. This time, he found a rusted anchor. He hadn't used his power to lift anything out of the water before, but he didn't want to keep asking Azarwrath for favors, so he tried to channel the water and condense it the way he did with air when he lifted things. In attempting to do so, he created currents, not unlike what he'd done when he'd created a tidal wave the week before. On a whim, he twirled them, making something similar to a small, controlled tornado.

The water rotated, forming an upside-down vortex that tugged the anchor from its resting spot, then lifted it far more quickly than Trip had envisioned. The anchor flew straight out of the water and up. He rushed to shift his attention from the water to the air, cushioning his rusty treasure so that it would float gently over to the beach rather than losing momentum and landing back in the water with a huge splash.

I'll give that extra credit for creativity, Jaxi said.

It would have been better and required less energy expenditure on his part if he had used my method, Azarwrath said.

You must be tons of fun as a teacher.

I've instructed numerous young handlers over the years. That stiffness had crept into Azarwrath's tone again.

Did they die of boredom after you wilted their eager little egos?

They became powerful sorcerers.

Are you sure some didn't die of boredom? Jaxi asked. *I suspect you of having a selective memory, Azzy.*

While they insulted each other, Trip used a combination of brute force and magical power to lever the anchor into the boat. Once it rested on the bottom, he melted it slowly, separating the quality material from the rusted exterior, then smoothing it over the hole in the bottom. He formed screws and did his best to seal what became a thin sheet atop the wood. Something like a rubber gasket would have been ideal, but he didn't want to spend the whole night scavenging the harbor for parts. If the rowboat leaked, it should be a slow leak, and they could get to the barge and back before it mattered.

He flipped it over, shoved it off the sand and into the water, and grinned like a boy when it floated.

"My lady," Trip said, extending an arm toward his new craft, imagining himself as her butler, offering her an arm into the family steam carriage. Or did she have a separate chauffeur for that? How many people worked for her family?

He pushed the thought out of his mind. Besides, he should imagine himself as a handsome suitor rather than a servant. In the fairy tales of old, the butlers *never* got the ladies.

"If we take a walk along the harbor together, is it going to be like this?" In the dark, Rysha's face was impossible to read, but she sounded amused. Maybe *bemused.*

"I hadn't planned to stop along the way to fix a boat, if that's what you're asking. I suppose I might be tempted to pick up interesting materials I found on the beach."

"Interesting materials found on the beach?" Rysha accepted his arm and assistance into the boat, though she could have easily jumped in without getting wet. "Or on the bottom of the harbor where they've been rusting for centuries?"

"Naturally, the most interesting finds would be the ones hardest to reach."

Trip brushed her shoulder as he sat on the bench beside her. She tensed, and a faint green glow seeped from Dorfindral's scabbard.

She muttered something unpronounceable—Trip knew the word and still regarded it as unpronounceable—and the light faded.

"I see Dorfindral objects to me flirting with you," Trip said.

He supposed it was silly, but he'd thought the sword might start reacting differently to him after he'd assisted Rysha in reprogramming it with new command terms. But it *had* tried to kill him the whole time he'd been doing it.

"You were flirting with me?" Rysha asked.

"Well, I made you a boat."

"This is for *me*?" She reached out and touched the wet wooden side, the barnacles still attached inside and out, including on their equally wet seat.

"I would have just levitated across if I'd been alone."

"Ah, I see. In that case, I may need to name this fine craft. Perhaps I shall name it after my mother."

"The mother who, as you said, objects wholeheartedly to your commission in the army?"

"Indeed." Rysha prodded one of the poky barnacles and smiled. "I think you forgot to scrounge oars off the bottom of the harbor."

"Not really." Trip channeled a tiny tunnel of wind behind them and pushed at the back of the boat. The wood creaked, making him doubt his assessment of the craft's soundness, but it moved forward.

It needn't last for long, he reminded himself.

"You're a talented man, Trip," Rysha said, leaning her shoulder against his. "I enjoy going on adventures with you. Even though my butt is now soaking wet."

"They say mutual discomfort is the way that harmonious souls bond."

"Wise words, even if you pilfered them from the songwriter, Lord Yaringtor."

"Pilfered? At worst, I paraphrased."

I think you should just put your arm around her and kiss her, Jaxi said. *Your flirting skills leave a lot to be desired.*

What makes you say that?

The fact that she didn't know you were flirting with her.

Thanks for the advice, Jaxi.

You're welcome.

After the boat cleared the docks, Trip manipulated the wind, turning them toward the barges. He angled out wide, hoping to come in from the far side and remain unnoticed. The warehouse wasn't well lit on the side opposite the nearby palace.

One of the guards walked out the front door of the warehouse and fished in a cigarette tin. Trip winced and wished there were clouds in the sky poised to conveniently drift in front of the moon.

Relax, Jaxi said. *We'll add some camouflage. You can focus on wooing your lieutenant.*

I'm not going to woo her when her butt is wet.

You're not much of an opportunist. Why don't you offer to dry her clothes? With a gold dragon as a sire, you should have a knack for warming things up.

Warming them up, or incinerating them with the fiery flames of the hells?

Given that your girlfriend's butt cheeks are involved, I suggest mere warmth.

The guard with the cigarette inhaled and watched the harbor around him, his eyes too alert for Trip's comfort. For a few seconds, those eyes shifted in his direction. He stopped manipulating the air, worried the man could see their boat. Or *sense* it. Trip didn't think he had dragon blood, but that might be hard to gauge if it was a small amount.

A rumble came from the street near the head of the docks, and a steam carriage rolled up, the metal gleaming under the street lanterns. As new and modern as the latest Iskandian models in the capital, it seemed an anachronism in a city set a couple hundred years in the past in all other matters.

Most other matters, Trip amended, remembering those high-speed armored boats that had been powered by Referatu magical artifacts, not unlike Iskandian fliers.

Four cloaked and hooded figures stepped out of the carriage. The night wasn't cold, so there was little reason for the hoods, unless the people didn't want to be seen.

Trip thought of the cultists and their raised hoods, but they favored white attire. These people wore darker clothing, and they chatted easily, a few laughs ringing out over the harbor. One laugh belonged to a woman. Was this the Silver Shark? She leaned against another figure, linking arms with him or her.

A couple of armed men also stepped out of the carriage. The broad-shouldered and silent types, they took up bodyguard positions.

On the warehouse barge, the guard dropped his cigarette, stamped it out, and hustled back inside.

Worried they wouldn't have time to snoop, Trip channeled the wind again, moving the rowboat to the far side of the barge and out of view from the docks.

A word of warning, Telryn, Azarwrath said. *The woman that just got out of the metal conveyance has dragon blood.*

"It doesn't look like we'll have much time to snoop," Rysha whispered, her gaze toward the docks.

Trip grimaced. "You're right about that."

CHAPTER 5

RYSHA CLIMBED OUT OF THE rowboat and up the side of the barge, with Trip giving her a boost to reach the railing. Fortunately, it wasn't that far above their heads. The waves were calm here in the harbor, and she doubted these vessels ever left its protected waters.

After turning the remains of the anchor into a chain and hook to secure their rowboat to the barge, Trip followed Rysha up to the deck. She marveled at his ingenuity, even if magical power gave him much more versatility than most engineers. Still, she wondered who else would have thought to dredge a boat from the bottom of the harbor and fix it up instead of "borrowing" one from somewhere else.

"Back door?" Rysha pointed toward the rear of the warehouse, the end opposite of where that guard had stepped out on deck. She didn't know if such a door existed, but it was dark and shadowy back there, so she would prefer going that way.

Trip hesitated. "The animals are in the back half of the warehouse."

"Are you worried they'll bark?"

"Bark, growl, croak, roar. All of that."

"Neither you nor the soulblades can magically soothe them?"

Rysha worried about dallying. She could hear the voices of the people who had arrived at the docks, and she also heard their steam carriage chug away. Rysha assumed they were coming out to the barges, and that she and Trip wouldn't have much time to snoop.

"I'll try." Trip led the way down the narrow aisle between the wall and the railing. The majority of the barge was devoted to the warehouse, leaving little deck space. "That woman has dragon blood, so I'll need to be careful about how much power I draw upon."

Rysha rested her hand on Dorfindral's hilt; an eager warmth emanated from it. The *chapaharii* blade had hummed on her hip as they'd approached the barge, no doubt aware of the animals if they had dragon blood. It seemed to know what they were talking about now because it thrummed under her touch, as if to say it was ready to guide her arms in battle.

"Can you tell if she's a trained sorceress? Or would she be a shaman out here?" Rysha hadn't gotten a good look at the woman and had no idea what nationality she was.

Trip didn't answer right away. He was probably consulting the swords.

"We can't read her," he said as they rounded the back corner and headed for an unassuming metal door. "That means she knows how to protect her thoughts, so she's had at least some training."

Trip laid a hand on the door, not checking the latch, at least not in the usual way. A soft click sounded as a lock unbolted. He pulled the door open and stepped into the shadowy interior.

Rysha smelled hay and animal droppings as she followed him inside. Life stirred nearby, rustlings, soft growls, and hisses coming from both sides.

Trip walked slowly, his hands spread instead of resting on his sword hilts, and he seemed to radiate a placating sense of serenity. Even behind him and oblivious to magic, Rysha felt it. It made her want to stretch out on a sheepskin rug with him, their bare toes touching as they lounged in front of a crackling fire. Amused, she wondered if the animals were experiencing similar feelings.

Her fingers brushed cold metal bars, and something growled at her. Something large.

She hustled forward to stay closer to Trip. Even though Dorfindral's battle-hungry signals were trying to override Trip's suggestions of relaxation, Rysha had no desire to fight these creatures. She had no idea why they were caged up in here, but she immediately disliked the woman for keeping them imprisoned.

Trip paused, and in the dark, Rysha bumped into his back.

"What's Dorfindral telling you about these animals?" he asked softly.

"It wants to kill them."

"Anything else? Can it tell... I sense minor magical artifacts—is it called an artifact if it was made in modern times?—embedded in some of their chests."

"My texts didn't mention modern artifacts," Rysha said. "Most of them were Iskandian textbooks and insisted magic and dragons didn't exist anymore." She almost launched into the three definitions her books had offered for historical magical artifacts—there were archaeological terms to differentiate between manmade and dragon-made ones, as well as devices of unknown origins—but she doubted Trip truly wanted an answer right now.

"I can't tell what they do, but Jaxi and Azarwrath believe they're for controlling the animals."

"I guess that makes sense. If you were ever going to let that thing in the back that's growling like a tiger out of its cage, you'd want a way to keep it from eating you."

"It's a lion. With wings."

"Then it's all the more likely to eat you." The idea of a winged lion intrigued Rysha, but she also found it scientifically puzzling that such a creature could have evolved. "Though flying is technically cheaper, energetically speaking, than walking or running, heavy creatures aren't designed to fly. It's why birds and dragons have hollow bones. I suspect a lion with wings would have a tremendous metabolic tax when flying. Like hummingbirds, but even more so. Did you know that when hummingbirds hover, they use as much as eight times more energy than when at their basal metabolic rate? I can't imagine how much effort a lion would have to expend to keep its body aloft. It would be ravenous all the time if it was flying often." Realizing she was rambling and this wasn't the time for it, she finished with, "Sorry, that information probably won't be useful for finding your little sister. Or Dreyak's murderer."

"Perhaps not, but you've ensured I'm not going anywhere near that lion's cage."

"I aim to be helpful."

They moved away from the cages and into an open area, and Rysha could make out a few shapes as the darkness grew less absolute. A door ahead of them stood partially ajar, letting in lantern light from whatever was in the next room. Trip headed toward the doorway, his boots barely stirring the straw that covered the floor. Without pausing, he stepped through, then turned toward the corner where a set of stairs rose along the wall and over the door they'd just come through.

Rysha peered ahead before following him, toward aisles and aisles lined with barrels, bolts of fabric, sacks of spices, grains, coffee beans, and who knew what else. The exotic scents in this area were far more appealing than the animal scents from the other room.

"Truly a warehouse," she murmured, then clamped down on her tongue.

A chair scraped on the floor on the other side of all those aisles. From her spot, Rysha couldn't see anyone, but lantern light was coming from the same direction as the noise, a corner near the far door. The guards likely had their card table set up there.

The Silver Shark is supposed to be a businesswoman, Trip said, responding telepathically. *Someone successful enough to pay off the enforcers and have laws made. At least that's the impression I got.*

Is anyone upstairs? Rysha responded silently. Not that she minded his gentle touch in her mind. Even though he was only sharing words, she couldn't help but remember the way he'd used a few tendrils of his magic when they'd slept together, touching her not just with his hands but with his mind. She lamented that they hadn't had a private night together since their first one in the cavern, because she wanted to experience that—experience *him*—again.

No, not yet. There's an office and a bedroom up here. If there are interesting documents, I'm sure they'll be in one of those rooms.

I like interesting documents, Rysha thought, bringing her focus back to the mission.

I know you do.

A playful feeling of warmth trickled into her along with the words, and she wondered if he'd sensed her wandering thoughts. Probably. It was quiet back here, and they were close, so what would distract him?

The four people that arrived in the carriage are on a boat on the way out here now, Trip added, stopping in front of one of two doors on a landing that overlooked the rows of towering goods. *We may only get a chance to snoop in one room. Office or bedroom?*

Office. But didn't you say you wanted to talk with the woman? This may be your chance.

Trip waved two fingers and again magicked the locked door open. *That was before I knew she had dragon blood and could hide her thoughts. I'm not an expert on the old-fashioned way of interrogation.*

They stepped into a tidy office, Trip closing the door behind them, and the warmth from a fire burning in a stove wrapped around them. Two large oil paintings hung on the back wall, and Rysha stared at them in surprised recognition, a pair of nearby lanterns providing enough illumination to see the landscapes. Though she hadn't traveled to Cofahre, she'd seen illustrations in books and knew the huge—and distinctive—granite mounds framing Lake Fallen Armies. She also recognized the Blood Fields with their signature orangish-red grasses and blue flowers.

"This woman is either from Cofahre or quite taken with it," Rysha said, aware of Trip moving straight to a desk and bookcases full of ledgers and scrolls.

"When I saw her in the paymaster's mind, I thought she looked Cofah." Trip followed her gaze toward the paintings. "Those are places in the empire?"

"Popular tourist destinations, yes."

"The army doesn't send us to tour the empire very often."

"I don't think Cofahre encourages Iskandians to visit their lands, regardless. But followers of the Soldier God often pilgrimage to that lake, and the Blood Fields are popular with painters." Rysha waved at the signature in the corner, though she wasn't familiar with the artist.

"It hurts my brain to think about bloodthirsty, conquering nations having painters." Trip pointed to another wall with much smaller sketches on them. "I think those lend further credence to the idea that she's Cofah."

Rysha adjusted her spectacles and stepped closer to that wall. The lantern light didn't brighten it as much, and it took her a moment to realize she was looking at wanted posters rather than artwork. They all featured the same woman, a dark-haired beauty in her twenties. *Grekka Amonosheir* was the name printed under the face on all of them. Was this the Silver Shark? Decades ago?

"I'm amused that they're framed," Trip said from the desk. "Grekka, huh?"

He'd either read them as he first came in, or his magic was enhancing his eyesight.

"If you did something dastardly enough to earn Emperor Salatak's wrath, wouldn't you frame the evidence and display it in your office?" Rysha pointed to the issuer's signature in the corner of the warrants. It had been Salatak himself rather than some lesser official in Cofahre.

"Pilots don't get offices. I suppose I could fit one in my cockpit." Trip opened a ledger on the desk, but paused before reading it, his head tilting toward the door.

Worried they would have to leave—or hide—soon, Rysha moved to his side to read the writing and skim the tidy columns of numbers.

"Grekka and her comrades have arrived on the barge," Trip said. "They're talking on the deck and getting a report from one of the guards. Jaxi is camouflaging us and will let us know when they come inside the warehouse, but I doubt we have much time."

"This is Cofah writing." Rysha pointed. "Our words, essentially, but the Cofah haven't lost their diacritical marks yet, the way we have."

He cocked an eyebrow.

She hurried to read the words instead of commenting on the language. Trip could have read them himself—aside from the diacritics, the Cofah and Iskandian alphabets were the same—but he wore an abstracted expression that meant he was using his senses.

"She delivered Dakrovian rum and Cofah wine to five inns and taprooms in the city today. Nails and ingots to a carpenter. Silk to a seamstress. And she's set to pick up cactus flower honey and ceramic roof tiles from the locals tomorrow."

"She sounds truly nefarious." Trip poked into drawers. "Where do we find her records of paying local mages to assassinate visiting relatives of the throne?"

"I don't know what the average person files such things under." Rysha delved into another set of drawers, quickly skimming the labels on the hanging dividers inside. "Here's a folder on the animals with a bunch of receipts in it. Nothing indicates where they originally came from, but some she rents to performers. Others go out by the hour for tracking purposes. That sounds somewhat nefarious."

"Maybe, but there weren't any claw marks on Dreyak's body, so I don't think the winged lion got him." Trip kept glancing at the door, even though they had closed it.

"Here's something about payments to the enforcers." Rysha flipped through pages in a folder, pulling out a few. "Ah, and a receipt for a sword that she paid them for. Five thousand vreks."

"A *chapaharii* sword?"

"It doesn't say, but this was only three days ago. It's hard to imagine any other swords going for that much money."

"Agreed. Grekka and the others have moved inside. They're discussing something at the table where the guards were gaming earlier, but I'm sure they won't stay there for long."

Rysha wondered how good Jaxi's camouflage was. Would someone with dragon blood walk right past them? What if she was in the room with them? It was late enough that the woman might go straight to bed, but the lit lanterns and fire in the stove suggested Grekka would head to the office first.

"We're either going to have to find a hiding spot soon, or confront them." Trip sounded nervous at the prospect.

Out on the beach, he'd suggested he could handle Grekka, but that had been before he knew she had dragon blood and mage training. Rysha assumed he was more powerful than she was, even if she was a sorceress, but also understood that he'd barely begun to learn to use his power.

Trip closed the drawers, looking like he meant to leave, but Rysha had pulled out more interesting papers from the file.

"Wait," she said. "These are receipts from the enforcer paymaster. She's paid to have people arrested—a fellow businessman, Aragatun Po, was detained three times this month, all financed by her. Lots of other people have been arrested too. Or, uh, I think this one for a thousand vreks was an order to kill someone."

"That's how business is done here, right? Is there anything about Dreyak? Obviously, that would have been a recent one."

"I know, and I'm looking, but nothing so far. There's not even anything that *might* refer to him, like a description rather than a name. She's very specific. All her targets are named."

"No copies of rewards put out for stasis chambers, either, I suppose."

"Not that I've found."

"Thanks for looking. Put the papers back." Trip pointed to the drawer. "We need to go."

Rysha slid the folder back into place and hurried around the desk, clunking Dorfindral's scabbard on the edge. She winced at the noise and hoped the woman wasn't right outside.

Trip eased the door open and stepped out on the landing, lowering into a crouch. The warehouse was a lot brighter now, with men with lanterns standing in the central aisle at the far end. Rysha, slipping out after Trip, recognized them as the two bodyguards from the docks.

She didn't see the original two guards, but the other four people from the docks also stood in view, their hoods lowered. Three were men, all with the bronze skin and dark hair of the Cofah, though the oldest fellow's hair was half gray. He was in his late forties or early fifties and also had a graying goatee, impeccably trimmed and shaped. He stood close to the woman, her lush black hair also holding a few gray streaks. Or silver, Rysha supposed, if one wanted to be poetic about it. Grekka, the Silver Shark.

Trip tugged Rysha toward the stairs, but slowly. None of the main four of the group faced the back of the warehouse or this upper level, but one of the bodyguards, his gaze roving about, peered toward the landing.

Trip and Rysha froze. Her hand rested on Dorfindral's humming hilt, and the blade sent aggressive feelings into her, making her want to rush down the stairs and challenge Grekka to a battle.

But it was basing its desires only on her dragon blood. So far, Rysha didn't have proof that this woman had ordered the baby kidnapped or had anything to do with Dreyak's death. Not yet. Grekka clearly had some slimy business practices, but that seemed the norm in this city. Rysha didn't feel justified in being her judge and executioner. Still, she didn't know if she and Trip would get out of here without a fight. She mentally told Dorfindral to stand ready.

A thrum of excitement came from the blade. It wasn't the stand down command it heard so often.

"I just want him dead," Grekka growled, turning so that her voice was audible from the back of the warehouse.

The bodyguard with the roving gaze must not have seen Rysha and Trip, thanks to the shadows. Or thanks to Jaxi's magic. His attention turned back to his boss.

"I don't mind competition, but he takes our rivalry too far," Grekka added.

Rysha wondered who she was complaining about. The man she'd had arrested three times? Some other business rival?

Trip had reached the stairs and descended a couple of them, but he paused and sank low to peer through the railing. The thick spindles might hide them if one of the bodyguards glanced back again, but Rysha would have preferred to keep going down, so they could escape out the back of the warehouse if need be.

"He's rumored to have a shaman working for him now," the graying man said. "It's not surprising he's eluding you."

"*Two* shamans," another man said. "Apparently, they fled Dakrovia after a dragon ate everyone in their village."

"Not everyone, clearly."

"*Almost* everyone. We're lucky dragons haven't shown up here yet, despite that idiotic cult praying every day and sacrificing virgins."

"Gods among men, do they still do that?" Grekka asked. "Heathens. I had one of their leaders killed a couple of years ago."

"There's always another one that sprouts up. They believe—oh, it's insanity what they believe. As if that dead dragon is going to come back to bless them."

"Actually," one of the younger men said, "I heard…" He paused, and the others turned curiously toward him. "It's nothing but rumor, I suppose. I've seen nothing to prove there's any truth to it yet, but I heard that someone showed up claiming to be the son of their dragon. Or maybe it was the dragon himself. What's his name? Agar-something. I forget. Apparently, he's telling the cultists to follow him, and he can lead them to great health and prosperity."

Rysha, crouching on the stairs beside Trip, stared over at him. She was fairly certain he hadn't tried to take over the dragon cult while they'd been in the outpost. True, she'd barely been conscious for that half hour after the tarantula bit her, but someone would have updated her on that development if it had happened.

He met her gaze, but only shrugged.

The door opened with a bang, and a furtive man scrambled in, clutching a hat to his chest.

"Ah, one of your terrified minions is here, Shark," one of the younger men said. "We'll leave so he can attend to you."

The woman snorted, but didn't object when the two younger men headed for the door, stepping around the newcomer, who looked down instead of meeting their eyes.

"Bhodian," one called back, looking at the man standing beside the woman. "Will you be at the palace later?"

"Of course."

"I've a business proposition for you. A private one."

"I'm always amenable to hearing business propositions."

Rysha shifted her weight and wished Trip could use his magic to direct the conversation back to this supposed dragon son that had shown up. Was that out at the outpost? Or here in the city somewhere? And how did it tie in with Trip? What other sons could there be that were old enough to make such claims?

"What is it, Delix?" Grekka asked the man now studying her feet— elegant leather loafers with tassels, specifically. "I'm assuming from your posture that your cousins failed to get the swords."

"Yes, ma'am," the man spoke, his voice so soft Rysha barely heard it. "And I lost Trelix and Selix and several of their friends."

"Lost?"

"Yes, ma'am."

"Didn't you say a couple of women carried the swords?"

Rysha's interest sharpened. He wasn't talking about...

"Yes, ma'am. They fought well." The man winced and bobbed his head. "Very well."

"Did the man that was seen with them, the one rumored to be a mage, return in time to help?"

Rysha met Trip's eyes again. This could only be about their group.

"No, ma'am. It was only the women. They fought *very* well."

"Or your cousins fought poorly."

"I think they were Iskandian soldiers, ma'am. Iskandians let their women go into combat."

"So I've heard, but that doesn't explain your cousins' failure." Her voice softened, and Rysha missed a few words. "...*your* failure."

"No, ma'am, but one of my spies was watching and saw something, something that will interest you. One of our rivals snuck in and got one, but there were others. *Many* others."

The gray-haired man, Bhodian, smiled and clenched his fist. He was behind Grekka, and she didn't seem to notice.

"Other whats?" she asked, her focus on Delix.

"Strange artifacts that looked like... she wasn't sure what," the man said. "But she knew they were magical and valuable. Selling them could gain you much more than selling those swords."

Bhodian nodded, still smiling.

"I doubt that," Grekka murmured. "Run along, Delix. I'm not paying you for failure. Get me those swords, and we'll talk again. If you find this powerful magical artifact that was taken, or any of the others, I'll consider making an offer on it, but I'm not interested in trinkets."

Grekka looked back at Bhodian, and he wiped the smile off his face and clasped his hands behind his back. He assumed a bored expression and shrugged a shoulder at her.

"Yes, ma'am," Delix said.

As the man scurried out, still clutching his cap to his chest, one of the bodyguards moved to stand next to the other one. He tilted his head toward the stairs, toward Trip and Rysha. Uh-oh. Had they been spotted? Trip had mentioned magical camouflage, but belatedly, she realized that wouldn't work on her, for the same reason he hadn't been able to float her across the harbor to the barge.

"What's the matter, Grekka?" Bhodian asked while the two guards conferred too quietly for Rysha to hear. "You're no longer able to afford to run your business if you don't collect more swords that loathe you?"

Maybe it was her imagination, but Rysha had a feeling he was trying to turn Grekka's attention away from the artifacts her man had reported on. The stasis chambers. Why? Because *he* was the one who'd ordered them stolen in the first place? If so, what was his connection with the Brotherhood of the Dragon, if anything?

"They'd loathe you, too, if they understood the world," Grekka said dryly.

"Such an unfriendly thing to say to the sexy man who keeps your toes warm at night. I have a team that can go out and find a sword or two for you if you need. Weapons unclaimed and buried in ancient ruins rather than in collections that require theft or murder to acquire."

"Doesn't sound nearly as exciting," Grekka said, though she sounded distracted. She was looking toward the front door.

Trip? Rysha asked silently. She was tempted to ask it aloud since he hadn't stirred in a couple of minutes. What was he doing?

Yes?

Is there something going on outside? And do those bodyguards know we're here?

Sorry, I've been trying to figure out the man. I can't read his thoughts either. Uhm, outside, it's quiet, with two men leaving in the boat they all came over in. Apparently, these two—Grekka and Bhodian—are staying here or on the barge next door. I think the palace belongs to the man, which is why I've been trying to read him, but I can't. He's even harder to read than the woman. If I didn't see him with my eyes, I'm not sure I would be able to tell he's there. I believe he's carrying some artifact that blocks me, but I don't sense it either. It's almost as if... He looked toward the *chapaharii* blade on her hip.

Maybe we should get out of here before we're discovered. Rysha glanced at the bodyguards, half expecting to see them striding toward the stairs. Oddly, they stood next to the woman and the man, also looking toward the front door.

Uh oh. Trip gripped the railing, as if he meant to stand and march down there, or maybe leap over it and to the floor. *I can't read the leaders, but I can read the bodyguards. The woman just told them there are intruders here and to let the animals out to deal with it.*

Abruptly, Grekka and Bhodian strode toward the front door. The bodyguards turned and sprinted toward the back of the warehouse.

Trip vaulted over the railing, tearing Azarwrath and Jaxi free as he dropped.

Rysha yanked Dorfindral from its sheath and raced down the stairs. One of the bodyguards ran to engage with Trip as the second man sprinted into the animal area. Grekka and Bhodian disappeared out the front door.

As Rysha charged toward the closest guard, he pointed a pistol at Trip and fired.

Jaxi incinerated the bullet in the air. Instead of attacking the shooter, Trip pointed Azarwrath toward the doorway leading to the animal area. Dorfindral buzzed angrily in Rysha's hand, making her certain the soulblade had hurled some magical power.

A thud and a pained cry came from the bodyguard in the back.

The one aiming a pistol at Trip fired three more times. Once again, Jaxi incinerated the bullets in midair, little orange bursts of light appearing between the two men.

Rysha was tempted to launch herself at the shooter, to keep him from firing again, but Trip had it handled. If she could get Bhodian, she could question him about the stasis chamber. She was positive he knew something.

Trip twitched Jaxi, and some blast of air must have struck the bodyguard, because his pistol flew from his hand. It bounced off a huge glass bottle on a shelf, then disappeared into the shadows. Trip glared into the animal area, and the bodyguard that had run in there was dragged out on his back by the scruff of his collar, some force Rysha couldn't see pulling him.

Trusting Trip had the two bodyguards under control, Rysha ran down the center aisle toward the front door. Though she feared she was picking the more dangerous fight by chasing a sorceress—and a man with a device or power to keep Trip from sensing him—she had the weapon to handle it.

Rysha sprang into the night with Dorfindral at the ready only to find the deck abandoned. A couple of people moved about on the lit docks across the harbor, but nobody remained outside on the warehouse barge.

She peeked around one corner. Their rowboat floated, still attached to the back end of the vessel, the silvery moonlight reflecting in the water around it. Good. They could get away if they needed to.

She peeked around the other corner, not expecting to find anyone on that walkway, either. But she was in time to see Grekka jump onto the railing and spring toward the palace barge.

The ships were close, but not *that* close. She shouldn't have made it—no human should have. But she sailed twenty feet and landed lightly beside someone standing in the shadows between two lights on a walkway. Bhodian?

Grekka paused and looked back, straight at Rysha.

Rysha thought of hurling Dorfindral at the woman—she was sure the *chapaharii* blade contributed to that thought—but she lowered the weapon. Throwing it would be a good way to lose it. She envisioned Dorfindral clanging off the railing and disappearing into the water. Or maybe Grekka would risk the pain to catch it and turn it in for a reward.

Rysha reached for the pistol holstered on her belt, but hesitated. She was the intruder here, and she didn't have any evidence to prove that Bhodian had ordered the stasis chamber stolen. She couldn't justify starting a firefight with the owners of these barges.

A warning buzz ricocheted through Rysha's mind, and she leaped back around the corner. A blast of air—or some kind of energy—swept through the space she had occupied. Dorfindral probably would have protected her, but she didn't mind evading the attack altogether.

She waited a second, then peeked around the corner again. Grekka and the man were gone.

As Rysha turned back toward the front door of the warehouse, intending to reluctantly admit to Trip that she hadn't caught them in time, he burst out, almost sprinting. The door slammed shut behind him, seemingly of its own accord.

She started to ask what had happened—surely, those two bodyguards hadn't been a match for him and the soulblades—but something crashed into the door. Whatever it was, it struck so hard the hinges rattled and the metal shook.

Trip whirled to face the door.

"What is it?" Rysha asked as something thudded against the door again.

A roar came from somewhere deep within the warehouse. An answering roar came from right on the other side of the door.

"Never mind," Rysha said, getting the gist.

"I stopped the two bodyguards, so I don't know who let the animals out, but a bunch of them are free now. A bunch of the larger ones."

"I think I can guess who was responsible." Rysha glanced toward the palace, but Grekka was nowhere to be seen.

Maybe she and Bhodian had climbed to one of those towers and were looking down at Rysha and Trip, sipping wine and waiting to see if either of them would be eaten.

"We're going to have to leave," Trip said, but his feet didn't move. He scowled at the door, as if he meant to do anything *but* leave.

Rysha understood. They hadn't found the stasis chamber, and they hadn't found anything to explain Dreyak's death or why someone would want him dead. Trip had to be frustrated that they had wasted their time.

He looked toward the floating palace. The deck remained empty of life, but it was drifting away from the warehouse quickly. Fifty feet away now.

He could still jump over there, as Grekka had. Was he considering it? Rysha had seen him levitate through the air across a hundred meters of rubble before. He'd also levitated *her* short distances when she'd been willing to throw the sword ahead of her.

The barge was too far away for her to throw Dorfindral to it, but Rysha nodded at Trip and said, "If you go, I'll find a way over there to help you."

As he opened his mouth to answer, the first animal raced into view, not from the door but from the walkway on the side of the barge, the same one that led to their rowboat. It was a great scaled panther like

Rysha had shot out in the desert. A small blue gem embedded under its throat glowed softly.

Rysha fired at the gem, certain it controlled the creature. Her aim was true, but the bullet bounced off. Powerful muscles bunched and rippled under the silvery moonlight as the panther bounded toward them.

Azarwrath flared in Trip's hand, and red lightning streaked toward the creature's head. The panther sprang straight up in the air, its speed so great that it blurred. The lightning bent, curving upward and around to strike it in the butt.

The panther screeched, twisting and slashing at the air behind it as if it could bat away the lightning. Gravity caught up to the creature and brought it back toward the deck. Rysha moved a few feet, realizing it would land right in front of them, and switched her pistol to her left hand so she could yank out Dorfindral.

The lightning must have hurt the panther, but it screeched and launched wild slashes as it landed. Jaxi hurled a fireball that struck it in the chest.

Rysha tried to find a way in close, to target the gem, this time with the magic-hating Dorfindral instead of her pistol. But the panther moved so quickly, its focus on Trip instead of her, that she couldn't find the right angle.

A thunderous smash came from the warehouse. The door flew outward, the hinges snapping off as if they were made of paper, not metal.

A roar preceded the appearance of another attacker, the great winged lion. Other shapes moved in the warehouse behind it. A *lot* of shapes. Had the sorceress opened every cage?

Rysha fired at the lion as it sprang into the air, its tawny, furred wings unfurling from its body. Her bullet struck it in the shoulder, but it didn't seem to notice. Its spread wings blocked out the moon as it flew toward her head, its legs curled underneath it. She fired again, unable to believe the lion didn't cry out when the bullets sank in. It didn't even alter its path. Its limbs and claws extended, slashing toward her face.

Rysha knocked the attack away with Dorfindral, the blade glowing a hungry green, then ducked and rolled to the side. As she tumbled away, she glimpsed Trip's glowing soulblades in the dark as he battled a second scaled panther. Where had that one come from? The first, charred and hardly recognizable, lay in a heap at his feet.

Up! Dorfindral seemed to cry into her mind, and Rysha found her feet more quickly than should have been possible.

She was just in time to meet a giant lizard scuttling toward her, its massive tail whipping from side to side on the deck as it ran. Its body was too low and its maw too long for her to see the gem embedded in its throat.

She slashed at the top of its head, expecting the blade to sink in deeply, but the creature's scales were like steel armor. The magical sword gouged in to some extent, more than a normal weapon would have cut, but not enough to crush bone and sink into the creature's brain.

Rysha had to leap to the side and almost bumped into Trip as he felled the second panther.

Let's work our way to the rowboat, he said into her mind as he faced a second massive lizard scuttling out of the warehouse. *She can keep opening those gates. We're not going to get the answers we seek tonight.*

Even though they were both busy fighting, Rysha sensed the defeat that laced his words. He was chagrined that he'd handled this poorly and that they would go away empty-handed.

"You can still go to the palace if you want," Rysha panted, slashing again at her lizard, hoping to damage it as she parried the alligator-like maw snapping toward her. "Get her and confront her. I'll be all right here."

"I'm not leaving you to fight the zoo alone. Come."

As Rysha blocked more attacks and did her best to find an eye or other vulnerable spot on the lizard, she followed Trip along the railing, heading in the direction of their rowboat. More animals waited on that walkway, including an ape beating its chest and yowling. The lizard chased after them.

Trip glanced past her. "Duck!"

The huge winged form of the lion streaked out of the night sky, claws outstretched. It came in right above the lizard snapping at Rysha's heels, and it might have gotten her, but its yellow eyes were fixed on Trip.

She flung herself against the wall, but also slashed the lion as it flew past. This time, she could see the gem blazing at its throat. Dorfindral slammed into it with a crack, and its glow went out.

Unfortunately, the lion continued to fight. It flew up so it could dive down again, determined to get to Trip.

He stepped past Rysha, Azarwrath and Jaxi sweeping in front of him to keep the lizard back as he met the lion's gaze. A great gust of wind slammed into the furred creature an instant before its claws reached him.

The invisible attack hit it like a locomotive. Crying in pain for the first time, the lion tumbled through the air, wings and legs tangling. It flew hundreds of meters to where the palace now floated, near the mouth of the harbor, and it slammed into a wall and crumpled to the deck.

A twinge of guilt ran through Rysha as she brought Dorfindral up in time to deflect another attack from the lizard. These animals might have dragon blood and might be stronger than typical, but they were still just animals. It seemed cruel to hurt them.

Yes, but they're deadly animals, Trip spoke into her mind. *We need to be careful. Here, stand behind me.*

Behind? Rysha roared and lunged at the lizard, not willing to be some damsel in need of protection. She could help him, damn it.

With Dorfindral's assistance, Rysha moved with impossible speed. Her blade plunged into one of the hungry reptilian eyes staring at her. Finally, the sword sank in more than an inch. The lizard screeched, an alien cry that reminded her of those awful half-dragon bats from the mountain as it hammered her eardrums.

I simply meant so you would be behind my barrier, Trip thought. *I can't make a bubble around you, but I can make a barrier that will cover our retreat, like a shield across the walkway.*

Rysha realized he was no longer attacking the animals. Half a dozen of them were trying to get at him from the other end of the walkway, but they struck an invisible barrier he'd erected and bounced back, snarling and howling in frustration.

There is nothing to be gained by killing more of them, Trip added.

Oh. Rysha scrambled closer to him.

He spread the soulblades, as if to mark the edges of the twin shields he'd erected on either side of the walkway. He and Rysha were sandwiched in the middle, but he moved the barriers as they moved, making their way to the rowboat.

More of the animals flung themselves at them, but they couldn't get through.

Be ready. I'm going to have to shift my barrier around to protect us as we get in. Some may slip past me.

I'm ready.

Dorfindral, still hungry for battle, echoed the thought in her mind.

That one may also be a problem, he added, his tone dry.

They had reached the rowboat, but an ape waited inside it, roaring and jumping up and down, threatening to knock the craft free of the barge.

As Trip shifted his attention to it, another ape on the walkway jumped onto the roof of the warehouse, ran two steps, then jumped down toward the walkway again, bypassing the invisible shield.

"Look out," Rysha ordered, planting her feet and raising her sword instead of leaping away—she didn't want to ram into Trip's back.

The ape tried to snatch her sword out of her hand as it dropped toward her. Gritting her teeth, she held the blade firmly and thrust upward.

The point jabbed into the ape's shoulder, but its weight and momentum were too great for her. She couldn't maintain her stance, and she stumbled backward into Trip.

He cursed, but she couldn't look to see if she'd interrupted some magic he was hurling.

Pinned between him and the ape, Rysha didn't have much room to pull her sword free. Hairy arms pummeled her. She twisted the sword, hoping to hurt the beast so it would pull back and run away. Its eyes were wild with fear and pain, but it kept attacking. Its gem pulsed and glowed, as it had on the lizard.

A paw clubbed Rysha in the side of the head, knocking her against the warehouse. She yanked her pistol free and fired at the ape's chest.

A ferocious roar came from behind her. It wasn't an animal; it was Trip. Before Rysha knew what was happening, all the animals on the walkway were hurled over the railing and into the water.

She almost lost her sword as an invisible force flung the ape away. But Dorfindral flared in defiance, and the strength to keep hold of the hilt flowed into her.

Trip whirled toward the rowboat as the ape still inside it leaped at him.

Fire appeared in the air all around the creature, reminding Rysha of the time Trip had battled flying automatons on the pirate airship. She thought it came from Trip rather than from Jaxi.

When it disappeared, nothing but ash trickled down from where the ape had been.

Trip sprang into the rowboat, the small craft rocking as he landed. He turned, his eyes gleaming with power as he faced Rysha.

"Get in." He pointed at the seat in front of him.

Even with Dorfindral protecting her from magic, Rysha felt the compulsion in that order and the power radiating from Trip.

She might have resisted him with the *chapaharii* sword's help, but she didn't want to. She jumped down, legs spread for balance as she landed on the slick metal bottom. Trip steadied her with a hand as the chain he'd made unfastened itself. He stirred up a gust of wind, and it pushed the rowboat away from the barge.

"Thanks," Rysha said.

Before he could answer, a gunshot came from the direction of the docks. A bullet struck Trip's shoulder, startling a shout of pain from him.

Rysha whirled toward the docks as he dropped the soulblades and sank to one knee. She pointed her pistol, but hesitated. There had to be fifty people lined up there, and she had no idea which one had fired. She couldn't indiscriminately shoot into the crowd. They must have been drawn by the commotion, gawking at the battle on the barge and at the animals still roaring and yowling from the water.

Sorry, Trip, Jaxi spoke to both of them. *I tried to raise a barrier around you two, but didn't adjust for Dorfindral and the fact that you were touching Rysha.*

I can obliterate those who seek to harm us, Azarwrath added.

"Just get our boat out of here." Trip gripped his shoulder, his eyes squinting in pain. "Please."

Toward the docks? Jaxi asked. *That's going to be problematic.*

"Take us out to sea," Trip said. "We'll find a place to land and circle around to walk into the city from the other side."

More shots fired from the docks. Rysha dropped low to make herself a smaller target. The rowboat had drifted far enough from the barge that it offered no cover, and they were vulnerable.

But the bullets bounced off a barrier this time, one that must have been stretched out to protect the rowboat instead of Trip and Rysha specifically. Rysha lowered her pistol, knowing she couldn't fire through the soulblades' shield. Even without the barrier present, she would have hesitated to fire into the crowd. She'd seen one of the men who'd fired this time, but the cowardly bastard was hiding behind someone else, someone who couldn't get away from him with so many bodies pressing in from the sides.

The rowboat sailed out of the harbor and toward the choppier water of the ocean, maneuvering inexplicably, at least to Rysha's eye. She was glad her presence aboard it wasn't keeping the soulblades from finding a way to steer it. She sighed down at Dorfindral, feeling she had been more hindrance than help tonight. If Trip hadn't been worried about protecting her, he could have simply wrapped himself in his bubble barrier and strode off the barge, levitated across the water, and escaped into the city.

He hissed in pain as the rowboat steered into rougher water. Rysha sheathed Dorfindral and knelt beside him, wrapping an arm around his back, careful to avoid the wounded shoulder he gripped.

He rested his head against her, his body tight with pain. Who healed the healer?

"I'm sorry," Rysha whispered, again feeling useless since she couldn't do more than offer her shoulder.

She glared at the floating palace before it disappeared from view and thought she saw Grekka out on the deck, glaring back at her. Rysha hoped one of her animals lost its gem in the water and ate her.

CHAPTER 6

*I*T'S REALLY NOT A PROBLEM, Jaxi spoke into Trip's mind. *I can handle it easily.*

That is not an approved healing technique, Azarwrath responded.

He's in pain. It makes sense to obliterate the source of the pain, and I can do so instantly.

Unless you miss and incinerate some of his organs.

The bullet is in his shoulder. How could I possibly hit an organ?

I have no idea what kind of aim you have.

Didn't you see me smack that ape in the face with a fireball? I aimed to shoot it right up his nostrils.

And you took off its entire head.

Via its nostrils.

Trip groaned.

Rysha's arm tightened around his back. She knelt beside him in the bottom of the rowboat, letting him lean against her as the soulblades navigated them down the coast and toward a beach at the southernmost end of the city. The arguing was driving him mad, but at least Jaxi and Azarwrath had lifted the little craft above the waves, so it was no longer being pummeled. It floated parallel to the coastline and toward that beach.

"Are you in much pain?" Rysha asked over the roar of the ocean.

"No," Trip lied. "I'm being tormented by arguing soulblades."

"They stopped including me in their conversation."

"Consider yourself lucky."

Trip leaned back, staring up at the stars as the boat floated closer to land. He thought he could remove the bullet on his own, but he wanted solid ground underneath him before he tried. He also wanted to make sure that no more would-be enemies would spring out and attack them while he was distracted. The people on the docks couldn't have had any idea who he and Rysha were—he highly doubted they'd been part of the Silver Shark's security team. More likely, they had seen the glowing swords and, having heard of the reward for *chapaharii* weapons, had hoped to claim one somehow. Or maybe they simply hated magic and had shot at him because it had been obvious he was using it.

Tears formed in his eyes. He told himself it was from the pain in his shoulder, but part of it might have been frustration. He hadn't wanted to hurt or kill simple animals, especially when he'd realized they were being compelled by those embedded gems to attack. Instead, he'd spent time trying to figure out how to remove the devices, time when he should have been focused on fighting. That had almost been his and Rysha's undoing. Finally, he had grown too frustrated by everything, and had simply hurled all his power at them to knock them into the water. He should have done that in the beginning. Or he should have run for the rowboat as soon as he'd realized what was happening. But it had been a struggle to shield Rysha when she held that sword.

Rysha with Dorfindral in her hand was a powerful ally, and he knew they would, with enough practice, figure out all the kinks of fighting side by side or back to back. But they hadn't had that practice yet. And half the time, he still questioned his own power and what he could do. At one point, he'd been tempted to create a tornado to obliterate the entire warehouse. If not for the unconscious guards and the animals that had still been caged inside, he might have done it.

He had tried to attack the floating palace when he'd realized Grekka was over there, using her mental abilities to unlock the animals' cages from a distance. But the wave of power he'd thrown at the other barge hadn't done a thing. It was as if she'd been wielding a *chapaharii* blade and somehow extending its influence to protect the palace all around her. It shouldn't have been possible. Besides, he hadn't seen anything in her hand. Maybe whatever had protected Bhodian from Trip's mind-reading attempts also protected his barge.

The rowboat settled onto the sand. Rysha released Trip, patted his back, then stepped out with sword and pistol in hand. She scanned the jagged dark boulders that rose up at the back of the beach. Houses started up a quarter of a mile away, and a path led between the rocks and toward them, but Trip didn't sense any people—or animals—nearby.

Rysha must have reached the same conclusion because she turned back, offering her arm as he levered himself out of the boat. "I'll stand guard while you heal yourself. You can do that, right?"

"I think so," he said, though he admitted it would be a lot harder to concentrate when *he* was the one in pain. But if he couldn't manage the task, Azarwrath had a healer's training. And there was always Jaxi and her willingness to incinerate the bullet... while it was inside of him.

"Good."

Trip grunted and settled on his back on the sand. A burst of fire burned within his shoulder, and he gasped, his back arching.

It's gone, Jaxi said. *Your organs are still there. You're welcome.*

Heathen, Azarwrath said.

You can't tell me that wasn't efficient.

As the pain faded, Trip slumped onto the sand again. Azarwrath used his power next, and healing warmth—a much more subtle and less painful warmth—filled his shoulder.

Relieved by the soulblades' help, Trip let his lids droop most of the way shut until only a thin star-filled crack was visible, with Rysha at the edge of it, standing ready to face any danger that might come down the path. She adjusted her spectacles, and he smiled.

He appreciated her watching over him, but he wouldn't have minded if she snuggled down next to him. Their clothes were damp from the spray of the ocean waves, and he shivered as his body cooled down.

The warmth in his shoulder faded, and he lifted his arm experimentally. It felt tender, but no longer hurt.

Thank you, he told the soulblades.

You're most welcome, Jaxi said.

I did the hard work, Azarwrath said.

And clearly want a reward for it. Maybe Trip will buy you a cookie.

Azarwrath sighed dramatically.

Trip wondered if the soulblades would be offended if he suggested they sometimes acted more like teenagers than centuries-old sorcerers.

"I'm better," Trip said when he caught Rysha looking down at him. He pushed himself into a sitting position, though his arms were weak. "I might need a few minutes before I can walk back."

"I would offer to carry you, but I've yet to meet any men who were willing to be carried by a woman. Except my brothers."

"You offer to carry men around a lot?"

"Just when they're tired and look like they were run over by a flier squadron."

Trip rubbed his face. "Your brothers let you carry them?"

"When we were younger, they did. We'd take turns toting each other around on our backs. We'd race along the trail by the lake, always forgetting that there were spots where the branches hung low. I managed to smack Krey's face on one while going full speed. Chipped his tooth. To this day, he's got a noticeable gap. Maybe you can heal it for him when I take you to visit my family. How are you at teeth?"

"I haven't tried to rebuild any teeth yet. It seems like it might be more challenging than tendon, muscle, and flesh." He warmed a little inside, pleased by her statement that she planned to take him to visit her family. He wasn't sure how that would go, but he wouldn't shy away from trying to get them to like him. Or at least, to decide he was acceptable for Rysha, likable or not. Noble or not. Maybe his three-thousand-year-old birth mother had been noble. He laughed at himself, doubting nobility had been a concept back then.

"You can do bones, though, right?" Rysha sat down, not beside him but behind him, her back to his. Probably so she could continue to watch the path.

"Yes, but bones usually fracture, rather than having big chunks gouged out of them. And they're on the inside where blood vessels can deliver the body's building blocks to them, to provide material for the repair process." He wasn't sure on the details so he didn't attempt to explain further. So far, he'd healed people intuitively. Maybe one of Sardelle's classes would discuss how bodies worked and the way to heal all the various parts of them. "If nothing else, I could probably fuse some other material to the spot, something like porcelain that could *look* like a tooth, so people wouldn't notice anything awry."

"I think that would improve his looks, but I'm not sure he would agree to it. Krey likes to think he's a big tough fellow who could handle himself in a battle and survive on the streets if he had to. He seems proud of that broken tooth, even if it was delivered by a wayward tree branch rather than some thug's fist."

"What does he do for a living?"

"He samples alcohol."

Trip snorted. "That sounds like something that could only be a job if you're noble-born."

"Possibly true. Basically, he oversees the cider, wine, and beer that's made from the fruit and wheat grown on our property. He makes sure things taste good and are ready to drink. We have a distillery and a winery near the highway. They're actually quite profitable for the family, I understand."

"I wonder if making money is an easier way to gauge success than... other ways." Trip thought of his goals, or the ones he'd held until the dragon revelation. To become a renowned pilot and a hero to Iskandia. To drive enemies away from its shores. To earn medals, to know he was making a difference to his country.

He always felt different from people like his grandparents, simple folk who enjoyed their work and simply wanted the freedom to create and live in peace, doing as they wished day to day. But how did one ever truly know if one succeeded at life? For that matter, how would *he* know if he succeeded? Would it be based on the number of medals he earned? How did General Zirkander judge success? Did he believe himself to be a hero the way the rest of the country did? Or did he analyze what he was doing every day and come up short sometimes?

"It is black and white if all you do is count nucros at the end of the year," Rysha said. "But my brother is very proud of what he does, independent of the money. He's always determined to make the best-tasting beverage and win medals."

"Medals for winemaking?" Trip imagined hanging a wine-bottle-shaped medal up in his room alongside an army one.

"Awards, anyway. Sometimes, medals are involved."

"Huh." Trip's legs felt stronger, so he shifted his weight to stand up. "We better get back to the room and check on Major Kaika. It sounded like the stasis chambers will continue to be targeted." He planned to suggest moving to a new hostel in the morning, if not sooner.

"Yes, and it *sounded* like that Bhodian knew something about that."

"Did it?"

"Well, not sounded, but looked. He clenched a triumphant fist when he heard that someone had gotten away with one."

Trip had missed that. He'd been too busy trying to read the man's mind and hadn't paid much attention to his body language.

He gazed back in the direction of the harbor, even though the terrain of the coastline hid it from sight. He was tempted to go right back out there and try again to reach Grekka and Bhodian. Bhodian, especially, if Rysha's instincts were right. But he would like to figure out a way to question both of them.

In addition to wanting to recover his little sister, Dreyak's death continued to haunt his thoughts, along with his concern that Cofahre would blame Iskandia for it. As often as he'd dreamed of being a great war hero, he admitted it would be unfortunate if something caused Iskandia to slide back into more troubled times, with the empire at their doorsteps again. His people had dragons to deal with already; they didn't need to add imperial conquerors. He might not know what success looked like, but he had no trouble envisioning failure.

"If Major Kaika finds a ship in the morning that's willing to take us home, what will you do?" Rysha asked as they started up the beach toward the path.

"I don't know." Trip hoped it took Kaika a few more days to find them passage.

"I understand wanting to find the little girl—I'm willing to stay and help you do that—but I think Kaika has a point that it's important to get the other ones home, especially now that we know people are looking for them. Possibly powerful people."

"I know."

"I'm worried about the babies because I want them to grow up healthy and happy, but I'm also worried... There's the potential for Bhodian or whoever is trying to get to them to use them against us. Against *you*. I'm a little alarmed by how many people in this city seem to be gunning for us right now."

Yes, and he hadn't helped matters by sneaking into a powerful businesswoman's barge, snooping around, and getting caught doing so.

"Just a little alarmed?" he asked.

"Yes, but it may escalate to a lot if we return to the hostel and find our room on fire."

"So long as Jaxi isn't responsible."

Rysha cocked her head. "Is there a reason she would be? Because she likes to fling fireballs?"

"And incinerate things. Don't ask where the bullet in my shoulder went."

"Hm, I suddenly feel fortunate to be walking beside you. With your body fully intact."

"I also feel fortunate to be walking beside you." He rested his arm across her shoulders.

I may gag, Jaxi announced.

So long as you don't incinerate anything else today, Trip thought, sighing at the interruption.

Rysha slid her arm around his waist as they maneuvered up the path, and that made everything better.

Nothing at all? What if there are enemies waiting around that bend? Or apes with nefarious nostrils that need the attention of a fireball?

Let the young man have a private moment with his lady, Azarwrath said.

Was that an order? It sounded like an order. I don't take orders from other sorcerers. Or anyone else.

Trip groaned, afraid another argument was forthcoming.

"You don't seem to be in pain anymore," Rysha said, "so I'm going to assume soulblades are squabbling in your head."

"You're coming to know me well." He kissed the side of her face.

"And the odd company you keep." She patted his chest.

"Are you including yourself in that category?"

"Absolutely."

Trip must have been exhausted after all the power he had drawn upon the night before, in addition to the energy his body had used to heal itself, because he didn't wake up until sun slanted through the shutters of their hostel room. He opened his eyes, immediately checking to make sure the disassembled wagon and stasis chambers were where he'd stacked them the night before, after their little group had changed hostels. A little twinge went through him at the visual reminder that one was still missing, that the night before had been a waste.

He didn't see Rysha and Kaika in the room and grew concerned until his senses assured him they were nearby. In the lavatory together.

He cocked an eyebrow, finding that a little odd. The attached lavatory was a tiny space with a hole in the tiled floor and a spigot on the wall, nothing more. How sad that he considered this room an upgrade from the first place they had stayed, which had only offered a chamber pot for biological needs.

Trip sat up, his back sore after sleeping on a thin straw mattress inhabited by bed bugs and centipedes—one had oozed out of a hole in the cover to bite him in the middle of the night.

A powerful sorcerer destroys such creatures before going to bed, Azarwrath observed, perhaps sensing Trip rubbing the bite.

As does an un-powerful one, Jaxi added. *In my day, vermin control was covered in the first year of Referatu training.*

Perhaps you could have covered it last night, Trip grumbled silently.

You didn't ask. I'm still waiting for you to master the workbook Sardelle sent along.

There hasn't been much time for homework.

Spoken like a man who wants to be perforated with bug bites.

"Just use one hand," came Kaika's voice from the lavatory.

"One hand is too hard, ma'am," Rysha said, her words strained.

"Because you haven't practiced that way. Look, watch me. You have to center yourself so you don't have to hold on with the other."

Trip pushed himself to his feet, though he wasn't sure if he should look in on the conversation or not. The curtain that hung from a rod over the doorway was only partially drawn, so they must not have been too worried about privacy, but he had his doubts about peeking into the lavatory.

He paused by the stasis chambers and rested his hand on one, gazing down at a dark-haired baby boy visible through the lid. He lay curled on his side and suspended in gel, but the way his thumb was stuck in his mouth made it seem he could stir to life at any moment. The boy looked a lot like the curly-haired girl who had been taken. Rysha had mentioned that they might be twins. Sadness grew in Trip's heart at the idea of the boy losing his closest relative, the only full-blooded relative he had. His mother, like Trip's mother, had to have died thousands of years ago.

"No amount of adjusting is going to make this anything other than awkward," Rysha said in the lavatory.

"I didn't say it wouldn't be awkward."

"You said it would feel *good*."

"I said it would feel good *afterward*. Once the pain stopped."

It was his need to use the lavatory that finally compelled Trip to venture toward the curtain. Otherwise, he would have let his curiosity about what they were doing remain unsatisfied.

He cleared his throat, and the women fell silent. "Can I, uh…"

"If you need to pee, come on in," Major Kaika said. "I'm sure Lieutenant Ravenwood wouldn't mind you lending her a hand."

"*Ma'am*," Rysha protested. "I don't need anyone's help. I'm just trying to find the right angle."

"Something Trip would be happy to help you with, I'm sure."

"Are we still talking about pull-ups?"

"What else would I be talking about?" Kaika's voice held a smile.

Pull-ups? Trip pushed aside the curtain and found Rysha and Kaika dangling from the water pipe that ran through the tiny room near the ceiling.

Kaika winked at him and pulled herself up and down three times, using only one arm. Rysha made a valiant effort, but she looked like she had been hanging up there for a while and was tired. She brought her other hand up, used it to help, and did a couple of pull-ups.

"Having a spotter *can* help you learn," Kaika said. "Don't you agree, Captain?"

"I just came to use the hole." Trip pointed at the lavatory's version of a toilet.

"We're not stopping you." Kaika switched hands and did a few more pull-ups on the other side.

Rysha dropped to the tiles, shaking out her arms. "I don't want to watch him pee."

"So don't watch."

"I, uh, think I need a rest." Rysha glanced at Trip as she hurried out, but she seemed embarrassed and didn't hold his gaze for long.

He didn't know if it was because of the conversation or because she'd failed to do the pull-up when he'd been watching. Maybe he would point out to her that it was unlikely that *he* could do a one-armed pull-up.

Kaika dropped to the floor and wiped rust off her hands. "This is a dubious gymnasium, at best."

Trip thought about pointing out it was unlikely the architect had intended it as such, but said only, "Yes, ma'am."

"I went to the docks while you were snoozing." She propped her fists on her hips and eyed him frankly.

Uh-oh. Had she heard all about their ineffective snooping? Trip hadn't explained much the previous night since he'd been tired and embarrassed about the result. Kaika had known he and Rysha had gone to the harbor, but she probably hadn't intended for them to draw the attention of half the city—or that of vindictive and prominent business owners with long reaches.

"I've secured passage for us on a steamer heading to Iskandia on its way to the empire. It's waiting for cargo now, but the captain plans to leave two mornings from today. He has room for three people and their belongings." She waved through the doorway toward the stasis chambers.

"That's good, ma'am." Trip meant it. Two days gave him more time to look. He'd feared she would find something sooner.

"Will you be coming with us?" Kaika lifted her eyebrows.

"As long as I find the stasis chamber first, yes, ma'am." He would go back to the barges, out to the palace one this time, and have a frank talk with Bhodian about that. And if he learned more about Dreyak's death at the same time, all the better.

Kaika frowned, and he feared she would see his words as evidence of disobedience. Maybe he should have said yes and assumed he *would* find his lost sibling by then.

It may be unwise to assume that, Azarwrath told him. Trip must have been letting his thoughts leak out. *While you slept, I scoured the city for many hours, attempting to sense the stasis chamber. The devices do not emit a strong aura, but since I am familiar with them now, I should have been able to locate it.*

But you weren't able to?

Unfortunately not.

Thank you for looking.

"I won't stop you from looking in the interim," Kaika said. "The seven gods know I'm responsible for you losing the thing in the first place, and I'll do my best to guard the others while you search, but we need to go home when the steamer leaves. Whether you've found the lost one or not."

"I understand, ma'am." And he did. He just didn't agree that he would go. But he kept that thought to himself. If he resolved his problems in the next two days, he wouldn't *need* to disobey.

"Before you leave to hunt, I need your help. I'm afraid I was followed back from the docks this morning. I'd left Eryndral in the room, so it wouldn't attract notice, but it didn't matter. I did my best to lose the boy, but there are eyes all over this city. I think we should move again, ideally to somewhere more defensible than these hostel rooms." Her lips turned downward. "A man was also lurking outside the room when I returned—he was trying to see through the shutters. I shooed him off, but I am getting irritated with people knowing exactly how to find us, Trip." Kaika gave him a scathing look, as if it were all his fault.

Maybe it was. Maybe the stasis chambers were acting as beacons. The *chapaharii* swords didn't give off much of a signature, so it was less likely that someone was sensing them from afar.

The night before, Trip had tested his ability to detect the stasis chambers from a distance, and he'd been able to sense them from a mile away. But he'd thought... Maybe it was arrogant, but he hadn't thought there would be mages in the city with his range.

Of course, a mage with a lesser range could have gotten lucky. Or sensed his team entering the city and then followed them. Trip hadn't been trying to hide his power when he'd first entered Lagresh, and Jaxi and Azarwrath also gave off magical auras.

"I want you to use your magical whiskers to find us a safe place to hole up until we can board the freighter," Kaika said.

"Whiskers?" Trip rubbed his stubbled jaw. He hadn't had a chance to shave yet today, but he'd been doing it every morning, even out in the desert, since that was dictated by the Iskandian uniform code.

"Senses. Like a cat uses its whiskers to sense things. Keep up, Captain, or I'm not going to encourage Lieutenant Ravenwood to let you spot her."

Judging by her smirk, she wasn't too irritated with him, but she was a tough woman to please. If the stories about her and Angulus being a couple were true, Trip felt a lot of respect for the king, respect that had nothing to do with dealing with diplomats and ruling a nation. Though, now that he'd seen firsthand how some other cities ran things, he had more respect for Angulus's ability to rule too.

"Yes, ma'am."

"I also want you to figure out a way to camouflage those baby boxes, to keep other sorcerers from finding them. I assume that's what's happening, right? They're oozing their magickness and others are spotting it?"

"I suspect so, but I don't know how to hide them long term. The soulblades and I can camouflage things temporarily, while we're focusing on keeping them hidden, but—"

"Figure it out, Whiskers. I have faith that you can do it." Kaika slapped him on the shoulder.

"I…" Trip had less faith. He knew sorcerers could make magical booby traps and create effects that endured after they stopped concentrating on them, but *he* never had.

"Come on. You made a locomotive out of scissors and nail clippers. This can't be that hard."

"Actually, I only used a ruler."

"Proof of your cunning and magnificence."

"I'm more comfortable when you insult me than praise me, ma'am."

"I would be happy to insult you. After you camo the baby boxes. Get to work."

"Yes, ma'am. Uh." Remembering his original reason for coming in, Trip waved toward the hole. "Can I relieve myself, first?"

"Keep it short." Kaika headed for the curtain but added, "Or I'll send Ravenwood in to spot you."

"*Ma'am*," came the aggrieved protest from the other room.

Despite the threats, Trip finished his business without any feminine interruptions. This was not, however, how he had imagined special missions for General Zirkander going. Admittedly, since he'd deviated from the main mission, he had nobody to blame but himself for how things were turning out.

When he stepped out, Rysha rose from a cross-legged seat by the wall, journals open on either side of her. She snatched one up and trotted over to him.

"I found a clue," she said.

"Oh?" Trip leaned over to look at the open page. This couldn't be about the baby or Dreyak, not if it was in one of those old journals.

"I actually found it yesterday, but it didn't have any meaning until we sailed out to those barges."

"Sailed? A flattering term for our damp-seated venture."

"Look." She pointed at a line two-thirds of the way down a page.

It was the more modern journal, the one from the dead man's pack in the dragon lair, so Trip had no trouble reading it. "...went to the *Tax Street* to pick up the purse for our supplies from our benefactor for this expedition. Eight lanterns, whale oil, two grappling hooks, two hundred yards of rope—"

"Not that part." Rysha thumped him on the chest. "*Tax Street.* I read this page the other day and thought that name was a clue even then. I was on the verge of running out to look for a map because it sounds like a road, right? But then when we sailed out last night, it was the name on the palace barge. Did you see it?"

Trip frowned, trying to remember if he had. The palace barge had been well lit, including the exterior hull, but he hadn't bothered to read the ship's name. He'd been more focused on the warehouse.

"Our benefactor for this expedition," Trip reread slowly.

"It doesn't say whether it's a man or a woman, but I have a hunch it's that Bhodian. It sounded like he owned the palace barge, right? Maybe he owned it twenty-five years ago too. Trip, we could have been looking at the person who financed the expedition that your mother went on. If so, he could have known about the stasis babies years—*decades*—ago. At the least, he would have known about your sire and had an interest in finding his lair."

"He could be the one who was chasing my mother too." Trip thought of the memory he'd seen in his grandmother's mind, of his mother being afraid that people were after her and wanted to take him away from her. "Who apparently wanted to take me away for..." He shivered. "Who knows what purpose?"

"*He* knows." Rysha closed the book. She bounced on her toes, beaming a smile at him. "We need to talk to him."

Her excitement sparked some similar feelings in Trip. He was intrigued by the prospect of learning more about his past and how his mother had found him, but even more, this seemed close to proof that Bhodian had an interest in the stasis babies. If he'd funded the expedition years ago and possibly tried to steal Trip away from his mother, wouldn't Bhodian have been delighted when a second chance to get his hands on the half-dragon babies came along? Even if he hadn't been the one to arrange the theft from the hostel, Trip wagered Bhodian knew where the stasis chamber had been taken. Maybe he even had it on his barge by now.

His thought of going out for a frank talk with the man returned. But what would be the result of confronting him? Trip already knew he couldn't read the man's thoughts. Further, Bhodian might be inclined to think of Trip as an enemy for sneaking aboard his girlfriend's ship and, however inadvertently, causing the deaths of many of her animals. And what if they weren't just romantic partners? What if they were also business partners? If so, those animals might have belonged to him, at least in part.

"Terribly exciting," Kaika drawled from behind them, "but let's not forget that someone needs to first help us find a new place to hide for two days." She waved toward the stasis chambers. "And don't forget the cunning and magnificent magical camouflage you're going to create for your little siblings, Trip."

"I thought *I* was cunning and magnificent, not the camouflage."

"Nah, I was just flattering you to boost your ego." Kaika was pointedly keeping her hand extended toward the stacked devices.

Trip exchanged wry smiles with Rysha.

"I'll do some more research," she whispered.

"Thank you."

Trip headed over to the stasis chambers, hoping Jaxi and Azarwrath could guide him in this. He would do everything Major Kaika asked, to the best of his abilities, but that night, he intended to return to the barges. He couldn't guarantee it would go well, but he intended to talk to Bhodian.

CHAPTER 7

R YSHA STEPPED THROUGH A RECTANGULAR entrance in the canal bank, entering a tunnel that fed water into the main channel. So far, her team had filled their canteens from public fountains and wells, so she didn't know where this water went. Maybe it was siphoned to some wealthier part of the city where indoor plumbing existed.

She did her best to balance on one of the narrow ledges to either side instead of stepping into the water. At the entrance behind her, the grate scraped back into place without anyone touching it. A rusty padlock refastened itself with a click.

"Seeing stuff like that hasn't stopped being creepy yet," Kaika said.

She and Trip were ahead of Rysha, the reassembled wagon full of stasis chambers between them, the wheels high enough to keep the water from reaching to the sides.

"Not cunning and magnificent?" Trip asked, the joke sounding a touch sad.

Rysha found Trip's arm in the shadows and patted it.

"No," Kaika said, "but if your camouflage works, I'll lend it those adjectives."

"It's working," Trip said firmly.

Rysha hoped so. He'd spent two hours that morning staring at the stack of stasis chambers in their hostel room while she and Kaika had taken turns watching the street outside, worried more trouble would find them. When Trip had finished, he'd said it was done and also that he had found a place that might work for hiding. At the least, he'd promised it would be easily defensible.

As Rysha eyed their dim surroundings, graffiti blackening the tunnel walls, she hoped it wouldn't be a sewer. If Lagresh even claimed a sewer system. Thus far, she'd only seen waste being left in alleys or going into pits. She was surprised people here weren't all diseased and dying. Maybe the sick were captured and sold to the same person who paid for dead bodies.

"Lead the way, fearless Captain," Kaika said, extending her hand into the dark passage.

Trip drew Jaxi, and she emitted a pleasant blue glow, illuminating the way as he strode into the tunnel. The wagon rolled after him without anyone touching it.

"Creepy," Kaika whispered to Rysha with a wink.

They fell in behind the wagon, since it took most of the space in the tunnel.

"I think you should let Trip know how much you appreciate him and his powers, ma'am," Rysha said, not wanting poor Trip to feel like an outcast. He didn't deserve that.

"You do? There are rules against senior officers being openly appreciative of lower-ranking officers, you know. We're supposed to haze them to make them stronger."

"A couple of weeks ago, you two were the same rank."

"Yes, but pilot ranks don't really count. They barely have to do anything to gain rank except sit in their chairs in the sky and shoot things."

Rysha scowled, not agreeing with that. She focused on the route ahead, on balancing on the narrow walkway while Kaika walked on the adjacent one.

"I'm not good at appreciation," Kaika said, glancing over at her.

The comment startled Rysha. "What?"

"Showing it, I mean." Kaika kept her voice low, the words for Rysha instead of Trip. "It's kind of backwards, if you think about it, because I've been on a lot of dangerous missions and lost colleagues. *Friends.* Some that I'd known for years and years and liked a lot as soldiers and people. You *should* show people like that appreciation, because you never know when you'll lose them. Or when you'll get killed yourself. In the past, after friends have died, I've found myself often regretting that I never told them I thought they were good people. And that I appreciated them." Kaika spread her arms in a shrug.

Rysha nodded, then realized Kaika wouldn't see it in the dim light behind the wagon. She offered an encouraging noise instead, hoping to hear more. She was surprised Kaika was opening up and wondered if she'd had a harder time than she'd let on escaping the brutes who'd been after her and the sword the day before. Or maybe Kaika was thinking of their frantic battle with those constructs in the dragon's lair. She had been in the thick of the fighting for longer than Rysha and had seen Blazer struck with that axe. Death and losing comrades might be on her mind for a reason.

"I don't know why it's like that," Kaika said as they turned right at an intersection, Trip seeming to have a map in mind. "It's just hard. It makes you feel vulnerable, I guess. And being vulnerable around enemies lets them know you've got a weakness, and then you're more likely to get attacked, more likely to get killed. Sometimes, the unit feels like a battlefield, too, when you're always trying to prove that you belong. You can't show that you have vulnerabilities—weaknesses—or someone will use them against you, try to prove you *don't* belong. After a while, it becomes a habit to hide them all the time. You forget how to turn that off, to be different around friends."

Rysha felt she should say something, but she didn't know what. She lacked the experiences that had shaped Kaika and suspected any advice she tried to offer would sound naive if not inane.

Kaika looked at Rysha. "The work turns you into something you weren't when you got started."

"Are you telling me I shouldn't stick with the elite troops training, ma'am?" Rysha thought about pointing out that she'd already seen death and lost comrades in the dragon attack on the city, but she hadn't yet lost anyone she'd been truly close to. Her grandmother was the only one, and that would have happened whether she'd been a soldier or not. By being a soldier, she might keep *more* instances like that from occurring in the future.

"Nope. It's just a warning so you're prepared for the day when you find it hard to show appreciation for a lower-ranking officer." Her voice grew so soft that Rysha barely heard the next comment. "Or a lover that treats you better than you deserve."

Rysha slipped on a patch of mildew and almost bathed her leg in the channel.

"Watch where you step, Lieutenant," Kaika said dryly.

"Yes, ma'am." Again, Rysha thought about saying more, but again felt her lack of experience keenly.

"And make sure you're on that steamer in two days," Kaika added. "The *Eternal Horizon*. They won't wait for us. I don't know about you, but I'm ready to go home."

Rysha hesitated to supply one of her prompt *yes, ma'ams*. The stasis babies weren't her responsibility, as her superiors would be quick to point out, and it wasn't as if she had the tie to them that Trip had. But if he hadn't located the little girl in two days, he probably wouldn't board that steamer. Would he want Rysha to stay and help with the search? He had the soulblades and magical power, but she believed she was better at research and ferreting out clues.

Kaika gave her a narrow-eyed look.

"I'm ready to go home, too, ma'am," Rysha said.

Kaika's eyes stayed narrow. She knew that hadn't been assent.

"Don't make me write you up when I get back, Rysha," Kaika said, frowning not at her but at Trip's back. "This early in your career, you'll get away with less than you might when you have a proven record and your superiors recognize you as a valuable soldier. Insubordination alone would be a reason for them to revoke your commission, but going AWOL?" Kaika's gaze shifted back to Rysha. "Don't give it up before you even know what you're giving up. It's worth it. Sometimes, it makes you harder than you want to be." A vague hand wave seemed to acknowledge her earlier words. "But you get to use your talents to help your country, not just for your own gain."

"I understand, ma'am."

Kaika looked expectantly at her. Waiting for a confirmation that Rysha would be on that steamer in two mornings?

"Thank you," Rysha said, since she couldn't give Kaika what she wanted, not yet.

Trip turned again, the wagon scraping on a wall as they entered a narrow passage. This one was dry, and he followed it around a bend and down a ramp. By the water channel, the tunnel had seemed newer and well maintained. Here, bricks that had crumbled from the walls dotted the ground, along with all manner of human trash. Rysha's nose wrinkled as the scent of urine and other waste grew noticeable.

"Taking us someplace classy to stay tonight, Captain?" Kaika called ahead.

"It'll be at least as appealing as the last two places," Trip said over his shoulder.

"Don't make promises you can't keep."

"Major Kaika said she would be disappointed if there wasn't a pull-up bar," Rysha said, though she wouldn't share that disappointment.

"I *didn't* say that. But it is true."

Rysha heard voices in the darkness ahead, and she fell silent. As they went down the ramp, the tunnel widened into an underground chamber full of half-crumbled walls, old and rusty machinery—was that the wheel to a mill of some kind?—and storage bins tipped on their sides. Stone columns ten feet in diameter rose to a high ceiling, supporting arches that stretched across it.

"What is this place?" Rysha wondered, then clamped her mouth shut when she noticed people camped among the ruins. Dozens of them. Maybe hundreds.

Here and there, lanterns burned and ragged blankets marked the boundaries of areas belonging to families or small groups. There were as many children as adults, hunkered down and whispering to each other.

"We camouflaged?" Kaika asked.

Nobody seemed to be looking in their direction even though they were an oddity with the blanket-covered wagon rolling along and nobody pulling it.

I am and the cart is, Trip spoke into their minds. *I can't camouflage you and Rysha directly, but I'm doing my best to make the path we're walking along appear particularly uninteresting to those in the chamber.*

"Uninteresting is good," Kaika said more softly.

Trip turned the wagon toward one of several tunnels with entrances located on the sides of the cavernous room.

By Rysha's estimation, they had dropped below sea level. It was hard to believe such a vast chamber could exist without having water in it. The columns and arches reminded her of Karudian architecture, and she wondered if some of those early ocean-going explorers had colonized this area before it had been turned into a penal colony. Maybe the existing city had grown up atop another.

The wagon barely fit through the new tunnel, and Rysha kept bumping shoulders with Kaika as they trailed it, their sword scabbards banging against their legs. Trip still had Jaxi out, lighting the way. Rysha eyed the walls, hoping for more evidence to support the idea that the Karudians had been here long ago. If they had been, this now-subterranean area could have existed before the dragon-rider outpost.

Trip turned again, the wagon scraping the wall and getting stuck before some force shoved it through the tight spot, leaving stone dust floating in the air.

"You *do* know where you're going, right, Captain?" Kaika swatted at a broken cobweb sweeping toward her nostrils.

"Yes, ma'am. I found a map earlier."

"Earlier? When you were sitting in the room and staring at the stack of baby boxes?"

"Yes, ma'am. My head was aching, so I took a break from the camouflaging assignment and went to what passes for a library in this city. It's more of an archives building, and you have to pay to access it. If you go in person."

"Are you saying you went with your mind?"

Trip glanced back. "If I say yes, will you call me creepy again?"

"You're not creepy," Kaika said. "Some of the things you can do are creepy."

Rysha snorted. She doubted that clarification would make Trip feel better.

"Would visiting a library with one's mind count?" Trip asked.

"Yes."

"Then I merely studied a pamphlet that I picked up while I was out last night," Trip said.

"Uh huh."

"Was that before or after we were attacked by magical animals?" Rysha asked.

"Before," Trip said firmly, then took a right at an intersection and led them to a dead end.

Kaika groaned. "I'm not helping you get that wagon turned around back here."

Trip walked straight to the dead end and placed a hand on the ancient stones. Rysha thought of the way he'd touched the ice walls in the dragon complex in the Antarctic, but this did not look like a place that had once been built by the great creatures. A dragon would have had to shape-shift into a miniature version of itself to make it through the tight tunnels.

Nonetheless, the wall swung inward, slowly, ponderously, and with a rumble that made it seem an earthquake was imminent. Dust trickled down from the ceiling, and Rysha sneezed. She rested a hand on the cool wall next to her in case the ground started shaking. But the stone door finished opening, and the dust settled with nothing more ominous occurring.

Trip walked in as though he had expected nothing less. The wagon trundled obediently after him.

Rysha and Kaika stepped through into a much smaller chamber than the one with the arches and squatters. It was illuminated with blueish light that came in from above, bright enough to make Rysha squint after the dimness of the tunnels. She stopped while her eyes adjusted.

Dorfindral sent a huff of displeasure into Rysha's mind. Had some magic been involved in the construction of the room?

"What the—" Kaika pointed upward toward… Rysha didn't know what to call it.

It looked like a pool with a glass bottom that was embedded in a stone ceiling, between arches and supports similar to the ones in the other chamber. Light streamed in, turning blue as it filtered through the water. The pool had to be open to the sky up above, but where in the city was it? Some park or garden? Did the Lagreshians even believe in such things?

It's the private garden of one of the crime lords in the city, Trip told her silently, smiling back from where he'd stopped under the pool. *Jaxi snooped around and says nobody in the twenty-person household, most of those people being his staff, knows this is under here. From up above, the bottom appears to be made from stone, and they toss marbles into the pool for luck.*

A magical illusion? Rysha asked, also speaking silently.

Kaika might think it odd if she answered aloud. She was stalking the perimeter of the chamber, peering into shadows behind posts.

Yes, one that's been in place for a very long time. Since long before the crime lord bought the sprawling compound up there.

"Major Kaika," Trip said aloud, "we're alone in here. The people who squat in the tunnels out there don't know this sanctuary is here."

"How did *you* know it was here?" Kaika continued her walk around the perimeter and kept checking all the shadows.

She stopped in front of a dragon statue on the far wall, another pool nestled in its lap. A real dragon wouldn't *have* a lap, but this one was chubby and squatted on its lower two legs with the stone vessel resting between them. Its wings stretched outward against the wall, and its head was tilted, its expression one of curiosity rather than the pomposity Rysha associated with so many dragons. Or outright coldness.

"She's beautiful," Rysha murmured, drawn across the chamber toward the statue.

Interestingly, this chamber didn't stink of waste like so many of the tunnels had. It might simply be because people didn't come in here, but it didn't even smell of dust and disuse. It had a pleasant earthy odor that reminded her of the woods back home in her family's valley.

"I was studying the map," Trip responded to Kaika, "of these tunnels down here. I hadn't originally known they were here, but I sensed them when I was searching the city and looking for the missing stasis chamber. You'd mentioned wanting something better than a hostel for us."

"Searching the city... with your mind?" Kaika asked.

"In whatever way you find un-creepy, ma'am."

"I'm going to pretend the swords were looking and just told you about it."

"It's less creepy when they use magic?"

"Yes, because they're not human. Humanish."

"Your logic is interesting, ma'am," Trip said.

"You're not the first man to call me interesting."

Rysha reached the dragon and slid a hand over the lower part of one wing as she peeked into the pool. Dorfindral continued to rumble discontentedly at her, but she didn't sense that an enemy was near. This seemed to be the sword's way of letting her know magic was around.

The pool was clear, no hint of algae or any other growth marring the bottom of the bowl. She could see her own reflection and realized it was the first time she had in days. Their rooms hadn't contained anything as luxurious as mirrors. She made a note to dig out her brush, since her bun was on the lumpy and frizzy side.

"This appears to represent Lyshandrasa," Rysha said, touching a plaque on the side of the statue, "the mate of the dragon that was carved into the stone of the meeting room at the bottom of the outpost. If I remember my history correctly, she was a hero and friend to humanity, though she wasn't one of the Iskandian dragons and didn't travel to our land. She favored desert climates, such as this." If she knew where Moe Zirkander had gone, Rysha would have asked him for more details on the dragon, as he'd seemed quite knowledgeable about this part of the world. "I wonder what she was truly like, legends aside. This is a rather whimsical-looking expression for a dragon, especially a female. They were often fierce, the dominant predators of the species." Rysha looked more closely at the face. "This one reminds me of Shulina Arya."

Trip came to stand next to her.

"Is it odd that I miss her?" she asked as Kaika finished her inspection of the chamber—the sanctuary, as Trip had called it.

"I don't think so. She's a lot friendlier than the other dragons. And she didn't suggest you become her minion."

Rysha quirked her eyebrows.

"The bronze dragon on the Pirate Isles made that offer to me."

"A minion? That's it? After all the help we gave him?"

"A *high*-level minion, if I recall correctly. I believe the job came with a hut and a mate."

Rysha stared at him, thinking he was joking, but he seemed serious. "With perks like that, it's no wonder so many humans are willing to worship dragons."

"I know I was tempted." His eyes crinkled. "He didn't say whether I got to pick my mate, or if one would be assigned to me."

Rysha sniffed. "He probably would have found you a pirate floozy with overly ripened melons on display."

Trip glanced toward her chest, then blushed and made a point of studying the fountain. She remembered her stint in the pirate costume and supposed it was unfair to judge those who displayed their... melons. For all she knew, Major Kaika had civilian clothes that flaunted her assets. Even though it was hard to imagine her in anything except a uniform with a rifle—and a half-dozen grenades—close at hand, she *had* been comfortable in that pirate clothing.

"Is there a way out of here if legions of people trying to get our swords show up?" Kaika stood under the pool, gazing up at it. "While this place is pleasantly quiet and doesn't smell, it was a long walk to get here. If we had to run with the wagon getting stuck at every turn in the tunnel, it would be tough. There also doesn't appear to be a back door, unless that counts." She pointed above her.

"I don't think we can go out that way as there's a lot of old, strong magic reinforcing the pool and ceiling," Trip said, "but there is a rusty ladder not too far away that leads to the surface. A lot of the people living down here come and go that way. We just wouldn't have been able to fit the wagon through the manhole at the top, so I brought us the long way."

Kaika puckered her lips.

"It's only for a couple of days, ma'am." Trip shrugged. "I thought it would suffice. With luck, nobody will ever know we're here."

"With luck? When has luck ever favored us?"

"We must have been lucky at least once," Rysha said. "We're all still alive."

Kaika's lips twisted and puckered a bit more. Once again, Rysha wondered if she'd had a close call the day before.

"I like to think my skills are what keep me alive." Kaika sighed. "All right, it's only for two days. If we stay holed up in here the whole time, maybe nobody will notice us."

Trip took a deep breath and faced her. "Ma'am—"

"Let me guess," Kaika said. "You don't want to stay holed up in here."

Trip opened his hand toward the ceiling, the blue light playing on his palm. "I have to use the time we have to find her."

"Her?"

"The baby. It's a girl."

"It's a three-thousand-year-old statue in a box."

"It's a three-thousand-year-old *baby* in a box. That can grow into someone just as normal as…" Trip started to point at himself, but maybe he decided he wasn't an exemplar of normal. "You," he finished.

Rysha looked sadly at him. She couldn't tell if Kaika was swayed.

"You did already tell him he could look, ma'am," Rysha pointed out. "This morning."

"Oh, don't remind me. I was feeling guilty because I lost the kid in the first place. All right, all right, you can go, Captain. But be *discreet* this time." Kaika pinned him with her gaze.

Trip turned his own gaze on Rysha. *She heard about last night's fiasco somewhere.*

I'm not surprised.

"I'll do my best, ma'am. And, just in case something happens and I'm delayed... I'll go alone."

"What?" Rysha asked as Kaika said, "Good."

"Trip, you need my help," Rysha said. "They're using magic, both of them, right? I have Dorfindral. And if snooping needs to be done, I'm good at reading and analyzing data quickly. I—" Realizing she sounded like she was spouting off qualifications for a job interview, she stopped, finishing only with, "You need me."

Trip smiled at her. "I don't want you to miss the boat because of me."

"We have two days. Plenty of time. It's not like those barges are going to sail out to sea with us stuck in the dungeon. Barges don't even *have* dungeons."

"It's evening, already, and it'll be night before I go out there. That means only a full day and a full night until the steamer leaves. Things happen. I don't want you to miss the boat. If it takes me longer to find the girl, then I'll follow after you as soon as I can. And accept my consequences for being late when I return." He met Kaika's gaze.

She nodded at him, approval in her eyes.

Rysha didn't approve, damn it. "Trip, you're being fatalistic. There's no reason to assume going back to the barges will take more than a night."

Unless he believed he was going to get captured. Why would he think that? He ought to be more powerful than Grekka. Even though the palace barge was an opaque box to him, it wasn't as if he *had* to go in. He could go back to the warehouse barge and wait for Grekka to come there. He ought to be able to use Grekka to get to Bhodian.

I hope not *to be captured,* Trip spoke into her mind, *but it would be foolish for me not to plan for the worst. I intend to stake out the harbor this evening and hope to get lucky, to catch Bhodian or Grekka coming or going so I don't have to go out to his barge. But if I don't... I will walk up and knock on his door if necessary. The soulblades have confirmed that they don't sense the stasis chamber in the city. Since none of us can sense the barge palace, that seems the most likely place to look for it. It's possible it's been taken out of the city, but I will start there.*

Yes, I understand, but why not let me come? Rysha hesitated. *Is it because you had trouble protecting me with your barrier last night? Because you couldn't use your magic on Dorfindral? Trip, if we have to fight the sorceress or some other magic—*

No. I know you're valuable, and I want to take you with me. But it's too close to the sailing. I don't want you to risk punishment—or worse—because of me and my quest.

I don't want to see someone misusing or hurting that baby girl any more than you do.

I know. Trust that I won't let that happen. And that I'll be right behind you if I'm delayed.

"If I'm not back in time," Trip said, turning to Kaika again, "please make sure the babies get to Sardelle. She's the only one I'm sure will… do the right thing."

Kaika spread her hands. "I'm just a cog in a machine, Trip, so I doubt I'll get any say, but most of our superior officers aren't assholes. I don't think they'll make a cruel choice. And I know Angulus won't."

"Good."

Rysha watched, feeling bleak, as Trip filled his canteen at the pool and gathered a couple of supplies to take with him. He walked to the door, waving his hand to open it, and stepped into the tunnel. He paused there, looking back at her. Would he change his mind?

Actually, I was hoping you would rush after me to give me a good-luck kiss.

Even though I'm grumpy and don't agree with you going without me?

Yes.

The petulant part of her almost crossed her arms over her chest and turned her back, but she worried she wouldn't see him again in the morning, that he knew something she didn't.

She didn't rush, but she walked through the doorway, hugged him, and kissed him.

He smiled against her lips. *Thank you.*

Your swords are poking me in the stomach.

Have I mentioned what a pleasure it is that you don't seem to mind that I have two swords that poke you in the stomach?

I knew you were odd from the beginning.

She'd meant to give him a chaste kiss, the simple good-luck kiss he'd suggested, but he slipped his arms around her and touched her lips so tenderly that her irritation faded. She stroked the back of his head, fingers twining in his hair.

Be careful out there, she thought.

UNRAVELED

I'll try. You know pilots tend toward recklessness.

What do powerful sorcerers tend toward?

Arrogance, probably.

You're doomed either way, aren't you?

He chuckled and drew back, resting his hand on her cheek. "I hope not."

He turned, heading down the tunnel.

"Trip?"

He gazed over his shoulder. "Yes?"

"I'll leave Dorfindral leaning against the wall so it's easier for you to reach me telepathically if you run into trouble and need help. I *will* come to help you. No matter when the sailing time is."

"Thank you."

As he disappeared around the corner of the intersection, he sent some tendril of telepathic power back to her, infusing her with his gratitude. *More* than gratitude. A warm tingle spread through her body, reminding her of the night they had spent together.

She wanted to spend *another* night with him, and she hated the idea of sitting back here and twiddling her thumbs while he risked himself. She understood that he didn't want her to risk her career—or her chance to get into the elite troops—because of his side trip, and she appreciated that he cared, but it was her choice. And she didn't truly believe it was a risk, no matter what he argued. A day and a half was plenty of time to poke around in a couple of barges.

"You all right?" Kaika asked as Rysha walked back into the chamber, drumming her fingers on her thigh.

Maybe she appeared agitated. At the least, she likely appeared oddly determined for a woman walking away from a kiss.

That was because she *was* determined. She wouldn't follow Trip out to the barges, but she decided she *would* go down to the harbor that night. That way, if something happened and he needed help, she would be close enough to give it.

"I'm fine, ma'am. I was giving him a good-luck kiss."

Kaika narrowed her eyes. "Was it not enjoyable?"

Kaika was either better at reading people than she was given credit for, or she'd come to know Rysha well enough to read her. Rysha did her best to wipe her determined expression off her face.

"It was lovely, ma'am, but two swords jabbed me in the stomach."

"A man with two swords is somewhat alarming."

"I'm getting used to it."

"Clearly, you're a remarkable woman."

Rysha grabbed her pack and sat on one of the stone dragon feet at the base of the statue, a bench of sorts. Aware of Kaika watching her, she removed the two journals and the rubbings she had taken at the outpost, hoping to make it look like she intended to spend the evening studying assiduously. No need for Kaika to stay awake all night to keep an eye on her young lieutenant....

A part of Rysha wanted to be straightforward and ask for permission to follow Trip to the harbor, but she was skeptical that she would get that permission. Better to slip out after dark after Kaika went to sleep. If she could. Kaika was as alert as any soldier.

"I admit to feeling bad about not offering to help him," Kaika said, surprising Rysha.

"You do?"

"I *am* the reason one of the boxes got stolen in the first place. I should have stayed in the room and fought with my back to them so nobody could get by."

"They got by both of us."

"Yes, but you're young and inexperienced. I should know better. I'm worldly and wise."

"I thought you were going to say old and experienced."

"No woman is going to call herself old."

"Mature?"

Kaika glared at her. "*Worldly.*"

"One of us could follow Trip down to the harbor tonight," Rysha found herself saying. Maybe she should get permission, after all. "Just to keep an eye on him from afar."

"On him or his two swords?"

"*Ma'am.*"

"Sometimes eccentricities like that get young women overly excited."

"I'm not excited. I'm practical. He's going to face at least one sorceress. He could use someone with a *chapaharii* blade nearby. And it wouldn't take more than the night. I won't miss making the steamer's departure time. I'll be there."

"Promise?" Kaika asked.

Rysha hesitated, realizing she hadn't agreed to that yet. When Kaika had brought it up earlier, Rysha had hedged, wanting to wait to see what happened with recovering the stasis chamber.

Was this what she had to do to gain permission to watch Trip tonight? Give her word on this?

Kaika watched her intently. Waiting.

Rysha was glad that Kaika cared and didn't want Rysha's career to be damaged or for her to lose any opportunities, but she couldn't help but feel she'd let herself be maneuvered into this situation, into having to give her word over something that was uncertain.

As she met Kaika's gaze and said, "Yes, ma'am," she knew she was committed now, that she did indeed have to be on that steamer.

She would just have to make sure that Trip retrieved the baby girl before then.

CHAPTER 8

T HE ROAR OF A LION drifted through Lagresh's streets.
Trip frowned. Had the animals he'd knocked into the water the
night before been allowed to roam free in the city? He would
have expected the magical gems to act as leashes that Grekka could
mentally tug on to bring the animals home. Maybe the lion was on some
independent hunt that had nothing to do with the previous night.

Trip stood across the street from the docks, watching the barges as twilight
deepened, and hoping Bhodian would leave so he could waylay him outside
of his stronghold. At the moment, a smaller ship was delivering cargo to the
floating warehouse. The palace was well lit once again, and Bhodian walked
out occasionally with a drink in hand and looked toward the other barge. Was
he waiting for Grekka to come over for a date? Unfortunately, he didn't look
like he intended to head into the city any time soon.

The roar came again, followed by a distant scream. Trip closed his
eyes and sent his senses up the hill and into the city. Normally, it would
have been difficult to find a single person or animal when so many other
people occupied the area, but since the lion had dragon blood and a
magical gem, it was easier to locate.

The lion was unwounded and lacked wings, so Trip didn't think it
was one of the ones he'd battled the night before, but it was huge and

powerful. It ran through an alley, roaring up at a woman stuck on the rooftop of a one-story building. Clad in mismatched rags, she looked like an older version of the young girl Trip had given a coin to. Definitely someone who lived on the streets and had a rough life. What could such a person have done to earn the Silver Shark's ire? Or was this simply some sport? Had Grekka rented out the lion by the hour to entertain someone who watched?

Loathing that possibility, Trip groped for a way to help from a mile away. Could he use his power over such distance?

The lion sprang into the air, almost reaching the roof of the woman's building with its bound. She raced to the other side as she glanced toward higher rooftops nearby, maybe believing the predator couldn't reach her if she climbed high enough. It seemed inevitable that it would find a way up to her current perch, especially since there were stairs on one side. The lion must not have spotted them yet.

The woman crouched at the edge of the roof, overlooking an alley. Trip sensed her intent, to jump down, sprint across, and climb up the next building, a taller building. Maybe she could do it before the lion reached her.

But even as she crouched to lower herself, the great predator raced around the corner. It leaped, and she rolled back on the rooftop. Its claws nicked the gutter before it dropped back down.

"Have to do something," Trip whispered, knowing the lion would find a way up there soon. It was determined to get its target.

He closed his eyes, formed a current of compressed air, and willed it to soar through the streets toward the woman. Debris flew into the air as it passed, doors banged open and closed, and dogs howled. Trip directed it through alleys and toward the woman's perch. He was aware of the lion rounding a corner, spotting those stairs, and racing toward them. From there, it would have no trouble reaching the rooftop.

Keeping his concentration, Trip willed even more wind to gather into his stream. As the lion sprang up the stairs and to the rooftop, he swept his channel of air under the woman.

She cried out in fear, arms and legs flailing as it lifted her. The wind sailed her across the street, upward to the higher rooftop, and halfway across that building before Trip let it dissipate.

The woman gripped the roof tiles on her hands and knees, panting in terror. Trip wished he'd warned her first, but he hadn't been certain he could lift her. At least she was safe now, assuming the lion would get tired of stalking her when it realized it couldn't reach her. He watched with satisfaction as the creature tried to emulate the route he'd sent the woman on. But the alley was too wide. The lion's leap only carried it part way up the higher building before it struck the wall and dropped to the ground.

Do you think it's wise to go out of your way to irritate the Cofah businesswoman? Jaxi asked, popping the balloon of his satisfaction. It felt good to have used his power to help a stranger.

If she killed Dreyak, she deserves to be irked. Trip still held on to the possibly delusional hope that he could somehow find his little sibling *and* get to the bottom of Dreyak's murder. Maybe if he could corner Bhodian *and* Grekka and get them to talk....

She likely deserves to be irked no matter what she did with Dreyak, but it might not be smart for you to be the one doing the irking.

Who else is going to?

Just be aware that you have comrades to worry about.

They can take care of themselves, but I am noting your objection.

Good. I do enjoy being noted.

Azarwrath cleared his throat in Trip's mind. *Few are watching the barges.* The loading had finished, the smaller ship returning to dock. *Perhaps it would be a good time to travel out there and confront these people.*

Both of them? Have you seen evidence that Grekka is out there?

Trip hadn't sensed her in the warehouse, but she could be able to hide herself from him with her magic. She might not have his raw power, but she likely had decades more experience in using what she had.

I do not know, but the man she was with last night is in the palace. She may be his female.

Or he may be her male, Trip thought dryly, imagining Rysha objecting to Azarwrath's wording. Jaxi would object too. *Grekka seemed to be the one in charge last night.*

I didn't see it that way, Azarwrath said. *Regardless, I still can't sense the inside of the palace. I do sense that there are fewer animals in their cages in the warehouse this evening.*

Trip grimaced. How many had been rented out to hunt people tonight? He knew the handful of deaths he and Rysha had been responsible for couldn't have emptied many cages. And he assumed the ones he'd knocked into the water had been recovered.

Trip let more time pass, his shoulder against a post supporting the main dock structure. He didn't truly want to go into the palace, and he kept hoping Bhodian would leave or he would catch Grekka returning home. But as the night grew later, that seemed less and less likely.

I think I'm going to have to go out there and knock on the door. Trip gathered wind again, this time to carry himself across the water. Wryly, he admitted he'd enjoyed the challenge of bringing the wrecked rowboat up from the bottom of the harbor and repairing it. But that had taken a lot of time, and without Rysha—and Dorfindral—he could move more quickly.

I do love it when you take us to dangerous places where our magic doesn't work, Jaxi said.

The wind ruffled Trip's clothing as it lifted him into the air. He needed most of his concentration to levitate—and make sure nobody nearby noticed him doing so—but he managed to ask, *You think your magic won't work in there? Just because you can't sense the interior?*

We won't know until you open the door and take us inside, but it reminds me uncomfortably of the magic dead zone. I hadn't planned to take another nap so soon.

How could Bhodian have created a magic dead zone just around his barge?

Perhaps by bringing some of the ore from the quarry and placing it within, Azarwrath said.

Trip should have considered that. It seemed an obvious explanation. Still, he hoped it was wrong. Perhaps Bhodian had some magical artifact that protected his home from prying mages, a camouflage similar to what Trip had created for the stasis chambers. Maybe Grekka had even made it for him.

Trip floated over the harbor, skimming above the gently lapping waves, without anyone noticing and sounding an alarm. Maybe that signaled that his luck would be good tonight.

His boots touched down on the deck of the palace in front of the double doors of the main entrance. From here, it seemed more like he was on a patio in someone's yard rather than the deck of a ship. He eyed the windows visible on the front of the structure, both at ground level and in the spires and towers above. Curtains were drawn, but light shone through from some of the rooms. He listened for voices or perhaps a phonograph playing music, but heard only the lapping of the waves.

Shall I try sneaking inside or just knock on the door and confront them? Trip asked, a dull ache starting up behind his eyes. It made him want to get this over with as quickly as possible. It also reminded him uncomfortably of the quarry.

Maybe Azarwrath was right. Maybe the palace's framework was made from that tainted iron ore. If so, was it enough to keep Trip from using his magic at all? Or would it be like it had been at the spring, with his senses going in and out?

Maybe he should try to sneak in through a window, find the stasis chamber, and get out? But without his senses, that could take hours. And he already knew Bhodian was inside. Trip would have to avoid him and however many other men and women worked on the barge.

Perhaps you should knock and invite the occupants outside rather than going in, Azarwrath suggested.

Trip was relieved he could still talk to the soulblades. *How will I do that? Point out the moon is lovely tonight and that they might want to look at it?*

The sorceress did *go in here last night,* Azarwrath pointed out. *If the place was extremely awful for someone with dragon blood and she couldn't use her magic at all, she probably wouldn't ever visit.*

True.

Trip drew a bracing breath, walked forward, and knocked.

A doorbell inside played a short eerie refrain. Or maybe that was an alarm. It wasn't as if he'd rung a bell.

The double doors opened inward on silent, well-oiled hinges. Trip crossed his arms to rest his hands on the soulblades' hilts.

But there was nobody at the door. Or anywhere in sight.

A grand foyer opened up, lit by a swan-shaped chandelier hanging from the high ceiling. A marble floor stretched back, offering space enough to host a ball. The barge itself wasn't that huge, and Trip estimated the foyer took up one-third to one-half of the interior space, at least above decks. There was a hallway and closed doors at the back of the room, and a staircase along that wall led up to a balcony and more closed doors. Bedrooms?

Interestingly, two large roll-up doors occupied the side walls. They looked more like something that would lead to carriage storage rooms than living areas. But why would people on a barge need anything except boats for transportation?

Trip tried to sense what was behind those doors, but his headache only intensified, and he couldn't see anything with his mind. He looked back toward the docks, reassured when he was able to sense things out there. He decided to stay where he was rather than walking in. If the front doors held some of the tainted iron, it might end his ability to sense anything at all if he allowed them to close behind him.

"Hello?" he called into the interior. "My name is Captain Trip. I'm from Iskandia, and I have a business proposition."

You do? Jaxi's voice sounded soft and far away.

No, but I thought the promise of business might intrigue them.

Unfortunately, nobody appeared. Trip tapped the soulblade hilts thoughtfully. He was reluctant to explore or even leave the threshold. Right now, if the doors started to swing closed, he could scramble out to avoid being trapped inside.

"I know where more *chapaharii* swords are located," he called.

It seemed as good a thing to offer to pique their interest as any.

A clank came from outside, not from the barge but from somewhere to its side. Trip leaned out and sensed the warehouse barge had drifted much closer. And was that a ramp that it had extended? A walkway for—

"Shit," he groaned, sensing animals rushing across the ramp before he heard the clacks of claws on metal.

Act quickly this time, Azarwrath warned. *Fling them into the water before they can attack.*

Yes, we'll help. Jaxi's hilt warmed as she summoned energy. *No hesitation.*

Trip hurled a blast of wind at the animals as two of the winged lions raced around the corner, the gems in their throats glowing.

Unfortunately, they flapped their wings instead of splashing into the water. Azarwrath hurled lightning around the corner at two more animals coming—panthers? Jaxi flung power at the ramp where the animals raced across. There were at least a dozen of them, scaled panthers, giant lizards, and apes, many of the creatures he'd battled the night before.

Cracks and clanks sounded as Jaxi tore the ramp from its hinges and hurled it out into the harbor. One of the lions flew up to avoid it. The other lion angled toward Trip and flapped its wings hard, aiming to ram into him.

Trip hurled another wave of power, attempting to both knock the lion away and throw more animals into the water before they reached him. He also braced himself, determined not to let them push him back into the foyer. Right away, he sensed that they wanted to do that, to drive him inside where he would have less access to his magic.

Just create a barrier in front of the door, Jaxi said. *We'll handle the rest. You should watch your back in case—*

Something wrapped around Trip's ankle from behind, and he didn't hear the rest.

He yelled in surprise as he was yanked off his feet before he could jerk away. As he flew backward, he drew the swords. He twisted in the air so he could hack at whatever gripped him. He expected a rope or a whip, but as he tumbled to the hard marble floor, he saw the truth. A massive snake was pulling him into the building. Though he couldn't get much leverage with it dragging him across the floor, he slashed at it anyway.

The soulblades glowed more softly than usual, but their blades sank into snake flesh. The creature pulled him a few more feet, but let go after the fourth strike. It reared back, coiling into itself. A flat head and yellow eyes stared at Trip as its forked tongue darted in and out. It hissed at him, seeming to challenge him.

Trip jumped to his feet, having no interest in accepting that challenge. He spun back toward the door, but lions and apes sprang across the threshold, blocking the way. Then the doors clanged shut, leaving Trip trapped inside with ten powerful predators.

"Should've known," he grumbled, whipping the soulblades up to defend himself as two scaled panthers sprang at him. Azarwrath had warned him that fewer animals were in their cages, but he hadn't considered that someone had been preparing the others to send over here, someone who must have anticipated his visit.

Trip dodged and deflected slashing claws as he glanced over his shoulder, afraid that snake would take advantage and strike at his back. But it had moved off to the side. Another snake had appeared in the foyer, also coiled, its head higher than Trip's as it hissed at him. It wasn't close enough to attack. Instead, it maintained its coil off to one side, across from the first snake.

As Trip frantically blocked attacks, he got the feeling that the snakes had opened the way and that the other animals were driving him in a particular direction. Toward one of those doors in the back?

Claws slipped past his defenses and raked his arm, shredding his sleeve—and his flesh. He growled and attempted to throw a wave of power at the animals, to knock them all back to the doors.

All he managed was a feeble puff of air that barely stirred their fur.

The soulblades also weren't as effective as usual. When he'd battled with them before, they had guided his hands, turning him into a master swordsman even though he had no experience. He sensed little bursts from Jaxi and Azarwrath, as they tried to add speed to his blocks, but it wasn't enough. He couldn't hold his ground, and the animals succeeded in driving him farther and farther from the front doors.

Trip glanced back again. He was definitely being angled toward one of those doors. What if he simply ran to it, opened it, and shut it in the faces of the animals? Nothing, probably. These powerful creatures could bash down a door. Besides—

The floor disappeared under his feet.

Trip swore as he pitched downward. He released the soulblades and grabbed at the edge of the opening, but it was slick with grease. His fingers slipped off. He fell into darkness, one flailing hand grazing the hanging trapdoor that he hadn't detected, its marble tile surface identical to that of the rest of the foyer flooring.

He expected to splash into the water under the barge, but he landed on the hard hull, the metal cold and unforgiving. Darkness enshrouded him, and he couldn't sense a thing. Metal clanged right above him, and he flinched and lifted his hands, expecting something to fall on him.

Nothing struck him, but when he jumped to his feet, he cracked his head on a low ceiling that he hadn't anticipated. No, not a ceiling, he realized as he patted around, fingers brushing metal bars. The top of a cage.

A roar came from above, one of the lions peering through the trapdoor opening. Even without access to his senses, Trip knew it was envisioning a tasty dinner entrée. But the trapdoor swung shut first, locking the animals out. And locking Trip *in*.

He explored the rest of the cage, looking for a way out, but all he found were metal bars all around him. When he shoved at the metal over his head, the flat top did not move. A well-designed cage, he admitted grudgingly. And he'd allowed himself to be placed right in it.

CHAPTER 9

R YSHA ARRIVED AT THE WATERFRONT several hours after the sun set and expected to spend hours waiting in the shadows, watching the palace to see if anything explosive happened. She didn't expect to find a battle underway as soon as the barge came into view.

She gawked at the chaos taking place out there, at lions, lizards, and apes racing from the warehouse barge across a ramp to the palace barge. That ramp was soon hurled into the air by some invisible power, but it didn't matter. The two barges were close enough that more animals leaped across. They all arrowed toward the man standing just inside the open double doors. Trip.

He wielded Jaxi and Azarwrath, the blades whipping about as he deflected bites and slashes, but the swords had a much duller glow than usual, and his movements seemed more frantic than expert.

A few people had gathered on the waterfront, drawn by the battle—the growls and yips echoed throughout the harbor. Others stood gaping from the deck of a large merchant steamer moored at the end of the docks—the vessel Kaika must have booked passage on.

Rysha ran toward the docks, wondering if she could persuade the captain to take her out to the barge. But there wasn't any smoke coming from his smokestacks. Firing up the vessel would take time, time that Trip might not have.

The palace barge wasn't so far out that a ride was necessary. Besides, whoever had let out all those animals would notice another ship coming out. That person might not notice a single small figure in the dark water…

"I knew swimming would be involved sooner or later," Rysha grumbled to herself.

She ran past the docks and turned onto the sandy beach where Trip had fixed the rowboat the night before. From down here, she couldn't see him anymore, but the roars and growls continued to emanate from the barge.

Rysha made sure Dorfindral was secure in its sheath, then tugged out the strap that would secure her spectacles to her face. Though she hated to delay, she also grabbed an oilskin bag she'd stopped to buy on the way here, having envisioned having to swim. She stuck her pistol inside and did her best to make the bag watertight, so the bullets wouldn't get wet.

Finally, she plowed into the water under the docks. Its frigid grip wrapped around her body, making her gasp, but the cold propelled her arms to greater speed. The sooner she got out there, the sooner she could climb out and help Trip. Assuming there was a ladder or a way up to the deck from the water.

She grimaced as she swam, realizing there was no guarantee of a ladder, but she vowed she would find a way up. She didn't know how Trip had gotten into trouble so quickly, but her gut told her that he needed her. Dorfindral was made to battle people—and animals—with dragon blood.

By the time she reached the barge, her breaths were ragged, and her arms and legs felt like lead. A clang sounded—doors shutting? The noise of the battle grew muffled. She still heard roars, but they sounded like they were coming from inside now.

Rysha swam around the hull, looking for a ladder or any handholds she could use to pull herself up. Finally, she spotted something.

Not a ladder, but the thick anchor chain that stretched from midway up the hull into the water. She swam over and pulled herself up with weary arms. The chain hole wasn't large enough for anyone to crawl through, but she managed to stick a boot in and use it as a foothold. She pushed herself up, stretching high, fingers brushing the lip of the railing. Growling, she leaped from the tiny, awkward ledge. If she didn't make it, she would simply try again.

Her fingers curled around the railing, only with one hand at first. But she flung her other hand up and also caught the railing. And then she dangled there, some part of the back of her mind laughing because this was the exact situation she'd been in when she'd had to get over that wall on the elite-troops obstacle course.

As she'd done then, she swung her legs from side to side, making a human pendulum. The railing was damp, and she had to be careful not to dislodge her fingers. Tedious seconds passed as she gathered momentum. Worry gnawed at her heart because the sounds of the battle had faded completely.

Finally, she twisted at the height of a swing and hooked one leg over the railing. That was enough. She pulled herself up awkwardly, almost falling over and onto the walkway.

Hot air washed over her, and she glanced to the side. Not air. *Breath.* Fangs snapped toward her.

She lurched back, tearing Dorfindral from its sheath. Her shoulder rammed hard against a wall, and she almost dropped the sword. But the *chapaharii* blade took over, slashing to knock aside a panther's snapping maw before her conscious mind could have summoned a defense.

Dorfindral flared, its green light shining in the creature's yellow eyes, and energy surged into Rysha's limbs. All the weariness from the hard swim evaporated, and she felt like climbing mountains. And slaying enemies.

She lunged away from the wall, meeting the panther in the air as it sprang toward her, its jaws snapping for her face. Rysha roared and swept the blade up and across with all her strength. The fangs almost made it to her, and she jerked her head back, but not before Dorfindral cut halfway through the panther's broad neck.

She jumped back, pulling the blade free as the animal dropped to the deck. It couldn't survive that injury, but it didn't know that yet. It bunched it muscles, preparing to spring for her again.

Rysha leaped first, the sword giving her greater speed than usual. She adjusted her grip and plunged the blade down from above, the point diving into the creature's skull. There was so much power behind the blow that she almost pinned it to the deck.

Afraid that others would have heard the battle, Rysha yanked the blade free and spun to look in the other direction. And then swore.

She'd expected more animals, but a woman stood there with twin ivory-hilted pistols in her hands. Grekka.

Rysha stared at the dark muzzles pointed at her face.

"I happen to know the magic of those swords does not protect the wielder from bullets," Grekka said in a faint Cofah accent.

"Actually, I *have* deflected bullets before," Rysha said, still in a fighting stance, still with Dorfindral raised in front of her.

"Not from this range, I wager. And not two at a time."

Rysha couldn't tell if the woman had an invisible barrier around her, but she doubted it, not if she meant to shoot. Even if she *did*, Dorfindral could pop it in a second, and Rysha could lunge in and knock the pistols away. She just needed to buy that second.

"It's a very good blade," Rysha said, then glanced over Grekka's shoulder and frowned, as if something was back there.

The woman smirked and didn't glance away. Belatedly, Rysha realized she would have magical senses, the same as Trip, and wouldn't need to look to know nothing was sneaking up on her. Too bad.

"Drop it," the woman said.

"And then what?" Rysha asked, easily imagining the woman shooting her anyway. At least with the sword in hand, she had a chance at deflecting those bullets or lunging forward and cutting into the pistols before they fired. Even now, Dorfindral hummed in her grip, urging her to take action, to slash at the vile sorceress standing in front of them.

"Maybe I'll let you swim back the way you came. I can't imagine there would be much of a bounty out there for an Iskandian soldier, especially a lowly lieutenant."

Rysha masked her face, not letting her unease show, but it worried her that the woman knew all about her. She wasn't wearing her uniform jacket or her rank insignia, and she hadn't been thinking about her rank or her job, so Grekka shouldn't have telepathically plucked the information from her mind.

"You couldn't know many royal secrets," Grekka said. "Though there are Cofah who like torturing Iskandians just because it's enjoyable. Perhaps you *would* be worth keeping to sell. I have some empty cages after last night." Her eyes narrowed.

"You know a lot of Cofah subjects, still?" Rysha asked, realizing she might get some information from the woman. "I heard you prefer to kill them when they come to visit."

A hint of confusion entered Grekka's narrowed eyes.

"Dreyak," Rysha said. "He was helping our people out. Is that why he's dead now?"

The woman froze, and *her* face became a mask. Rysha had expected a different reaction, a sneer perhaps. She could tell the woman recognized the name, but she couldn't discern anything more.

Before she could ask another question, a rapid clacking of claws on the metal deck came from behind her. Damn it, she had forgotten there would be more animals out here.

Her instincts told her to spin and defend her back, but she made her feet stay where they were. There was trouble enough in front of her.

Grekka's fingers tensed on the triggers. Dorfindral whipped across, and a clang sounded right after the cracks of the pistols. The sword deflected one bullet, but agony flared in Rysha's stomach—the second one had gotten through.

She lunged and slashed at Grekka. A pop reverberated up her arm, Dorfindral breaking the woman's barrier. But before Rysha could push the attack, something massive slammed into her back.

As she flew forward, the woman dodged to the side to get out of the way. Rysha's hand cracked against the railing, and her fingers flew open. Dorfindral fell from her grip.

Rysha hit the deck, a huge weight atop her, and she roared in pain and frustration—and realization. She hadn't just dropped the sword; she'd dropped the sword into the *harbor*.

Rysha tried to push herself up, having a ridiculous notion of diving after it and somehow finding it in the dark water and catching it before it fell too far to retrieve. But she couldn't budge an inch. Whatever had her pinned weighed far more than she did.

"Warrior gods be damned, woman," Grekka growled, her feet coming into view as she stepped to the railing to peer over. "You threw that sword in? Those are worth ten thousand karvots a piece."

"Sorry to inconvenience your finances," Rysha growled through the pain in her abdomen. The bullet was lodged in there. Seven gods, she thought, terror creeping into her limbs. A wound like that could kill her.

Hot breath hit the back of her cold, wet neck. Something splashed to the deck beside her face. Saliva.

"You will be," Grekka snarled. "Fuddy, have her for dinner."

Grekka stalked away as the weight shifted on Rysha's back, the animal's fanged maw lowering to her head.

Rysha's terror went from a simmer to a boil. Whatever was on top of her was going to kill her long before the bullet did.

A hatch creaked open in the darkness, and the quiet thud of boots on metal floated to Trip's ears. He lifted his forehead from the bars of the cage—the cold metal helped ease his headache somewhat, though it did nothing to alleviate his sense of defeat. He was trapped and couldn't draw upon any of his power.

He didn't know if the cage was made of the tainted iron from the quarry or if the entire barge was, but he had been a fool to come out here. He'd dropped Jaxi and Azarwrath as he fell, and he didn't know if they were down in this hold with him or up on the marble floor, getting slobbered on by the circus. Whoever was walking toward him would probably pick them up and sell them. Or maybe, realizing a soulblade couldn't be used against its wishes, the person would throw them over the side of the barge.

Trip slumped as he imagined having to tell Sardelle that he'd lost Jaxi. Assuming he lived that long.

The person who'd entered unshuttered a lantern. The soft yellow flame didn't provide much light, but it was enough for Trip to recognize the gray goatee. Bhodian.

He lifted the lantern and gazed at Trip. "I must say, you're a disappointment."

"Thanks," Trip said, refusing to show that the statement confused him, even if it did. "And who are you?"

Oh, Trip had his name, but he had no idea if it was a first name, a surname, or a nickname. Nor did he know where the man was from or what he truly wanted.

Bhodian's eyebrows drew together. "You don't know? Do you typically break into the boats of people who you don't know?"

"I didn't break in. I knocked on the door. And then I tried very hard not to enter, but your guard dogs shoved me in. No, technically, the guard snake dragged me in."

"Droofy," Bhodian said, smirking. "Or maybe it was Dorfus. They are some of Grekka's favorites. I've a fondness for them too. She lets me keep them as house pets even when I'm not expecting intruders."

"As I said, I didn't *want* to intrude. I just wanted to talk."

"Which is why you broke into Grekka's warehouse yesterday and snooped through her desk drawers." Bhodian raised his eyebrows.

Trip wished he had an answer for that, other than to wonder how the man had known the precise details. Or was it Grekka who had known?

Trip shrugged. "I believe she killed a friend of mine, and I didn't think she would come if I invited her to tea to chat about it."

"No? She's open to chatting about killing people over tea."

"Lovely."

Bhodian looked him up and down while Trip did the same to him. It didn't look like the man carried a weapon, but he wore a long coat that could have hidden pistols and daggers. Trip tried to sense his thoughts, but it was in vain. He couldn't sense his own foot right now.

"Why am I not what you expected?" he asked, not because he wanted a list detailing his disappointing attributes, but because Bhodian may have known Trip's mother. More than that, he may have financed the expedition that resulted in Trip being found and being born again into this new era.

"You're half dragon, right? The offspring of Agarrenon Shivar." Bhodian tilted his head. "I expected you to be immensely powerful. I thought it was the greatest vanity for me to attempt to arrange this trap. Quite frankly, I thought you would wave your hand and destroy my home."

Trip decided it wouldn't benefit him to share that he'd only started training to be a sorcerer a couple of weeks ago. And that he'd been an absentee student for most of that time.

"You seem to have gone to some lengths to magic-proof it." Trip peered to the left and right of his cage, trying to pick out Jaxi or Azarwrath in the shadows. He also hoped, no doubt in vain, that he might spot the stasis chamber tucked away in a corner.

"Yes, several years back, I was concerned about a competitor. We were engaged in a feud of sorts. I assumed it would end up with one of us dead." He smirked. "I didn't imagine we'd end up with adjoining barges and often working together on deals."

"You and Grekka work together? Then you might know why she killed a Cofah warrior named Dreyak."

It was ludicrous to expect the man to give him information, but as long as Bhodian was feeling chatty, why not try?

"Dreyak? That was your friend? Huh."

Huh? Trip would have stripped naked for the power to read the man's mind.

"It's a little hard to believe since you're Iskandian," Bhodian added.

"Well, saying we were friends may be going too far, but we worked together to destroy the dragon portal in the Antarctic." Trip wasn't sure if he should be sharing that information, but nobody had told him it was classified. He imagined all the world powers knew it had happened by now. Of course, calling Lagresh—or even the entire continent of Rakgorath—a world power was optimistic. Did these people have any idea what was going on with the dragons?

"You destroyed a powerful dragon artifact?" Bhodian raised skeptical eyebrows, looking Trip up and down again. "A day ago, I might have believed that, but after seeing how easily you fell into my trap…"

"Look, I'm an army officer and a pilot, not a sorcerer. As you saw. My team destroyed the portal." Technically, it might simply be buried under all the ice and rock, but Trip saw no reason to mention technicalities, especially to someone who made a living off turning a profit.

"Yes," the man said, his voice turning dryer than the desert beyond the city, "I've heard Iskandian pilots are often issued not one but two soulblades after successfully completing their training."

"That's a long explanation. One is along to spy on me."

Bhodian blinked a few times, then snorted. "You have a unique story, I'll wager. I'm half-tempted to stand here all night and talk to you, but you have knowledge that I seek, and it would be best to extract it sooner rather than later. I know you have other team members in the city."

"Extract it?" That did not sound promising.

"You could make it easy on yourself and simply tell me," Bhodian offered.

Trip gripped the cool bars. He had a feeling he knew what was coming next.

"The stasis chambers. I will soon have one, and I want the rest."

Soon have? Damn, did that mean it wasn't here on the barge yet? Had this been yet another wasted trip?

"Alas," Bhodian continued, "it seems they've been relocated. I want to know where they are."

"To do now what you failed to do twenty-five years ago?" Trip asked numbly.

"Indeed. Back then, I had no idea there were more of you in the dragon's lair. Zherie promised me you were the only one." He grunted. "Never believe a woman, especially if you're sleeping with her."

Trip rocked back on his heels at the naked admission, and at the horrifying notion that his mother could have found this crime lord an appealing bedmate.

"As I said, you're a disappointment, but if I had the opportunity to raise a number of those half-dragon babies from birth, or near-birth, I could ensure they lived up to their heritage, that they would learn young to wield the power necessary to make me a very wealthy man."

"Aren't you already a very wealthy man? You have a floating palace replete with trapdoors in the foyer to get rid of intrusive door-to-door salesmen. And mages."

"I have wealth. I do not yet have a legacy. But I will. History will remember Bhodian Ygadrenon. Born a pauper, but a pauper no more."

"Congratulations. How about you let me go so I can go home to defend my country from dragons? Believe it or not, I'm good at piloting and battling them." Why was he telling the man that? Trip groaned inwardly. He shouldn't feel the need to defend himself to this moneyed monster.

"I'm willing to let you go and do that if you tell me where I can find the stasis chambers and their occupants."

"So they can be raised by someone who wants to use them for their power?"

"Do you think your Iskandian king will allow something different to happen if you take them back to your homeland?"

"I haven't had a chance to discuss it with him yet, but they're my siblings. I will ensure they have good childhoods and good lives, to the best of my abilities."

"They will have good lives here with me. They will be valued for what they can do. I will treat them as the children I was never able to have, and Grekka will teach them. By the time they are your age, they will be extremely powerful sorcerers. They may rule nations."

"Doubtful. Now that dragons are back in the world, there will be a lot more half-dragon babies born, I'm sure."

Bhodian shrugged. "Then they'll be prepared to succeed in the new world that is upon us. And they will serve me loyally. I will have my legacy."

Trip wondered if the megalomaniac thought he could take over a major country. Iskandia? The empire?

"Tell me where they are," Bhodian said, his gaze hard as it held Trip's. "Despite your breaking-and-entering tendencies, I harbor you no ill will. I'm willing to let you go once I've acquired the babies."

"All of them?"

This man was a loon if he envisioned raising eight babies all around the same age. Eight babies with magical talent. His grandparents had had trouble enough raising Trip.

"Even the animals. Though Grekka will probably take those. She does love animals. She's quite put out with you for killing so many of her pets. I believe she would enjoy being present at your torture session."

"Oh, has that been booked? I thought we were still negotiating."

"I sense that you aren't interested in helping me. You disapprove of me. As odd as it is, you believe yourself superior to me."

Morally superior, maybe.

"I've seen that look before. As I said, I grew up in poverty. People looked down on me for most of my life. Now…" Bhodian clenched a fist and touched his knuckles to an amulet on his chest—it was probably made from the tainted iron and what had kept Trip from reading his thoughts in the warehouse. "People no longer look down on me. If they do, they're sorry." His head tilted. "I do wonder how much pain a half-dragon man can take before succumbing. Will you resist torture for longer than a typical human, or will your soft upbringing mean that you crumble as soon as the master executioner's tools touch your skin?"

"Should I be concerned that you've tortured enough people to know what's typical?" Trip asked, keeping his chin—and his bravado—up, even though his heart wasn't in it. He dreaded the idea of losing the stasis chambers—the babies—to this man, and it horrified him that Bhodian apparently already had the little girl. Or he would soon. Trip had to fight back tears at the idea of his siblings being raised by someone who only wanted to use them for their power.

"Very concerned, yes." Bhodian turned away from Trip and walked toward the hatch. "I shall arrange for you to be questioned within the hour."

"Good, I'd hate for there to be an unseemly delay," Trip called as the man disappeared from sight, swallowed by the shadows.

UNRAVELED

A hatch clanged shut. Trip leaned his brow against the bars again, hardly caring that they were likely the source of his headache. The tears he hadn't been willing to shed in front of his enemy came now, dribbling down his cheeks and splashing to the unfeeling hull at his feet.

CHAPTER 10

I F SHE COULD REACH HER pistol, she might have a chance.
The massive creature on her back—a bear?—dug its claws into
her shoulder, the pain almost making her forget the bullet wound
throbbing in her abdomen. She thrashed and kicked, trying to distract it
or dislodge it, but the creature must have weighed five hundred pounds.

It thwacked her on the back of the head, and the strap holding
her spectacles on her face snapped. They tumbled from her nose and
cracked on the deck. Even though her spectacles should have been
far down on her list of worries, she couldn't help but feel a surge of
concern that they would be broken. Then those claws dug in again,
tearing the back of her shirt and sinking into flesh. She screamed,
though she doubted anybody was around to help her. Wherever Trip
was, he was sure to have his own problems.

She pounded her fist into the deck as she thrashed again, trying to
work her other hand down to her pistol. With the bear pinning her, she
could barely lift her torso from the deck. Even if she reached the weapon,
she'd wrapped it in that oilskin. She would need time to unwrap it to fire.

Would a bullet even kill a bear charged up with dragon blood? She
had a dagger sheathed at her waist, too, but she was even more pinned
on that side, the creature crouching on her with its crushing weight.

Her fist cracked against the frames of her spectacles. An idea snapped into her mind. She grabbed the frames and smashed them to the deck, hoping to break the lenses. One side cracked. She flicked the broken glass out with her thumb, cutting herself but not caring.

A cold nose touched the back of her neck, and she shrieked, thrashing again. She twisted as much as she could, which wasn't very much, keeping the broken lens in her hand. She thrust her arm over her shoulder and slashed the lens toward that cold nose. It struck the bear's snout, but she couldn't tell if it sank in enough to hurt.

Until a roar pounded her eardrums.

The bear reared up on its hind legs, pawing at the air, or at its nose. Its weight still had her pinned, but she could lift herself enough to yank out the pistol. She tore one-handedly at the oilskin bag as the bear sank back down, one paw landing on her shoulder, pinning it again. With her left hand, she jerked the pistol free and aimed it, hardly able to point it in the right direction from that angle.

She fired, hoping the sound would scare the animal even if the bullet didn't land. The report thundered right next to her ear.

Again, the bear reared up, but this time, its entire weight left her.

Hardly able to believe her luck, Rysha pushed herself to her knees to shoot again. But a blast of pain came from her abdomen, and she doubled over. The bear was less than a foot away, on its hind legs and roaring in agony.

Rysha could only rise up enough to shoot it in the gut. She hadn't been sure if her first bullet landed, or where it had hit if it did, but she saw this one burrow into the bear's flesh.

The creature dropped to all fours, and she scrambled backward on hands and knees. If it charged...

But it didn't. It leaped over the railing, a huge splash of water sending droplets all the way up to pelt Rysha's face.

She gripped her abdomen, hot blood oozing through her fingers, and pointed her pistol up and down the walkway, certain some guard had been watching the whole encounter and had orders to put her out of her misery if the bear didn't succeed.

Without her spectacles, everything was blurry, but she didn't see anyone in either direction. That shocked her, especially given the sound of the gunfire, but she was surely due for some luck. She would take it. She just hoped she could use it.

Rysha wanted to break down and cry over the loss of the sword, but this wasn't the time. Trip needed her.

She patted around on the deck for her spectacles, a deck wet with water—and her blood. She told herself that Trip could heal her if she could just find him. If she could survive long enough to do that, she had a good chance of living. Of course, she would have to get him away from the barge so he could use his powers.

"One problem at a time," she whispered, her hand brushing broken glass and finally the frames of her spectacles.

She lifted them close to her eyes. One of the lenses remained intact. It was cracked, but when she set the bent frames on her nose, she could see. Sort of. But only out of one eye.

"The deadly and ferocious Lieutenant Ravenwood to the rescue," she muttered.

She tried to push herself to her feet, using the wall for support, but all the blood seemed to drain from her head. Her vision grew dark, and dizziness swept over her. She was aware of her knees hitting the deck, but it seemed to happen far, far away. She clawed toward wakefulness, terrified she would die if she let herself lose consciousness here, but blackness swallowed her.

When she woke, gasping in pain, she stared around, confused for a moment before her memories rushed back to her. She was still on the deck, still alone, but cold now. Very cold. She touched her abdomen, grimacing when her cold fingers encountered warm blood still seeping out.

She couldn't have been unconscious for long. Maybe she'd fainted because she'd stood up too fast.

"Sorry, Trip," she muttered. "Might have to rescue you from my knees." Wherever he was, he didn't answer.

The pistol lay on the deck in front of her, and she picked it up. Once again using the wall for support, Rysha rose, very slowly this time.

The blackness encroached again, but she paused, taking deep breaths, willing the moment to pass. She kept one hand to her abdomen, doing her best to staunch the bleeding. Her other hand was numb, but she kept her fingers curled around the pistol. She was well aware that she didn't have many more bullets. Had she been smart, she would have brought an extra box of ammo, but she'd assumed she would be using Dorfindral out here among a sorceress and magical animals.

"Worry about that later," she panted.

She eased down the walkway, her shoulder against the wall, and reached the corner of the palace. She'd gone toward the back of the barge instead of the front, hoping for an unguarded rear entrance. The deck widened, and she heard people shouting, but it was coming from the other side of the palace. She didn't see anyone outside in the back.

Leaving blood all over the wall she was using for support, Rysha made her way to a door. As she reached for the latch, a nearby roar made her jump.

"Get 'em, come on!" a man yelled from the other walkway.

"Just get them to my ship," a woman shouted. Grekka? "Once they're over here, I can control them."

More roars answered her.

Rysha almost ignored it all to go through the door, but she shuffled toward the corner, clenching her pistol tightly. If she had the chance to shoot Grekka while she was over on this barge where magic didn't seem to work well, shouldn't she take it? Rysha didn't know if she could act the role of a sniper and shoot someone in cold blood, but after the woman had left her to die, she didn't feel kindly toward her. And the blood trickling through her fingers was warm, not cold.

No less than eight animals roared and yowled on the side walkway. At the far end of it, a man with a whip and a huge prod with a glowing orange tip tried to coerce more animals into the narrow passage. At first, Rysha thought the prod was glowing with magic, and wondered how that could be, but then she realized it was from heat. That tool was more like a branding iron than a simple metal prod. As she watched, the man applied it to an ape's hindquarters. The creature jumped forward, yowling and beating at the wall.

Maybe this was why nobody had heard the gunshots, or, if they had, hadn't been able to go investigate. They had been too busy herding the deadly animals. At least the scene suggested to Rysha that she hadn't been unconscious for long.

She spotted Grekka, her black-and-silver hair gleaming under the palace's outdoor lamps. Unfortunately, Rysha didn't have a good shot at her. A winged lion stood in the way, its tail swishing as it faced the woman. The woman who was keeping complete chaos from breaking out by tossing what appeared to be cubes of meat into the animals' mouths.

"That mage hurled the ramp into the harbor," someone yelled from the warehouse barge. The vessel had lined up with the palace barge, side by side, and it was only a couple of meters away.

"Throw a damn board down," Grekka yelled.

"We'll get them across it," the man with the heated prod added with determination.

Rysha backed away from the corner. She might get a chance to shoot Grekka in the back if she waited long enough, but she also might pass out from blood loss if she lingered. Better to find Trip, especially if this maneuvering of the animals was keeping the crew occupied.

Thank the gods, the back door was unlocked. She didn't have bullets to waste shooting off locks, and Grekka would definitely hear a pistol going off that close.

Rysha eased the door open. There was a step up, and her stomach objected painfully when she lifted her leg. She lurched sideways, almost tumbling down a stairwell.

The stairs were to the left of a straight passage with a galley opening to the right. More animal noises came from the route ahead, and at the end of the passageway, a well-lit marble-floored room was visible. A humongous snake slithered into view, then continued out of it again. A man carrying something that looked like a rat on a stick trailed after it.

"Come on, Droofy. Your friends have all gone home. It's time to get back in your cage."

The snake handler didn't glance down the passageway toward Rysha. Fortunately. She looked into the dark galley and debated whether to try the stairs or to venture into that well-lit front room. She would have to deal with at least one person if she went that way. And one snake.

Voices came from down the stairway, and her ears perked. Was it her imagination, or did that sound like Trip? They came from too far away to hear words, but she was fairly certain…

Wincing, Rysha levered herself onto the stair landing. Her legs were going numb. This reminded her unpleasantly of the bite she'd taken from the giant tarantula. Though at least she'd managed to *kill* the tarantula. And hadn't lost a priceless magical sword in the process.

As she descended the narrow stairs, moving as quietly as possible, she realized the odds of her making it back up them without help were poor.

"Please be down here, Trip," she breathed.

A scream of pure agony echoed from below, and she fell against the wall. Her stomach sank. She'd never heard Trip scream in pain, but she was certain that was his voice.

She rushed down the stairs as quickly as she could, fighting pain with each step. At the bottom, a large cargo hold took up the entire lower level of the barge. A portable brazier in the center danced with flames, highlighting a man standing in front of a cage. Long tools stuck out of the fire, and the man held one that appeared to have been freshly removed, for the tip glowed cherry red. It was similar to the prod being used on the animals.

He pushed the red-tipped tool between the bars. The person trapped inside tried to dart away, but he'd been shackled, his wrists and ankles chained together and clasped to the locked gate. He couldn't move enough to avoid the prod or lift his arms enough to knock it away. His shirt had been torn open, and the scorching iron found bare flesh. He screamed again. *Trip* screamed.

Rysha gritted her teeth in cold determination and shifted to the side so she could shoot the torturer without risking hitting Trip. In the darkness near the stairs, she shouldn't have been visible, but she bumped something with her toe. The soft clunk was barely audible, but it was audible enough. The man—the torturer—whirled toward her, wisps of gray hair flowing about his head.

Rysha shot without hesitating. She had no idea who he was, but if he was torturing Trip, he deserved to die.

Her bullet slammed into his chest. He gasped and tumbled to the deck, clutching the wound. Rysha shambled forward as quickly as her own wounds would allow.

She kept her pistol trained on the man, doubting a single bullet had taken him out instantly. She was right. As she drew close enough to kick the torture tools out of the burning brazier, the man lurched up to his elbow.

"Look out!" Trip warned as Rysha fired again.

Her bullet struck the man in the throat just before he threw a knife, the sharp blade gleaming orange from the nearby fire. The hilt tumbled from his fingers, and he slumped back to the deck, his eyes closing. Though she thought he was done this time, Rysha kept her pistol at the ready as she moved to Trip's gate.

"If you're here to rescue me, I approve wholeheartedly," he said, his shoulders forced by the chain to slump. His eyes held pain, and she could see burn marks on his chest and abdomen.

"You're not upset that I followed you to the docks?" Rysha looked around for a key. Presumably, Trip couldn't magic the locks open right now.

"It depends on how injured you are." He frowned, watching a droplet of her blood spatter to the deck.

"I'll be fine as soon as a good healer attends to my needs." Rysha hoped he wouldn't notice her missing sword. She felt mortified for having lost it, and she couldn't guess how she would get it back. Given the size of that steamer docked in the harbor, the water had to be deep.

"Unlock me, and I'll see if I can find you one." Trip tilted his head toward the fallen torturer. "He's got the keys on his belt. He had a couple of brutes beat on me so he could get the chains on, but then they left. He's had me all to himself for the last ten minutes. I'm glad it wasn't longer."

It had been long enough. Now that she had a better look at him, Rysha saw that he had a split lip, and one of his eyes was swollen shut. He needed a healer as much as she did.

She gripped the cage, using the support of a bar to lower herself to kneel beside the man. A gasp escaped her lips, and she winced. She knew Trip would figure out how injured she was soon enough, but she didn't want to seem weak or cause him to worry.

"I shouldn't have come without you," Trip whispered. "We would have been stronger together. Especially here." His wave encompassed the barge.

"Maybe *we* should have babysat the kids and sent Major Kaika. She could have just blown up the whole place." Rysha found the iron ring with the keys on it. She tried to rise to her feet, but her legs wouldn't support her, and blackness swam through her vision again. Damn it. How much blood had she lost?

She turned on her knees toward the cage and fumbled with shaking fingers, trying to find the right key for the gate.

"Here," Trip said, holding his hand out.

She had the urge to say she could do it, but it was easier to drop the keys in his palm. Then she slumped down, leaning her shoulder against the bars, exhausted. Not for the first time, a trickle of fear flowed into her. She was still bleeding. Was it possible she was close to death?

Could Trip get her out of here when he was also injured? She didn't know if she could stand up again. If he did get her out—she hated the idea of him having to carry her—how far away would they have to flee before he could use his magic to heal her? And would he be able to do so without the soulblades to help? She had no idea where they were.

"I met the owner of the barge." Clinks sounded as Trip tried several keys in his shackle locks and in the gate lock.

"I'm guessing it didn't go well." Rysha tried to open her eyes, but she couldn't manage it. Resting her temple against the bars and not curling into a tiny ball was all she could do.

"Not particularly. He said he didn't have the girl baby yet, but that he would soon. And he wanted to know where the rest of the stasis chambers are."

"Is he looking for them now?"

"He didn't say, but I bet he is."

"Hopefully, nobody will find that ancient sanctuary, but we should get back and warn Kaika."

"Yes." A clank sounded.

Rysha forced her eyes open to see if Trip had gotten out, but she felt herself lifted up and her face pressed into his shoulder before she saw anything. She looped one arm around his back, but kept the other clasped to her abdomen, her legs curled in, the pain demanding no less.

"Thanks," she mumbled into his shoulder as he strode toward the steps.

She still gripped her pistol and decided not to put it away. She only had one bullet left, but she might need it.

"I think I'm supposed to say that to you." He bent before he reached the steps, and she tightened her grip on him.

Soft scrapes sounded as he picked something up. Two somethings. Jaxi and Azarwrath. They must have been what she kicked on her way in.

"You are," she agreed. "I rescued you."

"Yes, you did. We can both properly thank each other later. When you're bleeding less."

"Good idea." She closed her eyes again as he climbed the steps. "Go out the back. Grekka and her people were busy when I came down, and hopefully they still are."

He obeyed and soon stepped out into the salty sea air. The sounds of roars and yips had diminished, and Rysha feared the crew might have finished dealing with the animals. They could be looking for her now.

"Did you drop your sword on the deck somewhere?" Trip asked. Somewhere.

"Not on the deck." Rysha grimaced. "In the water."

"Oh."

He didn't say more. He didn't have to. He knew she would be in trouble for losing it, and he also knew it would be difficult to recover. Had it been some other tool, Trip might have located it down there and used his power to raise it up, but Dorfindral wouldn't allow that, even if it meant being lost on the harbor bottom forever, like all those wrecks down there.

"I don't see a dinghy or anything we can use to row back," Trip whispered, moving to the side of the barge where she'd originally come up.

"I swam out here."

"You're a tough woman. The elite troops will be lucky to have you."

The simple words almost made her cry. Even though it was her nature to dismiss praise—how could she even deserve it after she'd lost a priceless sword?—that he'd thought to speak it touched her.

"I think we'll have to swim back," Trip whispered. "I hear voices up front and—"

A bang came from that direction—a door being thrown open?—and someone shouted. "He's gone!"

"That didn't take long," Trip grumbled. "Brace yourself."

He shifted her so he could sling his leg over the railing. She tightened her grip on his shoulders, expecting him to jump in. He eased in more slowly, lowering himself over the side before dropping in, but the shock of the cold water still slammed into her like a wrecking ball. Fresh pain burst from her abdomen, and she lost consciousness.

CHAPTER 11

RYSHA WOKE TO THE NIGHT sky being an indistinct blur above her. She reached for her spectacles but bumped something else first. Someone's arm.

"Trip?" she whispered, her voice raw and raspy.

"Here," he murmured, his voice distant, as if he were concentrating on his magic.

And he was, she realized, aware of a warmth within her, focused on her abdomen. Was the bullet still in there?

Jaxi incinerated it, Trip spoke dryly into her mind. *Azarwrath finds this medical practice horrifying, but she does seem to have pinpoint accuracy. She hasn't yet missed and incinerated an organ.*

Very comforting.

I figured that was more of a concern in your case, since the bullet was lodged in your gut. But she promised she could deal with it more quickly than we could.

What happens to the ash that's left behind when a bullet is incinerated inside your body? Rysha asked, assuming something had to remain.

Judging by the long pause, Trip hadn't considered that before.

As she imagined him having a scholarly discussion on bullet ash with the soulblades, Rysha grew aware of the cold sandy beach under her back. He must have swum across the harbor with her in his arms. She grimaced, knowing she had been a burden, and hoped he'd been able to use his magic to make it less onerous.

You're never a burden, he murmured into her mind.

She knew he was reading her thoughts—maybe he couldn't help it when they were this close, and he was monitoring her body for signs of anything going awry—but she didn't mind. Especially with that warmth in her belly. It felt so much better than the pain from before. The backs of her shoulders tingled with healing energy, too, and she remembered the bear clawing her there.

Are you sure? she asked silently. *I've heard that six-feet-tall women aren't easy to carry.*

Not a problem for sturdy, able, and handsome army captains.

You used your magic, didn't you?

Maybe a little.

How does handsomeness help with carrying things?

It makes the woman want to hold on tightly. Always useful. Trip stroked the side of her face as the warmth continued to work within her, easing all her lingering twinges. *To answer the ash question— technically, it's a lead question—Azarwrath has decided that Jaxi used enough heat to truly incinerate the vast majority of it. If an infinitesimal amount remains, your body should be able to excrete it.*

Ah. There's nothing like having a man stroking your face and discussing excretion.

You did ask.

Rysha turned onto her side to look at him. He was stretched out next to her in the sand, facing her as he worked. Though she couldn't see much without her spectacles, she could tell they were under the docks, hiding in the shadows. She squinted out toward the water. She couldn't make out the dark warehouse barge, but the palace was lit well enough that she could see its blurry outline.

"Did my spectacles fall off while you swam?" she asked.

"No, I have them." He slipped his hand into his trousers pocket and withdrew them. "I was going to see if I could fix them, but that was before I knew one of the lenses was missing. We'll have to find some glass that I can manipulate to replace it. All that's around us on the beach are those spherical green floats washed up from fishing nets. Would it be hard to see through a green lens?" He handed the spectacles to her.

"Perhaps slightly distracting, but I have another pair in my pack back at the sanctuary." Rysha donned the spectacles she had here, noticing that the remaining lens was no longer cracked. She was touched that Trip wanted to fix everything for her, and reached out to pat him.

His chest was mostly bare, his shirt hanging in tatters. She remembered the fresh burn wounds she'd seen there and drew her hand back, not wanting to hurt him. Knowing him, he had healed her before bothering with his own injuries.

I thought I would wait for you to recover so you could bandage them, he spoke into her mind.

That doesn't sound as effective as magical healing.

But it would involve you touching my chest. This is appealing.

If you'd seen how close I came to failing the combat-medic course in the academy, you wouldn't long for me to handle your wounds.

Oh? What did you struggle with?

Asking why we were doing certain things during timed tests. I wanted to understand the reasons, not just do the procedures.

You weren't asking about ashes, were you? Trip pushed a wet clump of her hair away from her face.

Rysha marveled that he could see well enough in the dark to know there were locks plastered to her skin. Imagining herself extremely bedraggled, she vowed not to look in the clear pool when they got back to their hideout.

I asked whether the army had funded much medical research to determine if their awful bromine concoction was truly the best thing to smear on wounds.

And you thought you should ask the question during a timed test?

I did.

Trip rolled onto his back with a faint groan. *Azarwrath said he would work on my wounds for me. He's a good sword.*

Is there anything I can do to help?

Now that she could see better—at least out of one eye—Rysha looked toward the barges. She worried there would be a pursuit and wondered how long she had been unconscious. She and Trip were making a habit of needing medical care on beaches, but this one was far less private than the last.

Lanterns moved about on the decks of both barges. It appeared the crew was looking for them on board first. Trip was probably using his magic to camouflage them, but it wouldn't take those people long to guess that she and Trip were no longer on either barge.

Yes. Trip took her hand and laid it on his bare chest.

Rysha trusted it wasn't in the middle of a burn mark. *Am I just holding it here for support? Or am I fondling things?*

You can fondle whatever you like. He closed his eyes, his head resting back in the sand. *Especially things.*

She brushed her thumb along the curve of his pectoral muscle, but was afraid to let her hand roam until she knew the soulblade had healed him.

What was it like, Trip? Being tortured? I mean, I know it was awful, but was it harder than you thought it would be? Was it something you'd ever even considered? Being captured and questioned about state secrets? Or about the positions of your comrades? Were you tempted to tell him anything? Did *you tell him anything?*

Rysha made her mind stop spitting words. She hadn't intended to interrogate him about his interrogation. It just happened to be something she'd thought about often, especially after a surly elite-troops instructor had mentioned it was one of the reasons the idea of letting women into the unit was always met with resistance. As if men couldn't be tortured all the same ways women were, though in truth, she had no idea how often male prisoners of war endured rape. She'd stilled her curiosity and kept from asking for detailed statistics about types and frequencies of torture among prisoners of war. Mostly because the instructor had been an ass and would have glared at her, not because she hadn't wanted to know.

Honestly, Trip responded after a moment of consideration, *I hadn't spent a lot of time thinking about it, and since Bhodian's master torturer only had ten minutes to work on me before my valiant rescuer showed up, I was able to resist without too much trouble.*

Valiant, right. I bled all over the deck and collapsed at your gate.

You collapsed most valiantly.

Uh huh.

I can see how it would wear you down over time, Trip added. *Especially if you didn't know if there was any hope that you would escape. You might be tempted to talk if a reprieve was promised if you did so. If they said they would let you go.*

Is that what happened to you? Rysha noticed her hand had started wandering around Trip's chest and the ridges of his abdomen, despite her thought to keep it still. She did brush against a few rough bumps, but they seemed healed, scar tissue rather than open wounds. And he didn't stir or give any indication that her touches hurt.

He said he would let me go, yes. But... it was my siblings he wanted, my blood. Even though I've never met them, as far as I remember, I feel a connection to them. I'm all they have in this world. I couldn't have given them up, not after he said he wanted to use them to make himself more powerful. Maybe for less important things, it would be easier to give in, to let secrets escape in order to stop the pain. I don't know. There are some tests that you can't know if you'll pass until the moment is upon you. I don't know if there's a way to prepare.

That's what I worry about.

His eyes opened, his head turning toward hers. *About being strong if you're caught and tortured?* He laid his hand atop hers.

That and other things. I wonder sometimes if it's delusional of me to think that I have what it takes to be in the elite troops. I'm not exactly typical. Maybe I'm too far from the mold.

What mold? There's only one woman in the unit.

True, but she's mostly like all the men, like her fellow soldiers. Their outlooks and competence and abilities are what make them similar, gender regardless. I'm not really like any of them.

I bet if you asked Major Kaika, she would say she's often felt that she's not much like her comrades.

Maybe. Rysha had a hard time imagining Kaika ever having anything but confidence and swagger, and knowing she could make it. She'd heard the story of how she had been invited to try out for the unit in the first place. After being turned down for being a woman, she'd supposedly gone to the castle for an audience with King Angulus. She'd ensured he wouldn't forget her by demonstrating her abilities... by blowing up an urn in his waiting room. *Did you ever doubt that you had what it takes to become a pilot? Were you nervous when you started your training?*

I was fearless when it came to flying and didn't have any doubts about my piloting abilities—even when I was a rookie and should have. Flying always came naturally, if you can imagine that. He seemed to smile, but it was hard to tell in the dark. *My doubts were about my ability to be part of a team, to fit into a unit of people and work with* them. *I'd always sensed I was little like everyone else. I spent my whole life worrying people would figure that out.*

It's hard being atypical.

Indeed. He rubbed the back of her hand and gazed into her eyes.

She couldn't tell if he was exuding any of his power or not, but she had the urge to kiss him, to let him know she understood him—and was glad he understood her. This wasn't the time and place for it, surely, but nobody was rowing toward the beach yet…

While letting her fingers continue to trail along his chest, she lowered her lips to his. Then laughed because his were sandy. Or maybe hers were sandy. She rubbed her fingers across his mouth and dragged a sleeve across hers.

I love taking you to romantic places, he thought wryly into her mind.

The beach is supposed to be *a romantic place. Though maybe not when you're wet and cold and covered in sand because you were dredged through the harbor like chicken being coated with flour before going in the oven.*

Are you cold? He slid his arm under her and wrapped it around her back, pulling her down atop his chest.

A little. The temperatures are drastically lower than they are during the day here, aren't they?

Especially when you're wet.

Warmth emanated from his arm, more than simple body heat accounting for it, and it spread through her body, whisking away the cold while stirring sensations within her that made her want to press herself to him.

Rysha?

Yes? She brought her lips to his again, not noticing the sand this time, only knowing that she wanted to touch and taste, to thank him for swimming her to safety and healing her. And to thank him for not judging her for losing the sword.

I don't know if you've noticed something, but…

I've noticed it. I don't know if this is the ideal place to get naked, but it is starting to sound appealing.

Not that. He smiled against her mouth and gave her a playful nip. *Though I'm glad it's noticeable.*

It has been on my mind since you mentioned fondling things. Rysha supposed her aunt would have advised her to be coy and never let a boy know she was fantasizing about him, but it wasn't as if Trip couldn't read her thoughts.

I'm extremely glad to hear it, and I'm open to fondling, but I did want to say something first.

Mm? She was amused that they could have a full conversation while kissing.

All the things you've done these last few weeks... battling dragons and oversized mutant animals and sorceresses... these are things most elite troops who have served for decades have never done. I can understand having doubts about oneself, but if those people don't accept you into their program, they're idiots.

But I did all that with the help of a magical sword. Without Dorfindral...

What did you do tonight after *losing the sword?*

I stabbed a bear in the nose with a spectacles lens.

He snorted. *That's it?*

Thoughts of shooting the bear and escaping from certain death ran through her mind again, followed by shooting that torture expert and getting the keys to Trip's shackles. Maybe she should have felt disgruntled that he'd read her thoughts and knew everything she'd done, but a sensation of warm approval flowed from Trip as he experienced them. Approval and... attraction. He appreciated that she'd fought so hard to come help him, and he found it arousing too. He found *her* arousing.

Her body flushed with this knowledge, and her kiss deepened as she pressed herself more fully against him. His wounds must have been healed by now, because he didn't object. His other arm came around her, locking her to him. The idea of sex on the beach was growing on her, whether this was a romantic situation or not, and she could tell he wanted it as well.

A clang and a shout drifted across the water from the barge.

"Search the beaches and the city," a man yelled. "I want him back. And find those babies."

Trip winced, and Rysha reluctantly withdrew her mouth from his. They looked toward the water in time to see four rowboats launching from the warehouse barge. They were full of armed men, as well as some of those winged lions and scaled panthers. Rysha could see the gems glowing at their throats even across the water.

"That's Bhodian," Trip said. "And there's the woman—Grekka."

Rysha spotted her on the warehouse barge, barely visible since the deck over there wasn't lit brightly. She had her hands clasped behind her back, her chest thrust forward, a thin robe flapping in the breeze, her lush hair worn down. She looked like she was ready to take someone to bed, not lead a hunt. But then, she wasn't the one yelling orders. She observed as Bhodian stalked back and forth on his deck and the boats rowed away.

"I don't think they want us to fondle each other on the beach," Rysha said, sighing.

"That's rude of them."

"Most definitely."

Trip kissed her, tongue stroking hers enticingly, and for a moment, Rysha thought he wanted to see if they could continue without being caught. Or maybe he intended to sweep the rowboats out to sea so the searchers couldn't bother them.

"There's an appealing thought," Trip murmured, smiling against her lips again. But he pulled away and shifted her gently off him so he could sit up. "I already checked, and I'm not able to affect Bhodian, even out on his deck. He was wearing an amulet that I believe has some of the tainted iron in it. The whole framework of the barge is made from the stuff. I see those rowboats were built using some of it too."

"He must have pissed off a lot of sorcerers in his life to have felt he needed to take so many measures." Rysha stood up and brushed off sand. Her body wanted to go back to rubbing and stroking rather than trekking to their hideout, but she reluctantly acknowledged the moment had passed.

"Apparently, his relationship with Grekka started as a feud."

Trip slipped an arm around Rysha's waist as they climbed toward the waterfront street. She couldn't help but think that Dorfindral would have objected if she'd had the sword with her. She ought to appreciate its absence and that it meant she could more comfortably be close to Trip, but she was mostly reminded of her failure. What would Major Kaika say?

"She must have decided it was easier to work with him than fight him," Trip added.

"Work with him? I don't think that's all they do together." Rysha remembered their body language from when she and Trip had spied on their conversation in the warehouse.

"I didn't ask for details."

"You should cultivate a nosy streak."

She meant it as a joke, but he sighed, sounding sad rather than amused.

"Every time I ask questions lately and dig into my past, I get answers I don't like. Nothing is anything like I thought it would be, and not in a good way. Every week, I'm more disappointed by what I learn. Next, I'll probably find out that my grandparents, my *foster* grandparents," he corrected with a grimace, "run a drug cartel back home. Is it sad that I long for the days when I was Lieutenant Trip, pilot, and that's it?"

"Considering you just healed me of a wound that would have killed me, I am going to argue that you should embrace your powers and be happy to have had a scaled ancestor."

He sighed again as they crossed the main street and walked through an alley.

"But I will agree that you may want to stop asking questions and digging into your past."

"Good. I'm going to do that. I wish I could stop dealing with those two, too, but I still don't have any idea where the baby girl is. And Bhodian does." He pushed a frustrated hand through his hair, probably yanking pieces out. "I still don't have a clue about what happened to Dreyak, either."

Rysha wished she had learned more about that and had some information to offer Trip. Even without telepathy, she could feel his frustration.

"It's possible he just ran afoul of them for no particular reason," she suggested. "Maybe Grekka knew who he was and has a vendetta against those in the royal family, even bastards who were never publicly acknowledged."

"I wish—"

Trip halted so abruptly that Rysha almost stumbled. His grip tightened protectively, but then he let her go and turned back toward the harbor. They'd climbed several blocks up the hill from the beach, but the water was still visible between the buildings.

Rysha squinted, worried he'd detected someone following them. She could make out one of the rowboats drawing close to the beach, but didn't think any of the searchers had landed yet.

"That's interesting," Trip finally said.

"I might agree if I knew what."

"Grekka contacted me telepathically."

"To threaten you and curse my name for killing her bear?" Rysha asked.

"No, she said she wanted to meet me tomorrow. She offered to buy me lunch and named an eating house that's apparently in a nice neighborhood."

"Uh, why?"

"She said she has information about Dreyak that I would find interesting. She also says she knows where the stasis chamber is."

"That sounds like a trap to me." Rysha shuddered, remembering how willing that woman had been to leave her to be eaten by a bear. Yes, she had sneaked onto the barges, but that hardly seemed a crime worthy of being eaten alive. "She and Bhodian must want another chance to capture you and torture you."

"That thought did cross my mind."

"Are you going to go anyway?" Rysha feared she knew the answer.

"I can't sense the stasis chamber, Rysha. This is my only clue as to where it's located."

"It's not a clue; it's a trap. You must see it. She's been trying to kill us."

"I know."

"You shouldn't go."

"I know."

"Are you at least going to take me with you this time? To break you out of whatever cage they put you in?"

Trip smiled and squeezed her waist, leading her across another street and out of sight of the harbor. "Let's talk to Major Kaika and see what she thinks. Maybe she'll want to come rescue me this time."

She frowned. He'd said that casually, as if he didn't care which one of them helped him, but she feared he didn't think she would be as useful now that she didn't have a *chapaharii* blade to wield.

That's not it. Trip stopped walking and turned to face her, their chests almost brushing. *As I told you, I know you're extremely capable even if you don't have a special sword to wield.* He brought his hand to the back of her neck, rubbing it with his fingers as he gazed into her eyes.

Even in the dark, she felt his power, that he wasn't bothering to hide his allure now.

I believe you're right that it's extremely likely this is a trap. I don't want to drag you into trouble again. Or have you experience more of that kind of pain. He pulled her into a hug, and she leaned against him, drawn to him and also warmed by his touch.

She sensed his feelings, as if she could read his thoughts, and realized he was horrified at the graveness of the injury she'd endured. Since he'd been the one to heal her, he knew exactly how close she had come to dying. He believed he'd never forgive himself if she died because of something he had done. Or because she'd been trying to help him.

I'd rather die helping a friend, helping someone I love, than for no reason at all, Rysha pointed out.

Love? he thought with a note of wonder. He nuzzled the side of her neck, not seeming to mind that she had sand and seaweed stuck to it. *Does that mean you still want to take me to that little cottage on your family's estate?*

I wish we were there now. She ran her hands up his bare chest and pushed his shirt off his shoulders. *I'd really like to have sex with you in a bed sometime.*

Oh? Are beds proven to enhance the experience?

I don't know, but I believe rocky caverns, sandy beaches, and smelly alleys could de-hance it.

De-hance? My dear academic, I don't believe that's a word.

Not in Iskandian, but I know many languages.

Rysha leaned in to him, returning to the kiss they had started on the beach. Maybe it wasn't wise, but she had a hard time thinking about logical matters, such as if they were far enough from the harbor that they wouldn't have to worry about pursuit. Or if those animals would be able to magically track them. All she could think about was that she'd almost died and she wanted to celebrate life with this man. And the way he was rubbing her neck and kissing her was making her vow to use her last bullet on anyone stupid enough to interrupt them.

This alley isn't terribly smelly, Trip pointed out, sliding his hand down her back to cup her butt.

True. The sea breeze sweeps away the most noticeable offenses.

The same can't be said for the hostel rooms in this town.

Lamentably true.

And they wouldn't have any privacy if they returned to their hideout. If anything, Kaika would grumble and ask what had taken them so long, then pace around while stroking her weapons. A definite mood killer.

Perhaps I can make you forget that there's no bed here.

I do suspect you have that ability.

Let's find out.

The telepathic talk stopped after that, as concentration went toward other activities.

CHAPTER 12

AS TRIP AND RYSHA WALKED through the tunnels that led to their hideout, he didn't bother to hide his grin. In the dim lighting, he doubted Rysha would spot it, but she could probably sense contentment flowing from him. Oh, most of the night had been a nightmare, but being with her had made everything much, much better.

Maybe it hadn't been the wisest place for a union—it certainly hadn't been the most comfortable—but he'd needed a release for all the emotion welled up inside of him. He'd been frustrated at being captured and at not finding the stasis chamber. Then Rysha had appeared, grievously injured, and he'd been so distressed at her pain, but also so honored that she'd been willing to endure all that pain to come help him. He'd almost broken down in tears. When he'd gotten her to shore in time to heal her, to bring her back to full health, he'd been relieved beyond words. That time, he *had* broken down in tears. Fortunately, he'd staunched their flow before she woke up. Manly and heroic pilots didn't cry, after all.

At times, Trip hated this new and complicated side of himself, but if he had the power to heal people that were close to death, he couldn't regret that. The rest of it was worth enduring for that.

He'd already been brimming with emotion, and then she'd said she loved him. That was so much more than he'd ever expected. He wished now that he had said it back. He would find a time later. The perfect time. Back in the alley, all he'd been thinking was that he wanted to show her that he felt the same way, that it would be worth it for them to find a way to have a relationship once they returned to the capital and their respective units. Their respective lives.

If you're done basking in the glow of your recently reaffirmed romance, you might want to pay attention, Jaxi said.

To what? Trip asked.

They had almost reached the secret door. He sent his senses ahead, suddenly worried that something had happened to Kaika or the stasis chambers while they had been away. What if Bhodian's people had found their hiding place?

But Kaika wasn't the first person he sensed. Trip halted a few paces away from an intersection, the one that led to their dead end. Someone was in the tunnel, near the very spot where the secret door lay.

Rysha also halted. She squeezed his hand and thought, *There's light up there.*

Trip nodded and lifted a finger to his lips while he investigated more closely. He *did* sense Kaika in the sanctuary beyond the door, and he also detected the magic from the stasis chambers. This person between here and there seemed... unremarkable. Had one of the squatters wandered this way to explore?

The man did have an inquisitive mind, and he was peering at the walls, at some old paintings on them. His surface thoughts, musings of dragon clans, dragon-rider outposts, and ancient cultures reminded him of Moe Zirkander, though this fellow was younger.

Trip drew Azarwrath.

Oh, sure. Jaxi harrumphed. *Pick him when I'm the one who warned you about that man. Azarwrath was napping.*

I was not napping. I merely didn't think there was much danger. That person appears to have a gentle soul.

Follow me, Rysha. Trip nodded to the corner.

Rysha nodded back, drawing her pistol, her pistol with a single shot remaining. He smiled, remembering the thought he'd caught, of her deciding to shoot anyone who interrupted their mutual comfort session.

Mutual comfort? Jaxi asked. *Is that what it's called when you're rutting and groaning loudly enough to make the neighbors think some of those wild animals are loose in the streets?*

I see I left my vault door open.

Yes, you have a tendency to do that when you look at your lieutenant. All your lustful thoughts ooze out all over the place.

Rysha raised her eyebrows, no doubt wondering why Trip was taking so long to walk around the corner. He thought about explaining, but that would probably only encourage Jaxi to share her thoughts with Rysha.

I'm always happy to share my thoughts. I've had numerous handlers with varying degrees of sexual interests and abilities. One rivaled Major Kaika in breadth of knowledge. If you want some tips—

No, thank you.

Trip stepped around the corner. Actually, he rushed around it, eager to end the conversation.

The man he'd sensed stood at the dead end, poking thoughtfully at the ancient stones as he held his lantern up. He must have heard them because he turned, his eyes widening.

"Please, sir. Ma'am." He lifted his hands, his gaze snagging on Azarwrath, who had decided to glow red and paint the stone walls with his light. "I am a simple explorer. I have little coin and want no trouble."

Rysha lowered her pistol, her gesture startled. "Horis Silverdale?"

Trip frowned at her. *You recognize him?*

I do, yes. I was even thinking about him yesterday when we first discovered this sanctuary—well, about all my fellow students and professors, not him specifically. I thought it was a shame they couldn't be over here to see some of the things we've seen.

Trip considered the man. He *did* have a familiar Iskandian accent. And the face matched the accent: pale skinned, a scattering of faded freckles, and long copper hair pulled back in a tail. A few of the strands had escaped and fell to frame high cheekbones and a strong jaw. Trip didn't usually notice other men's looks, but the fellow was undeniably attractive, a day's worth of beard stubble somehow making him appear ruggedly handsome. When Trip had stubble, he just looked unkempt. The man wore a backpack bulging with books, a pencil behind one ear, and ink smudges darkened his fingertips. Trip wasn't sure *how* someone like that managed to look handsome, but he did.

"Yes, ma'am. Er…" The man—Horis?—quirked his head. "Are you Professor Ravenwood's other daughter? You seem quite familiar, but hm." He looked at her pistol and her seaweed-draped clothing. "The last time I saw you, wasn't it at the university in the capital?"

"I believe so, yes. I'm Rysha."

"Rysha Ravenwood, that's it." The man lowered a hand to snap his fingers, but looked at Trip's sword, and paused. "I had a class with your sister."

Trip lowered Azarwrath, but he wasn't sure he wanted to be friendly to an intruder inspecting the secret door to their hideout, even if Rysha did know him.

"I must confess," Horis said, "you're the last person I expected to find here, at the doorstep to the Sanctuary of Lyshandrasa the Lovely. At least, I hope I've finally found the sanctuary." He frowned at the cobweb-bedecked walls around him. "If I can't get the rubbing that Moe requested, he'll never deign to work with me."

"Moe... Zirkander?" Rysha asked.

Horis blinked. "Yes. You know him? He's not exactly, ah, sanctioned, shall we say? If you're still studying archaeology, I'm surprised you would be willing to speak his name, notorious treasure hunter and ignorer of boundaries that he is. But *are* you studying it? I'd heard you became a soldier." He looked at her clothing again—Rysha wasn't wearing her full uniform, as they were all trying to stay incognito, but her fatigue trousers and combat boots definitely didn't look like archaeologist wear.

"I did."

Horis yawned and wiped his eyes. "Forgive me. It's very late. If I didn't have a deadline—ah, but I'm sure you're uninterested in such matters." He peered at Trip, then stuck his hand out to him. "As your fellow— officer, is it?—said, I'm Horis Silverdale. *Lord* Silverdale, technically, but I rarely feel worthy of the noble treatment, I confess. You may not have heard of my family. We're up north, most of our land in the mountains. *Our* land, I say, but of course, I claim little of it. I'm the youngest of seven boys. I stand to inherit a lovely hill with three trees on it."

"Three? That's a respectable number. You could perhaps build a table with three trees." Rysha smiled at Trip.

He stirred, realizing he hadn't offered his name and might appear standoffish. She seemed to want to include him—and his table-making hobby—in the conversation.

"With one, if it's stout enough. And the wood is mature and strong." Trip sheathed Azarwrath, deciding he could be on guard without looking like he meant to skewer the man. "I'm Captain Trip." He clasped the offered hand, finding it soft and without callouses, what he would expect from a noble. Especially a *pretty* one.

"Your name is Trip? Well, you can't complain that it's unwieldy and difficult to pronounce." Horis smiled.

Trip tried to decide if he was being mocked.

"I don't mean to be forward," Horis said, "but are you hiding from someone? I don't have any weapons, so I'd like some warning if I'm likely to be embroiled in an altercation because I'm standing next to you. I can't imagine a reason for soldiers to be in these tunnels, otherwise. Unless—" his eyes grew puzzled, and he tilted his head, "—Moe didn't also send you to get rubbings, did he? I understood it was a test of sorts, but I didn't think there was a lineup of people eager to work with him. Especially soldiers."

Rysha's brow furrowed, and she glanced at Trip before answering Horis. "We actually did run into Moe Zirkander a couple of weeks back, but he didn't make any requests of us. He actually helped us locate something."

"For a commoner, he's an uncommonly good resource." Horis smiled at his wordplay.

If Moe is in town, Trip told Rysha silently, *I wonder if it's possible he would have heard anything about the stasis chamber.*

His expertise is ancient history, not modern crime, Rysha thought back. *Though I would be curious to find him and learn if those girls we rescued found safety.*

"I note you didn't answer my question," Horis said, his tone turning dry. He glanced past them toward the intersection, as if he worried trouble would come stomping down it. "If there's some danger, and I could possibly convince you to find *another* dead end to hide in, I would be most appreciative. There's surely nothing of military significance down here."

"We're not being followed. Probably." Rysha looked at Trip.

He shook his head. He hadn't checked recently, but Jaxi or Azarwrath should have warned him if someone was coming. Even so, he would prefer not to stand out here indefinitely, as it was possible someone would hear them talking and wander this way.

"I don't have much time," Horis said. "I'm supposed to meet Moe at the waterfront tomorrow. If I prove my archaeological abilities by finding the sanctuary and taking a rubbing of a plaque he said would be inside, he's agreed to take me on the expedition he's putting together. To find the Forbidden Treasure of Amon Akarth. This is, he said, a test of my worthiness. I admit, it's a touch galling to have to prove my worth to a commoner, but these are not our grandfathers' times." He smiled at Rysha, as if certain she would feel a similar lament for the lost golden age of the nobility.

She did smile back, which made Trip uneasy. He wanted to get rid of this fellow, not establish a rapport with him. Even if he was exactly what he said—and so far, Trip didn't sense Horis lying—having him here might draw attention to the area and jeopardize the mission and the safety of the babies.

Besides, Trip found it suspicious that this Horis had shown up, knowing about and wanting to explore the sanctuary, at the same time that Trip and the others were using it as a hideout. He'd had the sense, from the way it was hidden and undisturbed inside, that few had discovered it over the centuries. Admittedly, he'd felt clever for examining negative space and finding it himself. If he learned that Moe Zirkander had ambled by the week before, and countless others visited it every year, he would feel less clever.

"I know it's unseemly for me to want to join forces with a treasure hunter, and I hope you won't tell my grandmother, but as I implied, my financial future is somewhat in question. Finding Amon Akarth could be a great boon, even if I received only a small percentage of the gold and silver reputed to be inside. I also wouldn't mind having my name put down in the history books as one of those who discovered it." He looked warmly at Rysha.

Their gazes held for a long moment, which made Trip uneasy again, this time for reasons that had nothing to do with the mission.

"I don't think you'll find your sanctuary back here," Trip said. "Rysha and I were hoping to have some private alone time, so if you could move your search elsewhere, we would appreciate it."

He wondered if he could employ his power to convince Horis to leave. Would it be wrong to use a little mental persuasion in order to keep their hideout secret and the stasis chambers safe? Even though Rysha recognized the man, that didn't mean he wasn't a threat. He admitted to needing money. What if this seventh son who stood to inherit a mere three trees had heard about the reward for the *chapaharii* swords? Bhodian probably had a reward out for the rest of the stasis chambers too.

"In a tunnel?" Horis peered around, flicking a finger at a dangling cobweb. "It's rather musty."

"We enjoy exotic bed-free locales," Trip said.

"*Trip.*" Rysha swatted him on the arm. Her cheeks were pink.

Hells, he hadn't meant to embarrass her, just convince this interloper to lope somewhere else.

"That sounds somewhat primitive," Horis said dubiously.

"Yes, that's me. I believe you'll find what you seek down another tunnel." Trip tried to use some of his power, imagining an underground ancient dragon sanctuary located on the far side of the city. He did his best to convince Horis that he wanted to go over there to look for it.

Horis smiled brightly at him. "Oh no. I'm quite convinced it's here. Would you like to see my map? I consulted three older maps and a number of ancient texts from the pre-Lagresh era, some from as far away as Eastern Cofahre. I found some excellent references in the appendix of *Dragon Outposts and Magical Sanctuaries*. Are you familiar with that text? I'm quite proud of the map I created from a time period when maps were crude and inaccurate. I'm very resourceful. Moe Zirkander would be a fool not to take me on his expedition. Do you want to see my map?"

Trip shook his head, but Rysha stepped forward, eyeing the book Horis had pulled out. "I wouldn't mind taking a look."

"*Rysha.*" Silently, Trip added, *Don't encourage him.*

He's not going away, Trip. I have a feeling he'll camp out here until he finds the secret lever. And we can't just leave. Is Major Kaika still in there?

Yes.

Trip frowned as Horis opened his journal and showed off his map. Rysha had come forward to stand next to him and look at it. She had the most intrigued and fascinated expression on her face, one that promptly made Trip wish *he'd* made a map. Even if he hadn't perused ancient texts and appendices, he could have used his senses to create an accurate one of the area.

"Our hideout is inside the sanctuary you're seeking," Rysha told Horis, and Trip fell against the wall. "My colleague is simply being wary, but I can show you the plaque. It won't take you long to do a rubbing. And then, as a favor, would you mind if I accompanied you to meet Mr. Zirkander tomorrow? I have a couple of questions for him."

Rysha, Trip said sternly into her mind.

What? Moe can tell us about the girls, and he might know more about Dreyak's death too.

Trip rubbed the back of his neck. *Jaxi, what do you think of this man?*

Nothing special, but I also find his appearance suspicious. It seems possible he's hoping to collect your new friend's reward.

I don't sense that in his surface thoughts. Do you? Trip could try to probe more deeply, as he'd done with the vile cult leader down in the bottom of the outpost, but he shied away from that. He remembered the pain his forced intrusion had inflicted and the way blood had trickled from the man's nostrils as he had unintentionally caused physical damage. This man hadn't declared himself an enemy. Yet.

No, Jaxi said. *I only sense that he's passionate about relics, knows exactly what Ridge's daddy looks like, and that he's interested in your lieutenant's boobs.*

What? Trip almost blurted the word out loud.

You can't be surprised. Your clothing is still damp, and that shirt is nicely form-fitting on her. Most of the blood washed out in the harbor too.

Trip rubbed the back of his neck again, telling himself he was above worrying about such things, but he couldn't help but scrutinize the Iskandian nobleman to see if he was checking out Rysha's chest. It was hard to tell with Horis's face tilted toward the pages, but he could easily be sneaking peeks. And he was standing closer to her than he had been a moment ago.

What do you think, Azarwrath? Trip asked.

They are nice.

What?

Her cogs, as you once called them.

Trip rubbed his neck harder. *I meant about Horis's thoughts.*

Ah. On the surface, he seems exactly what he says, but there is something elusive about his mind. I find it hard to pin down his specific thoughts. I just get a general impression of archaeological interest and excitement toward a potential treasure hunt.

Yes, me too. Any thoughts about what that elusiveness could mean? Does he have dragon blood?

Azarwrath hesitated. *I'm not sensing it, but it's possible. He could have a small amount. Perhaps he's learned to hide it, since having dragon blood in your country is not, I understand, a good thing these days.*

It wasn't when Sardelle first came out of her stasis chamber, Jaxi said, *but we're attempting to instill in the populace a new appreciation for those with dragon ancestors.*

"It's a lovely map." Rysha seemed to notice that she'd moved closer to Horis—or more likely that Horis had moved closer to her. She stepped away, which Trip liked, but she gave Horis a friendly smile, which he liked less. "I would love to see the reference books you brought with you." She waved to his backpack. "But I'm afraid my comrade and I are leaving the city soon, so we don't have much time for extracurricular activities."

Comrade? Trip could see her not wanting to call him her lover, especially since he'd figured out they were officers—they should be perceived as conducting themselves professionally—but "comrade" seemed so platonic.

"Such as being actively romantic in a tunnel?" Horis raised his eyebrows.

"No. Tri—Captain Trip was only joking."

"I would love to show you the other texts I brought along." Horis smiled shyly at Rysha. "There may be some you're not familiar with. I'm something of a collector and have amassed an eclectic library. And perhaps you could show me your texts."

Trip squinted at him, trying to decide if that was a double entendre.

"This isn't an archaeological mission for us," Rysha said. "Not exactly. So I didn't bring research texts along."

"None at all? With your interest in such matters, that's hard to believe. You haven't discovered any interesting tomes here have you?"

Rysha hesitated. "Nothing of note."

The door ground open, startling Trip.

At first, he thought Horis had done something—mentally if not physically—to pull the switch. But Kaika appeared in the doorway, her pistol in one hand and Eryndral in the other. The sword glowed an impressive pale green in the dim tunnel.

"What's with all the *chitchat* outside our secret hideout? You two didn't know that secret hideouts come with a no-blathering-at-the-front-door rule?" Kaika frowned at Horis. "And a no-inviting-strangers-to-visit rule?"

Trip stirred, watching her sword and Horis's startled reaction to it. Was the blade glowing for *him*? Or for Trip?

Kaika turned her frown on Trip, and he saw that urge to attack him come over her, her eyes growing fierce as the sword no doubt reminded her for the thousandth time that slaying him would be particularly fine. He telepathically ordered Eryndral to stand down. Kaika may have been giving the order at the same time. The pale glow faded significantly.

"This is Horis Silverdale, ma'am," Rysha said. "I recognize him from—"

"Silverdale?" Kaika gave Horis a longer look. "Guess I should have guessed. You have the family looks. You one of the younger brothers?"

"Indeed, ma'am." He bowed low. "Are you of the nobility? It sounds like you know my family."

"I knew your brother Fyothor at one time. A brief but vigorous and satisfying time." Kaika smirked.

"Fyothor, ma'am?" Horis scratched his head. "Did you mean Fyodontor, by chance?"

"Ah, yes, that's it." Kaika waved as if she'd forgotten, but Trip sensed that had been a test for Horis. "I can't remember the names of all the men I've slept with."

Horis peered past Kaika into the dark sanctuary. With the sun long gone from the sky, no light filtered down from above, but a lit lantern rested on the stone floor.

"Horis needs to take a rubbing of the plaque in our sanctuary, ma'am," Rysha told Kaika.

"What sanctuary?" Kaika shifted to stand in front of the open door. "This is just a dark hole where I've been waiting for my subordinates to reappear while cleaning out the dirt under my nails."

"Dark hole?" Horis protested. "I can see Lyshandrasa the Lovely presiding over it even from here. Won't you let me look around? I won't tell anyone that it's been usurped by the Iskandian military as some kind of base of operations. And fingernail salon."

Rysha snorted.

Trip told himself it would be pathetic of him to feel threatened because another man's jokes tickled her humor. He wasn't that insecure. He was, however, still suspicious of the man.

"I told him he could come in," Rysha admitted.

"Why?" Kaika frowned again.

"In exchange, he should be willing to take me to meet Moe Zirkander in the morning. Moe helped us once. He might be able to help us again."

"I'm happy to take you to see him." Horis smiled and slipped inside past Kaika, not appearing alarmed that her hand tightened around the hilt of her sword.

Are the stasis chambers covered, Major? Trip asked silently, coming to stand beside her.

Kaika seemed startled by his telepathic contact, but she recovered and replied. *Yeah, I threw the blanket over them before opening the door.*

Horis went straight to the statue, not seeming to have any interest in the devices in the wagon.

Trip still couldn't read any deception in his surface thoughts. All he could tell was that Horis seemed a touch smitten with the dragon and looked forward to treasure hunting with Moe.

I do not think this is a good idea, Telryn, Azarwrath said.

I agree, but I'm not in charge now that Kaika has come out. Fortunately, she's looking at him like she's thinking of flaying him with her sword. Trip approved of that look.

You may be mixing up her looks, Jaxi told him. *She's actually thinking of removing all his clothing with her sword so she can see what he looks like naked. Admittedly, they're both predatory expressions.*

Ew.

He is *handsome. Like a young Ridgewalker Zirkander. Though I doubt Ridge ever wandered around with ink on his fingers and a pencil behind his ear.*

"Lieutenant Ravenwood," Kaika said, eyeing the empty scabbard at her waist. "You seem to be missing something."

"Yes, ma'am. It's a long story. Actually, it's a short story that ends in the creation of a difficult problem with a solution I haven't discovered yet."

"It sounds complicated."

"I'm afraid it will be, but I'll figure things out before we have to leave." Rysha grimaced.

Trip touched her arm. *We'll find a way to get it off the bottom.*

In time to catch that steamer with Major Kaika?

Let me think of some ideas. I can locate it. I just can't be the one to go down and get it.

Any idea how deep the harbor is out where those barges are? Rysha asked.

Yes. Trip had checked while they'd been resting—and healing—on the beach. *About two hundred feet.*

Rysha groaned next to him, and he didn't blame her.

I think the deepest I've gone is twenty or thirty feet, she replied. *In the lake back home. I don't suppose you've learned how to shape-shift into a dolphin yet?*

Even if I had, I wouldn't be able to touch the sword. Unless I grabbed it with iron tongs. Trip remembered doing exactly that in the tunnel to Agarrenon Shivar's lair.

You want to shape-shift into a dolphin with hands to hold tongs? Maybe Sardelle will give you extra credit on your homework if you manage to do that.

I think I'd have an easier time building you a diving suit. Or a submarine.

Building a submarine? *In a day? Trip, that can't possibly be easier than turning into a two-handed dolphin.*

I should think one hand would suffice.

Whatever gets me that sword back, Trip. Rysha smiled, but her smile had a bleakness to it, like she didn't truly believe they could retrieve it.

She was wrong about that.

CHAPTER 13

"H E'S MORE INERT THAN HIS brother was," Kaika observed when Rysha woke up early the next morning. She nodded across the chamber to where Horis was snoring.

He'd been painstakingly methodical in taking his rubbing of the plaque the night before, insisting on making several copies. He'd yawned the whole way through it, and he'd fallen asleep before finishing. He now lay on his back, papers sprawled all about him.

"Maybe he's meditating," Rysha said, pulling herself into a sitting position against the wagon that held the stasis chambers. "Loudly."

She'd dug out her spare set of spectacles as soon as she'd gotten back the night before, so she could see their guest well enough. His presence in the city had startled her the night before, perhaps because they'd seen so few other Iskandians here, and she still found it surprising.

"While resting his hand on that dragon's toe?" Kaika asked.

"It's not any worse than kissing a ball."

"I don't think Leftie's meditating when he does that."

"Hoping to get meditative with a woman, maybe." Rysha smiled, finding she actually missed Leftie, Duck, and Blazer.

She wondered if they had flown back to a peaceful Iskandia or if they'd found dragons attacking the country. Had King Angulus been relieved by the extra *chapaharii* swords they'd brought home? Or had he been disappointed that they hadn't brought Trip's sire?

"I don't think *meditating* is what Leftie does with women," Kaika said, then lowered her voice. "Maybe we should wake Trip up and roll his siblings out the door. There's too much interest in this place, and we still have another…" She pulled out a dented pocket watch that had survived their numerous battles. "Just under twenty-four hours before boarding time."

"Too much interest? There's just him." Rysha pointed at Horis's back.

"That's too much. I'd kick him out, but then he might tell people he's seen us. I'm more inclined to lock him in."

"*Ma'am.* I know him and his family. My sister dated him—or tried to date him. I'm not sure he ever agreed. Either way, we can't lock him in a three-thousand-year-old shrine. Does that door even have a lock?"

"We could shove a boulder in front of it."

"He's from Iskandia. The *nobility*." Realizing Kaika probably didn't care one way or another about the nobility, Rysha added, "He said he'd take me to see Moe."

"How is Moe going to help us with any of our *many* problems?" Kaika frowned at Rysha's empty sword scabbard, perhaps finding Dorfindral's loss more of a problem than the missing baby or Dreyak's mysterious death.

"I don't know, but he helped us before. If he's been here for a while, he may have some good ideas about where to find things in the city."

Rysha yawned. After staying out so late and nearly getting herself killed, she was tempted to go back to sleep and hope the world would leave them alone for the rest of the day.

No such luck, Jaxi spoke into her mind.

Rysha twitched, startled by the contact. Maybe Jaxi was speaking to her because Trip was still sleeping. He had taken the first watch, then collapsed in exhaustion, his head crooked up on his pack. It did not look comfortable. His belt and soulblades lay next to him.

What's wrong? Rysha asked, glancing at Kaika to see if she had also received Jaxi's communication.

No, just you. You're Trip's snoffle buddy now, so that makes me more likely to speak to you.

That's how you determine who's worthy of your words?

That and how grouchy people are when I contact them. Listen, you might not have much time. I've been periodically reaching out to make sure nobody is sneaking up on us, and I noticed all the squatters have moved.

All the people in the chamber we originally came through?

Yes. I'm debating if I should wake the snoozing dragonling.

Probably.

"Major?" Rysha said, pushing herself to her feet. "I think you're right. Let's pack up and find another spot. Maybe we can get aboard the steamer early. I saw it in dock last night."

Rysha hoped the steamer's captain hadn't seen *her.* He might not want to take on passengers who had challenged two of the most powerful people in the city. And their magical guard animals.

"Fine with me." Kaika frowned at the snoring Horis, maybe wondering if they could sneak out without him waking up.

There are two people that just came into that open area, Jaxi thought. *They're wearing some of those white cultist outfits. I'm waking Trip.*

Rysha wondered how soulblades woke people up. She imagined Jaxi zapping him in the butt with a magical shock.

I gently nudge his mind into a state of alertness, Jaxi informed her. *But if you ever want his butt zapped, I may be willing to accommodate.*

Uh, that's all right.

Trip rolled to a sitting position, his dark hair mussy, and grabbed the swords. "We have trouble coming," he said, glancing at Kaika and Rysha. He seemed surprised to see them standing up already.

"I heard." Rysha grabbed her pack and slung it to her shoulders.

"You know about the men lurking suspiciously out there?"

"Jaxi told me." Rysha kept her voice low, doubting they should openly talk about magic in front of their visitor, who could wake up at any moment. Even though she knew him, that didn't mean he would be comfortable hearing about such matters. Few Iskandians were.

"Jaxi's talking to you?" Kaika tugged on her own pack and snapped her sword and pistol belt around her waist. "Why didn't she talk to me?"

"You don't snoffle with Trip."

"I don't know what that is, but if it's like being his soul snozzle, I'm not interested."

"My what?" Trip asked.

"Soul snozzle," Kaika said. "It's what Jaxi calls General Zirkander."

"I don't need to hear things like that about my commanding officer." Trip faced the exit, his eyes taking on a distracted quality.

"So, we shouldn't talk about the rumors that say he's a thorough and inspired lover, either?" Kaika winked at Rysha.

"They're only rumors, ma'am?" Rysha asked. "You've slept with dragons but not generals?"

"Oh, I've slept with generals. Colonels. Majors. Sergeants. Sergeant Majors. The delightfulness of variety is what makes life worth living. But I didn't meet Zirkander until after he was Sardelle's soul snozzle. Alas, he's monogamous these days from what I hear."

Trip gave them a pained expression, grabbed the handle of his wagon, and headed for the secret door. "We can't go out the back way with my cargo—up the ladder—so we'll have to risk going past the people in the large chamber. I'll do my best to camouflage us."

"We should warn—" Rysha pointed at Horis only to find him sitting up and stacking papers.

"Please forgive me," he said. "I was *exhausted*. But I believe I've taken rubbings sufficient enough to please even the most demanding professor. Or treasure hunter."

"Wonderful," Kaika said.

"I truly enjoyed visiting this shrine, I must say. Do you know it holds a piece of the long-dead dragon's essence? I wouldn't have minded knowing her. She was reputed to be friendly to humans and all dragons, even lowly bronze dragons." Horis's lips twitched wryly. "A rarity among dragon kind."

"Uh huh," Kaika said. "We're clearing out. Apparently, there's trouble afoot."

"You better come with us," Rysha said, not wanting Horis to be trapped in here by some trouble in the tunnels. "What time are you meeting Moe at the waterfront?"

"Oh, I'm not late am I?" Horis pulled out an expensive-looking gold pocket watch. "Ah, no. I still have three hours. Very good."

"Those two men in white are running away now, toward the exit tunnel. We may want to hurry." Trip depressed the indiscernible button in the wall that opened the door, then dragged the wagon through. "I can create a barrier around myself, Rysha, and Silverdale, but Major Kaika…"

"I know," Kaika said. "Eryndral and I are on our own. But why do you think we'll need a barrier? What were those people doing out there?"

"I just have a hunch there'll be trouble."

There will be, Jaxi said, the words for all of them. *They left little boxes. I'm not the demolitions expert that Kaika is, but I believe they are explosives.*

"Explosives?" Kaika asked as the group moved into the tunnel. "If you show me one, and if there's a countdown, I might be able to stop it. But it's probably better just to get out of here before they go off."

"Explosives?" Horis asked in alarm. "Near the sanctuary? There could be damage!"

"Damage?" Kaika asked. "It could be obliterated."

"After standing protected by magic for thousands of years? That's obscene."

Rysha tended to agree. She hoped the sanctuary's magic would protect it. Why were people setting explosives under the city? In the hope of killing Trip and getting to the stasis chambers without having to deal with him? What if a rockfall buried the devices? Or damaged them irreparably? Bhodian wanted the stasis chambers for himself; he wouldn't reward anyone for destroying them.

They made it out of the maze of tunnels and into the larger area. A few spread blankets remained along with piles of trash, but the space was eerily quiet in comparison to how it had been the day before. Had the men setting the explosives warned the families to leave? Or had the people simply sensed trouble and fled?

"I don't see the explosives," Kaika said, looking around as the group followed Trip at a jog.

He was pulling the wagon instead of floating it magically behind him, and it bumped and clanked on the uneven rock. Maybe he needed all his power to keep a protective barrier up and look for enemies.

"The people who left them are waiting for us at the canal exit," Trip said.

"You sure they're waiting for *us*?" Kaika peered left and right as they walked, eyeing the rock piles. "Maybe they're just admiring the view of the water."

"They're aiming rifles and pistols back into the tunnel," Trip said. "Exactly where we're going to come out. Assuming we escape before the explosives go off."

"I feel particularly unloved in this city," Kaika said.

As they neared the ramp that led out of the large chamber, an explosion roared from one of the rock piles behind them. White light flared in the air, blinding in its intensity.

Trip whirled, raising a hand as Kaika crouched down in a ball, her arms protecting her head. The storm of rocks that flew through the air struck an invisible shield before reaching her. Trip might not have been able to include her in a bubble barrier, but he must have created a wall between their group and the explosion.

Unfortunately, another bomb went off farther up the ramp. And then another, one that had been placed against a stone pillar. It crumbled, and one of the huge arches spanning the ceiling came down. Rysha stepped closer to Trip and the wagon, wishing she could do something to help. In addition to the roar of the explosions, rocks crashed down all around them, the noise cacophonous.

"Look out!" Horis yelled and sprang toward Kaika. She was still hunkered in a ball.

He dove into her, pulling her several feet to the side as she yelled in alarm. An instant later, a massive stone block that weighed tons fell free from the ceiling and slammed into the ground where she'd been.

Rysha stared. How had he known?

Trip cursed. "I'm adjusting my barrier to protect us from above too. Everyone get close."

So much dust clouded the air that Rysha couldn't see more than five feet. Someone bumped into her. Horis pulling Kaika along with him.

"I'm fine," Kaika barked. "Don't manhandle me. Unless a bed is involved and I ask for it. I—" She broke off in a fit of coughing.

Rysha didn't hear the booms of any more explosives going off, but there had been at least four, and they'd started a chain reaction of damage. Huge slabs of rock continued to crash down as the ancient arches gave way. Light slashed in from somewhere above, but it was so hazy that Rysha couldn't see much. Long seconds passed as the chamber quaked and more and more collapsed. She couldn't believe how many slabs tumbled down from the ceiling. How far underground had they been?

Fortunately, Trip's protective barrier deflected the rocks that fell from right above them. He'd even found a way to protect Kaika.

As the rocks finally stopped falling and the dust settled, Rysha realized two things. The ramp leading back to the canal was buried in rubble and what had once been an underground chamber was now an open pit with sunlight streaming in from above.

She squinted up, half-blinded from the brightness, but the picture gradually came into focus, buildings ringing the pit and a few people standing at the edge, gaping down into it. Now, she understood why the ceiling had seemed to have a ridiculous amount of material to drop. It hadn't just been the ground above them, but all the buildings built atop that ground. They were now broken into millions of pieces, bricks, stone, tiles, and even furnishings piled high in the pit.

"Whoever set those explosives," Kaika said, her words punctuated with coughs, "did *not* know what they were doing."

Rysha shook her head slowly, shocked by the devastation. "Why would Bhodian have approved this? Why would anyone? Destroying a city block just to get to us? To capture the stasis chambers?"

"Stasis chambers?" Horis looked at the wagon, the half-barrel-shaped devices stacked atop it appearing undisturbed under their protective blanket.

Rysha didn't reply, realizing she shouldn't have roused his curiosity about them in the first place.

Trip lowered his hands—lowering the barrier, as well? "He may *not* have approved it. Maybe people seeking the bounty got overzealous."

"Or maybe someone wanted to *destroy* them, not collect them," Kaika said.

Trip arched his eyebrows. "Destroy? To what end?"

"How would I know?" Kaika asked. "But I'm sure not everybody in the city works for this Bhodian. That was an insane amount of power. You don't set off explosives like that if you want to *capture* someone."

"Even if that someone is a mage?" Rysha asked. "They may have anticipated Trip being able to protect us."

Kaika's expression was skeptical. "Maybe, but Jaxi said men in those white cultist outfits set these bombs, didn't she? The Brotherhood people have been after us since we got to town."

"Technically, they were after Trip when we first landed on that beach," Rysha said.

"Perhaps we should move elsewhere to discuss this," Trip said quietly, nodding up toward the people gaping down from above. He also scrutinized Horis.

Rysha nodded. Horis looked more puzzled and confused than suspicious, and he had saved Kaika from being crushed, so Rysha was inclined to think well of him, but they shouldn't be speaking of their mission in front of him.

"Yes," Kaika said. "Let's go see if we can board the steamer early. If we can't, I'll sit our load down on the docks and shoot anyone who comes near."

Rysha snorted but did not disagree. They could join Horis when he met Moe, and being at the harbor would put her close to Dorfindral. She and Trip could work on a way to retrieve the sword.

Except that Trip was going to a lunch meeting, one that was probably a trap.

She grimaced. She'd almost forgotten about that.

"While we're there, we can drop hooks into the water to see if we can retrieve something valuable." Kaika gave Rysha a pointed look, clearly contemplating the same thing.

"You seek to retrieve something that's underwater?" Horis asked. "I put together an archaeological expedition once where we pulled up ancient treasures from the depths of Skarborah Bay. We pulled up a lot of ancient junk, too, but as you know, even middens can contain interesting insights about the past." He winked at Rysha. "I would be glad to assist you if you seek something out in the harbor here. We developed some techniques that you might find useful."

"*I* will help you with the retrieval," Trip said coolly, frowning at Horis instead of looking at Rysha.

"You're both welcome to help," Rysha said. "Trip, we could start right away if you skip your lunch trap."

"Trap?" Kaika said. "Did someone forget to mention this?"

"We'll fill you in, ma'am. On the way to the docks, I guess." Trip turned his frown onto his cargo wagon.

Rysha had no trouble reading that expression, that he didn't like the idea of having the stasis chambers out in the open, even if there was a blanket covering what they were. By now, half the city probably had a description of his wagon and knew how much of a reward was being offered for it. And *more* than half the city seemed to know about the *chapaharii* swords.

"Let's head there now." Kaika nodded toward the far side of the pit, to a man in white gazing down at them from the edge. "We're easy targets down here."

"I can find us a way out," Trip said, but he didn't move immediately. He pinned the white-clad man with a stare. Their eyes met and held. After several seconds, the man turned and walked out of sight.

"Mental manipulation?" Rysha asked quietly.

"Yes. It works on *some* people." Trip glanced at Horis, the gesture surprising Rysha.

Horis wasn't paying attention. He'd pulled out a book and was flipping through it.

"I believe I have a map somewhere that lists the depths at various locations in the harbor," Horis said. "Perhaps it would be helpful."

"Perhaps," Rysha said, though Trip had already told her the sword had fallen in a spot two hundred feet deep.

Horis beamed a smile at her. He certainly seemed eager to please.

"My mental suggestion won't last for long," Trip said, turning his back on them and waving his hand to lift the wagon up to float over the rubble.

Rysha and Kaika headed after him. Presumably, he could lead them out of the pit—or float them to the streets above.

Horis, not obviously disturbed by this show of magic, strolled over the rocks as if they were as easy to walk on as pavement, and he whistled as he perused an atlas.

"That is more than personal cargo," the steamer's first mate said, waving at the wagon, though he kept glancing at the smoke and dust cloud hovering over a certain block in the city. The captain and numerous crew members were on the deck of the large iron ship, also studying the dubious horizon. "If we can find room for it, it'll cost extra."

Kaika made a point of not looking in that direction. Trip and Rysha were doing the same thing. Horis seemed oblivious to it all and was still studying the atlas. If he truly thought he could help retrieve Dorfindral, Rysha would be happy to let him do so. She didn't see how Trip could build a submarine today, especially since he would leave soon for his lunch date. Who knew how long that would take? And should she go with him to stand guard?

She wanted to keep an eye on Trip—she didn't trust Grekka one bit—but she also felt obligated to retrieve her sword. The last thing she wanted was to report to King Angulus that she'd lost one of the country's most valuable resources.

"Cost extra?" Kaika jammed a fist against her hip. "You already want to charge us a fortune just to spend an extra night on your boat."

"We are a shipping business, ma'am, not a passenger transport. Space is at a premium, reserved for cargos that can bring us a return." The first mate, a dark-skinned man with curly black hair, pointed at the hazy cityscape. "Do you know what happened up there? We've heard everything from a dragon attack to Cofah or Iskandian bombs."

"Why would Isk—another country want to bomb your city?" Rysha asked.

According to the country flag painted on the hull alongside the steamer's name, *Cyan Rooster*, it claimed Rakgorath as its homeland.

"To take it over and add it to their collection of colonies, no doubt."

"Look, we'll give you five extra nucros," Kaika said. "That's it. The cargo can stay in our cabin."

"Cabin?" The first mate lifted shaggy black eyebrows.

"Don't we get a cabin?"

"Passengers sleep in the hold. There are hammocks."

"You're charging us five hundred nucros for *hammocks*? On a voyage that's only three days?"

"You're welcome to talk with the other captains here if you find our fares unpalatable." The first mate extended a hand to encompass the rest of the docks. A few local fishing ships occupied slots, but there weren't any other vessels that traveled across international waters.

"Funny," Kaika said.

"Here's the map of the harbor I mentioned," Horis said, coming to stand next to Rysha, his shoulder brushing hers.

She nodded and looked, but she also eased a few inches away so they weren't touching. Her sister might have mooned over him a few years back, but Rysha had no interest in the nobleman.

"It should be useful," she said, not mentioning that Trip could sense the *chapaharii* blade down there and point them to the exact spot. They had already spoken too openly about magic in front of Horis.

"I have many useful resources," Horis said, smiling at her.

Rysha caught herself staring back at his gaze, noticing how lively and appealing his warm copper eyes were, and how nicely they matched his hair. Had his hair always been that richly colored? She couldn't remember.

"Perhaps you'll see fit to share *your* books with me eventually. I do so love books. Especially old ones from far off places." His smile seemed genuine, and he radiated enthusiasm, but a warning bell clanged in the back of Rysha's mind.

This was the second time he'd seemed certain she had texts along that he wanted to see, as if he knew she had a couple of journals in her pack. She didn't see how he could. She hadn't taken them out in his presence, and as far as she knew, they weren't magical, so they shouldn't be giving off any kind of aura.

"If you visit my family's manor sometime when we're both back in Iskandia," Rysha said, "I'd be happy to show you all the books my mother has collected. As you know, she's the real archaeologist in the family. She sometimes trades some of our family winery's best vintages for rare historical astronomy and mathematics books. Those are her favorite subjects."

"Ah, yes. I appreciate the invitation." Horis looked like he might say more, but he turned as Trip walked up to them.

Trip's expression was flat and hard to read. Rysha hoped he hadn't heard her invitation to Horis. She hadn't meant it to sound like she was extending an offer of friendship—or anything else. She'd simply wanted to veer Horis's interest away from her pack and whatever he thought she had in it.

It was hard to believe he knew about the journal from the old exploration team, but even if he did, why would he want it? He hadn't been ogling the stasis chambers or even paying attention to them, so she didn't think he was aware of or interested in Agarrenon Shivar's offspring.

"While Major Kaika negotiates our fare, I'm going to my meeting." Trip was being deliberately vague, Rysha suspected, and he looked at her, not including Horis in the conversation. "I want to arrive early enough to check for trouble."

"A good idea, but don't you think that Kaika or I should go with you?"

"Major Kaika appears to be busy." Trip looked at the argument still going on between her and the first mate. There was a lot of fist waving. "And you have something important to retrieve."

"That can wait. Besides, you haven't built me my submarine yet."

She meant it as a joke, but he winced.

"I apologize. I've been trying to think about solutions, but there have been distractions." Trip didn't look at Horis specifically, but did let his gaze brush over him as he turned toward the smoke above the cityscape—those explosions must have started some fires. "I had a discussion with my friends—" he tapped the soulblade hilts, again being vague, though Horis seemed educated enough to know what they were, "—and actually think I could hold my breath long enough to get to the bottom, grab something with iron tongs, and get back up."

"That seems highly unlikely."

Trip arched his eyebrows.

Rysha pushed her spectacles higher on her nose. "It's true that the natives on Jonga Junga use weighted stones to descend up to a hundred feet—they collect the soft sea sponges unique to their island chain and trade them around the world—but they also practice diving a *lot*. Visiting explorers have timed them, and many can hold their breath for five minutes, long enough to drop down and cut the sponges off the bottom. Five *minutes*, Trip. At one hundred feet. If you want, I can calculate how long it would take you to descend to two hundred feet and pluck something off the bottom with tongs, but I can't imagine you holding your breath that long."

She reached for her pack so she could pull out pencil and paper, but Trip stopped her by resting his fingers on her wrist.

"I wasn't planning to do it without help," he said, tapping a soulblade hilt again. "But I have no problem with you cogitating on alternative methods while I'm gone. If you can retrieve it without my help, I'm certainly willing to forgo getting wet again." Trip looked like he wanted to give her more than a wrist touch in parting, but he glanced at Horis and lowered his hand. "I'll be back soon."

Rysha, her mind busy running gravity calculations, didn't notice Trip leaving until he had already crossed the waterfront street into the city.

Trip, you have a death wish, she thought after him.

No, he surprised her by replying. *I just like being rescued by beautiful, mathematically inclined women. Do try to avoid being shot in the process the next time you rescue me. I don't like seeing you bleeding.*

And I don't like having your sword incinerate things that are inside of me.

I'm sure your body is working that lead out of your system as we speak. We're not going to talk about excretions again, are we?

No, I don't want to distract you further from your math equations. Trip sent an image along with the words—actually, it was more of a sensation—of him pressing his lips to hers. A tingle went through her body as if he were right there.

After that, math wasn't what she had on her mind. She glanced to the side and found Horis gazing at her. He couldn't know what she'd been thinking, but she blushed anyway, afraid she'd had some dreamy—or lustful—expression on her face.

"You can use my pencil if you like." Horis lifted the one he kept behind his ear and offered it to her.

"What?"

"For your equation."

"Oh, thank you." Rysha lifted a hand, intending to wave away the offer, but Kaika was still arguing with the first mate, so why not?

It would only take a moment to factor in gravity and buoyant force to estimate how long it would take Trip to descend if he had a weight dragging him down. She had no idea if magic could grant him the ability to hold his breath longer than average, but she could help him by figuring out the numbers. Maybe she should run them on herself too. She'd been the idiot who dropped the sword, and she wouldn't need special tongs to pick it up if she went down. She would be more buoyant than he was, thanks to more squishy curves and less muscle, but if the soulblades could help him hold his breath, maybe they could also help her?

She accepted Horis's pencil and was surprised when a little charge of electricity seemed to go through her when their fingers touched. She looked at him, suspecting him of doing something, but he merely lowered his hand and gazed at her blandly.

She'd always felt a charge when Trip touched her and assumed it was part of the chemistry they had. Feeling a tingle from a relative stranger's touch made her uneasy. She knew some of her body's attraction to Trip came from his dragonness, his *scylori*, but Horis couldn't have that, could he? Trip and the soulblades would have sensed it if he had dragon blood, and they hadn't said anything about that to her.

Besides, she knew him and knew his family. She'd never heard rumors of them being accused of witchcraft.

Even if he did have dragon blood and somehow was trained as a sorcerer, what would he be doing here, poking through ruins and wanting to join Moe Zirkander on a treasure hunt? Unless that was all a ruse, and he'd come looking for their team because he wanted something. If he had, what could it be? That journal? He hadn't asked about it specifically, but he did seem to think she had books he wanted to see. Would a sorcerer need to physically hold a book to read it? Couldn't he just see into her pack with his mind?

"I'm not a poor mathematician," Horis said, his gaze innocent as she scrutinized him. "If you would like to run your answers past me, I would be happy to double check them."

"I'll keep that in mind. Thank you."

"All right, Lieutenant," Kaika said, walking over. "We and our cargo can board early."

The first mate stood behind her, smiling as he counted coins.

Kaika should have asked Trip to use his mental manipulation skills on the man to see if they could get a better deal. Then again, Trip probably would have objected to that. He hadn't hidden his qualms about using those powers, and Rysha didn't mind. She admired him for questioning whether or not he should do things he was able to do.

"I see our cargo hauler isn't around to help get it on board and unload it," Kaika grumbled, scowling in the direction Trip had gone, then turning her scowl on Horis. "We're not paying your way, nobleman."

"I would never ask such a thing, Major. I am here for a meeting, as you'll recall." Horis tilted his head. "However, it is still two hours away. Lady Ravenwood, shall I join you on the ship and help you with calculations for retrieving this item that is of value to you?"

Rysha hesitated. *Could* he help her? Truly?

As he gazed into her eyes, she found herself forgetting her earlier skepticism about him and nodding slowly.

"We can get it without you," Kaika said.

"I do not mind helping. Let me see if the first mate will allow me aboard to visit with you or if I also must pay a fare." Horis walked over to the man.

"Ravenwood," Kaika said in exasperation, "have you given him a firm no?"

"Ma'am?" All Rysha could imagine Kaika referred to was Horis's interest in the journals, but Kaika hadn't been close enough to hear those subtle requests, had she?

"That you don't want to have sex with him. I *assume* you don't. You seem content with your perky pilot."

"Of course I don't, ma'am."

"Then you better let him know so he stops trailing you like a faithful hound."

"He's not trailing me."

"Well, he's not trailing *me*. And he's definitely been studying *your* ass and chest, not Trip's."

Rysha's cheeks warmed again. "I don't think that's what he wants."

"Trust me, he wants you."

"I mean, I don't think that's why he's sticking with us. I'm the one who asked to come to the harbor with him to meet Moe. But aside from that…" Rysha lowered her voice. "I believe he may have figured out I took a journal from the man in that exploration party who died in the dragon lair. I don't know how—I didn't tell anyone except our team. But he's hinted that he'd like to see what's in my pack."

"I'll bet."

"*Ma'am.*" Rysha was irritated that Kaika kept suggesting Horis wanted a sexual relationship with her, mostly because she was positive he wanted something else. She knew she wasn't ugly, but it usually took a unique man to appreciate her physical assets. A man who didn't think her odd when she got excited by the idea of creating instruction manuals for magical swords.

"Just pay attention, Lieutenant. Being oblivious to things like that can get you in trouble." Kaika jerked her thumb toward the wagon. "Now help me move our cargo, hopefully for the last time. At least until we get to Iskandia."

"Yes, ma'am."

CHAPTER 14

T RIP EYED THE RESTAURANT ATOP the rooftop of a hotel from the street below. Cheerful yellow-and-orange-striped sun umbrellas provided shade for those dining above while girls and boys wandered from table to table with fans to further cool off the patrons. A decorative wrought-iron railing surrounding the rooftop had barbs and spikes subtly incorporated into the pattern.

Trip supposed the diners wouldn't want the riffraff from the streets climbing up to assault them while they ate. Not that such events seemed likely. He had traveled three miles inland to reach this neighborhood, far from the rough areas where he'd thus far spent time, and there were steam carriages and rickshaws waiting in front of the building, the drivers polishing their conveyances or their own shoes while they waited.

Think they'll let me in? Trip asked doubtfully.

Use your scylori *and command them to let you enter,* Azarwrath said. *You are the son of a dragon. If you wish to dine at a restaurant, you shall do so.*

Or he could just brush his hair and rub the soot off his face, Jaxi put in. *He doesn't look too disreputable now that he's changed into a shirt that doesn't reveal all of his chest and abdomen.*

Rysha liked that shirt. Trip licked his fingers and rubbed his face, hoping to clean off any lingering soot, then scraped his fingers through his hair. Dust and shards of rock tumbled free.

No, she liked being able to see what was under *the shirt. No woman would find a shredded, bloodstained shirt appealing.*

The sorceress Grekka is seated on the left side of the restaurant, Azarwrath said. *At a table by herself, drinking what appears to be a dark red wine. A cabernet? Does this benighted land have vineyards somewhere? The food at the other tables looks half-promising. Telryn, I insist that you sample a number of the culinary offerings within. If there is an actual chef... My palate has longed for good-tasting food for ages.*

I see you're putting a lot of effort into checking for traps, Jaxi said.

There are two chefs in the kitchen. And a dessert chef. Telryn, you must order a dessert. I wonder what the local specialty is. Please, nothing with cactus pads.

Fine, I'll look for the traps, Jaxi said.

I sense one of those magical creatures nearby, Trip said, his own senses extended, not just to the restaurant but to the streets and buildings around it. *Actually, I sensed its gem controller first, but I believe it's one of the winged lions. It's atop the roof behind the restaurant. I suppose that's more of a turret.*

I think the lion is Grekka's bodyguard, Azarwrath said, having apparently wrenched his attention from the kitchen. *It doesn't look like it's poised to leap on unsuspecting diners.*

What about suspecting diners? Trip asked.

You have proven that you can handle her lions.

I've also proven that her snakes can handle me.

There is no tainted metal here, and I don't see the man who ordered you tortured.

Trip nodded. He had already checked for Bhodian since he had no trouble envisioning them sitting at the table together and holding hands as he walked up. He had also checked for the stasis chamber and hadn't felt it. He hadn't expected to, but he felt disappointed, regardless.

"Might as well get this over with then," Trip said and strode across the street to the entrance of the hotel.

He entered the building without being confronted, but a waiter—or maybe that meaty fellow was a bouncer—stood with his arms folded across his chest in front of the stairs leading to the rooftop deck. He wore an eye patch, and a long scar stretched down one of his bare forearms, as if someone had once thought it would be a good idea to extract his ulnar bone with a dagger.

Trip attempted to exude confidence and a right to be there as he approached the bouncer.

The man's gaze snapped onto him and held. Trip braced himself, expecting a sneer and a challenge, especially if he hadn't succeeded in wiping away all the soot. Further, the bouncer might object to someone with two swords entering his peaceful restaurant. Trip had thought about leaving them behind, but only briefly. He was far too likely to encounter trouble at this meeting to be without the soulblades' assistance.

The bouncer's lips parted, but not in a challenge. His gaze lingered, as if he found Trip… mesmerizing.

Was that his *scylori* at work? He hadn't meant to exude whatever it was that seemed to draw people. He just wanted the man to let him pass.

"I'm meeting the Silver Shark for lunch," Trip said.

"Yes, sir," the bouncer said and promptly stepped aside, gesturing for him to ascend the stairs.

Trip hurried up, aware of the man's gaze following him. More than that, when Trip glanced back, he caught the bouncer looking at his butt.

He stubbed his toe and almost fell face-first onto the stairs.

You needn't be so alarmed, Jaxi spoke dryly into his mind. *Handsome dragonlings attract both sexes.*

Always? Trip deliberately avoided brushing the bouncer's thoughts, not wanting to chance upon any lewd images involving him.

Not always. Sometimes, people will just pay extra attention to you and be eager to do as you wish. But if you happen to fit a person's preferences, sexual interest is very common.

Are you saying that man is…

You're not discriminating based on looks are you? Jaxi did that dry tone extremely well.

No, I just thought—never mind.

Trip reached the top of the stairs and looked around for a server to guide him. He thought about dampening his aura, but he might need it again to get past further gatekeepers.

Since he'd already sensed Grekka from below, Trip looked across the tables to her corner. She must have been watching the stairs—or she'd sensed him as easily as he sensed her—because her gaze was already locked on to him. She smiled when their eyes met, then looked him up and down and licked her lips.

He knew he didn't appear that dapper and handsome, especially since he'd been wearing his last undamaged shirt in the explosion, but if *scylori* could improve his desirability, maybe it was worth continuing to use it during this lunch. He remembered the way the Cofah sorceress, Kiadarsa, had been attracted to him, drawn by his power rather than his looks, apparently. She had been willing to answer his questions when she'd been under his influence. If he'd asked the right questions, he would have learned much earlier that the Cofah had been at cross-purposes with Trip and his team. But he hadn't known what he'd been doing then—hells, he hadn't been doing anything, just being himself. Now, he could possibly choose to use his power to get information about Dreyak—and keep Grekka from springing whatever trap she planned.

Come here, young and sexy, Grekka purred into his mind.

He sensed her trying to use some magical compulsion on him, but it didn't affect him at all. That reassured him. At least if it came to a battle between the two of them, he ought to have the upper hand, lion lurking on the rooftop notwithstanding. He had Jaxi and Azarwrath. Other than the lion, she had nothing.

No, he realized, sensing a magical artifact on her person. She did have something. She wore a slender dagger in a scabbard tucked into her boot. It lacked the aura of a soulblade, but it definitely had magic about it. He would be aware of it, but he didn't see a reason to fear it.

Trip lifted his chin, waiting a moment so she would know that he wasn't obeying her. He was tempted to order *her* to come to him, but that would be silly. They would end up standing at the top of the stairs instead of sitting at a table. Besides, several other diners had turned to look at him, including a woman in her eighties studying him from head to toe with even more interest than the bouncer had shown.

The name is Trip, he told Grekka, walking toward her.

A waitress smiled shyly as he passed, and stepped aside.

Less than a minute using his *scylori*, and he felt like a conspicuous ass disturbing people and drawing far too much attention to himself.

Does this come more naturally to others? Trip asked the soulblades.

Your friend Leftie doesn't seem to mind being the center of feminine attention, Jaxi pointed out.

I don't think that happens quite as often as he thinks it does.

Embrace your power and your heritage, Telryn, Azarwrath said. *You go to face another mage. It is important to establish dominance.* A little surge of pride or perhaps pleasure emanated from the soulblade.

Trip remembered their conversation back in the Antarctic when Azarwrath had admitted he wanted to be with a powerful sorcerer rather than settling for someone like Kiadarsa. Trip suspected the soulblade would prefer it if he always strode around with his aura on full display, with people drawn to him. Or drawn to serve him. Trip couldn't imagine anything that would make him more uncomfortable.

He thought Azarwrath might comment, but maybe the soulblade didn't hear his thoughts. He was trying to keep them locked down so the sorceress wouldn't hear them either.

I'm glad you came. Grekka patted the empty seat next to her.

It was positioned scant inches from hers instead of on the other side of the table, the way others in the restaurant were arranged. Lovely. They could sit side by side and gaze out on the city while she fondled his leg.

I almost didn't. Your friend tortured me last night, you know. And you tried to kill someone I care about. Trip adjusted the chair as he sat down, putting a few more inches between them.

A misunderstanding.

Grekka waved over a waiter, one who'd been standing a few feet away and looking in her direction. Was his only job to serve her table? She pointed to the empty glass in front of Trip.

Do you find it unfortunate when your misunderstandings result in people being tortured? Trip watched as the waiter filled his glass to the brim with red wine. Imbibing alcohol seemed a particularly unwise thing to do while drinking with the enemy.

Grekka must not have agreed because she took a deep swallow from her glass to finish off the wine in it. The waiter filled it again before stepping away to a discreet distance.

That was Bhodian who had you tortured, she pointed out. It seemed she wanted to have their entire conversation telepathically. Maybe because people were still craning their necks around, looking at Trip.

After your animal menagerie forced me into a trap.

His idea, not mine. And I charged him for the use of my animals, as any good businesswoman would.

Grekka waved her hand toward the people eyeing Trip, and he sensed her exuding power, convincing them to find their own tables more interesting. He didn't think she had a lot of dragon blood, but she'd clearly had training and knew how to use what she had.

Aren't you partners and lovers? Trip asked bluntly.

Of course we're partners. And we share our beds occasionally. But not exclusively. I take other lovers. She smiled at him, and again, he felt her trying to compel him to come closer.

When he didn't comply or respond, she scooted her own chair closer to his. He thought about scooting farther away, but what a ridiculous game that would be, of him inching away and her inching after him, all around the table. Besides, he needed to take charge if he wanted information.

Even though Azarwrath's words about dominance made Trip think about dogs raising their hackles and marking territory, he wouldn't be surprised if that was essentially how it worked in the world of the magical.

Tell me, he thought, gazing into Grekka's eyes and trying to compel her.

Belatedly, he realized he should have been more specific. What if she told him all about the lovers she'd taken in her life? She had to be fifty years old, but she was still a beautiful woman, and he had no doubt there had been many.

I admit, I was happy enough to lend Bhodian the animals, though I worried you would kill some of them. And you did. *You and that snooping wench with the* chapaharii *sword.* Grekka's eyes narrowed.

The snooping was my *idea,* Trip thought coldly, feeling a surge of protectiveness toward Rysha. This woman had hurt Rysha—*shot* her—and forced her bear to attack her. That had almost *killed* her.

Forgive me. Grekka dropped her head and rested her hand on Trip's thigh.

At first, he thought it was a sexual advance, but her shoulders shrank, and she truly seemed to be seeking forgiveness rather than trying to seduce him. Had she sensed his anger? He was being careful to keep his thoughts in the bank vault, but maybe his aura had changed somehow.

Forgive me, Grekka repeated, *but after you came without invitation and snooped in my office, I thought you deserved Bhodian's ire. If that involved torture and death, so be it. I've not risen to such a powerful position by being afraid of killing those who stand against me. I believed you some business enemy's spy or, when we researched you, even Iskandian spies. I thought your king or someone high up in your government might have an interest in my business, that perhaps I'd crossed your people somehow, and that I needed to show strength so they wouldn't think me an easy target. That is the way of things here. You must be strong. Always.*

Trip tried to sense if she was telling the truth or if this was some act to distract him. She had her thoughts walled off, just as he did, but he found he could glimpse fragments, images of that night and what she had been thinking.

Her hand stirred on his leg, and another thought slipped free of her wall. She was enjoying the feel of his thigh muscle and wondering what it would be like to sleep with someone so powerful, the son of a dragon. What magic they might experience in bed together.

He flushed with embarrassment and discomfort, and threw out an image of her pulling her hand back. She did so, so swiftly she smacked her knuckles on the table hard enough to scrape skin away and draw blood. He winced. He hadn't meant for her to hurt herself. Seven gods, he was awful at this.

Forgetting his earlier vow to leave the wine alone, he took a long drink.

Grekka sat quietly in her chair, her head down, her hands in her lap. Trip glimpsed the waiter looking at her, a shocked expression on his face. This wasn't how her dinner dates usually went, the man's reaction said.

Trip sensed the lion atop the rooftop stirring and wondering if it should leap to its handler's defense. But Grekka must have ordered it to stand down, for the great cat sat on its haunches again.

I apologize, Trip told her after he collected himself. *But I have someone already.*

Someone who liked to sleep with him because of who he was, not *what* he was.

I see. Did she? She sounded puzzled, as if she couldn't imagine it. Or imagine having only one lover, perhaps.

I am not a spy, Trip thought. *A personal quest brought me to this continent, and I came to this city because I was looking for a friend.*

Her gaze lifted to his. *Dreyak.*

Yes. Did you kill him?

Grekka was so surprised, she gripped the table, as if to keep herself from falling out of the chair. *Of course not. His death may have been my fault, but I assure you, I didn't intend for it to happen.* She looked away, out across the rooftop and toward the city. *I should not have met with him openly where others could see. There are no innocents in this city. It has a million eyes, all for hire.* She looked toward him. *It was Bhodian mentioning that you claimed friendship with him that made me realize I might have made a mistake. It seemed unlikely since you're an Iskandian, and he was always loyal to the emperor and Cofahre. For reasons I can't fathom.* She snorted and sipped from her glass.

Explain.

He was my son.

This time, Trip was the one who almost fell out of his seat. *What? How—I mean, I know how, but we're a long way from Cofahre.*

People do move occasionally. Grekka arched an eyebrow, but her humor didn't last long. She gazed out on the city again as she continued on. *More than thirty years ago now, I was one of Emperor Salatak's concubines. It was neither prestigious nor enjoyable, but I was young, and I believed differently then. I thought it was an honor to have been chosen, especially when Salatak came to see me regularly. He was moderately handsome back then. But even in my idealistic youth, I was there for more than honor and definitely for more than him, though I admit I had a silly infatuation with him. There was a woman in his court who taught magic to those with dragon blood. Salatak hated her and hated everything to do with magic, but his mother was still alive then, and she was the one who thought it would be wise to have all those with power trained. He didn't know I had power, but I did. I approached her, and during the days, when my services were not needed, I received my training. It was worth staying for that reason alone.*

Trip nodded, though he hadn't meant for her to tell him her whole story. He needed to be careful when he was exuding his aura and making suggestions to people.

We took measures to ensure we didn't become pregnant, but accidents happened. Even though Salatak had three wives during his rule, and he legitimized all the children produced in those marriages, he would not give anything to the bastards born in his harem. He magnanimously told me he wouldn't have my son killed, and that my boy would even be raised to serve his legitimate children. That's when some of Salatak's allure wore off for me, but that isn't what made him an enemy to me.

Though she still gazed toward the city, her jaw clenched, and her eyes grew hard. *He found out I was training with Lakrai and that I had dragon blood. Not only did he refuse to touch me after that; he ordered me to leave his court. And to leave my son, Dreyak, with him. I fought that and tried to sneak away with him in the night, but his bodyguards caught me. They ripped Dreyak from my arms and threw me out of the palace. All I could hear was my baby crying as they carried him back inside in their oversized calloused hands.*

I'm sorry. Trip felt sympathetic even though the woman had caused him so much trouble and had hurt Rysha. He had to admit that he could understand how, from her point of view, they had been the intruders. The enemies. If he had walked up, asked her about Dreyak, and introduced himself as a friend of his, they might have avoided so much. Instead, he'd made assumptions and jumped to conclusions.

Grekka didn't seem to hear his comment. *I left,* she went on, *since I had little other choice. At the time, I thought I would one day get Dreyak back and raise him outside of the palace and far from Salatak's influence, but that was before he started trying to have me assassinated.*

What? Why?

I don't know if someone turned his ear or if he decided this on his own, but he believed that I would use my magical powers to seek revenge on him, that I might even try to assassinate him. He believed he had to have me killed first, or that's what I was led to understand from the women back at the palace that I maintained contact with after I left. Grekka shook her head. *He sent four different assassins after me. If not for the small amount of power I claim, I would have died to their daggers. I'm fortunate that they weren't his best assassins. He either didn't think he needed his best to kill me, or he wasn't willing to spend that much money to pay the best.*

Either way, I believed I had no choice but to leave the empire and hope he didn't care enough to have me hunted to the far ends of Linora. I ended up here, thousands of miles from his influence, and in what I suspected was the last place he would look. As far as I know, no assassins have sought me out here, but I never forgave him for what he'd done. I vowed that, if I ever got a chance, I would drive a dagger into his heart.

Some people forgive or forget. I do neither. Of course, I never thought I would get a chance to go through with my vow. Grekka looked at Trip for the first time in several minutes. *But then the Iskandians kidnapped him and exiled him to an island not far from here, if you can imagine that.*

That was before I was out of the flight academy, Trip shared, not wanting her to believe he'd had anything to do with that, though she didn't seem displeased by it. If anything, there was a smug smile on her lips.

Was it? I'd heard they had a dragon along and ten sorcerers.

Trip snorted. There weren't ten sorcerers in all of Iskandia. He wasn't sure if Sardelle had been on that mission or not. But she would be at most one.

I didn't care how it was done, Grekka continued. *Just that, for whatever reason, your king decided to store Salatak here. Within my reach.* Her fingers tightened around the stem of her wine glass. *At first, I merely sent people to observe. He was marooned on an island, so it wasn't easy to spy on him, but he had Iskandian guards, and some were willing to talk for the right amount of money. Now and then, supply ships came in. He was well cared for, though certainly not to the degree he was accustomed. I doubt your king felt he needed a harem to attend his needs.*

Trip had no idea how monarchs and emperors were usually treated when foisted into exile, but he didn't imagine that harems were typical.

While my people were observing him over the months, it occurred to me to be mature and magnanimous and let Salatak live. Then I acquired this dagger from a colleague. It seemed a perfect weapon to use on him, a magical blade once made for a preeminent assassin during the First Dragon Era. For the first time, Grekka touched its hilt, acknowledging the dagger's presence in her boot. *Even so, I was still of a split mind when I had my people sail me out to his little island. By then, there were only two Iskandian guards with him. It was easy to knock them out and slip into the stone cottage he'd been given near a lighthouse. I walked right up to him, startling the piss out of him. I was surprised he recognized me after all those years. Decades.*

She loosened her grip on her wine glass. *If he'd asked for forgiveness or even acknowledged that he'd overreacted and made a mistake, I might have let him live, however pathetic his life in exile was. He was, however inadvertently, the reason I became the woman I am.* She waved toward the city and the harbor, perhaps to encompass her barge and all her business dealings. *Had he been smart, he might have even asked me to help him escape the island and take him back to his homeland. But I think that year in exile had broken him. It was a perfectly hospitable prison, but a prison is still a prison in the end. To have no freedom and nowhere to go after having been the most powerful ruler in the world? Yes, it broke him. And all he did was growl at me and spit his bitterness. He accused me of being the one who helped the Iskandians capture him.*

What did you do? Trip asked, though he knew the answer already. He remembered Dreyak saying that he'd sensed Salatak's death a couple of years earlier and had come out here to confirm it, to bring back some proof of it, so that his people would allow Prince Varlok to finally and officially be named emperor.

I killed him. He said something snide and that I'd never use the dagger on him, that I wouldn't have the guts to kill him with a real weapon instead of meddling and conniving with magic. Grekka drew the slender dagger and laid it on the table, the blade simple and unadorned. *He didn't know it was a magical dagger, not that its magic has anything to do with making killing easier. But I didn't need it to be easy. He lunged and tried to knock the blade from my hand. I blocked him and stabbed him in the side. When he tumbled to the floor, screaming and cursing my name, I slashed his throat and finished him. I can only imagine what the Iskandian guards thought when they woke up and walked in on that. I was long gone by then, the vow I'd made twenty-five years earlier fulfilled.*

So, Dreyak came here, seeking you out? He must not have known you did it because it was still a mystery to him when last we talked.

He didn't know I did it, and he had no idea I was here. He didn't have any memory of me, of anything but being raised by surrogate mothers in the emperor's court. Grekka stared bleakly at her wine glass. *I know he was only a year old when I left, and I shouldn't have expected anything else, but I suppose I thought his blood might somehow sense my blood. The dragon part of it, anyway. And maybe he did sense it. When I learned he was in the city and sought him out—we had dinner in this very restaurant—he listened to what I said. He didn't seem sure if he should believe me or not, about any of it, but my story did match up with what he'd sensed from afar about his father's death.*

Grekka lifted a shoulder. *I offered to bring him the dagger, since I knew it would show the death of the last person it had killed.* She touched the blade. *I hadn't thought to dig it out and bring it to our meeting then. I should have. If I had, maybe he would have come back to my barge and stayed with me instead of returning to whatever room in the city he'd gotten. I found out about his death the next morning. I believe Dreyak was targeted right after meeting with me, that someone overheard us... that someone learned he was important to me. You, Captain Trip, should be thankful I'm speaking to you telepathically so nobody can overhear this time. I didn't want to be so intimate with Dreyak when he didn't yet believe we were related, but... it was a mistake.*

Who killed him? Trip asked.

An enemy of mine. I have many of them. I received a letter the next morning, bragging about stealing my son from me. I have vowed to kill the man who sent it, as I am positive I know who it was. And as you can see, I fulfill my vows. I was considering using this blade, but I believe I shall give it to you.

To me?

If you are a pilot as well as a sorcerer, it should be easy for you to get the blade to the Cofah imperial court.

Easy? Trip couldn't think of anything less easy. He would be shot for sure. All right, he and Azarwrath could create a barrier and prevent that fate, as long as they were prepared, but by now, Prince Varlok might have ten dragons working with him and nesting on the rooftops of his palace.

Trip didn't voice his concerns, telepathically or otherwise, but she must have read his dubious expression.

If you are Dreyak's friend, then you should do this for him. I cannot return to the empire. Though Salatak is dead, the warrant on my head remains. It is the one place in the world I do not do business. But with your power, taking the dagger to Varlok would be simple enough. He will know what to do with it.

There is something that was taken from me. You mentioned it when you spoke to me last night. Trip touched his temple. *I'm not leaving this continent until I find it.*

The stasis chamber. Yes, Bhodian has kept a few things from me, but I tend to catch up with his secrets sooner or later. He doesn't wear that amulet all the time. I know where the device is. I can get it for you.

When? Trip tried to keep his tone casual, but he couldn't help but lean toward her, wanting to shake the answer out of her. *We leave soon.*

I can get it by this afternoon. Providing you do this favor for me.

Trip leaned back in the chair. As he'd said, he couldn't leave without the baby girl, but could he make this promise to Grekka? He had planned to return promptly home, not to visit yet another continent. His people needed him in the air and fighting dragons, especially since he'd failed to secure one as an ally. They wouldn't let him wander off again as soon as he got back.

Touch the blade, Grekka said. *You'll see why it can provide the proof that Dreyak sought.*

Trip hesitated. A part of him still suspected there might be some trap in place for him here, even though his senses told him that Grekka had been telling the truth.

Touch it, Telryn, Azarwrath said. *I recognize it, and it is what she says, an assassin's blade. There were many of them in my day.*

Trip laid a finger on the dagger.

An intense vision washed over him, almost stealing his awareness of the restaurant and those around him. Instead, he was in a simple stone cottage, the sea breeze warm and salty, the furnishings simple but clean and comfortable. Two people stood in the main room, Emperor Salatak—Trip recognized him from the newspapers—and the woman now sitting with him. The emperor's death played out exactly as she'd described, except that the blade flared with a strange black light as it sank in, and it seemed to relish drinking the life force of its victim. The emperor died with Grekka watching him, her face grim rather than pleased, and then the vision went dark.

Trip pulled his finger back, awareness of his surroundings returning. He was glad nobody had attacked him during that interlude.

The dagger will retain that vision and share it with others until it takes another life, Grekka explained. *It was designed that way so that an assassin could return from a mission and prove to his employer that he'd succeeded.* She pulled out the sheath for the dagger, slipped it inside, then pushed both toward him. *Take the blade. Take it to Varlok.* She squinted at him. *Will you do that?*

She didn't attempt to manipulate him again, but Trip did sense her trying to read him, to see if she could trust him to do this thing. It meant more to her than she'd revealed. She had only just been reunited with Dreyak when he'd been killed, and it had been because of her, because he'd come to see her. Prince Varlok didn't mean much to her, though she remembered seeing Salatak's eldest son around the palace when she'd lived there, and he hadn't been a horrible young man. This was about Dreyak, though. She felt she owed him.

Trip picked up the dagger. *I can't promise that I will go personally, but I will make sure it gets to Prince Varlok one way or another. The weapon handily shows that Iskandia had nothing to do with the emperor's death, other than Angulus exiling him in the first place, so it would be good for my country if the Cofah knew this. I would do it only because I knew Dreyak, and he helped us with a difficult mission, but now you can see that I have multiple motivations.*

Good. I will make sure your stasis chamber is delivered to the waterfront this afternoon. Grekka signaled the waiter, as if to say the conversation was done, though she did add, *I wouldn't want piddling Iskandians to get credit for Salatak's death under any circumstances.*

Trip snorted.

"Now," she said, speaking aloud as the waiter approached, this time with plates of food instead of wine, "let us sit in companionable silence and enjoy our meals."

Finally, Azarwrath thought, and Trip felt the soulblade stretching his senses toward the plates, examining what they were being served. *I thought we would never get to dine. On a chef's fare. Delightful.*

"And then we shall discuss this odd notion you have of only keeping one lover." Grekka smiled slyly at him. "That is very un-dragon-like, you know."

She probably meant it as a joke, but Trip thought of all the strange half-dragon babies in those stasis chambers, and he shuddered at the idea of being *dragon-like*.

CHAPTER 15

R YSHA SQUINTED AT THE FADED words on the journal page, wondering why an expedition leader had thought pencil was an acceptable medium for making records. Her dim surroundings didn't make reading any easier. Too bad the first mate had shooed his passengers below decks, saying his men needed the space up top for cleaning the steamer and loading coal for their journey. The tiny porthole letting light into the crate-, barrel-, and hammock-filled cargo hold was on the small and stingy side.

She supposed she should be happy there *was* a porthole, at least on this end of the hold. After being ushered below, Rysha had left Kaika in the dark nook their group had been assigned, feeling guilty about foisting stasis-chamber guard duty on her again, but Rysha needed the light.

She had already solved her diving equations, and now she was sketching alternative ideas. The idea of sending Trip—or herself— down to the bottom without any kind of protection worried her. There would be more water pressure down there, and she hadn't read of any accounts of humans going deeper than those Jonga Junga divers, even in diving suits with oxygen tubes that ran back to the surface. Though she believed breathing while underwater and under pressure would cause more problems than simply holding one's breath, if one could hold it long enough.

Rysha would prefer to come up with another plan so they wouldn't have to take the risk. If Trip could sense exactly where Dorfindral was, couldn't they lower a chain or a cord with a grasping hook on the end of it? True, it would be hard to manipulate from so far up, and she couldn't imagine how they could even do so if it was at the end of a two-hundred-foot chain, but with Trip's engineering expertise, it seemed plausible. More plausible than building a submarine, though if they had more time, he would probably enjoy that challenge. He'd certainly taken to creating the small locomotive that had pulled the fliers out of the magic dead zone. But that had taken three days, and he'd had more help than he would have now. Surely, a submarine would be even more complicated to build.

"I've finally found you alone," came a dry voice from behind her.

Horis? His Iskandian accent had disappeared, changing into something else, an accent that she couldn't place.

Rysha grimaced, Kaika's warning fresh on her mind. She didn't smile as she turned to face the man, not wanting to encourage him in any way.

But when their gazes met, she almost gasped. He had changed.

Oh, he looked the same, his face alluringly handsome, his eyes attractive and appealing. But they were more than that now. They were captivating. Rysha had a hard time looking away. He radiated power, the way Trip sometimes did. But even more so.

The first inkling that this might not be the real Horis Silverdale entered her mind.

"It's been irritating trying to get close to you when your guard dog hovers by your shoulder all the time," he said.

"And why do you want to get close to me?" Rysha raised her voice. "Major Kaika, are you still in the hold?"

Horis smiled, a wolfish smile, and he looked her up and down, his gaze lingering on her chest.

Unease plucked at her senses, and Rysha backed up, but she could only go a few feet before her shoulder blades hit the porthole glass. Even though Horis radiated power in a manner similar to Trip, she didn't feel drawn to him. She felt… afraid.

Major Kaika didn't answer. Rysha realized she didn't hear any voices or sounds that would indicate other people were in the hold. There had been earlier. It was a large ship with a crew of two dozen. How had Horis gotten rid of everyone on this deck?

"You took something from the dragon-rider outpost," Horis said, walking closer, his steps slow like those of a predator stalking its prey.

Rysha reached for her sword before remembering it was on the bottom of the harbor. She rested her hand on her pistol hilt instead, lifting her chin and trying to appear unafraid, even though she suspected—no, she was certain—that shooting this man—or whatever he was—would do nothing.

"An old journal that has instructions for rituals and the founding constitution for the Brotherhood of the Dragon," he said.

"Why would you care about that?" Rysha's grip tightened on the hilt as he stopped in front of her, close enough to reach out and touch her.

"The cultists have proven themselves skeptical about my right to rule over them. Their minds are easily manipulated, but even so, it would be much easier if they believed I was the one they'd waited for all this time. Agarrenon Shivar. That is what I told them, and I showed them my dragon form, a slightly more golden hue than typical, but they are skeptical, you understand. Apparently, other interlopers have tried to position themselves as one of his descendants over the years, so they're suspicious of people claiming a right to rule them. If I could not only quote from their foundational material but return the stolen tome to them, I suspect they'd more easily believe I was their rightful leader. Then they would be faithful to me even if I was away for a time and my mental influence wore off." His wolfish smile deepened.

Rysha stared at him, trying to grasp what he was saying—and if she could believe any of it. He couldn't mean...

"They were most distraught to lose their foundational book." Horis tilted his head. "Why did you steal it?"

"To study it. I intended to return it."

"It *is* fascinating reading, isn't it? I have been perusing it while it's been in your pack. Even though the true Agarrenon Shivar disappeared before my time, I find myself intrigued by the things he did, the religion he created around himself, and the humans who so willingly served him. The humans he so thoroughly enjoyed." Horis looked at her chest again, his gaze staying there this time. "It is strange. In my natural form, I have no attraction for humans, nor any interest in rutting outside of mating periods, when females in heat display themselves and make the request. Not that this happens much to bronze dragons."

His lip curled, and it slowly dawned on Rysha that Horis wasn't lying. He was *complaining*. By the gods, was he truly a dragon?

"Bronze females always seek a silver or gold mate," he explained, "so their offspring have a chance of being born with their traits. Then the status is much greater for them. Few females want to mate with bronze males, no matter how powerful we are, no matter how cunning. But right now, I find that I do not care much. Perhaps Agarrenon Shivar was wiser than his contemporaries gave him credit for, to create his own religion, his own worshippers, and to have females whenever he wished." Horis licked his lips. "I find my arousal is frequent in this form. I even wake with the desire to mate. It is strange, but I have also found it satisfying thus far. Pleasurable in a way that mating with other dragons is not."

He reached toward her breast.

Rysha couldn't back up any farther, but she whipped up an arm block and attempted to stomp on his instep. She managed the block, but then a wall of power slammed into her. It plastered her against the hull, her head clunking the glass of the porthole. If only it were large enough that she could escape through it.

"Major Kaika!" she yelled again.

"Your friend with the sword will not hear you. Nobody will. I've created a sphere of silence around us. So I can get the journal." He pointed toward the pack slumped against the hull by her feet, but he made no move to open it. "And so I can sate myself upon you."

She growled and tried to spit at him, but her tongue was as restrained by his power as the rest of her. The way her arms were flattened to the hull made it impossible to punch, impossible to gouge his eyes out as she desired.

She should have listened to Kaika and stayed far away from the man. Why had they even let him come along? Had he used his mind powers to manipulate her? Kaika should have been immune with the sword, but Rysha was vulnerable right now. And Trip—how had he not known? How had the *soulblades* not known?

"Bronze dragons are crafty," Horis said, grinning and stepping forward. He lifted his hand, and she could neither shift her body nor block him as he grasped her breast. "We are used to hiding what we are. You do not want to mate with me?" He cocked his head, stroking her. "This is surprising. Thus far, the females have been eager to please me. It has been extremely satisfying. I understand Agarrenon Shivar more each day, and I've vowed to take what he created. He is long gone and cannot object. All the females here will be mine whenever I wish."

"Lucky them. Just take the journal, you asshole," Rysha bit out, forcing the words around her poorly working tongue. She was horrified at how this had gone bad so quickly, and terrified because, with all the training she'd endured to enter the army and then the elite troops, she couldn't do a damn thing to fight the magical power smashing her against the hull.

"I will take you first. I have admired that you are a warrior woman and not so malleable. Your spirit is appealing. I long to take the other one, too, but her foul sword guards her from my wiles."

"*Wiles*? Is that what you call forcing yourself on a woman?"

"Hm, yes, it is rather unappealing to use force. I wish you to wrap your legs around me and groan and beg as the other females did. There need not be force, only pleasure." He dragged a finger around her breast, making her body tighten and tingle, responding to his magic, not to him.

She gritted her teeth and closed her eyes, not wanting to respond and not wanting a damn thing to do with him. What would Trip think if she had sex with some megalomaniacal dragon? And why hadn't she gone with him? This asshole dragon had already admitted he wouldn't have tried this if Trip had been around.

Kiss me, the dragon spoke into her mind.

"Screw you."

That too. He chuckled and pressed his body against hers, his lips coming down on hers, hard and eager. She was still flattened to the hull with little control, but she managed to bite his lip. He chuckled again. *You will succumb. Once you've known a dragon as a lover, you'll want no other. You'll wish to be my female and mine alone. You'll—*

He spun away from her, the force disappearing even more quickly than it had come.

A shadow lunged in from beside Horis. Kaika. Eryndral blazed intense green in her hands.

She leaped past a hammock and swung at Horis's head.

He was fast and would have ducked but Rysha kicked him in the ass as hard as she could. He pitched forward, and the sword sank into the top of his head.

He roared and flung himself at Kaika, moving with blazing speed. She tried to dodge, but grew tangled in the hammock. He caught her with a glancing blow, enough to knock her head back into a support post.

That didn't keep her from whipping Eryndral across in front of her. Horis had started to lunge after her, but he leaped back, landing in a crouch.

Rysha yanked her pistol free and fired. She hoped he wouldn't have his defenses up, that her bullet might slip through. But it clanged off, as if he were made from metal instead of flesh.

Kaika regained her balance and stabbed at him, a mix of feints and determined lunges meant to skewer him. His reflexes were fast, but he had no weapons, nothing to parry with. He sprang back, and Rysha thought Kaika might catch up with him, might drive that blade through his chest.

But metal screeched right beside them, and one of the support posts tore free from the ceiling. It toppled toward Kaika.

"Look out!" Rysha barked, grabbing Kaika as she jumped backward. Rysha pulled anyway, wanting to make sure Kaika cleared the post.

It slammed to the deck, tearing two hammocks free from the ceiling along the way. Kaika barely seemed to notice that she'd almost been flattened. She snarled, leaped over the fallen post, and landed in a crouch, Eryndral's green light filling the hold.

The light, however, landed on nothing. Horis was gone.

Rysha slumped back against the hull, lifting a hand to her face to wipe the taint of the jerk's mouth from hers. Her hand was shaking. Her whole body was. She couldn't believe how close she'd come to being forced against her will, to being violated by a gods-cursed dragon.

"You all right?" Kaika looked at her but kept the sword out, pointed toward the stairs the dragon must have fled up.

"Yeah," Rysha croaked, though she wanted to say no. She felt disgusting all over after that, and more than ever, she lamented that Dorfindral was at the bottom of the harbor.

"I think he went up, but we better check on the stasis chambers."

Rysha nodded, grabbed her pack, and holstered her pistol, for all the good it had done. "Right behind you."

"I knew that bastard was trouble. He's a sorcerer, right? Eryndral gave me a little buzz when I first saw him in the tunnel, but Trip was there, too, so I wasn't sure the complaint wasn't about him. And then the sword's objection disappeared completely. Do you think Horis knows the *chapaharii* command words? I bet he does. He probably transmitted them telepathically."

"Probably. He said he was cunning." Rysha snorted. "Also that he's a dragon, not a sorcerer. And definitely not the real Horis Silverdale. He must have read my mind and plucked out someone to emulate who was familiar to me but not *too* familiar." She wagered Moe Zirkander wasn't anywhere nearby, either, that the dragon had used his name to make her more likely to want to keep him around.

Judging by the cursing that Kaika emitted, she agreed with Rysha's conclusions.

Rysha was relieved. She felt like a fool for having been pinned up against the wall and manhandled—dragon-handled, damn it—but she would have felt even worse if the others didn't believe her, didn't believe that she'd been helpless because her foe had been too powerful.

"That's a relief," Kaika said when they reached the other side of the cargo hold. "They look like they're still intact. Given how many people have been trying to destroy them, I thought Horis might want them dead too."

"He might." Rysha peered into one of the chambers, at a tiny boy baby locked in the gel-like substance inside. She had no idea how to tell if the devices had been tampered with, but as Kaika had noted, the little indicators on the outside still glowed, seemingly to suggest power was flowing to the occupants, keeping them alive. "He just wanted something else more."

"You?" Kaika arched her eyebrows.

"No, the journal I took from the outpost. I should have guessed. Twice, he suggested I should open my pack so he could examine my books. I thought he wanted the *other* one."

"Did you give it to him? I happily would have."

"No. I probably would have, too, to be honest, but he, uh, got distracted." Rysha shivered at the memory of his hand groping her breast, of being able to do nothing to stop it. It had been even worse when he'd started using his magic and making her body respond. Seven gods, would she have willingly had sex with him eventually?

Kaika grunted. "Maybe they get as stupid as whatever creatures they shape-shift into when they do that."

"As affected by hormones and instincts, anyway," Rysha murmured. "They needn't worry about reprisal, so they must feel they can do whatever they want with impunity."

"If he tries that again, I'll impune the hells out of him." Kaika raised Eryndral. "What do you think happens to a dragon if you cut off his flesh pole when he's in human form?"

"The history books I read didn't cover that."

"A pity."

A yell drifted down from the deck above.

Kaika eyed the stairs, but then looked at Rysha, her pack, and the stasis chambers. "Eryndral is letting me know there's a dragon and that it wants to slay it. And I want to slay it too. But I'm afraid that if I leave you here alone, or leave the stasis chambers here alone, he'll come back. For you *and* them."

Rysha wondered if Kaika's suspicion about someone wanting the stasis chambers destroyed altogether was right. How long had this bronze dragon been here, influencing the cultists? Had he arrived after she and the others had explored the outpost and taken the journal? Or had he already been here then? Maybe he was the reason the cultists wanted Trip dead and had been calling him a usurper. Maybe the bronze dragon knew he carried the blood of Agarrenon Shivar and feared the cultists would consider him a worthy successor. Or maybe he worried one of the babies inside would grow up and become a successor. At the least, they might have the power to see through the facade the bronze dragon had to be creating, his trick to get the cultists to believe *he* was Agarrenon Shivar.

Rysha touched the side of one of the devices, again peering in at the tiny baby. How awful to be so young—not even six months, she wagered—and to have so many people vying for him. Some wanting to use him, some wanting to kill him.

"It's not fair," Rysha murmured.

"Dealing with dragons never seems to be," Kaika said.

Another yell came from above decks, this time followed by a scream. Rysha grimaced. She had a feeling the injury the bronze dragon had received from Kaika's blade had only incensed it. It would be back, and it would get what it wanted.

"You should go up there and see if you can find a way to fight him, ma'am," Rysha made herself say, though she wanted nothing more than to ask Kaika to stay with her and the babies, to make sure they were protected. "And if there isn't a way, if he's not coming within the sword's range, you should go get Trip. I'm sure as soon as he knows about this, he'll rush down to help."

Kaika glanced toward the stairs, back to Rysha, and back to the stairs again, clearly torn.

"Go," Rysha urged. "I'll sit here and see if I can figure out a way to get my sword off the harbor bottom while you're gone."

Kaika snorted. "*That* would be helpful." She moved toward the stairs. "I'll just go up and check, see if he's up there. I'm not going way into the city to fetch Trip while you're down here unprotected, but if our pretty boy Horis is on deck, I'm going to shove this sword down his throat."

"Don't forget to properly attend to his flesh pole," Rysha called after her, forcing herself to sound brave, even though she was still shaky and afraid.

"Flesh pole, then throat," Kaika's voice drifted back down. "Got it."

Rysha slumped back against the stasis chambers. She wanted to do what she'd promised Kaika she would do, but her brain felt frazzled. How was she supposed to figure out a way to retrieve something two hundred feet under water? It wasn't even straight down. She would have to swim or sail over near the barges and take some guesses as to where it had gone down, especially if the barges had shifted their positions since that night.

You think about too many things, female, a voice sounded in her head. Horis, or whatever his name was, and his accent from another place and another time.

I am Xandyrothol, the dragon said, *and I shall have that journal, if I must tear that ship to pieces in order to get it. Spare your friends' lives by bringing it up here and tossing it to me.*

Tossing it? Had he switched into his dragon form?

Is the journal all you want? Rysha wished she could believe that were true. If it were, she would willingly toss it to the dragon and leave these people to deal with him and the cult. Half the population seemed to be *in* the cult.

I will still accept you if you wish to toss yourself to me as well. He chuckled into her mind at the same time as a great wrenching sound came from above. Was he attacking the ship? *Fortunately, changing into my natural form took away that pesky animal arousal, and I can think more clearly, but I would gladly save you for later.*

I hear getting hit in the head with swords takes away arousals too.

Perhaps. Another chuckle. *Mine was quite strong and sizable. Is that not what human females desire?*

I desire you to leave this ship alone. If I bring up the journal, will you promise to do so?

She couldn't believe she was trying to negotiate with a dragon. He could tell her anything, and how would she know if he was lying? It wasn't as if she could look into his eyes to gauge his trustworthiness.

Of course, he purred into her mind. *Bring it now.*

Though he spoke softly, the words rang in her mind like a command, a command that could not be resisted. She caught herself taking several steps before she realized she'd done so.

Growling, she gripped a post to stop herself, then stalked back to her position by the stasis chambers. She couldn't trust the dragon, and she couldn't leave the babies unprotected.

You can trust me, he promised, purring again, and she could feel the power of those words, the way she wanted to obey them. It was as if her brain existed outside of her body, and her body kept trying to do as the dragon wished, to walk up those stairs with the journal in hand.

If you fear for those babies, you need not, the dragon added. *If you swear to take them to another country, I will stop trying to harm them. It was only when I believed they would be raised here and that these humans might consider them worthy heirs to their sire's cult that I worried. As if half-dragon bastards could be worthier than I. Xandyrothol the Great.*

Xandyrothol. It sounded like the hoity-toity name that a pharmacist would give to a cough syrup in the hope that he could charge more for it.

Promise me you'll remove them from these shores and give me the journal, and I'll bother you no more.

Rysha closed her eyes. Even her brain was tempted this time. It seemed a logical request. But it chilled her that the dragon had admitted to being behind at least some of the attempts to destroy the stasis chambers, sending his ill-won minions after them. How could a decent person—a decent being of any kind—order babies slain?

Come, Xandyrothol growled into her mind, a hint of impatience accompanying the word.

A boom rang out in the distance. One of the cannons that defended the harbor?

Rysha clenched her jaw, reminded that she and Kaika weren't alone here, not if the dragon had revealed himself. Everyone in the city would fear him and want him gone. Even his own minions, most likely. Would they be disappointed when their returned god turned out to be a lowly bronze dragon instead of the gold their founders had written about?

Lowly! I am Xandyrothol the Great. I fooled you, and I shall fool them. And I shall take everything I want, including all the humans here. They shall worship me and serve me for all eternity.

Another boom sounded. Even as Rysha hoped cannonballs were slamming into the dragon's butt, a massive squeal of metal and a tearing sound came from the hull right next to her.

She jumped back as talons pierced the side of the ship, pinpricks of light piercing the darkness.

Rysha's instincts yelled for her to run, but she couldn't leave the babies undefended. She pointed her pistol at those talons, even though it was a useless gesture. She would die here, but what else could she do?

CHAPTER 16

T RIP HADN'T IMAGINED HIMSELF ACCOMPANYING Grekka home after their lunch, but they were both going toward the harbor, so he found himself sitting in a steam carriage across from her as the driver navigated the bumpy streets of Lagresh. Fortunately, Grekka hadn't put any more effort into seducing him, or whatever she'd been trying to do. After she had given him the dagger, she'd seemed satisfied that she'd gotten what she wanted. He had also done his best to dampen down his aura, since seduction attempts happened far more often when he was using his magic or showing off his power. His dragonness.

Claws scraped on the roof of the carriage.

Grekka smiled fondly upward. Trip was glad the winged lion was riding up there rather than in the carriage with them. It was not a small creature, even with its wings folded against its body.

"Ma'am?" the driver's voice came through a horn mounted in the corner. He sat atop an exterior bench in the front, steering the carriage and also keeping the fire burning to heat the boiler. "There's a road block ahead of us. Shall I turn around and take a different route?"

A low growl drifted down from the rooftop.

Grekka's eyes narrowed. "What *kind* of road block?"

Instead of looking out the window, Grekka gazed upward, her eyes growing distant.

Assuming she was checking with her senses, Trip did the same, though he didn't yet feel suspicious. He assumed that any road block would be a result of the block-wide pit in the middle of the city that had been created earlier. Maybe the driver hadn't heard about it yet and hadn't known to go around.

But when he stretched out with his senses, he realized they were several blocks from the pit. Something else had happened at the intersection ahead of the steam carriage. Water overflowed from a broken fountain in the center, and mobile obstacles had been placed to force traffic to detour around.

"There aren't any enforcers up there," Grekka said, her eyes closed to slits. "Usually, there would be for something like that."

Trip wasn't sure how she could tell without opening the door and looking at uniforms, or the lack of uniforms, on the people out there. He sensed several armed men.

In white, Azarwrath said. Apparently, the soulblade had the ability to sense colors and clothing styles. Trip would have to work on that.

Two in white, Jaxi said, *and others in simple local clothing, but all armed. I believe these may be more of your Brotherhood friends.*

Friends, right.

"We may want to avoid that intersection and go around," Trip said aloud.

He didn't want to explain to Grekka that the Brotherhood of the Dragon had been attempting to kill him since he stepped foot on the continent, though she might already know, given that she'd learned his and Rysha's names and ranks easily enough.

"Ma'am?" the driver prompted. "Two armed men are heading this way. Not enforcers."

"I know, but the alternate routes down to the harbor are also blocked. It seems a pit has appeared in the middle of the city, utterly *destroying* some of those routes." Grekka quirked an eyebrow at Trip.

"You don't seem surprised about that," Trip said.

"News travels fast."

"Do you know who was responsible?" It occurred to him that he might be able to get some information from her, now that they were allies of a sort.

"Don't you?"

"I saw cultists, but I don't know who sent them or why they want me dead."

"The *cult* sent them. It's been active of late, since their dragon god has presumably returned."

"*What?*" Trip gripped the bench he sat on.

Grekka held up a finger. "Davors, attempt to drive through the men and the intersection. I paid for an armored carriage for a reason."

A roar came from above, and Trip sensed the lion springing toward the approaching men. They yelled and veered in different directions. The lion chased after one. Unfortunately, more men approached.

"Shoot anyone who deters you, Davors," Grekka added. "My crest is on the side. They should know better."

"Yes, ma'am," the driver responded, a hint of glee in his voice.

The carriage surged forward, and Trip's back thumped against the bench cushions.

"I believe the dragon's name is Agarrenon Shivar," Grekka said, her expression not changing as the carriage accelerated, thumped against something, and lurched from side to side.

A gun fired, a bullet clanging off the side by the door.

"That's impossible," Trip said, flattening himself against the cushions so he wouldn't be a visible target to someone shooting through the window. The metal frame of the carriage was likely bulletproof, as Grekka had suggested, but the windows appeared to be made of glass. Thick glass, but glass, nonetheless. "He's dead. I saw his bones. He's been dead a long, *long* time."

Grekka twitched a shoulder. "Then someone else has taken his place and convinced those fools to follow. Someone or something."

"Something? A dragon?"

"It could be, or perhaps a human is seeking to trick them. However, in more than twenty years, I've never seen the cult this active in the city. I think it would take more than a human. With hundreds of dragons now in the world, I imagine they're all fighting for territory, seeking to carve out a niche for themselves. It would be handy for one to find a cult, an outpost, and a whole religion already established and waiting for a dragon to appear."

Trip thought of Bhrava Saruth and his claims to be a dragon god. He would probably love having a cult. But it couldn't be he. Trip hadn't sensed his arrival in the city, nor had he detected any other dragons around. And he should have if they were within fifty miles.

"I haven't sensed any dragons here," he said.

"Nor have I, but dragons can be crafty."

Trip remembered the silver dragons in the Antarctic that had shape-shifted into pigeons. They'd had their auras dampened down so much that he'd barely been able to pick them out of the flock.

More guns fired outside, and two of the carriage wheels rose up on something, pitching Trip against the side. A boom erupted, rattling the windows and making the whole vehicle quake.

Trip sensed more people in the intersection now, all with rifles and pistols pointed at the carriage. And he also sensed someone with grenades. Gunshots sounded from nearby—the driver firing as he tried to navigate them through the water flooding the intersection.

The carriage ran into something, and its steam whistle blew. They stopped moving.

"Do I have to do everything myself?" Grekka growled, drawing a pistol and reaching for the door.

Trip narrowed his focus to the man with the explosives. His target was preparing a second one to throw. Trip started to channel the wind, intending to knock the weapons out of his grip, perhaps hurling them all the way to the harbor where they could splash into the water, but someone else attacked first. Fire flared around the man, and the grenades blew up in his hands.

Trip winced, glad he wasn't looking with his eyes. It was bad enough that he sensed the gory and instant death, and the injuries to the two men who had been standing close.

Enemies, Azarwrath said, and Trip realized he'd lit the fire. *Do not coddle them. They've chosen to make an enemy of you. Destroy them or let them live at your peril.*

Stunned by the harsh verdict, Trip didn't leap out of the carriage after Grekka right away.

For once, I agree with Azzy, Jaxi said. *Also, something is happening back at the steamer. I think your lieutenant and maybe your stasis siblings are in trouble.*

Trip growled, the news hardening his feelings. He sprang out of the carriage as he raised a barrier around himself.

He splashed down in ankle-deep water. The carriage had run into the fountain, and Trip saw the reason why as soon as he took a few steps away from the door. Their driver lay slumped on his side, a bullet in his forehead.

Gunshots fired, and he sensed them hitting someone else's magical barrier. Grekka's. She stood on a ledge circling the fountain and glared defiantly all around her. Though she gripped a pistol, she attacked with her mind, somehow keeping her barrier up at the same time. The water rose up in a wave and slammed into two men pointing pistols at her. It washed their weapons from their grip and toppled them onto their backsides.

Trip sensed that Grekka wasn't using a tremendous amount of power, and probably didn't have that much to draw upon, but she knew how to use what she had well.

Less subtle, Trip hurled a wave of power at a group of men on the other side of the intersection. He wasn't sure if they were all enemies, but one wore the cultist attire and pointed a rifle in his direction. The man fired, but too late. His bullet went skyward as Trip's power slammed into the group, hurling all the men down the street. They flew more than thirty feet before landing.

That reckless battle lust that always lurked within him, ready to spring to the surface and revel in fighting and defeating his enemies, threatened to burst forth and start making decisions for his conscious mind. He willed it to stay tamped down. He needed to be in full control here. He didn't want this to become a bloodbath.

With precision, Trip ripped firearms out of people's hands, using channels of air to fling them onto rooftops. If his enemies had no weapons, they couldn't attack him. They *should* run away.

Though he hadn't yet drawn the soulblades, they weren't content to hang idly from his belt. Jaxi hurled a fireball toward a rooftop on a corner where a sniper crouched, firing at Grekka. Three branches of lightning left Azarwrath's scabbard to slam into three different targets, all wearing the cultist white.

Trip lamented that the soulblades didn't seem to mind if blood was spilled.

"There he is," someone taking cover in a doorway yelled. The man pointed at Trip. "The usurper. Our god said this man wants to take his position, that he claims a right to rule us. You know that isn't true. There is only one god, Agarrenon Shivar! Kill him!"

These people are insane, Jaxi said as Trip sent a wind attack through that doorway to strike the speaker in the chest. It hurled him back into the building and hopefully into silence.

But it was too late. The cultist had already gotten his message out. All the people who'd been firing indiscriminately at the carriage, at Grekka, and at the lion that occasionally ran through the intersection, turned their focus on Trip alone.

He channeled more of his power into maintaining his barrier, worried some of those bullets might get through. He spotted another man gripping a grenade. That *definitely* might get through.

It will not, Azarwrath snarled.

A second later, the grenade blew up, still in the man's hands.

Trip looked away as pieces of his foe's body splattered the walls and against the white clothes of his overzealous comrades.

That's barbaric, Azzy, Jaxi said. *You could just wet the fuse so it won't go off.*

Trip had the sense that Azarwrath, coming from a long-past era, didn't know much about fuses or how explosives worked, just that fire would detonate them.

All Azarwrath said was, *We must make them fear us if we want to leave an impression, to teach them to leave us alone.*

More gunshots fired from the rooftops. Trip frowned and knocked the snipers from their perches, again separating them from their weapons.

I don't think these people are impressionable, Jaxi said.

Trip couldn't believe that more zealots kept running this way. Why wouldn't they flee for their lives when they saw their comrades being killed?

I think someone may be coercing them into this attack, Jaxi said. *Or perhaps coerced them earlier in the day, and it's sticking. It must be nice to have that kind of power.*

"I am not here to usurp your cult," Trip yelled, attempting to throw his own power into his voice, both to make it louder and also to give what he said more weight. He had no idea how to manipulate an entire crowd, but he did his best to make his words sound persuasive. "I am a simple traveler, and I plan to leave soon. Save your attacks for true enemies. No good will come of this."

Someone flew across the intersection and smashed head-first into the ancient warrior statue in the center of the fountain. Trip caught Grekka's grim and satisfied look. He also sensed her weariness. She was drawing on her power a great deal, both to attack and defend; her reserves had to be running low.

"Stop attacking," Trip roared, spreading his arms. "We are not your enemies. Leave us be and lower your weapons."

More gunshots fired. A lot of people were down, dead or wounded, but the holdouts continued to fire.

Jaxi, how do I make my words more powerful? Am I having any effect on them at all?

It's hard to manipulate minds that are all riled up like that, Jaxi replied, *but as I said before, I believe there's some manipulation already in effect. Manipulation powerful enough to override what you're attempting to do.*

Whose?

Jaxi hesitated. *I don't think you want to know.*

Trip waited for her to explain as he disarmed more men. He was tired of the bloodshed, especially now that he knew someone was manipulating these people and forcing them to attack, so he did his best not to do permanent damage.

Sensing Grekka's barrier flagging, Trip stepped closer to her. He pushed her defenses aside so he could extend his around her. A few more gunshots rang out. Trip focused on the snipers' rifles and bent them in half with his mind.

Frustrated beyond measure, he looked into one man's eyes and mentally yelled, *Go away!*

To his surprise, it worked this time. The man dropped his bent rifle and sprinted away.

There you go, Jaxi said. *You just have to be extremely pissed to have enough power to override a dragon.*

A dragon? Was *that* who was responsible?

I'm afraid so, Jaxi said. *I've confirmed it. As soon as you're done here, hurry down to the harbor.*

Is Rysha there?

Yes, and she's in trouble.

Trip cursed and flung a wave of power to flatten the handful of attackers left around the intersection. He didn't bother disarming them.

"I have to get to the harbor," he blurted to Grekka. "Can you defend yourself?"

"Yes." Though she appeared weary, she straightened her spine and waved for him to go.

As Trip took off, sprinting down the most direct street to the waterfront, Grekka added a few words in his head.

I doubt they'll bother me now that you're leaving the area. Expect to receive an invoice before you depart the city. For the damage to my carriage.

He snorted since it sounded like a joke, but he couldn't be certain. She was a shrewd businesswoman, after all.

As Trip tore down a street that had emptied, thanks to all the violence a few blocks back, he sent his senses ahead of himself, afraid of what he'd find.

To his surprise, he immediately felt the overpowering aura of a dragon. The great creature was flying over the harbor. Where had it come from, and how had he missed sensing it before? The skirmish at the intersection had only been a mile from the waterfront. Had he been *that* distracted?

Now, the creature's aura affected him so profoundly that he could barely focus on sensing other things. It seemed impossible to believe he hadn't noticed the dragon before if it had been anywhere near the town.

But as the water and the docks came into view, he cursed, for there was no mistaking the great golden form flying over the harbor.

That's odd, Jaxi observed. *He doesn't feel like a gold.*

Trip shook his head. He didn't care if the dragon was purple with green polka dots. All he cared was that it was diving down, its talons outstretched. And its target was the steamer where Trip had left Rysha and Kaika and his siblings.

The dragon didn't land on the upper deck where crewmen fired rifles and artillery weapons at it. Instead, it perched on the side of the ship and drove its talons into the hull, as if it meant to dig out some prize.

Fresh worry slammed into Trip's gut. Where had Kaika and Rysha put the stasis chambers? And where were *they*?

Rysha? he cried with his mind, projecting her name toward the ship, then scouring it with his senses, searching for her.

Trip! she responded as he found her, right behind the hull the dragon was trying to get through.

She was alone with the stasis chambers, alone without a weapon that could harm a dragon.

Hide, Trip ordered, his legs pumping faster and faster as he ran down the hill. *I'm coming for you!*

He wished he could turn into a falcon or a giant hawk and streak down there to attack the dragon. He concentrated, just in case he could will himself to shape change. With some of his magic, that had been all he'd needed to do to call upon it.

But nothing happened except that his lungs burned and his thighs felt like lead. Maybe shape-shifting was something one had to spend time studying, like the fish in that workbook.

I can't, Rysha thought back, a wave of bleakness accompanying the words. He got a glimpse of what she saw, of the dragon tearing open more of the side of the ship with its powerful talons. For a creature of such strength, it was as easy as opening a fish tin. *If I don't defend them, he'll destroy them easily.*

Trip sensed her standing in front of the stasis chambers and pointing a pistol at the dragon. She fired when his maw thrust through the hull, his massive teeth so close they would be able to snap down on her.

Better them than you. Rysha, I love you. Don't you dare get yourself killed.

I'll try not to. I love you too.

He wanted her to hide, to let the dragon have what it wanted if it could save her. As horrified as he was by the idea of sacrificing his siblings, he couldn't lose her.

But he sensed that she wasn't moving. She wasn't hiding. She was determined to fight to keep the dragon away from the babies.

Damn it, Rysha!

CHAPTER 17

R YSHA FIRED AT THE MASSIVE dragon maw snapping toward
her. Apparently, Xandyrothol had forgotten his interest in mating
with her. Now, he exuded a predator's instincts, his desire to
defeat and destroy all enemies, including the spawn of those vile gold
dragons. Oddly, *he* appeared as a gold dragon instead of a bronze. Some
trick for the sake of his would-be minions watching?

Hot breath blasted Rysha's face. Her bullet didn't bounce off
an invisible shield, as she thought it might, but it struck the back of
the dragon's throat and did nothing. It didn't seem to penetrate at all.
Xandyrothol's tongue came up, his jaw snapped shut, and she feared he
swallowed the bullet.

A single copper eye glared at her through a hole torn in the metal hull,
then shifted toward the stasis chambers. Metal squealed as the dragon
thrust his neck farther inside, turning it so his head pointed toward his
new target.

Rysha fired again, aiming for his eye. But the dragon closed the lid
before it struck, and the bullet was deflected.

Xandyrothol's maw opened, as if he would devour the stasis chambers.

"No!" Rysha yelled.

She fired over and over until the hammer clicked, the chamber empty.

The dragon jerked his head back just before his fangs came down on the devices. Rysha gaped. Had one of her bullets actually done something?

Xandyrothol yanked his head out of the hold, more metal warping and squealing, as a yell came from somewhere above.

Rysha ran to the gaping hole in the hull in time to see Major Kaika falling from above. No, she had *jumped* from above.

She landed astraddle the dragon's neck and drove Eryndral downward. The glowing sword succeeded where bullets had failed and sank deeply between his scales.

Rysha screamed and clenched a triumphant fist, praying Kaika had done enough, or that she would be able to stab him over and over, driving the blade deep enough for a killing blow.

But Xandyrothol reacted instantly, twisting and flinging his neck—with Kaika straddling it—toward the steamer. He twisted so she would smash right into it. Kaika had been in the process of yanking Eryndral out so she could strike again, but she saw her fate coming and jumped to her feet.

Briefly, she managed to balance atop his neck, even lifting her sword to strike again, but that neck flexed and twisted faster than a whip. Kaika couldn't hold on, and it flung her toward the ship. She cracked against the hull so hard that Rysha feared the blow had broken her neck.

Kaika plummeted into the water below as Xandyrothol flew upward, like an eagle that meant to come around for another dive, to sink its talons into its recalcitrant prey.

Down in the water, Kaika lifted her head.

"Come back, you scaled bastard," she yelled, waving Eryndral.

Rysha smiled at her defiance, but then a ship came out of nowhere. One of those fast armored boats that had attacked Wolf Squadron. There was nobody in the wheelhouse—the dragon had to be propelling the craft forward, and at top speed.

Rysha yelled a warning, but she was too late. The boat slammed into Kaika, knocking the sword from her hands. It disappeared into the water, the same way Rysha's had. Worse, the force also sent Kaika flying sideways. She landed with her face toward the sky, but her eyes closed and her mouth open.

Was she unconscious? Dead?

Tears ran down Rysha's face. What now?

Gritting her teeth, she dug into her ammo pouch to load more bullets. A useless gesture, she knew, but she couldn't think of anything better.

"Wait," she muttered and dove for her pack. She could give the dragon the journal. Maybe it was too late—and maybe he wanted to destroy the stasis chambers no matter what—but she might get lucky. "It has to be time for some luck."

A shadow blotted out the light coming through the holes in the hull. As she turned, certain she knew who stood there, the dragon landed. Between one second and the next, he shifted form from the great scaled dragon that couldn't fit inside to a human who could. Horis. No, a doppelgänger of Horis.

"You've retrieved it for me," he said. "Excellent."

A thump sounded at the top of the steps leading into the cargo hold.

Horis growled and stretched a hand toward Rysha. An invisible force tugged at the journal. She clamped down on it, refusing to let go without striking a deal.

Light came from the steps, Trip running into the dark hold with Jaxi and Azarwrath glowing in his hands.

Horis jerked his chin toward him, and something akin to a hurricane gusted past Rysha and toward Trip. Even though she wasn't the target, she stumbled away, knocked into a post.

Trip halted at the bottom of the stairs and glared past several hammocks and toward Horis. He or the soulblades must have raised a barrier because the wind didn't stir his hair. But he grimaced, as if in pain. From the effort of blocking that blow?

Horis's cold gaze landed on him, and Trip stuttered forward, legs carrying him toward the dragon in awkward little steps. His grimace deepened.

Rysha growled and fired at Horis.

Her bullet hit an invisible field and bounced off, burrowing into the ceiling. Useless.

Or was it? It seemed to distract the dragon for a split second.

Trip growled, and Horis-Xandyrothol dropped to a knee. A fireball tore through the air, incinerating hammocks as it passed, and nearly burning Rysha's eyebrows off. It slammed into the kneeling human figure.

Rysha backed farther away, though she hated leaving the stasis chambers. For the thousandth time, she wished she had Dorfindral. Even if she could have done nothing else, she might have rested her hand on the devices and protected them with the blade's power.

Lightning streaked across the hold as the fireball dissipated, revealing Xandyrothol standing again, neither flesh nor clothing even slightly charred. Rysha groaned.

Then the dragon's eyes tightened and filled with confusion.

Shoot now, Trip cried into Rysha's mind.

She fired immediately, trusting he'd changed something. Her bullet slammed into Xandyrothol's shoulder, and he cried out in pain, just as a human being would do.

Rysha fired three more times, hoping to take advantage, to finish him off, but he got his barrier back up, and the bullets bounced off again.

Xandyrothol roared savagely, and Trip flew through the air, hurled by another blast of power. He soared past Rysha, arms flailing, and slammed into the stasis chambers. She winced as they wobbled, threatening to topple over. A snap sounded, followed by a wisp of smoke coming from one. Seven gods, would they be destroyed right in front of her eyes?

Xandyrothol's lips curled into a smile as Trip slumped to the deck, dropping one of the soulblades. He kept the other in his grip, but he had crumpled to his hands and knees, panting. It looked like some great weight had landed on his back and would force him flat any second.

Rysha ran and jumped over him, hoping to distract the dragon if nothing else. She fired one more time, though she wasn't surprised when the bullet ricocheted away before hitting him.

Cold copper eyes settled on her, and she saw her death in them.

Before Xandyrothol could attack, his head was knocked back, as if a sledgehammer had struck him in the face.

Trip leaped to his feet and lunged at Xandyrothol with one of the soulblades. Azarwrath. The tip stopped a foot in front of the dragon, as if it had met a stone wall. But lightning streaked out, wrapping all around the invisible bubble encompassing Xandyrothol.

Trip stood like a statue, the point pressed against the barrier, as Azarwrath's lightning danced and crackled, attempting to find a weak spot. All the while, he held the dragon's gaze. They glared at each other, eyes tight, jaws clenched, engaged in some mental battle.

The barrier disappeared, and Trip almost fell forward, the soulblade's tip leading. Rysha thought it might skewer the human-shaped dragon. But Xandyrothol whipped his hand up faster than the eye could see, and he caught the blade in midair. He pushed back, and it appeared he'd gained the upper hand.

Until Trip roared, thrusting and wrenching with his arms, tearing the blade free. Xandyrothol flew out the hole he'd entered, disappearing from sight.

A splash arose from below, reminding Rysha that Kaika was down there, possibly drowning.

"Good to see you," she blurted to Trip as she rushed to the hole in the hull to check on Kaika and the dragon.

Trip panted an unintelligible response, looking like he would fall over at any second. Rysha could only imagine what doing mental battle with a dragon was like.

"Any chance you can help Kaika?" Rysha squinted into the water, then spotted her. She'd floated away on the current. "There!"

Even as she pointed, the bronze dragon arrowed out of the water, his wings flapping, flinging droplets in every direction.

Rysha groaned again. She may have shot the human version of Xandyrothol in the shoulder, but the dragon appeared uninjured as those powerful wings beat, carrying him into the sky.

Cannons fired from the artillery stations on either side of the harbor. Rysha didn't even look. She knew those cannonballs wouldn't strike the dragon or bother him at all.

Trip held a hand toward Kaika, his eyes closing to slits in concentration. "She lost her sword?"

"I'm afraid so. They're both on the bottom of the harbor now."

He grimaced, but didn't speak again. Kaika floated out of the water. She hung as limp as a rag doll.

"Is she alive?" Rysha asked, afraid Kaika might have inhaled water and drowned.

"Yes, but unconscious. She's got a huge knot forming on her head."

Rysha slumped in relief. "Being run over by a boat will do that to you."

Screams came from above them as a shadow blotted out the sun. Xandyrothol. He wasn't done with them yet, but instead of returning to their hole in the hull, he dove toward the deck of the steamer.

Rifles fired, and cries of agony sounded. Metal ripped, torn free, and Rysha feared the dragon would destroy the vessel out of anger or revenge. Or just because it enjoyed causing havoc.

Kaika floated through the hull, coming to rest at Trip's feet.

Rysha wanted to check on her, but he knelt first, touching a hand to her forehead.

Will you check the stasis chambers? Trip asked silently. *I think we're going to have to move them, but I sense that they were damaged. I'm worried that... I'm just worried. I can't lose any more of them.*

Remembering that smoke, Rysha ran toward them.

Greetings, Storyteller! an exuberant voice cried into her mind, and she tripped, catching herself on the stasis chamber stack.

Shulina Arya?

Yes, it is I. I was sent to check on your progress. There is much dragon activity on the west coast of Iskandoth, and threats have been made by numerous aggressive conquerors. Your king wishes all of his great warriors back in the country to defend it.

Great warriors. Rysha almost scoffed, feeling anything but that right now.

No other dragon was willing to venture to this dark land, Shulina Arya continued, *but I was curious about it and also wanted to see what you were doing. It's actually a bright land. There is much sun, and there are many dolphins and whales playing in the ocean along its shores. I do sense the magic dead zone, but you are not in it. This is wonderful. Oh, but there is a bronze dragon where you are. Are you battling with it? Humans are quite fragile. I do not believe this is wise.*

No, it's not wise at all. He gave us little choice. Is there any chance you can help us get rid of him? I'll tell you whatever story you want to hear.

Oh? I asked Bhrava Saruth if he knew the tale of how the first dragons became bonded with the first human riders, but he did not. He said humans likely flocked to the dragons to worship them. I know this is not true. The legends say they respected each other and treated each other as equals, but I would like to hear the human stories.

I can absolutely share what was recorded in our histories. If I survive this day.

I am flying toward you, but I am still many miles out over the ocean. I shall arrive soon. A bronze is no match for a gold dragon! Even one who is tricking people into believing he is a gold. Do you see that illusion he is maintaining? How audacious!

He is definitely that, Rysha thought.

"Shit," Kaika groaned. She sat up and rubbed her head, water pooling on the deck underneath her. "Was that a dragon that ran me over?"

"An armored boat," Rysha said.

"I'm not sure if that's worse or not."

"Armored boats don't breathe fire."

"I guess that's a perk."

"The bronze dragon can't breathe fire either," Trip said.

"I jumped onto the back of a *gold* dragon," Kaika said.

"It was fooling you."

"It fooled me *and* hit me with a boat? That's it. I want it dead." Kaika looked around. "Damn it, I lost the sword, didn't I?"

"Losing priceless artifacts in the harbor has become trendy," Rysha said without humor.

Another wrenching of metal came from above, and something humongous splashed into the water, creating a wave so great that it rocked the steamer.

"What was that?" Rysha spread her legs for balance.

"One of the smokestacks," Trip said grimly.

"Shulina Arya is coming." Rysha hoped it would be soon enough.

"I know."

"She said she'd help if I tell her a story."

"Sounds like a good deal."

"That's the female dragon?" Kaika asked, rubbing her head again.

"Yes, ma'am. She came to check on us." Rysha decided not to mention that there was trouble at home, and Angulus needed all his great warriors back. Without the *chapaharii* blades, there wasn't much she or even Kaika could do. And they had more immediate concerns.

She rested her hand on one of the stasis chambers, wondering how she was supposed to tell if they continued to function.

"I'm starting to like that dragon more and more," Kaika said.

Another huge splash came from below, and again, a wave rocked the steamer.

"I'll like her even more if she arrives in time to do something about that," Kaika added.

Rysha peered into the stasis chamber she touched, but the light was too poor for her to make out the baby inside. The device was cool to the touch. Hadn't it been slightly warm before?

"They were damaged," Trip said, his eyes toward her, a distant aspect to them. "And I have no idea how to fix them. Maybe in time, and with a technical manual, but... there wasn't one that came with them."

"I'm not sure they wrote technical manuals back then," Rysha said. "Paper hadn't been invented yet."

"They could have carved it into clay tablets," Kaika said.

Trip's expression grew helpless and bleak as he stared at the stasis chambers. Rysha wished she knew what to say, some useful suggestion to make. Could they uncork them? Would the babies survive the process? It seemed they would surely die if they were left inside in those gels. If the magic wasn't providing... whatever it provided, they could end up being entombed in there and dying before they got a chance to live.

Something slammed into the side of the ship, and the deck pitched alarmingly. Snaps and groans came from the steamer's frame. A great tearing noise ripped through the air.

"Abandon ship!" came a yell from above decks.

The stasis chambers started to slide sideways. Trip jerked a hand up, and they halted.

A wave splashed against the ship, this time high enough that water washed in through the holes in the hull.

"Can you float them out of here, Trip?" Rysha gripped a post for support—and to keep her legs from being swept out from underneath her. "We need to get to safety."

Wherever that was.

The pitch of the deck grew steeper and steeper. Finally, the steamer tipped over completely. More snaps and cracks sounded, this time from outside. They must have smashed down on the dock.

"Yes," Trip said, "but wait a second."

"I don't know how many seconds we have," Kaika growled, also holding a post. Water flowed into the hold from multiple directions now. There had to be holes on the other side of the ship too.

Trip twitched his fingers, and Jaxi, the soulblade that had been dropped before, flew out of the water and into his hand. He spun toward the hole, climbing out to stand half on the hull, somehow keeping his footing on the impossible perch.

He raised both swords, and fireballs and lightning streaked out once again.

"Oh yes, this is the perfect place for a last stand," Kaika growled.

Storyteller, I have arrived! This bronze dragon is making an awful mess.
I noticed.
Such carnage. What does he hope to gain?
A cult.
What?
It's a long story, which I will happily share on the way home. Just—
can you please help? If you stop him, Trip, Kaika, and I will be extremely
grateful. Rysha almost promised that those stasis babies would be, too,
but would they even survive?

Tears threatened at the thought that her team had taken them from a
safe if forgotten home in that dragon lair and brought them out into the
world to possibly die.

Of course! Do you wish to ride with me? We can go into valiant
battle together.

I... Rysha hadn't expected the offer and didn't know what to say.
Despite all the craziness going on around them, including Trip hurling
attacks out into the harbor and water pouring in from all sides, a surge
of excitement went through her at the thought. She'd dreamed of flying
into battle on a dragon's back since she'd been a little girl. *I lost my*
sword. She formed an image of Dorfindral in her mind.

She couldn't go into battle without it. What would she do? Sit on
Shulina Arya's back and polish her scales while the dragon did all
the work?

We will get it! A simple matter! Then we will fly after the bronze and
smite him and drive your sword into him.

The dragon sounded even more excited by the notion than Rysha.

Though Rysha didn't think retrieving the sword would be that easy,
Shulina Arya spoke again before she could voice objections.

Stand next to your mate, and I will retrieve you. He is valiantly battling
the bronze now by himself. We must hurry if we wish to participate!

Her mate? Trip?

"Major Kaika, can you watch the stasis chambers?" Rysha pushed
through the water, gripping the shredded and charred remains of
hammocks to pull herself toward the hole where Trip balanced, hurling
his magical attacks.

"It does seem to be my lot in life." Kaika swam over and gripped
one of the devices, devices that were defying gravity to stay in one spot.

Trip's doing? "And now that I lost my sword, what else can I do? All my explosives are underwater too. This day is *not* going well."

Rysha understood Kaika's feeling of helplessness all too well—and how unusual it must be for the capable and confident major—but she couldn't stop to commiserate with her. She reached the hole and pulled herself out beside Trip. He was almost fully standing on the exterior of the hull now. The steamer had pitched over, flattening the dock beside it.

Rysha crouched on the smooth, wet surface, careful not to slip. Trip, standing with his legs spread and the soulblades raised, looked down at her. The wind whipped at his hair and his clothing, and he almost glowed like a sun from all the power that poured off him.

The dragon, now appearing bronze instead of gold, wheeled in the sky and screeched. When it tried to dive toward Trip, talons extended, it struck an invisible barrier, one much larger than usual.

He seemed to be protecting the entire ship as well as attacking the dragon with the soulblades. People who had fallen in the water gaped at him and the dragon as they swam for the shore. Others scrambled along the remains of the dock toward the waterfront. Cannons still boomed ineffectually.

The soulblades had stopped hurling fireballs and lightning from their tips, maybe because the attacks couldn't go through Trip's barrier, but explosions of light and energy appeared in the sky all around the dragon, making the creature dance as it flew.

Rysha, almost mesmerized by Trip, who once more looked like some powerful sorcerer of old, didn't notice Shulina Arya's approach until she was almost on top of them. Rysha twitched in surprise when the great gold dragon alighted on the hull beside them. Trip wasn't surprised. He must have lowered his barrier long enough for her to fly in.

Jump atop my back, Storyteller, Shulina Arya said, crouching low.

Rysha hesitated, afraid she would slip and pitch into the water, but a magical force swept under her and lifted her from the deck. She tamped down the startled scream that almost escaped her lips. Great warriors did not scream before going into valiant battle.

She'd ridden Shulina Arya before when they'd left the ice caves in the Antarctic, and remembered there was no saddle or reins. Magic would keep her astride the dragon's back. Even though she knew that, she flattened herself and spread her arms, trying to find a handhold.

Wheeee! Shulina Arya cried as they sprang from the ship and flew into the air over the harbor.

In all the hundreds of history books Rysha had read that revolved around dragons, she couldn't remember it ever being mentioned that they made such exclamations as *whee*. She wouldn't complain. She was glad Shulina Arya wanted to help her.

Do you know where the sword is? Rysha asked, wondering how she could explain when even she didn't know exactly where she'd lost it.

I can sense two of them, yes. Hold your breath.

That was all the warning Rysha got. She glimpsed the bronze still flying around the capsized steamer, trying to get to Trip—and perhaps to those stasis chambers—and then the water appeared straight below them. She grabbed her spectacles to keep them from flying off as they plunged into the blue depths. If physics had been the only thing at work, Rysha would have been hurled free when they hit, but magic kept her aboard the dragon's back as the icy water wrapped around her.

They plunged into darkness so quickly that she grew disoriented. An intense ache pierced her ears as they descended, but it disappeared almost immediately. The dragon's magic?

The bright green glow of a blurry sword came into view, the blade leaning against the silt-covered remains of a wreck. Seven gods, they'd made it to the bottom in five seconds, if that.

I can't touch it with magic, but you can grab it. Shulina Arya tilted on her side so Rysha could reach it.

She couldn't see well with her spectacles in her hand, but the glow was hard to miss. She stretched, fingers brushing the hilt. Before she touched it, she knew this was Eryndral, Kaika's blade, instead of hers, but it didn't matter. They needed to recover both.

Got it, Rysha thought, clenching her teeth as the foolish sword tried to convince her to slay Shulina Arya. *The second should be by those barges.*

Yes, I see. I shall swim like a dolphin!

Later, when Rysha wasn't holding her breath and hoping she wouldn't run out of air, she would ponder with some bemusement why a dragon might find dolphins so appealing.

Because we didn't have oceans in the other world, Shulina Arya thought, laughing into her head. *Water is fantastic. And there are so many brilliant creatures. Did you know that deep down in the ocean trenches, there are all manner of incredibly bizarre creatures? There is your sword, Storyteller!*

Rysha grinned despite the terrifying darkness rushing past all around her and the fact that her lungs were starting to long for air. That *did you know* had sounded so much like one of her own *did you knows*. After being mocked by a former love interest, Rysha had tried to stop using that phrase, but it hadn't lasted more than a few weeks. She always wanted to share what she knew and never could understand why people weren't as fascinated by quirky facts as she was.

I see it! Rysha thought, spotting the green glow in the darkness.

Dorfindral lay among sponges and strange tentacled creatures attached to the rocks. Again, Shulina Arya tilted so Rysha could reach the weapon without moving from her back.

When her hand wrapped around the hilt, Rysha not only felt Dorfindral's desire to slay dragons, but she experienced a feeling of triumph over their reunion. She wasn't sure if it came from her or from the sword, but she once again felt that she could matter, that she *could* be a great warrior.

You matter even without the sword, Trip's calm voice sounded in her head. Or maybe he was weary instead of calm. He sounded like he barely had the energy for this telepathic contact. *You're a far greater warrior than you believe.*

I appreciate the support, but shouldn't you be focused on that dragon?

Yes, but I wanted to make sure your exuberant dragon hadn't drowned you. You've been down a while.

Her lungs agreed.

I need air, Shulina Arya, she thought. *And to slay that bronze dragon.*

Yes, it will be most glorious.

They shot upward, toward the light of day and the battle.

CHAPTER 18

T HE BRONZE DRAGON WAS WOUNDED.
Trip would have felt exultant, but he was so weary, he could barely keep the soulblades from slipping out of his fingers. Their attacks had grown weaker, too, and he knew they didn't have unlimited reserves. Trip tried to take solace in knowing he was keeping the dragon from doing further damage to the steamer and the people around the harbor, but shielding so many while also attacking was intensely draining.

Give me the journal, and I shall spare your siblings, the dragon whispered into his mind.

Xandyrothol. He'd introduced himself earlier, before promising to destroy the babies and to eat Trip. It had been a while since he'd made those threats. Now, he was trying to deal. Trip sensed the dragon was weary, too, and scared now that Shulina Arya had arrived. He didn't seem to know if the gold was a threat or not. Shulina Arya hadn't physically engaged with him yet. Maybe she hadn't said anything to him at all.

"Trip," Kaika called from inside the hold. "Your baby boxes are underwater, and I'm not sure if things are working anymore. Can you get us out of here? I don't want to leave them."

Fresh fear rushed into Trip's heart. He remembered hearing something break when the dragon had hurled him against the stasis chambers. He still sensed some power coming from the devices, but he could tell they had been damaged. He worried the occupants might even now be dying, as his sire had, trapped within his own giant stasis chamber deep in that mountain.

"Yes, but we may be vulnerable while I do it," Trip called back.

"I can't believe I don't have any bombs to throw at that hairy dragon's ass."

"Hairy?" Trip sheathed the soulblades, crouched, and gripped the hull under his feet, the edge of the hole the dragon had made. He concentrated on expanding the opening, melting and forming the metal to create a gap he could levitate the stasis chambers through.

"I'm sure it was hairy when it was human."

Xandyrothol flew back and forth, staring down at Trip, a predator sensing an opportunity.

Guard us, please, Jaxi and Azarwrath, Trip thought, dropping his barrier because he needed the concentration for this.

We will, Azarwrath replied firmly.

Jaxi moaned into his mind, sounding exhausted. The hilts of the soulblades warmed Trip's thighs through his clothing and their scabbards, as if they were overheated horses in need of a stable and a rubdown.

I'm less inclined to protect you when you compare me to a horse. Jaxi sniffed, managing to sound indignant through her fatigue.

Are you saying you wouldn't like a rubdown later? A nice oiling, perhaps? Trip stood, the hole wide enough now.

As long as it doesn't take place in a stable. I prefer a more serene setting.

We are shielding you, Azarwrath said, *but we can't protect the entire ship.*

I think everybody is out, Trip thought.

Kaika climbed out beside him, dragging all three of the team's packs, as Trip focused on releasing the stasis chambers from the magical straps he'd created to hold them in place. The devices slid deeper into the hold, fully immersed in the water. He prayed it wasn't too late to keep the babies inside alive. He couldn't fail in this, damn it.

Feeling his power flagging, he gritted his teeth as he lifted the devices through water and against gravity. They floated into the air and toward the hole.

"He's coming down." Kaika clenched her fist, as if she would punch the dragon.

A wave of power crashed into the soulblades' barrier as Xandyrothol plummeted from the sky, seeing his chance to get at Trip, to kill him and all those with Agarrenon Shivar's blood in one final attack.

Keep that barrier up, Trip urged the soulblades, sensing that it was weakening, that it might drop and let the dragon cruise through.

As the stasis chambers floated into the open, Xandyrothol's eyes seemed to light up. Trip quickly lowered the devices to the water, using a tendril of his power to ensure they would float for a few moments, and threw all his remaining energy into strengthening the barrier.

Power buffeted it, rocking him back on his mental heels. But it held.

The dragon must not have expected it to stay up, because he struck the invisible field and bounced off, as if he were a trampolinist. Before he reached the apex of his bounce, an invisible locomotive seemed to smash into Xandyrothol from the side.

He was hurled across the harbor like a cannonball, his wings furling tightly to his body and his tail clenching. He smashed into Bhodian's palace with so much force that he destroyed the entire structure. Wood flew in a million directions, and the barge sank below the surface before popping up again.

"Did *you* do that?" Kaika asked.

Gawking, Trip shook his head. He would have if he could have, but—

I did that, a female voice spoke into Trip's mind. *And it was fun!*

Shulina Arya's golden form streaked up from the depths of the harbor, sloughing rivers of water. Rysha sat astride her back with not one but two *chapaharii* swords gleaming pale green in the sunlight. She wasn't wearing her spectacles. Trip hoped she hadn't lost another set. He also hoped she could see.

"I am definitely starting to like that dragon." Kaika waved to Rysha, probably hoping she would drop off Eryndral.

But Shulina Arya flew straight for the half-destroyed barge where the bronze dragon struggled to rise from the wreckage of the palace. She opened her great fanged maw, and flames roiled out like water sprayed from a fire hose. They completely engulfed the barge. The bronze managed to erect a tiny barrier around himself, keeping the flames from striking him.

Trip decided he needed to focus on getting the stasis chambers to safety instead of feeling smug that Bhodian's barge was being annihilated by crashing dragons *and* fire. He summoned what little energy he had left to levitate them out of the water and toward the beach. Azarwrath lifted Trip and Kaika with his own power, pushing them in the same direction.

While he concentrated, Trip watched Shulina Arya and Rysha. They weren't done with their bronze foe yet.

The female dragon swooped toward the smoke and flames, tilting in a smooth maneuver that brought Rysha close enough to their enemy for her to slash the swords over her head, to strike Xandyrothol's barrier.

Though nothing visible happened, Trip sensed it popping. Shulina Arya flew in a tight circle, her back to the bronze dragon, giving Rysha more chances to attack with the *chapaharii* swords.

And attack she did. She leaped up, defying gravity to stand atop Shulina Arya's back and wield both blades.

If Xandyrothol tried any magical attacks or defenses, they did not work. He attempted to block Rysha's attacks with his wings, but her swords slashed in and bit deep, battering the dragon.

As ferocious and terrifying as Trip had found Xandyrothol when he first ran to the docks, and as much damage as the bronze had done, he seemed pitiful next to the larger gold dragon. And Rysha… She was magnificent. She looked just like some epic dragon rider of old, like she belonged in that exact spot.

Trip smiled as he watched. He'd meant what he told her, that she didn't need magical weapons to be a great warrior, but he understood why she felt so much more powerful with them. Injured and exhausted, Xandyrothol was completely inept at fighting her off.

The bronze sprang into the air, leaving the smoldering ruin of the barge, and tried to fly away, but Shulina Arya gave chase. She was relentless, and he was injured, barely able to gain altitude as he did the aerial equivalent of limping away.

Shulina Arya opened her maw again. This time, when the fire rolled out, Xandyrothol couldn't muster a defense. An inferno engulfed him, and for long seconds, he was invisible, hidden behind curtains of flames.

When she finally ended the attack, only a blackened husk of a dragon remained, like some unrecognizable piece of meat that had fallen through a grill to the coals and been left to burn. The dead dragon dropped into the harbor and sank, much as the nearby barge was doing.

"That was impressive," Kaika said as she and Trip landed on the beach next to the stasis chambers. The rest of the beach was devoid of life, as were the docks. The crew of the steamer and the citizens of Lagresh had fled far into the city to let the dragons battle between themselves. "Though it would have been more impressive if I'd had my sword and been along for the fight."

"It was wonderful," Trip said. "Do you think she'll still share a bed with me when she's a famous dragon rider?"

"Does she share one with you *now*? There haven't been many beds on this journey, unless you count the cactus pad mattresses in the hostel. Even your grandparents just gave us the rug in front of the fireplace. Except for Leftie, who hogged the couch for himself. He is *not* a gentleman."

"Do you think she'll still share an alley with me then? Or a cave?"

Kaika curled her lip at him. "An *alley*?"

"I would have taken her to a hostel if the rooms here weren't so abysmal."

"The alleys certainly aren't better. Hells, Trip, if she shared an alley with you, she's probably yours for life."

"Really?" He managed a smile, despite his weariness. He felt ridiculously bolstered by this third-party observation.

"Really. Go check your baby boxes."

Trip wanted to drop to his back in the sand, his entire body numb and exhausted after all the power he'd called upon, but he forced his legs to carry him to the stasis chambers. He fell to his knees and fought the intense headache pulsing behind his eyes to check on them.

As he ran his senses along the magical components, he identified damage to several conduits. One was severed. A couple of the tiny power sources had burned out. Already several of the chambers weren't working.

He swallowed, dread hollowing a pit in his stomach. He didn't think the occupants had died yet, but surely, they would if he couldn't fix the damage. Or... what if he simply took all the babies out? If his mother had done it, it couldn't be that hard. But what would he do with them *here*? In this awful place? It wasn't as if that steamer would be leaving in the morning to carry them to Iskandia. Not now. Probably not ever.

He laid his hand on the side of a chamber with a human baby girl inside, tears forming at the idea of not making it in time, of losing his siblings before he even got to know them. He'd already lost one, unless Grekka kept her word. Unless—

Look up, Azarwrath said.

Trip did so, and his mouth fell open. The single missing stasis chamber floated across the waterfront street and down the beach toward him. He spotted Grekka standing next to the open door of her battered steam carriage.

Do not forget your promise, she told him silently, meeting his eyes.

I won't.

The stasis chamber settled in the sand next to the others, and Trip jumped to check it. The dark-haired girl was inside, and the device appeared to be functioning normally, despite dents in the side that hadn't been there before. He sagged with relief. He'd started to give up on ever seeing the little girl again.

Thank you, Grekka. Trip looked up, but she had already disappeared into her carriage, and it was rolling back up a street and into the city. Perhaps the harbor was too chaotic for her right now. He was glad that *her* barge hadn't been destroyed in the battle.

"Now we just have to figure out how to get all of you home," Trip said, patting the stasis chambers.

Perhaps your new dragon friend can give you a ride, Jaxi suggested.

Three people and two dozen stasis chambers?

Dragons use magic to carry people, not muscles. And they fly fast. I wouldn't be surprised if she could get you back to the capital by dawn.

I don't know her very well. It seems a presumptuous thing to ask.

Just offer to build her a dolphin toy, Jaxi said. *If we get back soon, you should have time to get Sardelle's advice on these things. Or just take all the babies out. And get Sardelle's advice on that.*

Trip felt somewhat heartened that there was someone he could turn to, even if they still had to fly across an ocean and a continent to get to that person.

Shulina Arya landed on the beach, and Rysha slid off, both swords still in hand. She ran over, handing Kaika her blade, then dropped down beside Trip.

"Are they all right? Did you get them out in time?" She'd returned her spectacles to her face.

"They're damaged. We need to get back as soon as possible."

I will take you, Shulina Arya announced into their minds. *I was sent to get you.*

You were? Trip looked toward the dragon.

She perched atop a log, preening under one wing like a gold egret. *Hm, not precisely. I was invited to a meeting with Bhrava Saruth and your king and some of your generals, and someone said, 'I wonder what happened to Captain Trip and his plan to bring back Agarrenon Shivar, because we could use an elder dragon's help now.' Bhrava Saruth said he wouldn't go to* Rakgorath-ilthin *to check because of the magic dead zone, but I'm far braver than he, and I intended to show it. So, I volunteered, and here I am!*

Shulina Arya twisted her head upside down to do something to the bottom of an outstretched wing. It couldn't be preening exactly, could it? Dragons did not have feathers. Surely, scales didn't need straightening and cleaning. Though Trip *did* see her pull off a piece of seaweed and toss it to the sand.

"That dragon has a flexible neck," Kaika observed.

Do you think you can carry all three of us back and all these stasis chambers too? Trip asked the dragon. *They were damaged.*

"Maybe she can fix them." Rysha touched the device with the dark-haired girl inside. "You got the missing one back?"

"Yes, thanks to Grekka."

Rysha's lips thinned. Trip could understand why she wouldn't want to thank Grekka for anything.

Shulina Arya turned her long neck and brought her head over to peer into the chambers. It was alarming how large a dragon head was up close, and Trip made a point of not looking at her fangs.

Kaika came over to stand next to Shulina Arya and touched her scaled neck. The gesture surprised Trip until he realized Shulina Arya had the same aura—*scylori*—as other dragons. The *chapaharii* blades might dull its effects for Rysha and Kaika, but this close, they must still feel the pull. Trip certainly felt the draw of the dragon's power, even though she wasn't performing any magic, other than perhaps sensing the stasis devices.

I do not know how to repair these, Shulina Arya announced. *I do not believe this magic was used in the other world. I do not know anything about machines, only about science. My sires were scientists. They taught me about animals and geology and climates, mostly in the world where I was born, but they also told me about Serankil. They always believed dragons would return to this world one day.*

"Did you say sires?" Rysha asked.

Yes, if you will tell me the story of the first dragon riders on the way back, then I will tell you how two bronze dragons saved me from my mother—a nasty female who was going to sacrifice me to a volcano because she thought I was born too small and weak.

Trip eyed the dragon from head to taloned toes, having a hard time imagining anyone ever applying those adjectives to her.

Climb on. I can carry everyone and everything back. I am barely tired after battling that weakened bronze. He was half-dead already. Shulina Arya turned her large violet eyes on Trip, and he felt the draw of her power even more, for a moment believing he would do whatever she wished if she but asked. But he imagined himself securing his bank vault around his mind so he wouldn't be affected, and the pull lessened.

Your sire was a gold, yes? He must have been very strong. I did not believe humans could battle dragons at all.

He was a gold. And... Trip thought of the cult, of all he'd seen, of all his sire had apparently reveled in. *A complete ass.*

Shulina Arya pulled her lips back, revealing more of her fangs. Had he offended her? He forced his feet to stay where they were, though the temptation to skitter back came over him.

Many dragons are megalomaniacal, Shulina Arya said. *That is why I was so excited to meet humans. They are much more fun to play with. Come now, yes. You will all ride?*

Rysha scrambled up her side first, as easily as if there were stairs leading up the dragon's back. "We will come. Thank you, Shulina Arya."

"I think Major Kaika has to stop fondling her neck first," Trip said, following Rysha up.

Kaika, who'd seemed half-mesmerized by the stroking, yanked her hand down and scowled at them. "I was just checking the structural integrity of our ride. Three people and all our gear on one dragon seems excessive."

"Trust in the magic," Rysha said.

Trip settled behind her on the dragon as Kaika climbed up. He looked to their packs and the stasis chambers, thinking to lift them himself, even though his headache wanted nothing more to do with magic. But Shulina Arya beat him to it. All the gear rose from the beach and floated in the air above the base of her tail.

Ready? Shulina Arya asked.

"Ready," all three of them said, Kaika settling behind Trip.

The dragon sprang into the air and flapped out to the ocean, the city and the harbor falling away quickly behind it. Trip was glad to leave Lagresh and Rakgorath. It seemed they had been there for months instead of a couple of weeks.

He touched the cargo pocket where he'd buttoned in the magical assassin's dagger, reminded that he hadn't completed the mission he'd given himself. Not yet. He hoped General Zirkander and the king would agree that the blade should go back to Cofahre. No matter what his nickname was, he was tired of going off on his own and disobeying orders. He was ready to return to his flier and rejoin Wolf Squadron, perhaps one day becoming the hero to the people of Iskandia that he'd always longed to be. He was less ready to oversee the second births of all the babies floating behind them, but that seemed inevitable now. He would do his best to make sure they had a promising future and someone to care for them.

Kaika slapped Trip on the shoulder. "Is this even better than you imagined? Being sandwiched between two beautiful warrior women?"

"Two beautiful women who are soaking wet and draped in seaweed?" Trip asked.

"Every man's fantasy, I assure you."

Trip gave her a salute, but rested his hands on Rysha's waist. There was only one woman in his fantasies.

EPILOGUE

RYSHA WOKE TO SOMEONE SHAKING her shoulder gently. "Trip?" she mumbled, blinking her eyes open. The last time she'd been awake, it had been dark, with Shulina Arya flying them across the ocean. Dawn had come, but clouds surrounded them, and she couldn't tell if they were over water or land.

"Yes." The shoulder shake turned into a light squeeze. "Your dragon just flew by the hangars."

His tone had a dryness to it, but it took her a moment to realize why.

"You thought we should land there and report in?" Rysha asked.

"There or in the citadel. I bet General Zirkander is already at work. I sense a couple of other dragons at the edge of my range, not Bhrava Saruth or any of the friendly ones."

Shulina Arya must have been descending because they dropped out of the clouds, and Rysha could see the sea, the harbor, and the capital sprawling up and down the coast below. Though she'd flown over the area with Wolf Squadron a couple of times now, she still found it breathtaking to see the city from above.

"Would you like to suggest to your dragon that either of those places would be excellent stopping points?" Trip looked over his shoulder, either at Kaika sleeping against his back and drooling on his jacket, or at the stasis chambers, still floating along over Shulina Arya's tail.

He sounded tired. Had he dozed at all during their long flight? Or had he been trying to figure out how to repair the ancient devices?

Rysha couldn't imagine repairing anything while riding a dragon across an ocean. "She's not *my* dragon, Trip. You're telepathic. Did you ask her to take us to the army fort?"

"You tell her stories. She likes you." He squeezed her shoulder again, then lowered his hand. Rysha wouldn't have minded if he had left it there. "I did actually suggest to her that we should report in, but her response was very muzzy."

"Muzzy?" Rysha had never encountered a muzzy dragon.

"Maybe sleepy is the correct word. She mumbled something about tarts, and I got a sense that she's barely staying awake. I'm back here, rubbing the soulblades and staying prepared in case her magic falters and we need to save ourselves from falling out of the sky."

"Rubbing the soulblades? Do they like it?"

"Jaxi seems to. I'm less certain about Azarwrath. Perhaps *you* could rub him, and he'd feel content."

Rysha rubbed her face instead. "If Shulina Arya is tired—and I can imagine why after flying us so far—and wants tarts, then we both know where she's going."

Rysha couldn't blame the dragon for being tired. They must have flown for twelve hours or more, and Rysha hadn't been able to tell stories *all* night. She had dozed off after four straight hours of sharing the origins of the Cofah empire, along with Iskandian hypotheses as to why so many of their emperors had acted crazily throughout history—lead-poisoning due to their aqueduct construction practices was among the most recent ideas put forward.

"General Zirkander's house?" Trip asked.

"Sardelle's kitchen, more specifically."

"The general may have already gone to work. We won't be able to report in from the kitchen."

"No? Aren't the two soulblades you're rubbing telepathic? And, for that matter, aren't *you* telepathic?"

"Well, yes, but... I don't think that's an acceptable way to report in after a mission. You're supposed to go in to your superior officer's office, click your heels together in front of his desk, and salute."

"Maybe you can click your heels together in front of the oven and send a mental image of your salute."

"Is that how they do it in the elite troops?"

"They would if they had telepathic swords."

As Shulina Arya swooped low and flew over the city walls and into the less densely populated suburban area outside, Rysha grew more certain of their destination. She leaned forward and patted the dragon's neck, silently letting her know that she thought this was a perfectly fine place to land. If they had to, she, Trip, and Kaika could walk or borrow a horse to ride to the fort. But shouldn't they see Sardelle first, regardless?

"Can you tell if Sardelle is at their house?" Rysha glanced past Trip to the stasis chambers. "She'll be the most likely one to help with our problem."

"I know. I'm just worried we'll get in trouble if we don't report in right away."

"Trip, you were willing to go AWOL in order to solve the Dreyak mystery. Don't you think it's hypocritical for you to worry about being slapped on the wrist for not reporting in promptly now?"

"No."

She turned, arching her eyebrows.

"I mean, if we *were* AWOL, I would, but technically, we came back as soon as we could. With your dragon's help, we're getting back even earlier than we would have if we'd ridden on the steamer. And Blazer ordered us to the city to catch transportation, so I am not AWOL, nor was I. I was simply doing research during the time we had to wait for transportation."

"Are you going to become a barracks lawyer, Trip?"

"Not unless it pays well." He grimaced. "I've been thinking about what's going to happen when these babies come out of their chambers, especially now that it looks like they'll all come out at once. Sane people don't raise eight children at a time. I'm sure it makes you crazy, not to mention that it has to be expensive. Rysha, captains don't make that much." His expression grew even more glum. Or maybe that was daunted.

Rysha imagined that he'd spent the night trying to figure out what he was going to do.

Better than poking into her mind. She didn't want him to find out that she'd been manhandled by that scheming bronze dragon. Forced to *kiss* him. The whole scenario felt like a failure on her part, and she vowed to keep it to herself.

"I'm sure you could use your burgeoning magical powers to earn some extra income," she said. "I can say from personal experience that your healing skills are already quite effective. There must be people all over the capital in need of healing."

"It seems uncharitable to charge sick people to heal them."

"Then don't charge the truly sick people. But you could charge to fix people's minor inconveniences. Like warts, bunions, and toenail fungus. Two nucros per wart."

Trip appeared more horrified than enlightened by this entrepreneurial suggestion.

"I'm *positive* there's a need," Rysha said. "Not everybody is going to ride all the way out to Bhrava Saruth's temple for healing, and it sounds like he's an infrequent presence in the city. Besides, do you think a dragon who thinks he's a god would heal toenail fungus?"

"I... really have no idea."

"It's an untapped market, Trip. I assure you."

The familiar street that Zirkander and Sardelle lived on came into view, the pond at the end and the tall trees behind their two-story cottage unchanged from the last time Rysha had been there. She hadn't truly expected anything to have changed—it had been less than three weeks since they left, even though it seemed like it had been months—but she had worried that dragons might have attacked the capital during their absence. She was relieved that the only smoke wafting from the city came from people's chimneys.

Shulina Arya alighted not in the yard but on the peak of the roof. Behind Trip, Kaika stirred, looking around in bleary confusion. The house and yard appeared much different from this viewpoint.

The dragon's head fell backward, almost clunking Rysha, and Shulina Arya yawned noisily. Birds in the nearby trees squawked alarmed protests.

"I didn't know dragons yawned," Kaika observed.

"I didn't know majors drooled." Trip wiped at a moist spot on his shoulder.

"This mission has been quite the learning experience, hasn't it?" Rysha asked. "Shulina Arya? Uhm, can you help us down?" She could slide off easily enough and skim down a drainpipe, but getting Trip's cargo safely down would be more of a challenge. Though she supposed he could handle that with his magic.

She'd no sooner had the thought than the stasis chambers floated slowly down to the yard to land in the trimmed green grass. Rysha wondered if Sardelle was awake yet, or if she would be startled out of sleep by a surprise dragon arrival. Surely, Jaxi would have let her know they were coming.

Shulina Arya didn't answer Rysha. Her long neck bent so that her head pointed toward one of the ground-level windows. That was the living room, wasn't it? If the door to the kitchen was open, she might see through to it, but Rysha had a hard time imagining baking going on this early in the morning.

Tarts? Shulina Arya asked.

Maybe she'll have some leftovers, Rysha thought.

Trip slid off the dragon's back, then hopped over the edge of the roof. He landed in an easy crouch next to the stasis chambers, his touchdown no doubt softened by magic.

A baby cried inside the cottage. Well, if Sardelle hadn't been awake before, she was now.

Rysha and Kaika tossed their weapons and gear down, then Rysha slung her leg over Shulina Arya's back to slide off, but magical energy lifted her into the air before her boots touched the slanted roof. Kaika blurted a startled oath as she was also lifted. They sailed off the roof and descended to the yard as the front door opened.

Sardelle stepped out, rocking her baby in her arms as her toddler trailed her out and stood behind her skirt to peer into the yard.

From the threshold, Sardelle looked at the dragon still gazing in her window. Shulina Arya rotated her upside-down head toward her, violet eyes large and sleepy.

Tarts?

Even though the question came out as hopeful, or maybe imploring, that typical dragon compulsion accompanied it, and Rysha couldn't imagine anyone saying no.

"Hm," Sardelle said, then looked toward Trip, Kaika, and Rysha. Maybe she had the wherewithal to ignore a dragon.

Rysha wished she had tarts or something sweet to give to Shulina Arya after the favor she'd done them all.

"Ridge has already left for the fort," Sardelle told them, "though I see why you came." Her gaze shifted toward the stasis chambers. "Blazer reported that these would be coming, and Jaxi woke me when you were about fifty miles away. Ah, a couple of the units appear to have failed."

"Yes, ma'am," Trip said. "I was able to weave some wiring back together and fix a couple of breaches in others, but the power sources are beyond me. They're not like anything electrical or mechanical. But I believe the… offspring are all still alive and haven't yet come out of the hibernation, even in the broken ones. I'm not sure how much time there is."

As Sardelle nodded and came forward, a tray floated out the front door. It turned toward Shulina Arya's lowered head, then settled on the grass below.

"I keep waiting for things like that to stop seeming weird," Kaika whispered, standing beside Rysha.

"Is a tray full of floating pastries any weirder than a dragon flying you across the ocean?"

"I believe so, yes. The legends all mention people riding dragons. They don't mention floating pastry trays."

"The historians back then weren't nearly thorough enough for my liking."

Tarts!

Sardelle looked at Shulina Arya. "Yes, mango and strawberry. I'm trying to keep some on hand for when we have house guests."

Shulina Arya's long and large tongue slipped out, proving surprisingly dexterous as it plucked tarts from the tray and tossed them one at a time into her mouth. The toddler—Marinka, Rysha remembered—remained on the stoop, half hiding behind the doorjamb as she watched the tongue in action.

"It is a challenge when one's house guests have extra-large stomachs," Sardelle added, then turned back to the stasis chambers.

Trip pointed out a few things and murmured to her, a broken conversation that Rysha had trouble following. She suspected it was half out loud and half telepathic.

As this went on, Dorfindral sent disgruntled sensations into Rysha's mind, the sword irritated by all the magic about, magic that Rysha wasn't leaping to destroy. She didn't want to deal with repeating orders for the blade to stand down, so she simply unbuckled the scabbard and leaned it against the side of the house. It ought to be safe here.

Tylie appeared on the threshold, ruffled Marinka's hair, then came out and offered to hold Sardelle's baby. When Sardelle relinquished the little one, Rysha thought Tylie might take him back inside, but she instead walked around the stasis chambers and peered in the top of each one.

"Some of these are animals," she said brightly, as if this was delightful news.

Rysha remembered how they'd been attacked ferociously by the dragon-blooded animals that Grekka had spent who knew how many years collecting from around the world. She felt significantly less delighted at the idea of half-dragon animals.

"Most of them," Trip told her. "There are eight human, er, half-human babies. Five girls and three boys."

"I believe we'll have to... hatch them soon." Sardelle rested her hand on the side of one device. "The occupants in even the undamaged chambers are showing some signs of distress."

Trip locked his concerned gaze on Sardelle, and Rysha felt for him. This shouldn't have been his responsibility, but who else's could it be?

"I've had a few days' warning," Sardelle went on, "though I didn't expect to have to act so quickly. I've spoken with a few mothers in the area that are nursing right now and could add another mouth to the dinner table, as it were. Myself included, of course."

Of course? Rysha wasn't sure *she* could imagine suddenly having to breastfeed three-thousand-year-old babies that were half dragon.

"Seven gods, I forgot about milk," Trip said, bringing the heel of his palm to his forehead. "I wasn't sure how old they are, or, uh, how long babies need milk. I don't know anything about..." He swallowed and lowered his hand. "But I'll learn. I don't want them to be raised in an orphanage. I want to take care of them."

"In between working full-time as a pilot and learning to become a sorcerer?" Sardelle quirked an eyebrow at him.

"Yes. I mean, I could give up one of those things if I had to." Trip threw an anguished look toward the sky, and Rysha couldn't imagine that piloting would be the "one" he would choose. "But I'll have to figure out a way to feed them and house them. Babies don't drink milk indefinitely, right? They need food eventually. And I don't think they can stay in the barracks..."

"Your thoughts on this matter are noble," Sardelle said, "if naive, but I suspect this may be a situation requiring a village to raise a child, or children, I should say."

"I can help with the animals!" Tylie grinned. "This one's a monkey. And that one is a seguano lizard. Isn't it fascinating that they all look like their mothers rather than their sire? None are little dragons, are they? I wonder what powers they'll have. I've been taking veterinary courses at the university, but dragon-blooded animals weren't discussed."

"Until now, they've been rather rare in the world," Sardelle said. "And very distant descendants of dragons. These will be quite different."

"I know, but I would love to help. I wonder how intelligent they'll be."

"I don't want them just stuck in a zoo," Trip said, "but I don't know how... I admit, I'm already daunted by the idea of raising eight babies, ma'am. Maybe my grandparents would consider moving to the capital to help. Though it's more expensive over here, isn't it? They might not be able to afford it."

"I understand the property values on this particular street have gone down dramatically," Sardelle said dryly, looking toward the weed-choked lot across from their house. Rysha hadn't noticed any activity in the other houses on the small, dead-end street when she'd visited previously. "Perhaps you could negotiate with the owner of that lot over there and build something on it. Something with a lot of bedrooms."

"Maybe Pimples could help," Kaika said, smirking. "Have you met him yet? He's in Wolf Squadron. He designs houses as a hobby. Of course, I don't know if any have actually been built."

"What happened to the property values?" Trip asked, seeming puzzled. He must have grown accustomed to magic quickly and forgotten that other people saw it as something terrifying, if not outright evil.

"It's the oddest thing. After we moved in, almost all the renters and homeowners on the street moved away." Sardelle gazed blandly toward Shulina Arya.

After demolishing the tray of tarts, she had dropped down to the yard where she now lay, eyes closed and curled up like a dog with the end of her tail covering her snout. Previously, when Rysha had seen her around the city, she'd been in her golden ferret form, but maybe she'd been too tired to consider shape-shifting.

"Given the size of that dragon lawn ornament," Kaika murmured to Rysha, "I think the adjacent land owners would have to *pay* people to live in their houses."

"I don't know why. I imagine having a dragon nearby keeps the vermin down," Rysha said.

"Do dragons eat vermin? I've only seen them eat cheese, tarts, and sheep."

"I'm not sure, but the vermin should be too scared to make homes near a dragon lair."

Kaika smirked. "I wonder if anyone has told General Zirkander that he's living in a dragon lair."

"I suppose we should wait and see what Angulus has to say before making long-term plans," Sardelle said. "He and Ridge are on their way."

Trip blinked. "Here?"

"Yes. Jaxi warned Ridge you were coming at the same time she told me. He and Angulus were at the citadel, waiting for you to report in."

Trip shot Rysha a dirty look. "I knew we should have gone to the fort first."

Rysha lifted her hands. "I wasn't piloting. Shulina Arya wanted tarts. If General Zirkander wants dragons to visit his office, he should keep a tart supply at the fort."

"I think that's the primary reason he *doesn't* keep food of any kind in his office and was horrified when his mother brought in Spring Blooms Fest cookies the other day. Dragons have excellent noses."

I'm convinced they're part dog, Jaxi spoke into Rysha's mind, or more likely, everybody's minds. *Have you seen the way Bhrava Saruth sniffs people?*

"Yes," Trip promptly said. "He's the one who told me who my sire was. After smelling me."

"Maybe dogs are part dragon," Tylie said. "Or have a common ancestor."

A raven flew over the house, circled the gathering, then landed on her shoulder. She didn't appear surprised. A pet? Maybe she *would* be a good person to help raise half-dragon animals. But poor Sardelle. She wouldn't want more than a dozen cages in her house, would she? The cottage was two stories, but it wasn't *that* large. Rysha believed there were only three bedrooms. And no animal-raising rooms or sheds out back.

"Ah, they're almost here." Sardelle nodded toward the street, though nobody had come into view yet.

Now that full daylight had come, the sun hiding behind clouds, Rysha occasionally heard a steam whistle or shout from the arterial street farther away, but this lane remained quiet and untrodden. Diminished property values indeed.

"I've sent for our resident dragon-blooded scientist, too," Sardelle added. "Tolemek. He wasn't up yet, but he'll come over shortly. I believe I'd like his help when it comes to removing the babies and, ah, pups— whelps?—from the devices. He may even have some familiarity with them, as he's quite well read on ancient magic now, especially when related to science and medicine. I believe these stasis chambers would qualify under that heading."

Trip didn't seem to hear her. His gaze was locked on the empty street. Finally, the clip-clop of horses at a trot grew audible. He shifted from foot to foot and tugged at the hem of his uniform jacket.

It sounded like a *lot* of horse hoofs. Rysha imagined an arrest squad coming to take Trip and his siblings away, but Sardelle merely smiled toward the road. Rysha realized that if the king was coming, he would have bodyguards.

Yes, she was right. Angulus, wearing his state robes and a hat decorated with gold trim and the Iskandian royal emblem, came into view. General Zirkander rode next to him in a pressed undress uniform. Eight armed men in the king's guard uniform surrounded the pair as they advanced down the street. Zirkander wore his usual irreverent smirk, especially when his eyes met Sardelle's, and seemed more bemused than daunted by his royal escort.

The king stopped right next to Rysha, startling her until he dismounted and Kaika flung herself at him. Rysha supposed that was confirmation of all the rumors that proclaimed them to be lovers. When their lips locked, it was a certainty. Angulus must have worried about Kaika being gone on this special dragon-finding mission, especially when Blazer and the others had come back without her.

"This isn't how reporting in usually goes," Zirkander told Trip. "The lower-ranking officers go to the location of the higher-ranking officers, not the other way around."

Zirkander glanced at Kaika, as if to inform her, too, but she was clearly busy, so he waved a dismissive hand in her direction.

"Yes, sir. Our transportation—" Trip glanced toward the empty tray near the window, "—craved sustenance."

As Zirkander walked toward Trip, Rysha stepped away from Angulus and Kaika to give them their privacy. They were murmuring to each other now, lovers' murmurs.

Rysha thought about joining Trip to offer him whatever support he needed, but he, Sardelle, and Tylie were clustered around the stasis chambers, pointing and discussing while updating Zirkander. Not wanting to interrupt talk of magic and how to raise young babies, something with which she had no experience, Rysha headed over to Shulina Arya instead. It amused Rysha that none of the king's guards had batted an eye at the dragon's presence in the yard. Such things seemed to be expected at this house, at least by those in General Zirkander and Sardelle's immediate circle.

Since Shulina Arya's eyes were closed, she probably wouldn't mind someone leaning against the side of the house beside her. The toddler had wandered back inside, and an argument over the proper use of game pieces wafted out. Rysha remembered Sardelle's young students and guessed they were babysitting at the moment.

Of course you can rest beside me, Storyteller, Shulina Arya spoke into her mind, one violet eye opening. A sleepy violet eye. *I will make you a spot.* She thumped her tail, as if to offer it as a bench. *How did the dragon riders and dragons of old find accommodations at the end of a day joined in valiant battle?*

The riders had bedrooms in the outposts, I believe. And the dragons had... well, our textbooks call it a stable area.

A stable! As if a dragon is the same as a horse?

Most likely the dragons had a different term for it.

I should think so.

Shulina Arya thumped her tail again, and Rysha climbed on it, turning around so she could lean against her side. She wasn't positive it was all her idea. Shulina Arya, though much friendlier than other dragons, had that power about her, power that inadvertently, or maybe intentionally, compelled others to obey her. Still, Rysha found the spot comfortable. The dragon didn't radiate body heat, like a horse or dog might, but she radiated *something*. Rysha had the sense of being protected and felt safe and oddly content.

Where do you usually sleep, Storyteller?

The barracks at the army fort.

Barracks? I have seen this place. These dwellings are not dissimilar to stables.

This is true. Aunt Tadelay had said almost the same thing when Rysha announced her intention to join the military.

It is not a suitable habitat for an honored dragon rider.

I'm not a dragon rider, though, Rysha thought. *Just a very new lieutenant in the king's army.*

You rode a dragon last night!

Yes, and we appreciate it very much, but I wouldn't presume that you want to fly me around all over the place.

If you tell me more stories, I will certainly fly you places. And we will go into battle together. Did you not enjoy utterly destroying that obnoxious and destructive bronze dragon?

I did, Rysha admitted, *especially after he tried to force himself upon me.*

As soon as the words came out, she wished she hadn't said them. It would be worse if Trip found out, but she also hated to admit to Shulina Arya or anyone else how weak and helpless she'd felt without Dorfindral in her hand.

No man forces himself upon a dragon rider! Shulina Arya's voice thrummed with power and indignation, almost hurting as it bounced around inside Rysha's skull. But it grew less certain when she added, *That is true, isn't it? I admit that I wasn't alive during the first era of dragons and riders.*

Rysha smiled. *It does seem unlikely that anyone would want to risk the ire of a gold dragon. Especially a female dragon. You are larger than even Bhrava Saruth.*

Of course I am. My mother was wrong in believing me a runt. Shulina Arya rose to her full height and spread her wings, dwarfing the house behind her. She shifted her tail to the side, urging Rysha to slip off.

Several of Angulus's guards noticed and fingered their weapons uncertainly as they glanced back and forth from their liege to the dragon.

Human king, Shulina Arya announced in a booming telepathic voice.

Almost everyone turned to look at her, Angulus included. Only Trip looked at Rysha instead, lifting his eyebrows.

Not certain what was coming next, Rysha could only spread her hands.

I, Shulina Arya, friend to all humans who approach in peace and enemy to those who bear me ill will, have decided that Rysha Ravenwood will be my rider. You must do what must be done to make this official.

Horrified that the words had come out as an edict, and to her king no less, Rysha cleared her throat. "We say please," she whispered to the dragon. "And call him sire."

"A dragon rider?" Angulus asked, his tone hard to read, but he didn't look like he appreciated having edicts issued to him. His cool gaze turned to Rysha.

She wished she had Dorfindral in hand so she could strike a noble pose, one of a great warrior ready to go into battle. At the least, she wished her uniform were less rumpled, ripped, and plastered with dried seaweed.

"We were just discussing the possibility, Sire," Rysha explained, feeling even more dwarfed than the house by the dragon wing stretched over her head. "I didn't request it, but... we did go into battle together against a bronze dragon."

"They were magnificent, Sire," Trip put in.

Rysha smiled at him, appreciating the support, even if she doubted his words meant much more to the king than hers did. And Shulina Arya's? Rysha didn't know. The dragon hadn't been here that long. Had she even spoken with the king before?

"If you are interested in having a rider," Angulus told the dragon, "I am certain I could find you a suitable and very experienced warrior. Colonel Grady has been practicing with his *chapaharii* blade."

"And he writes those ballads," Zirkander said. "Maybe he'll do one to immortalize the Iskandian ally dragons. He just needs to find some words that rhyme with dragon. Pun? Stun? Bourbon?"

"You're not helping," Angulus told him.

"Sorry, Sire. It's early, and I was interrupted before I finished my coffee." Zirkander didn't appear contrite in the least, especially when Sardelle swatted him and he merely winked at her.

I have chosen my rider, Shulina Arya announced to them all. *You will continue to train her to help her become a great warrior, and she will continue to tell me wonderful stories all about the history of dragons in this world. Her tales are brilliant. A lieutenant is far too lowly a rank for such a great storyteller.*

"Ah, we have minimum time-in-service rank requirements," Zirkander said, looking at Kaika. "Hasn't she only been out of the academy for four months?"

"Five months," Kaika said.

"Well, that changes everything."

Shulina Arya had fallen silent, but her long neck lowered, and she stared steadily into Angulus's eyes. It was possible they were speaking privately, but Shulina Arya might be attempting to influence him with her power. While Rysha appreciated that the dragon wanted her as a rider, she didn't like the idea of tricking the king or forcing him to agree. She wanted to earn the position and for everyone to believe she deserved it.

You do *deserve it,* Trip said silently. *Just make sure there's room for me in the bed with you and your dragon.* He winked. *In case we decide to* use *a bed sometime.*

I'm sure a dragon wouldn't want to sleep in the bed with us!

No? Trip shared an image of General Zirkander lounging in his own bed in his pajamas and socks while reading a newspaper. There was a gold ferret draped over his lap.

Had he plucked that image from Zirkander's mind at some point? It didn't seem to be supposition.

We'll figure something out. I do know she's not interested in sleeping in a stable.

What if you put a mattress in the stall and called it a guest house?

Trip.

Just trying to figure out how many buildings I need to put on that little lot over there, if I can get a good deal on it. And can start making money on the side. How many warts do you think I'd have to heal to buy a piece of property?

Thousands. You better find something people are willing to pay more to have healed.

Corns?

Human king, I assure you this is the right decision, Shulina Arya said, her tone more conciliatory than before. Less demanding. *Rysha Ravenwood will make a most excellent rider. And we will protect your country together from foul and treacherous dragons who disguise themselves as humans and dragons high above themselves.*

Angulus's eyebrows drew together, and he appeared to be focusing quite hard to keep his thoughts clear, but he managed an offhand tone as he stuck a hand in his pocket and said, "Zirkander, is this dragon trying to influence me?"

"I believe so. Yes, Sire."

"She has tart crumbs between her teeth."

Shulina Arya's eyes narrowed. As friendly as she was, it would probably be wise to remember *what* she was.

Rysha didn't point that out. She mostly held her breath and waited to hear what the king would say. Even though she had never truly expected anything like this, she couldn't deny the thrill that ran through her at the idea of officially being assigned to ride Shulina Arya into battle, with Dorfindral in her hand, ready to cut down enemies.

"I see that, Sire," Zirkander said. "Do you think it'll be Lieutenant Ravenwood's job to provide those tarts when she's her rider?"

Angulus narrowed his own eyes, but at Zirkander instead of the dragon. Maybe he'd expected a less irreverent answer. Though, from what little Rysha knew of the general, she wasn't sure why he would.

"If they truly defend Iskandia's shorelines, *I'll* provide them," Angulus said.

Rysha straightened. Did that sound like consent?

"She, however, will be responsible for cleaning the crumbs out of the dragon's teeth."

"Seems fair, Sire," Zirkander said.

"Very well. I'll have the orders drawn up." Angulus looked at Kaika. "Who's her commanding officer?"

"Major Fwen in the 39th Artillery for now, Sire," Kaika said. "It'll be Colonel Dyre if she passes the elite troops training. Assuming she's going back to that." Kaika spread a hand, as if she wasn't sure if this was a promotion, a transfer, or simply a special designation.

Rysha had no idea, either.

"Oh, she's finishing it," Angulus said. "If she doesn't pass the tests, I will have to insist that another be chosen for this elite position of dragon rider." He lifted his chin, looking at Rysha and Shulina Arya.

Rysha felt panic well up inside of her. She'd intended from the beginning to pass the tests and officially be invited into the elite troops, but she'd missed so much of the training that she feared being able to make it this year. If she failed, did that mean she would lose this opportunity? That Colonel Grady would ride Shulina Arya while making up horrible rhymes for dragon?

Excellent, human king. Shulina Arya lowered a wingtip to Rysha's shoulder. *My rider will easily pass all tests you have for her. She is extremely capable.*

Clearly, Shulina Arya didn't sense her panic.

"Good," Angulus said, smiling slightly. "Then it won't be a problem."

Rysha couldn't tell if he believed she would pass and approved of that or *didn't* believe she would pass. And approved of *that*.

"Also, my name is Angulus."

Human king, Angulus, yes. Shulina Arya lowered her wings and dropped to all fours. *There should be a ceremony to make this official. With baked goods.*

"Let's just see if your rider passes her tests first," Angulus said.

Rysha could feel that panic threatening to bubble to the top again, but she forced herself to nod and look confident in her ability to pass any test placed before her. After all, she wouldn't want Shulina Arya to be bereft of pastries.

As daylight faded, Trip paced back and forth on the walkway in front of General Zirkander's house. He felt like a father waiting for news on the delivery of his baby.

He had provided as much assistance as he could with the stasis chambers and removing Agarrenon Shivar's offspring—they had started with the animals to ensure they had it down—but once the scientist Tolemek had arrived and the stasis chambers had been moved inside, Trip had felt like he was in the way. It had stopped being a matter of mechanical things, where his expertise lay, and a matter of squalling babies and pups and whelps and foals and... whatever baby lizards were called.

Earlier, he'd watched seven women, most with small babies of their own, arrive and enter the house. For nursing duty. Would they stay here to do that or take the babies back to their own homes? He wasn't sure. That did seem more realistic than his thought of raising all eight together in one house, especially since *he* couldn't provide milk, but he wasn't certain how he felt about the babies being separated. Further, how had Sardelle recruited people? The women didn't have dragon blood—he and Azarwrath had checked. What would they do if the babies they were nursing did something... odd?

Had *he* done odd things when he'd been a baby, or had his quirks not come out until later? He imagined toys floating across a room behind a nursing mother.

Even if the babies acted normally for the first few years, how would he pay these women back for feeding and caring for them? Making toys hardly seemed sufficient. He touched his cargo pocket where the fish puzzle he'd made was still secured. It was hard to believe it had survived all he'd been through, but he'd checked on it during the flight back. There had been a few dents to work out, but that had been an easy task. He wasn't sure when to give it to Sardelle. Before his next tutoring session? After all the babies were out? It seemed such an inadequate gift.

"Hello, Trip," General Zirkander said, strolling off the road and down the walkway.

He'd ridden back to the fort hours earlier with Angulus, and Trip realized it had to be the end of the workday now.

"Sir." Trip came to an attention stance and saluted him.

"You going to come back to work tomorrow or loiter in front of my house for another day?"

"I don't know, sir. I mean, of course I will come to work, but I need to make sure everything—everyone—is taken care of. And... I have no idea how to do that." He turned what was surely a bleak expression toward Zirkander, then immediately regretted it. He shouldn't be foisting his problems onto his CO. Zirkander wasn't even his direct commanding officer. If he was going to foist problems on anyone, it ought to be Colonel Tranq, Wolf Squadron's leader. Even if he barely knew her.

"Sardelle, Angulus, and I have been discussing that. Blazer gave us some warning, you know. Did the surrogate mothers come?"

"Yes, sir."

"They all live in the city and are willing to take one or two of the babies to care for as long as they need a mother's milk. I think one woman even lost her baby in childbirth just a few days ago and was glad to have one to take its place. Sardelle figures they won't do anything dragonly for the first couple of years, but even so, she made sure to select women who aren't concerned about magic. Several of them— don't hold this against them—are among Bhrava Saruth's devotees. I don't think any of them believe he's a god, but they bring him treats in exchange for his blessings. You can visit the children any time, of course. And once they're old enough to start learning magic… Well, Sardelle has been longing for more students." He snorted. "She's had a terrible time finding people in Iskandia with enough dragon blood to learn how to do magical things. Those who purged the Referatu three hundred years ago did an efficient job of it." His lips thinned.

"So, they'll be adopted, sir?" Trip asked. That probably made sense, especially while they required a mother's milk, but a twinge of guilt flowed into him at the idea that he might be abandoning them.

"Unless you object. It seemed the most logical choice. Trip, I know you're a capable young officer, and apparently, you're becoming a capable young sorcerer, but you don't strike me as someone ready to raise eight children."

"No, sir, but I want to do the right thing."

Adoption into families where they would have other siblings sounded better than going to some strange orphanage, but Trip was still skeptical. It felt like shirking responsibility. He supposed he could still be a part of all their lives—the mothers wouldn't object to that, surely— and he could make toys and give the parents money if they needed it. He doubted he would become a great healer of warts, but Rysha was right. He ought to be able to find some way to make extra money with his unique skills.

This is a wise choice, Telryn, Azarwrath said. *Raising babies is women's work.*

Only if the women want that work, Jaxi instantly responded. *There's nothing that says a man can't help with childrearing.*

Trip had returned Jaxi to Sardelle that morning, but since the soulblade was in the house, it wasn't as if Jaxi was too far away to participate in discussions.

I do agree with Ridge that Trip would be an awful father, she added.

That's not exactly what he said, Trip protested.

"The right thing for you is to be in the sky and hurling fireballs at dragons that want to take over Iskandia," Zirkander said.

"Has that been a problem, sir? While we've been gone?"

"Right now, they're avoiding the capital, thanks to all the *chapaharii* swords located here, but we've received reports of dragons eating livestock all over the country. A few have attacked towns and killed people too." Zirkander pulled his cap off and scraped his fingers through his hair. "I heard your sire was an ass, but it's too bad he's dead. We could have used an ally that has sway over dragons. Bhrava Saruth is useful to have around, and Shulina Arya seems exuberant, but I doubt either of them has the influence to sway other dragons. We're going to have to find another solution to protect Iskandia, to protect young dragonlings being born today." He waved toward the house. "The only good thing to come of these dragons is that Cofahre is having as much trouble with them as we are, if not more. Prince Varlok should be too busy with them to contemplate invasions of Iskandia, at least for the foreseeable future."

"Oh," Trip blurted, remembering the dagger and the mission Grekka had appointed him with. "I forgot to tell the king this morning. I should have. I've been distracted."

"I can't imagine why."

Blushing, Trip found his pack, dug out the dagger, and shared what he'd learned from Grekka.

"Do you want to touch it, sir?" he asked in the end—he didn't think a person needed dragon blood to receive the blade's vision.

"I try to avoid touching other men's daggers."

"I'm serious, sir."

"I know. You should laugh more. Have fun."

"Ry—Lieutenant Ravenwood said something similar to me."

"Maybe she's wiser than her five months out of the academy suggest."

"That's definitely the case, sir." Trip almost said that she was certainly wiser than he, but Zirkander would likely agree with that, which wouldn't be good for his morale.

"Bring it with you tomorrow morning." Zirkander waved at the dagger. "We'll take it to the king. *He* can touch it. He was the one who thought up the exile, after all. I suppose that's not much of a state secret at this point, so I can share that information with you."

"I assumed nobody else would have been brazen enough to kidnap an emperor."

"I'm a little more concerned about finding a way to get these dragons to leave our country alone right now than worrying about the Cofah," Zirkander said.

"I wish I could say that I'm sorry we didn't find my sire, but after all I learned about him, I'm not."

"I see. Well, we'll figure out another way to get the dragons to leave us alone. Perhaps Wolf Squadron can drop tarts onto other nations' continents to lure them all to distant shores."

"Rysha might lose *her* dragon if we did that."

The front door opened, and Sardelle stepped out into the deepening night holding her baby wrapped in a blanket in her arms. She gave a sideways nod to the left, and a porch light flared to life.

"We have all the animals and all the human babies delivered," Sardelle said, "if you can call it that. Some are almost a year old. Trip, would you like to come in and meet your siblings?"

"Of course." He squeezed his hands together, feeling excited and nervous and like he would throw up all at the same time. How had he come to be so invested in siblings he hadn't known existed until a couple of weeks ago?

"The plaques didn't come with names. Perhaps you can assist us in naming them, Trip. Before Ridge's mother comes to visit." Her eyes crinkled.

Trip didn't understand the comment until Zirkander smirked and said, "Rosemary, Tarragon, and Lavender are perfectly fine name suggestions for a little boy."

"Perfectly fine name suggestions that we ignored."

"I thought it would be nice if my children went through their school years without being teased," Zirkander said.

"That's unlikely to happen."

"Because all children get teased or because they're *my* children?"

Sardelle's lips curved up. "Yes."

Zirkander made a disgruntled sound.

"Trip," Sardelle said, "would you like to hold your little sister?"

"Oh? That's one of them?" He blushed, feeling silly for not having realized. But he hadn't been sending his senses out to check, and from what he'd seen, the auras of newborn babies were rather indistinctive. They were vague blobs of life to his sixth sense.

Babies don't get interesting—and less blobby—until they're older, Jaxi said as Trip walked tentatively toward the stoop.

Yes, I seem to remember you mentioning you don't start to like them until they're age twenty-five or thirty, Azarwrath said.

Age is no guarantee that I'll like them. The odds are just better that they'll start to talk about something besides themselves by then.

Trip ignored the soulblades and stepped up beside Sardelle to peer down at the bundle. The baby girl was mostly wrapped up, but her face was visible, her dark green eyes identical to Trip's—and their sire's. She was looking at the porch light Sardelle had turned on, and he wondered if she sensed that magic had been used to light the wick.

He couldn't tell how old she was, other than to note she was larger than Sardelle's baby. Her eyes were more alert, and she smiled when she focused on Trip. It probably had nothing to do with him—maybe she'd liked the porch light—but he found that encouraging.

"Do you want to hold her?" Sardelle asked.

"Is it all right?" Trip looked down at his hands, thinking about all the battles they'd been in lately, all the violence they'd helped perpetrate. It had been in service to his country, but he wondered whether it was appropriate to touch such new and innocent life after handling rifles and swords.

"It's not much different from holding a screwdriver or pliers," Zirkander said. "Babies just squirm a little more than tools."

"You're so helpful," Sardelle told Zirkander.

"That's why they made me a general."

"You'll do fine," Sardelle assured Trip. "After you hold her, we'll go in to see the rest of your siblings, and I'll introduce you to the surrogate mothers I found. If you object to any of them, you can let me know, but they're already eager to have more children in their households." She tilted her head toward the living room.

Trip stuck his head through the doorway to look. Four women sat on Zirkander's giant made-from-scrap-flier-parts couch, and three others were in chairs, all chatting amiably, all holding babies to their breasts to feed them. Their unabashedly bared breasts.

Trip jerked back, his cheeks flaming, and stumbled off the stoop. He hadn't meant to look in and intrude on their… naked parts.

"Maybe he's not ready to hold a baby, after all," Zirkander noted.

"Are you appalled by the couch or the women breastfeeding?" Sardelle asked Trip, her blue eyes twinkling.

"Uh. Well. I've seen the couch before." Trip waved, looking for words to articulate his embarrassment, but decided he would be better served by not talking.

"This is what happens when you're raised as an only child." Zirkander's eyes did some twinkling too. "If you're not around when little brothers and sisters come out, you don't get an education in the mysteries of womanhood. Until later." He quirked an eyebrow at Trip. "*Much* later, in some cases."

Trip's cheeks continued flaming. He was fairly certain his commanding officer now believed he was a virgin. Or close to it. "I just haven't been around many babies. Or mothers."

"*You* were an only child, I seem to recall," Sardelle told Zirkander.

"Exactly why I understand why Trip just put a boot print in your flowerbed."

"Oh well. There are dragon talon marks in it too."

A giggle came from the baby in Sardelle's arms.

Trip stepped back onto the stoop, turning his shoulder so he wouldn't accidentally look through the doorway again, and Sardelle shifted to hand the little girl to him. He took her with the utmost care and only after making sure he couldn't possibly fall off the stoop and into the flowerbed again.

The baby giggled again.

"Is she always cheerful?" Trip asked. "Or is she amused by me?"

"Probably the latter," Zirkander said. "I've noticed that small children are inordinately tickled when I stumble, trip, or otherwise hurt myself in front of them."

"Some of your commanding officers have that reaction too," Sardelle said.

"The world is a cruel place."

Trip wasn't quite sure what to do, but he rocked the girl in his arms. He thought about trying the cooing and oohing noises that people always seemed to make when holding babies, but he would feel goofy doing that in front of his commanding officer.

The baby stretched a hand up toward his nose. Not certain if she wanted to grab it or to investigate his face in general, he lifted her higher and bent his head. A finger poked into his nostril.

"Is this normal?" Trip asked.

"Your nostril or a baby with inquisitive fingers?" Sardelle asked.

"I guess she'll let me know if the nostril isn't."

The baby giggled again and lowered her finger. Maybe it was silly, but Trip felt as if they'd bonded somehow. She had investigated him and found him acceptable. Even though he still worried about what kinds of people the babies would grow up to be, some of the tension eased from his shoulders as he rocked her. Sardelle had known how to handle eight babies needing milk, and the king hadn't mentioned raising them to be used against the enemies of Iskandia. For now, the world seemed... if not peaceful, then at least tolerable. Maybe even hopeful.

Trip started to think of toys and maybe educational games he could make for the children as they got older. He hoped he could find time to build a few things before he was sent off on another mission. Even though he couldn't fault Shulina Arya for showing up and helping them, he had been a little sad that he hadn't needed to build a submarine to retrieve the swords.

"Do you want to name her?" Sardelle asked. "She's the oldest of the girls."

"Uhm, do you think Zherie would be all right? That was my mother's name. She was more adventurous than I ever realized when I was a kid."

"It's a lovely name," Sardelle said.

"If he doesn't want to go with Tarragon, it's all right," Zirkander said.

"Ready to come in and meet the mothers, Trip?" Sardelle asked.

"You better ask them to drape blankets over themselves," Zirkander said. "He has the look of a rabbit about to flee from a wolf. Trip, if you'd prefer, we could have a beer in the duck blind."

"No, sir." Trip attempted to smooth the alarm off his face. He'd faced enemy dragons and enemy sorcerers. He could handle breastfeeding women. "I'm ready. I want to meet them and make sure..." He almost said he wanted to make sure they were worthy of raising his little siblings, but that seemed presumptuous. The gods knew *he* wouldn't have been ready for the challenge. "I want to introduce myself and make sure they know I'll do everything I can to help." Inspired, he added, "I can help them create playrooms for the babies. Or build cribs with toys integrated into them. Do they need any new gear or equipment for their houses, do you think?"

Trip wasn't sure yet what kind of "gear or equipment" babies or mothers taking care of babies would need, but he would do some research. There had to be all manner of useful gadgets for childrearing.

"*We're* still waiting for a new coffeemaker," Zirkander said. "In case you're making a list of handy things to do before your next mission."

"Do you know when that mission will be, sir?" Trip was glad to be done with Rakgorath and hoped not to go back any time soon, but he missed his flier and itched to be in the sky again, in a craft under his own control.

"Soon." Zirkander's face lost some of its affability. "Soon."

Trip, sensing the general knew a lot more than he did, decided he better make the coffeemaker and baby toys soon. It sounded like Wolf Squadron would be up in the air again before long.

THE END

Printed in Great Britain
by Amazon